TOXIC

WES DEMOTT

Admiral House Publishing

Copyright © 2016 by Wes DeMott

Names: DeMott, Wes.
Title: Toxic / by Wes DeMott. — 1st ed.
         p. cm.
Description: Admiral House Publishing trade paperback edition. |
Miami : Admiral House Books, 2016.
Summary: A Sierra Club researcher's death exposes the depths of American corporate greed and governmental corruption.

ISBN 978-0-9851741-8-7 (hardcover) |
ISBN 978-0-9851741-6-3 (trade paperback) |
ISBN 978-0-9851741-7-0 (e-book) |

BISAC: FICTION / Thriller / Suspense. | FICTION / Thriller / Legal. | FICTION / Political.

1. Environment—Fiction.
2. Police Militarization—Fiction.
3. Federal Bureau of Investigation—Fiction.
4. Criminal Corporate Polluters—Fiction.
5. Extraordinary Rendition—Fiction.
6. Civil Liberties Abuse—Fiction.

Cover Art by James Moore / Stacyjoart.com

Please contact WES DEMOTT about interviews or speaking engagements through the contact information at: WesDeMott.com

Printed in the United States of America
ADMIRAL HOUSE PUBLISHING
10 9 8 7 6 5 4 3 2 1

Other Works By Wes DeMott

THRILLERS

VAPORS

THE FUND (*Vapors* in paperback & all foreign languages)

WALKING K

THE TYPHOON SANCTION

HEAT SYNC

ACTION/ADVENTURE

TORTUGA GOLD — Mayday Salvage and Rescue #1

THE SHRINE OF AKUMAL — Mayday Salvage and Rescue #2

LITERARY FICTION

LOVING ZELDA

AWARD-WINNING SHORT STORIES

The Fortune Teller

Seventeen Days on a Raft

Chapter 1

"Oh, I am *so* going to get you bastards!" Jeff Roberts shouted, then slammed the file closed and leapt out of his chair. "We're going to nail you this time."

He spun around twice, too excited to know what to do until he raised his fist in the air and shouted "Finally!"

Jeff logged off his computer with the screen still showing his smoking gun, the absolute proof and the emotional pull that would get them the win in court. Montessa Chemical Corporation would lose. And at least a tiny bit of Montessa's global criminal behavior would be punished.

He wanted to call Claire and celebrate with her, but there was a good chance her phone was bugged. He thought about calling Robyn, but it was too late to startle her when he was this jacked up and his whole body hummed with excitement. So he grabbed a beer, popped it open, and watched the courtroom scenario play out in his mind. Montessa's lawyers, slicker than snot with their thousand dollar briefcases and ivy league degrees. Unbeatable, almost. But Jeff had them now. He *had* them.

He needed to calm down and get some sleep, so he ran the tub full of hot water. Drank another beer and climbed in, making a mental note to clean his nails before showing up in court. He slid down in the tub and covered his face and stayed there, watching himself kill it in front of the jury, his cardboard boxes beating the crap out of those damned leather briefcases.

When he ran out of air he surfaced, but hadn't even opened his eyes before the forty caliber slug splattered half of his head against the wall.

Chapter 2

The tiger shark came reluctantly alongside the *Bella Sabrina*, a 36-foot sport-fisherman anchored nine miles off Marco Island in the blue-green waters of the Gulf of Mexico. Jack's refuge, where everything felt better and cleaner, just as it always had, even when he was a small boy alone in his skiff off Key West.

"Keep your rod tip up," Jack said to the angler. "He's still pretty green but I'm going to grab the leader."

The men in the fishing party gasped as the apex predator rolled on his side and flipped water into the boat with his enormous tail before making another powerful run, ripping the steel leader out of Jack's hand.

"Now move toward the bow," Jack shouted as he grabbed his tail rope. "Get him up again and I'll try to rope him."

"Confirm that I'm moving to the bow," the angler grunted as he strained against the tiger's relentless struggle, and then Jack knew for sure he was a veteran, too. Maybe Iraq or Afghanistan or maybe one of the few who'd served in Africa. Jack wondered, briefly.

The tiger turned and came back fast, the angler cranking like crazy to keep the line tight. He attacked the hull, banging his thousand-pound body hard into the keel before surfacing again, right beside Jack, his broad head shaking back and forth while his tail slapped the boat, giving Jack a chance to reach down into the frothing water and loop him. He planted his feet to the deck and pulled tight as he hauled the animal backward toward the stern, then threw two turns of the rope around a cleat.

"Keep him against the hull," Jack said as he snapped a photo, then read "Eleven feet four inches" off the ruler he'd marked at the waterline on both sides of his boat. As he said, "and nine foot ten to the fork of the tail," he grabbed the tagging dart attached to a long wooden rod, loaded a stainless steel tag, held the pole about three feet from the shark, aimed beside the dorsal fin, and stabbed hard. The shark thrashed his tail and splashed the men, but the tagging was perfect.

"The hook is down too deep but will rust out quickly. Get all the pictures you want 'cause I'm cutting him loose."

Jack reached over the side and ran his hand along the back of the thick shark's striped body, from the dorsal fin to the tail, and slid off the tail rope. Then he moved to the tiger's gaping mouth and clipped the leader, smiling as the tiger lapped the boat and headed for the depths.

"Nice job, everyone. Give me a minute to fill out the card."

While his party celebrated, Jack wrote the length, species, sex, weight, and angler's name on the NOAA 3x5 card assigned to that tag. He was filling in the latitude and longitude of the hook-up when his cell phone rang.

The caller ID said CHAINSAW, even though his friend, Mike Roberts, like Jack, was trying his best to distance himself from the violence of their past. Jack just hadn't edited his directory.

"Yeah, Mike. What's up?"

"Jeff is dead." Powerfully said by a powerful voice hiding overpowering pain.

Jack waved for the men to quiet down, then pressed the phone hard to his ear. "What?"

"Cops say he killed himself."

"Jeff killed himself? There's no way."

"That's what they said, Jack." A crack in that strong voice. "They say my beautiful boy climbed into his bathtub and put the barrel of a .40 caliber pistol to the side of his head. Squeezed the trigger and sent a hollow-point into his brain."

"Jeff hates guns. It would never happen. Ridiculous."

The line went silent. The anglers stared. A frigate bird circled overhead as the wake from a distant boat slapped *Bella Sabrina's* hull.

"Mike?"

"I'm still here, and I'm glad to hear you say that because I think it's a lie, too." The voice now hard, tempered like steel with the resolve that once had inspired men to follow him and Jack into battle. And then it wavered. "But . . ."

"But what?"

"Claire broke Jeff's heart a few weeks ago."

"What did she do?"

"She left him for some high-paying job in Atlanta, was all Jeff said."

"You think there's more to the story?"

"Probably. No way to know."

"Could that screw him up enough for him to shoot himself?"

Mike said nothing so Jack dialed it down. "For Jeff to take his own life?"

"Who knows?"

"We both saw it happen in Afghanistan."

More silence. Then, "No, Jack. I think Jeff was stronger than that."

"Yeah, me too."

"Which means I've got to go find me a killer."

Jack turned away from the fisherman, making it private. "You're a good fighter, Mike, but you're not an investigator and we both know it. What's your plan? Roll into town and crack skulls until a confession leaks out of one?"

"It's effective."

"At getting you arrested or killed. Look, you stay put. I'll go find out what happened."

"While I sit around on my ass? Smarten up, Jack."

"How's Marilyn doing? How are the kids holding up?"

"Leave them out of this."

"The way you're leaving them out?"

"Jack, you best be careful."

"Don't puss out on them, man. Not now when they really need you. Be the strong dad and husband they've come to expect."

Mike mumbled something.

"What? I didn't hear you, Mike."

"I said they're pretty busted up."

"You'll do them more good than you will Jeff. He was still living in Virginia?"

Was still living. The words had to hurt bad. Jack knew it. Jack felt it.

"Yes." Quiet. Sad. "Roanoke. Still saving the world with the Sierra Club."

"I'll head there now. Tell his landlord to expect me. Give both me and your family forty-eight hours, Mike. You'll still be plenty pissed two days from now, I promise."

More silence as Jack started his boat, hit the windlass switch to raise the anchor, and turned back to shore, slow enough to keep the wind noise down so he could hear. He glanced at the anglers and said, "We're heading back early. Emergency. Sorry."

"One question, Jack."

"Yours to ask, Mike."

"Can you still do it?"

Fair question, because Jack really wasn't sure. His Marine commanders had done serious damage when they'd silenced his challenges in Afghanistan with a bomb, and not just to his body. So all Jack knew for certain was that through eleven months in Afghanistan and sixteen excruciating months in various V.A. hospitals, he'd survived and done well by getting hard, mean, and ugly. It was nothing special, really. In truth, getting mean was a horribly human trait. Ten years in the FBI had softened or hidden or, more likely, civilized it, but he was willing to bet the ability was still there because the poison still came to a boil on very rare but just as regretful occasions.

"Yes, Mike. I can do it."

"Okay, I'll accept that. Because if someone murdered Jeff..."

"Yeah, Mike?"

"I want blood, Jack. I want gallons of blood."

Chapter 3

Jack flew into Atlanta late and caught an early morning flight to Roanoke. He'd hoped to sleep on the lay-over but didn't, his mind too busy conjuring scenarios and what-ifs that could have led to Jeff's death.

He stared out the window as the plane made its final descent, impressed by the natural beauty surrounding Roanoke, and understanding why Jeff would want to live snug in that narrow valley between the Blue Ridge Mountains and the Alleghenies, with the Roanoke River dividing the city that adopted its name. Chestnuts, oaks, and maples, leafy and green, stood in contrast to the tropical slash pines and cabbage palms of his home.

Driving toward town he saw boulders and rock faces he could imagine Jeff climbing, signs pointing to hiking trails, and of course the fast moving river with its spring current of melted snow rushing toward Albemarle Sound and the Atlantic, while slower water in shallow eddies provided safe and nutrient-rich spawning grounds for the striped bass and trout, their tiny offspring gaining size and strength in the safety of the shoreline vegetation before moving to more open water.

A hawk, hiding from its prey in the late morning sunlight, passed overhead as Jack parked his rental car at

Jeff's apartment building, an old square two-story that would have made a great fraternity house if anywhere close to a college, its broad covered porch with fat white columns and a deck on top almost begging to have a Greek-lettered banner strung across it. Only the frail black man sitting on that porch like an old but dependable sentry challenged the image.

Jack walked up the steps, smiling at the man. All the time he'd been traveling he'd been wondering how best to find out if Jeff had really killed himself, and in a sad way he hoped Jeff had pulled his own trigger. Dead was dead. Jack knew that better than most, and he sure knew the lure of suicide better than most. And since the why no longer mattered to Jeff, suicide would provide a tidy if uncomfortable answer. But if he hadn't killed himself, then the why had the potential to be life-changing for Jack, taking him back to a place he'd gone to and left many times before.

As the black man rose carefully from his rocker he said, "Well, young man, I'm going to take a chance and call you Jack Wells, even though I reserve my right to doubt that's who you are."

Jack smiled and the man smiled back, a bright set of teeth mitigating the heavy toll that life had charged to his face.

"Jeff's dad must have told you I was coming?"

"Mister Roberts said a man named Jack Wells was coming to see Jeff's room. He said the man was about thirty-five, and I reckon that's about how old you are. But your hair is much longer than he said, and it sure isn't light brown."

"Grown out by Mother Nature and bleached out by the sun."

"Aren't those two things the same? You want to take off those sunglasses for me?"

Jack removed his Ray-Bans, appreciating the old man's care in doing things right, which probably explained the well-kept appearance of the old building. More likely, it also meant he'd seen the consequences of being careless.

"You sure got the blue eyes he described all right."

Jack grinned. "They could be contact lenses."

The man grinned back. "Could be, I suppose. Would you go through that much trouble?"

"I would if I needed to, but I didn't."

"No, no, I don't suppose you did. And I don't imagine you'll have any trouble telling me Jeff's favorite kind of music then."

Jeff loved Southern Rock music from the '70's. Jack was sure of it because he'd been the one to turn him on to it, the same way Jack's own dad turned him on to it years before, when things were still good between them. Molly Hatchet, .38 Special, Marshall Tucker, Blackfoot, and Lynryd Skynyrd—especially Skynyrd, and especially when the band's survivors performed live with the horns backing them up. Twice Jack had driven to Jacksonville to join Mike and Jeff at concerts of the legendary band from the town's tough west side, and both times he'd promised himself to do it again.

"I'm happy to tell you what he liked, but do you mind telling me something first?"

"I'm a very old man, my boy, with nothing to hide but my cigarettes, and them just from my wife. So ask away."

"Why the questions? Why are you so suspicious?"

"Who's to say I'm suspicious?"

"Suspicion may not be the right word, but you are protecting something. Or hiding something."

The old man looked irritated as he glanced back at a window behind him before saying, "You know what, young man? Now you're starting to sound just like my wife. And you want to know something else? I don't need another wife. Let's walk a bit."

He headed past Jack toward the steps of the porch, and Jack followed. "Been married a long time?" he asked.

"Sixty-two years of beautiful co-dependency. I've never been able to understand why depending on each other gets such a bad rap."

"I wouldn't know. And Southern Rock."

The old man looked up as he took the steps one at a time. "Yeah, Southern Rock, that's what he called it too. But Jeff didn't hang out a Confederate flag or collect Dixie cups. He didn't act the fool and was very respectful about the volume. I even took a liking to some of the songs, especially that one about flirting with disaster that has the line, 'My life is running faster.' I kind of hate how true it is, though."

Jack wanted to help him with the steps, but wouldn't. The old man's slow and careful struggle was a ritual of defiance, a stubborn determination to not let those five wooden steps imprison him at home.

"There's been too many people by here already, Mister Wells. That's why I want to be sure about you. All good people, I suppose, but I never assume that from the outset 'cause there's plenty of bad ones out there. I learned that on streets where both the lessons and the liquor was hard."

"Call me Jack."

"In that case I'm Theodore, like Roosevelt, you know. Theodore Blanchet. The T at the end is silent as a brother at a Klan rally. Like I said, too many people coming by. Those are gawkers driving by now, but they live down the street so it's understandable."

Jack looked up at a car of young people, staring as they passed as if trying to understand death by studying where it happened.

"But there just hasn't been enough cops," Theodore said, and then he burst into a laugh that came from deep down in his stomach as the irony of his words clashed with his own black history. "Man, I'd get thrown *all* the way out of the NAACP if I got heard saying there weren't enough cops. You keep that to yourself now, and definitely don't tell my wife 'cause she really don't trust 'em." He was still smiling as he navigated the bottom tread. "There, that wasn't so hard. My wife still watching us?"

Jack looked back. "Yes, sir."

"My girl is always looking out that window, making sure I get my exercise. She doesn't say much, though, even if she does catch me lazy. Now walk toward the corner with me. If she does happen to ask, tell her we went the entire distance. I did it twice already before she got up but don't tell her that 'cause she needs something to help her feel useful, and that's pretty damn important at our age."

Theodore shuffled past a bush and out of his wife's sight and immediately pulled an unfiltered Camel from his pocket and lit it. "Want one?"

"No thanks."

"Good for you. Cops came right after I called them."

"So you found Jeff's body?"

"I did. Heard the shot and went running. Well, not running, you know, but—"

"What did you find?"

Theodore pulled off his cap and rubbed his wiry gray hair. "Jack, have you ever seen a man shot through the brains with a large caliber bullet?"

"I have, yes sir."

Theodore looked surprised. "Well then, I guess I don't need to explain much to you about how it looks."

"Suppose not."

"At least that nice boy was polite enough to get into the tub and aim toward the wall so as not to spray his brains all over the room. It sure made the clean-up easier, and I guess everybody appreciated that. His girlfriend wasn't around no more, either, which was good 'cause I'd of hated for that sweet child to see that mess."

"Did you see the gun?"

"I'm old but I'm not blind. It was right there on the bathroom floor so of course I saw it. What kind of dumb question is that from a smart young man like you? His death wouldn't have been labeled a suicide if the gun was missing, now would it?"

"Do you know guns, Theodore? Know anything about automatics? Specifically, do you know that the gas blowback re-cocks the pistol and seats the next round?"

Theodore shook his head. "Son, I grew up in nasty places where I saw a lot of bad things, and the worst of those bad things almost always involved guns, just like now. So the answer is yes, I know how an automatic works."

"Good. I didn't mean to insult you. So I assume you know why I asked."

Theodore nodded. "The pistol was on the floor, like I said. The hammer was back, cocked. No one had de-cocked it for safety. It was just the way a dead man would have dropped it."

"And the police already let you clean the place?"

"Suicide took away any reasons to consider it a crime scene. I thought I'd have a bunch of ugly yellow tape all over the place, but nothing at all. They took away Jeff's body and that was that. Cops left with the coroner. My insurance company sent out a cleaning crew first thing this morning."

Jack made mental notes. He was anxious to see the room but he didn't want to push, so he waited for Theodore to finish his cigarette and scatter the unburned tobacco into the neighbor's flowerbed.

"You said there were too many people."

"I did, but I guess that's not what I meant. All the gawkers came by, and a news crew set up in the yard for a bit. I wouldn't let 'em inside. A few of Jeff's friends hung around on the porch last night and felt bad together. Some cried. Bernadette made lemonade and took it out to them, but even good lemonade like Bernie's can't do nothing for an aching heart."

"But no forensics team came out, or detectives other than the first responders?"

"At first the cops were going all kinds of *Law and Order* at my house, separating me from Bernie so we wouldn't combine our stories. Of course, they had no way of knowing that Bernie was so rattled that she still hasn't said anything about what happened, not even to me."

"I can imagine it's tough on her."

"Those cops were looking around with special lights and stuff I don't understand, and then just as a detective was about to question me, our Chief of Police showed up with those crazy weird eyes of his. He saw that the dead boy was Jeff and declared it a suicide without hardly looking around, like he was some kind of a master sleuth. And once the word suicide rolled over his lips, why would the rest of the policemen keep investigating it as murder?"

"But you don't think it was suicide?"

Theodore gave him a long look, then turned back to his house. "Come on."

Jack walked along beside him, down the sidewalk and up the steps. Theodore opened the screen door and said, "We have company, Bernie," but kept moving without waiting to see if his wife would come to the open door from the front window.

Jeff's apartment was on the first floor at the back of the house. As Theodore opened the door the smell of strong chemical cleaners made both of them turn away. Then Theodore led the way in.

Jack moved slowly through the apartment, looking for something that might provide any kind of clue that Jeff had killed himself, in case Theodore was wrong. A Dear John letter, a stack of overdue bills, drug paraphernalia, graduate school rejection, anything that made suicide believable, but he saw nothing. If not for the fact that a young man had just died in it, the apartment and its furnishings had a good and happy feel, especially because so many pictures showed Jeff hugging a very attractive woman Jack presumed to be Claire.

Theodore shuffled to the bathroom. The door was closed. He put his hand on the knob and said, "You knew Jeff, so you're immediately going to stop wondering why I doubt it was suicide. It took me a while to piece it together, but hell, you're a lot younger than me and maybe even a little smarter."

As he opened the door he pointed with one finger and said, "Jeff sat right there with his back at that end of the tub. I didn't bother to point out it was the wrong end to the cops 'cause they didn't care no how."

Jack stepped past the man and into the bathroom. He only had to glance at the tub to know the truth. He turned to Theodore, who was staring at the tub and sadly nodding his head. "You're right," Jack said, his voice not much more than a whisper. "Jeff probably wouldn't have been able to kill himself while sitting in the tub like that."

Chapter 4

Jack took the downtown exit off Interstate 581, turned right on a tree-lined boulevard, and turned again down Market Street toward the Sierra Club's office. As he got close to downtown the sidewalks and crosswalks became brick pavers, all of them busy with pedestrians moving from the striped blue-and-white awning of one business to the striped blue-and-white awning of another. Like most small cities with reinvigorated central business districts, the master-planning had succeeded in making everything look safe and inviting, but in doing so created a bit too much conformity for Jack.

The Sierra Club was on the edge of the downtown business district, located in one of the city's hundreds of red-brick buildings that was typical of Roanoke in every way except for the armed guard posted at the entrance, watching Jack. A light breeze blew a small spiral of trash around the lot as Jack walked across it, creating an impression that Sierra had chosen this as a good place to start cleaning up the earth, or at least that part of it.

Jack must not have looked threatening to the guard because he opened the door for him. He read the lobby directory and then ran the stairs to the third floor. In all the scenarios Jack had gone through his mind on his layover in

16

Atlanta, he'd never considered that within an hour of getting to Roanoke he would be sure Jeff was murdered, and that changed everything. He was no longer there to find out *if* Jeff killed himself. He was there to find a killer.

But he had no idea whom he should talk to, or whether to talk to them as allies or suspects or witnesses. He had no leads. The police had already closed the case and moved on. And Mike was only five hours away in Jacksonville, getting more restless and deadly with every hour he stayed behind to help his hurting family.

Jeff's body hadn't yet been buried but his murder already felt like a cold case, and so Jack decided to be direct and challenging, make people uncomfortable, maybe even say things to them he knew were wrong just to see if they'd correct him. If they did, it would lend credence to everything else they said, helping him establish who to trust in his investigation. But if they went along with a lie, he would put them on his list of suspects, simple as that, at least for now.

He'd learned the tactic a long time ago at the FBI Academy, yet seldom used it because it was so badly at odds with his love of the truth. He much preferred setting the elaborate traps that so often made him successful, but he didn't have the time or the necessary data to do that now.

"Good morning, sir," a friendly old receptionist said with a sad look in her eyes, forcing the cheerfulness into her greeting as if she'd only just realized she was supposed to be pleasant. "I'm Theresa. How can I help you?"

"Hello, I'm Jack Wells."

"Welcome to Sierra Club, Mister Wells."

"I'm a friend of the Roberts family. Is there someone here I could talk to about Jeff Roberts?"

Jeff's name startled her. She stared but didn't say anything as her demeanor decomposed, her battle moving from finding words to fighting tears to simply staying at her desk. It took less than a minute for her to lose them all and walk out through a door that clicked locked behind her, leaving Jack alone in the lobby.

He waited, pacing the room, looking at posters of wolves and whales and other wild things that needed protection from the greatest predator the world has ever known. He picked up an old brochure about the Keystone Pipeline and was reading about the threats it posed when a well-dressed man in his mid-sixties, with white hair and penetrating brown eyes, came out and introduced himself as Preston Harmon.

"Nice to meet you. I'm Jack Wells."

"Good afternoon, Mister Wells," Harmon said, looking Jack over like he might know him from somewhere. "I'm told you're here about Jeff. Are you a family member?"

"We were friends as close as family, if that makes any kind of sense to you."

Preston Harmon smiled slightly. "In the best of ways it does. In which case I'll say that I'm very sorry, for all of us. Am I correct in assuming that's you posing with Jeff in the photo in his office?"

"Holding up a sailfish? Cigars in our mouths like we're both Hemingway?"

"That's the one, yes. That's why you look familiar. It's nice to meet you, too. Sorry it's under such circumstances."

"It's a sad time for sure."

"We're all still in shock around here."

"Shock or disbelief?"

Harmon showed surprise at the question, and it was definitely genuine. "Shock, Mister Wells. In my line of work I can't afford the luxury of disbelief. Now please, let's go to my office. If you like I'll get you some coffee, and I believe there's cake in the break room if you'd care for a piece. It's Janet's birthday, but under the circumstances no one feels like celebrating."

"Black coffee would be nice if it's not too much trouble. Thank you."

Jack followed Harmon out of the lobby and down a hall with its walls covered in posters of wildlife and wilderness. They passed several offices where people in casual clothes glanced up at them from their desks, and one office where an angry voice cited legal precedents from behind his closed door.

"I'm surprised you're in a suit, Mister Harmon. Everyone else seems to be in Merrell's or Columbia."

"I have to be in court later today. Otherwise," he said as he opened the last door down the hall, "I'm a jeans and flannel kind of man. Here's where I contribute my small part to saving the world. Please make yourself comfortable."

Harmon's office was a trophy case of awards and plaques and photos, and Jack recognized most of the places and events from the news. One was a magazine picture of Harmon at the Deepwater Horizon site, his face red and angry as, according to the caption, he argued with an EPA official about the use of dispersants that merely caused the oil to sink to the bottom where it would continue its devastating damage to the Gulf under four thousand feet of water, out of the public's view. A marine biologist friend of Jack's at Sarasota's Mote Marine Labs expected the oil's damage to sea beds and coral colonies to impact Gulf fish and wildlife for decades, if not centuries, and Harmon appeared to be arguing the same point, his one hand gesturing toward the depths while his other held up an oil-soaked chunk of hard sea bottom.

Jack sat down and Harmon sat beside him instead of behind his desk.

"We were all shocked by Jeff's death, Mister Wells."

"Jack."

"All right, Jack. We were truly shocked, especially since no one would have ever considered him suicidal. We still have a great deal of trouble accepting it, but the police are absolutely certain, and when I demanded a copy of the death certificate as soon as it becomes available they said the coroner had no doubts about the cause of death either, even though it will take a few days to make that an official report."

"And the gun? Where did Jeff get a gun?"

"I have no idea. No one here ever saw him with one, and as you might imagine, ours is not really a gun culture, although some of us here do hunt and many of us fish."

"I find that interesting."

"Our goal is to preserve the beauty of this world, Jack, not put it off limits. Jeff loved to fish, but I never heard him express an interest in guns."

"His father taught him to hate them. His dad isn't a hunter, though, and never had the chance to use them for sport, so his opinion is biased. He could only relate guns to the carnage of war, which is ugly, of course."

"Of course. I see. But the Chief of Police said a gun was on the floor below Jeff's hand, as though it fell there after he pulled the trigger. I'm told the lab is waiting for confirmation that it's the same gun that killed him, but the Chief said it was pretty obvious, being that it was a large enough caliber to do so much damage, it was just out of reach of his hand, and it had recently been fired. All of which makes us feel even more guilty for not spotting a clue to Jeff's unhappiness, for not preventing it somehow. After all, every one of us at Sierra have dedicated our lives to protecting vulnerable things."

"There's not much you can do to protect a man from himself."

Harmon rose out of his seat, but stood silent while he considered his response before saying, "I'm compelled to disagree with you, Jack, and I'm trying my best to do so respectfully. The protection of life depends upon our respecting it, and central to that is our respect for our own lives. But I never saw anything in Jeff that indicated a lack of self-respect. Anything at all."

"Thanks for the correction," Jack said, staying seated, "but did you really know Jeff well? Or was he just one of many people working here?"

Harmon took off his glasses and cleaned them, put them back on and adjusted them precisely.

"Somewhat like you said earlier, Mister Wells, in that all of us here at Sierra are, perhaps, closer than family. I know and love everyone with whom I've fought this battle for all these decades, so I can assure you that Jeff was not just one of many in this organization, if that's what you're asking. In fact, he and many of the other young people working here engender a great deal of parental pride in those of us who are a bit long in the tooth. We admire their amazing promise and enthusiasm, not yet beaten down by the truth."

"Meaning?"

Harmon raised an easy fist to his face and dropped his chin onto it as the formality of his posture crumpled. "Meaning only that we're fighting in a world that's dominated by a fossil fuel industry that owns or dominates Washington and the media, and we're losing this war at an accelerated rate now that some corporate-sponsored cable news outlets make environmentalists sound like crazy, tree-hugging alarmists."

"I can see that."

"No offense, Jack, but anyone with a modicum of intelligence can see that cable *news*, if that lofty word can be so applied, has done a fantastic job of convincing half of America that the two billion tons of pollutants we pump annually into the air we breathe doesn't contribute one iota to the crisis of global warming. Or should I say climate change, which is the new PC word for it since it elicits less of a knee-jerk reaction, the way Affordable Care Act gets far less of a negative reaction from people than Obama Care."

"Climate change does sound better."

"It makes it sound predictably evolutionary, doesn't it? Yet it's a distinction without a difference if agenda-driven cable news continues to convince Americans that global warming doesn't exist in the first place, or that nothing needs to be done about it. I actually saw a bumper sticker recently that said, 'I love Climate Change,' if you can believe that."

"Isn't there a reasonable basis for doubt?"

"Of course there is, Jack, and it's called ignorance. Even the Defense Department has declared global warming a grave security risk, and one of their biggest concerns for the future."

"So I've read."

"The Maldives, Seychelles, and Kiribati might well be underwater by the end of this century, and lots of coastal cities, including Norfolk, Virginia, where the U.S. Fifth Fleet is headquartered at the largest naval base in the entire world, will be partially underwater. Oceans have gradually risen eight full inches, and every year we see more wildfires, more animals migrating north, and more droughts, storms and floods, all because of a one-degree average increase in temperature. Two degrees will cause a near-total collapse of society, especially since the Artic is heating up twice as fast as the rest of the planet. If even a small amount of the carbon on the Arctic floor gets released into the atmosphere, well, as Dr. Box said in his now-famous tweet, "We're fucked."

"If all that's true, people will get the message soon enough, don't you think?"

"Of course they will, Jack. The willful ignorance people express so passionately today as they ridicule groups like ours in their support of *clean* coal—" He laughed. "What a stroke of marketing brilliance it was to pair those two odd words together."

"It does sound good."

"Black, filthy, polluting coal. Nothing clean about it. Anyway, all doubts about scientific warnings will have long been eradicated by the time major cities along the U.S. East Coast start becoming swamps again, but of course by then it will be much too late."

Jack sat quietly, thinking about what Harmon was saying and wanting to know more. But he had a job to do, a killer to find, and a gorgeous island waiting for him when he was finished, so his interest would have to wait.

"What was Jeff working on? The last email I got from him was a satirical editorial he'd written that defended the rights of corporations to exploit the environment. Something about a corporation saying access to water was not a human right."

Harmon laughed lightly. "Yes, that was a brilliant piece and cleverly written, but I kept him from submitting that to the magazines because I disagreed with the underlying premise that corporations are bad."

"Really? I'm surprised."

"You shouldn't be. Do you really believe that corporations set out with the intent of damaging the environment? Of course they don't. Sure, they have lots of good reasons to be against the Sierra Club and other groups like us, but corporations, even if only on an intuitive level, realize that we're all residents and trustees of the environment, even those people who work for polluting corporations. Earth is our home, so all of us are naturally inclined to want to protect it, not unlike the way we're naturally inclined to protect our kids, or our personal property. The problems occur when that motivation comes in conflict with other motivations, profit being chief among them."

"Corporate profits?"

"I'm simply talking about money, Jack, nothing more than the amount of cash you probably have in your wallet. Companies are big targets and easy to blame, but we don't have to travel very far from where we're sitting right now to find pollution-related birth defects, flammable water right out of the tap, dramatically decreased lifespans, and shockingly high infant mortality. Yet folks in those communities willingly overlook those incredible hazards because they need a job to pay their bills for food and doctors and school supplies."

"Jeff wrote an article a few years ago on towns that protect the polluters who employ them, even as the by-products of those very same companies were killing them."

"I've seen it play out many times myself, where we've succeeded in closing heavy polluters and then the folks who lived in those towns lost their jobs. Their homes became worthless and the tax base shriveled, which meant schools closed and essential services were cut. The residents had no money to move, so they stayed there and suffered. Our well-intentioned protection of the environment cost those people dearly, so they, too, have understandable reasons to hate us. I'm sympathetic to that."

"Being hated can be a dangerous line of work."

"Quite true, and often our most dangerous adversaries are not the companies we target, but rather those very citizens I just mentioned, along with the town councils, real estate firms, and developers of nearby communities. When they join forces with a company we've chosen to put in our crosshairs, ours becomes quite a formidable challenge."

Jack's pool of suspects for Jeff's murder was already undefined, and Harmon had just expanded it exponentially.

Harmon took a deep breath and smiled. "Of course, it could also just be that I'm getting old."

"It is a pretty pessimistic outlook for a man in your position."

"My outlook is formed by forty-six professional years of realism and hardened by a great many defeats, but I rarely share it with people. I'm a bit depressed today over Jeff. I dedicated my life to this work. I have no family of my own, so when I lose someone from my Sierra family, especially someone like Jeff, it hurts. You are right though, in that I can't afford to sound pessimistic. I need to inspire my co-workers. I need to have faith in our goals."

"What did Jeff do here?"

Harmon breathed deep, then rubbed his temples thoughtfully. "I'll take your word, and the picture in Jeff's office, to indicate you knew him well, which means that you must have known he was very easy to like, with an excellent ability to get along with people. Everyone always wanted to help him, and that enabled him to access a great deal of information."

Jack remembered Jeff asking questions about the FBI so innocently that Jack had trouble refusing, then putting Jack on the spot a year or two later with perfect recall as he asked for more details and justifications.

"He was good with people."

"He was more than good. I've never seen someone so young with so much natural skill that was so well developed. Robyn—"

"Robyn?"

"Yes, Robyn Thomas, our head legal council. She was Jeff's mentor and he reported to her. But she needed to do very little mentoring. I would often sit in on meetings where she and Jeff and others would speculate about how to develop evidence of an environmental violation, or recruit a solid witness, and as we threw out ideas Jeff would offer up some very simple approach. Then he'd make it happen, just by getting people to talk to him."

Jack couldn't help but smile. "Yes, that was Jeff all right."

"He was quite amazing."

"And what was he working on recently? Of course, I'm sure you realize, Mister Harmon, that what I'm really asking is what you think got Jeff killed."

He'd given Harmon a good opening, and so he quickly added a way out, "Or what you think might have made him kill himself?"

Harmon leaned back and smiled. "Ah, that's good."

"What?"

"That you're not quite convinced he killed himself, either."

"Mister Harmon, I'll ask you straight up. Overlooking all the evidence that it was suicide, and factoring in what you knew about Jeff, do you believe Jeff might have been murdered?"

Jack watched for the response. It didn't matter so much what Harmon gave as an answer, but the way he answered would be important.

Harmon thoughtfully tented his fingers in front of his mouth as though keeping it from moving until he was ready. Jack waited.

"I don't want to believe that Jeff killed himself. But I know he was upset over a troubled relationship. Their break-up hurt Jeff. And his work suffered when his girlfriend took the job in Atlanta and moved away."

"Hurtful stuff, for sure."

"But now I would like to know what you think, Jack."

Jack was going to stay pretty close to the police department version, with just him and Theodore knowing the truth for now. "Let's just say I have a little bit of trouble seeing Jeff as the kind of guy who would commit suicide."

"Please, let's be honest. You don't believe for one second that he killed himself."

"If you have another theory, I'd love to hear it."

Harmon walked to the windows. He stared out for awhile and then turned and leaned against them. "It's an absolute insult to call it a theory, Jack. An insult to so many good people."

Jack didn't know what to say, so he said nothing, which was apparently what Harmon expected as he paused with words so ready on his lips that they could have been a prayer.

"I've lost three people this year, Jack, just from the offices in this region. Three wonderfully devoted people who worked and gave their lives in the struggle to protect the air we breathe and the water we drink. That number is a bit larger than most offices because we have so much of the country's industry near here, often in tucked-away places where it's easy to get away with major legal violations."

"I never would have guessed this work was so dangerous. And to be honest I find it hard to believe now. They weren't all presumed to be suicides, I'm sure."

"Have faith in what I'm saying, Jack, but no, not all were suicides. Jonathan is believed to have drowned, even though he avoided the water and his body was never recovered. Jessica was killed in a crosswalk by a hit-and-run driver who was never caught. And of course there's Jeff, whose cause of death is yet to be determined for sure. All of them died just before filing a suit against a major polluter, or presenting their proof in a court of law."

"Are you suggesting some kind of conspiracy?"

"Conspiracy? No, that's ridiculous."

"Then what?"

Harmon stared as though he wanted to tell him everything. Then Jack saw him shake his head, very slightly, but enough for Jack to take as a sign he didn't think Jack was ready for truth without a lead-in. "Nationwide we've lost twelve people this year. Just Sierra Club alone."

"Incredible."

"Internationally, if you count all the groups protecting animals, water, air and land, about a hundred dedicated people are murdered every year doing their job. And keep in mind that number does not include accidental deaths, real suicides, and murder for other reasons, such as a jealousy. Those people were murdered while actively protecting the environment, pure and simple. Yet there's prosecution in only about ten percent of those murders."

"Again, I didn't know. I don't think I've ever heard anything about it, except for a Belgian prince getting shot to pieces working as a game warden protecting gorillas in the Congo."

"Quite a brave man he is, too, but you only heard of him because he was dedicated enough to go back to the Virunga National Park after he healed. Otherwise you wouldn't have heard of him, or any of our losses, because if word got out that two people a week died trying to make sure our air or water is clean, even our most skeptical adversaries would be tempted to ask questions."

"I suppose that lack of attention makes their deaths easy to overlook."

"Let's use Jeff as a painful example. His death is in the local papers today. There will be an obit here and in his hometown paper. After that, he'll be forgotten by all but family and friends like us."

"And that happens regularly in your world, Mister Harmon?"

"Sometimes in warring nations we'll lose a dozen workers at a time, and it's important to remember that all of them are non-combatant environmentalists, not soldiers. They're there to save elephants or apes or a potable water supply upon which a town or village depends for survival."

"I can imagine that's a dangerous environment."

"But clean water isn't only the problem of mud-hut cultures. Phosphate fertilizer run-off recently polluted the drinking water that comes from Lake Erie, and Lake Erie is a mighty big body of water to pollute. And look at the use of Chloramine in Flint and hundreds of other cities. Jesus, just to save money, those governments used stuff so toxic it strips lead and copper from our pipes and dumps it into our water glasses."

"Dangerous in a whole other way."

"But at least in war zones the fallen are credited with the reasons they put themselves in harm's way. None of them are shamefully labeled as suicides."

Jack sat silent, trying to stay focused on Jeff. It was hard.

"Mister Harmon—"

"After indulging me on that diatribe, please call me Preston."

"All right, Preston. Please tell me why you think Jeff is dead?"

Preston thought about it, staring out his windows as he worked out an answer. "Jack, even after all I've said, I have no choice but to go with the evidence. The police say it was suicide, the facts are compelling, and I've certainly seen enough young men and women do tragic things over a love gone wrong. I don't want to accept it."

"But you do?"

"Yes. I'm afraid that I do."

"You mentioned a mentor of Jeff's."

"I did. Would you like to speak with her?"

"If she's here, yes."

Preston stepped to his desk and picked up the phone. "Robyn, I have a gentleman in my office who'd like to speak to you about Jeff." He hung up and smiled.

A minute later Harmon's door opened and a woman stepped in, and for a couple of beats Jack forgot all about the reason he was there.

Chapter 5

Robyn Thomas led Jack to her office three doors down. She was almost as tall as he was, with a lean, strong body. Her brown hair was long enough to be feminine but short enough to look professional, and her eyes were almost as green as the new spring leaves on the trees outside, giving the impression that any work other than environmental protection would be a waste of her destiny.

She was in her early thirties, younger than Jack by only a couple of years, and walked ahead of him with the elegant self-assuredness of a woman who'd earned her way to command, her head high and her shoulders back.

As Jack followed along behind her he had a crazy-rare feeling that he could easily be talked into letting this woman take him anywhere. He'd always been popular with women, and as a standout first baseman at the University of Florida he'd gotten a fair amount of media attention that attracted lots of female attention, giving him a broad palette of experiences. But seldom had any of those experiences combined so many of the essential elements that made him feel the way he did right now, walking three steps behind Robyn.

Robyn didn't look back as she asked, "Do you live in Roanoke, Mister Wells?"

"No."

"Are you a detective?"

"No."

"Are you a one-word kind of fellow, Mister Wells? Or did a cat get your tongue?"

She glanced back and smiled and he felt himself flush.

"My dad taught me to do more listening than talking around powerful people."

"The suit is for court," she twisted her wrist to check her watch, "where I have to be soon."

"Preston also mentioned court. I won't take much of your time. You're a lawyer?"

"Environmental Law. And your father should have taught you not to discriminate, that you should listen to all people with respect."

"I believe I do, Miss Thomas." He needed to get some traction with her. And even if he didn't need to, he wanted to. So after a pause he added, "Or is it Missus?"

She glanced over her shoulder at him and pretended to look annoyed, using a lifetime of practice to make sure it didn't look genuine. "For the purpose of our discussing Jeff, does it matter whether I'm married or not?"

"It might. You never know what might turn out to be important."

"In that case it's Miss Thomas. Or Robyn."

She'd made a play by offering up her first name, but he was enjoying their game too much to take the hand-off. "Well, Miss Thomas, just to set the record straight between us, I've never considered the recognition of power as being discriminatory."

She nodded as she walked ahead of him, her hair bouncing against her shoulders. "Yes, of course you're right, it isn't. I was just kidding you, although I do believe what I said about discrimination."

"No argument from me."

"I was really just trying to make small talk."

Jack grinned and decided to throw the long bomb. "This feels kind of like a first date. You know, all awkward but interesting."

Robyn stopped instantly and turned. It took Jack a second to react, bringing him close enough to get a nose full of her perfume.

"What? No, Mister Wells, I'm making small talk because you're here to talk to me about Jeff, and that's going to be hard enough for me to do without first getting to know you a little."

"Oh." Jack said, forcing his eyes to stay even with hers. "Of course."

Then she cocked her head slightly and smiled. "Although under better circumstances I suppose some awkward first date talk might be fun."

She turned quickly and walked away, her high heels clicking the floor and attracting his eyes that followed her legs to the hem of her tight but professional skirt, at which point he wanted to hit himself for forgetting about Jeff, even though he knew Jeff would smile and tell him to go for it. If Jeff was alive.

Robyn opened her office door and walked in, leaving the door for Jack to close or not. He closed it and then checked to make sure that it latched to show he wanted to be alone with her.

The walls were covered with awards and photos, like Harmon's. None of the men in the photos seemed like a boyfriend. The only children were in groups, working as volunteers. The rest of the photos were of Robyn with co-workers, including some of her with Harmon that went back a decade or more.

She leaned back against the front of her desk with her arms folded over her chest. "As I said, Mister Wells, I don't have much time."

"Jack."

"Preston and I have to be in court in an hour."

"Does court have something to do with Jeff's death?"

"Yes and no. We're not going about Jeff's death, but rather as a direct result of it. We're going to plead for a continuance on the very important lawsuit Jeff filed against the Montessa Chemical Corporation and its parent, Montessa International."

"Why is a continuance necessary? Don't you have his files?"

"We do."

"So why can't you still go to trial with Montessa? Aren't they the weed killer company?"

"Yes, that's some of what they do. You're sure you're not a lawyer, Jack?"

"I'm not. But I like to think I know a little about the law."

She smiled beautifully as she rolled her eyes, pretending to soften the sting when she said, "Doesn't everyone think they know the law?"

"That's because laws," he shot back, smiling at her exactly the same way she smiled at him, "were built upon very human understandings of what's right and what's wrong. They were intuitive to us at the outset and still would be if lawyers didn't profit by complicating and manipulating them."

He kept smiling as he watched her closely to see if a simple argument of reasonable merit could offend her.

Robyn nodded as though she liked that he'd defended himself, or maybe that he'd attacked her. She was clearly a fighter and used to taking a hit, and that made her even more attractive to Jack.

"Well," she said, starting out slowly, "the problem we have today is that our case, Jeff's case, is based almost entirely on his nearly perfect compilation of compelling evidence. Evidence, I might add, of which Jeff was understandably proud and very anxious to present in court. He wouldn't have missed this trial for anything."

"Preston has accepted that his death was suicide, but it doesn't sound like you do."

Her voice rose with her as she pushed off the desk and stood very erect. "Of course it wasn't—"

She cut herself off, but her eyes had already sent a message Jack had seen many times before. She had revealed what she truly believed, but then she'd tried to hide it, probably for one of the three classic reasons. She either doubted what she believed, or she distrusted him, or she had good reason to be afraid of speaking out.

"It probably was suicide," she said. "Who am I to speculate? He was badly shaken by a relationship gone wrong."

"Did you know him well? Ever go over to his house for a party or anything? I know he was in a serious relationship with a woman named Claire, but I don't really know the details. Do you know her?"

"Claire Statler was a local news reporter. A good one. I don't think Jeff ever had parties. I've certainly never been invited to his house for one, or for any reason for that matter. I doubt any of us here have because he just wasn't a party kind of guy."

"You said his girlfriend *was* a local reporter?"

"Claire got an offer to anchor the news desk at NBC's Atlanta affiliate, which is obviously a much bigger market. It was a great opportunity for her. Jeff said she'd make three times what she earned here in Roanoke and have a much better chance of advancement."

"But he didn't want her to go."

"Of course he didn't, but it's not like they fought about it. Jeff was too nice for that. He supported her decision to move one hundred percent, even as it was breaking his heart."

It was easy to believe what she said because Jeff always wanted whatever was best for everyone else, putting himself near the end of the line. "Couldn't Jeff have transferred to Atlanta? Certainly there must be environmental issues there, too."

Robyn rolled her eyes again, but this time she frowned as she did it. "Oh, God, yes, of course. Jeff could have gone anywhere he wanted with us, or with any of the big organizations. But he had his teeth too deep into Montessa's skin. He couldn't wait to see this case through."

"Is that the reason you doubt it was suicide?"

"I said that it probably was suicide."

"You did, that's right, but you don't believe it."

She swayed forward and back as she thought about what to say, then looked up at Jack and said, "As bad as it makes me sound, I guess I want to accept that he really did kill himself over Claire. But I have two reasons to have my doubts and no matter how hard I try I can't seem to shake them."

She turned and pointed at several stacks of documents on her desk. "This stuff is the first reason. These documents represent a very intense year's worth of work that should have culminated in a sweeping Department of Justice investigation into Montessa's chemical-handling procedures, and probably ended up with several criminal convictions, especially as it spread to countries more concerned about the environment than America, countries with harsher penalties."

"And Jeff played a part in it?"

"He did far more than just play a part. Jeff was integral to the initial procurement of the evidence that forms the basis of this suit."

"And that would be...?"

"That Montessa is even more careless in their storage of chemical by-products than Freedom Industries. Jeff started out just wanting to get their local storage tanks cleaned and brought up to federal specifications, until he learned how globally careless Montessa was."

"Freedom Industries?"

"The criminally careless company that spilled 10,000 gallons of crude chemicals into the Elk River near Charleston, which is not far from here, and only got fined $7,000 for poisoning the drinking water of 300,000 people and causing $61 million in losses to businesses."

Jack was reminded of the BP oil spill, and how its horrible effects were slowly showing up in the water he loved so much, and how the TV commercials of BP executives saying how much they'd helped rescue the environment made him want to puke, since most of their help was at gunpoint. "Sounds like Freedom got off easy."

"Don't they all? How can you expect otherwise when Congress protects them? The tiny fine they paid was an insignificant percentage of the economic benefit they derived by polluting." She grabbed a spreadsheet off her desk and tossed it to him. "These are the companies we're targeting right now, ranked in order of their threat to our health and well-being. The dollar amount on the right shows the pittances they've been fined. The one in front of it, the one with all the zeroes and commas, is how much profit they made through the illegal behavior that lead to those fines. Not total profits, mind you, but just the specific profits they're earned through ignoring the environmental laws in place."

Jack looked at it and saw several familiar names, but he'd never heard of most of them.

"Jeff's research proved that a far greater hazard than the Elk River spill exists near here at a Montessa storage field. He was the primary link in the chain of custody of that evidence. So without him to testify we're back on our heels trying to still make some kind of a case."

"Should I wish you good luck?"

"The words would be wasted. We've already resigned ourselves to the fact that we won't win. The judge will throw it out and Montessa will keep on polluting, as they do all over the country and all over the world. You're sure you're not a detective?"

"I'm a charter fishing captain from Marco Island, Florida."

She leaned forward as a smile came to her lips. "Do you see many dolphins out there in the water?"

"Every day. I see dolphins almost every time I go out. They play in the wake of my boat and often leap in it. Sometimes they leap right beside the boat and look me straight in the eye. They're amazingly curious."

Robyn seemed to find peace in that, as though dolphins symbolized the rationale for all the pain and challenge and death associated with Sierra's work. "I absolutely love to see dolphins play and interact like that. But I suppose everyone loves them."

"I believe you're right. The Japanese love them for food."

She made a disgusted look. "It's a pretense for slaughtering them. Very few Japanese eat dolphin."

"I didn't know that."

She smiled. "Happy to enlighten you. Now, before we talk much further about Jeff or Sierra or anything else, Captain Wells, since you're not a lawyer or a detective I'd like to know why you're here. Preston asked me to speak with you and I've enjoyed our little chat, but please tell me why I should invest any more of my time in you."

"I....wow." He looked her over. "Are you really as tough as you seem?"

She leaned toward him as her smile took on a sly twist. "No, not really." Then she leaned back and said, "Well?"

Jack reset himself the way he had as a federal agent during tough cross-examinations by sharp lawyers paid a fortune to keep wealthy clients out of federal prisons, focusing both eyes straight ahead, squaring his shoulders, and then forcing a smile to make his face relax.

"I'm a good friend of the Roberts family. Jeff's dad asked me to look into his death." Jack paused as they both looked down.

"It is such a tragedy, regardless of how it happened."

"Yes it is."

"But why didn't Jeff's dad come himself? I would have come if it had been my son."

"Do you have a son?"

"I don't."

"Mike's staying home to help his wife and his other kids get through this."

"Good for him."

"And good for Roanoke, because you people wouldn't want him here. Mike's hurt and angry and those emotions make a man with his background extremely dangerous."

"And you, Jack?"

"I'm hurt and I'm sad."

"Not dangerous?"

"Not to you, certainly. I hope I'm not perceived as dangerous to anyone."

Robyn looked skeptical as she moved behind her desk and sat down. "So you are that rarest of all living things? A peaceful man?"

It would have felt great to say yes. "No."

"But can I assume you are trying?" She picked up a document from one of the piles of papers to use as a prop, feigning interest but not looking at it.

"I am."

"I guess that's good enough. Now you'll have to excuse me because I need to organize what little of this evidence we can still use against Montessa." She looked at her watch. "I really have to get going. How will you spend your afternoon, Jack?"

"I'd like to talk to Jeff's girlfriend, Claire. Do you have a number for her?"

"I do, but I've called her a dozen times and she doesn't answer. I can't say as I blame her."

"In that case I just might go out to Montessa Chemicals. It seems a good place to ask a few questions. Anyone in particular I should talk to there?"

"You'd need a subpoena to talk to any of those murderous bastards other than Julius Reed."

"Murderous?"

"I shouldn't have said that, but they cause so many deaths it's hard to see them differently. Please don't mention anything you saw or heard here."

"Of course not."

"Their regional office is east of town, toward Smith Mountain Lake. Take State Road 116. There's a sign for it." She shrugged. "Not that it will matter much if you share our conversation. They already know what we have against them. They know we're going to lose."

"I would never repeat anything you told me to them."

"And you must be cautious out there."

"That's rich coming from you."

"What's rich?"

"Your warning me. I'm a fisherman from Florida, here just long enough to get some answers about Jeff. It sounds like you, on the other hand, live at the tip of the spear of this war."

She waved it away. "It's really nothing. All of us long ago accepted the risks of the job and got used to them. Now, good luck to you, Captain Wells. If I can be of some help to Jeff's family or you, please ask, although I can't imagine how."

"Can we speak later, Miss Thomas? Perhaps over dinner?"

"It's going to be a long afternoon in court."

"I'm sure. Besides, you'd probably find it hard to be good company after that." He stood and turned to leave.

"Let's say six o'clock at The Lodge. It's just west of town. Call me Robyn."

As Jack walked to the door he turned in time to see her smile.

"Oh, one last thing, Robyn." It felt good to say her name.

"Yes?"

"The second reason?"

"I'm not following you."

"You said there were two reasons you had trouble believing Jeff killed himself."

She put down the paper and spoke slowly. "His girlfriend, Claire Statler, was an odds-on favorite to win a Pulitzer Prize for Investigative Journalism for the thoroughness with which she went after Montessa with Jeff. That's a very big deal, as I'm sure you can imagine."

"I'm guessing it can solidify a journalist's career."

"Exactly, and she was at the top of a very short list of likely recipients, particularly since this story has such worldwide implications for Montessa. She and Jeff swapped a lot of information, made a great team, and between them uncovered more than Sierra could have ever expected. Or Montessa could have anticipated, for that matter."

"Couldn't she still get the Pulitzer?"

"No."

"Why not?"

Robyn stood like a prosecutor delivering the final line of a closing argument to a breathless jury.

"When Claire Statler walked away from Roanoke she killed the story that could've won her the prize. She walked away from it, too."

Chapter 6

A small army of private security contractors protected *Montessa Chemical Corporation, a Division of Montessa International, Appalachian District Home Office.*

Jack read the sign a couple of times as he listened to the gate sentry talk on a phone to gain him access. Another soldier used a mirror to check under his car for explosives while his German Shepherd sniffed and scratched at it.

"Step out of the car," the sentry said as he hung up the phone and stepped out of his guard house. "We need to perform a pat down and vehicle search. You have the option of declining but the procedure is necessary for admittance."

Jack wanted to back up his car and leave. He'd already gone through enough paranoid theatrics at the airport, pulled randomly from the security line to perform the *Threat Level Orange Ballet* while a herd of shoeless passengers watched, working their way through the maze that kept TSA busy collecting pen knives and water while well-known airport employees were cleared to roam the airport and tarmac with a "Hey there, Fred" level of security.

But he'd promised Mike he'd learn the truth about Jeff's death, and now that he knew for sure that Jeff had been murdered he would submit to whatever was necessary to find out who did it. He owed it to Mike and he owed it to Jeff, even though it violated his personal rule to serve ideals and entire populations but never individuals, because protection on an individual basis was too black and white, with a single death making you a failure.

He slowly got out and stepped away from the car, as directed, and let the guards have it their way, one of them scanning him with a wand and then patting him down while another guard with an assault weapon at port arms carefully watched his eyes and his hands.

Their uniforms identified them as SILT contractors, a small security company Jack knew from Afghanistan that had ballooned in size in Iraq. They'd changed their name twice since the early days of those wars, trying to distance themselves from the bloody illegality of their actions, but anyone who paid attention to the news, especially news that involved the military and military contractors, would know their sordid but profitable history. They'd killed far too many civilians in Iraq, operated outside the restrictions placed on the military by its strict rules of engagement, and got rich for doing both things, their billion dollar no-bid contracts protected by the color of flag and guaranteed by the gutless patriotism of a terrified nation.

In the early days of the war Jack met a Wackenhut bank guard who'd been hired by them and sent to Afghanistan, earning a hundred and fifty large and a month's paid vacation even though he'd never been in the military or done anything more dangerous than locking and unlocking a bank's front door. But the quality of SILT contractors had improved as the business of war gave it a decade to work out its rough spots, right up to the point where SILT had evolved into its apex form, purely mercenary and extremely good at it.

"Mister Reed has approved your entry, Mister Wells," the SILT said with a fuck-you attitude before looking over at the SILT with the dog and mirror, who nodded. He turned back to Jack. "You'll need an escort. Get in your car and pull up to the force protection barricades. Turn off your vehicle. Leave the keys in the ignition but wait in the car." He sneered a "Thank you" as if hating the fact that Jack had been authorized to go beyond him.

"Over there?" Jack asked naively as he pointed.

The SILT pointed too. "Right over there."

"Right over there by the...what did you call it...force protection?"

"Yes, right...over...there." The SILT leaned into the window so it would just be him and Jack. "Are you trying to be a smart ass, Wells?"

"Are you trying to be a dick—" he looked for a name on the uniform but didn't find one. "Whatever your name is? Or does being a dick just come naturally to you? Maybe you're a third or fourth generation dick with a long and proud family heritage of dickishness."

The SILT reached into Jack's car, but Jack pushed his hand away as the other SILT with the dog hustled around and shouted, "Aaron, the man's been cleared to go in so back away and let him go." He pushed Aaron out of the way and said, "Begging your pardon, sir," as he handed Jack his license.

Jack said "Thank you, sir" to the second SILT, hitting the word sir hard to show that respect cut both ways, exactly the same as disrespect.

He pulled forward and parked the car and waited, looking around the compound while he did, and the more he looked the more obvious it became that no actual manufacturing took place in the four-story brick and glass building Montessa had built like a bunker among the sensually rolling hills and endless views of gorgeous trees in the full bloom of spring. This building was a command post, protected exactly the way a command post should be, with dogs and fences and men with guns, giving Jack a very familiar feeling.

Two other SILTs, walking the perimeter of the fence line, approached the gate from opposite directions, gave a quick report to Aaron at the entry gate, then proceeded on. Ten minutes later Jack heard a phone ring, and immediately after that another SILT with a Doberman walked out of a distant guard house and over to Jack.

"That way, sir" he said, motioning toward a white-painted path with red borders that crossed the parking lot and approached the building. Jack moved slowly out of his car and followed the path, with the SILT five steps behind him until they got to the door, where he stepped in front and punched a code into the keypad. The front door buzzed and he opened it for Jack.

In the lobby, another SILT at a reception desk made yet another copy of Jack's driver's license, and took a photo of him that he laminated onto a badge. He handed it to Jack and said, "Make absolutely sure this is clearly visible at all times."

"Okey-dokey."

"That way," said the SILT with the Doberman, and so Jack took off walking toward a second set of locked doors. But he'd only gone a dozen or so steps when the SILT stopped at a door just down the hall where a small sign said, Mr. Julius Reed, Vice-President, Public Affairs.

"You are instructed to go inside and wait."

The soldier waited for Jack to open the door and go inside, and as the door slowly closed he heard the dog's claws tapping back down the tile floor toward the entrance.

A white-haired woman looked up from her computer and smiled. "Make yourself at home, Mister Wells." Then she grinned as though the idea of her waiting room being comfortable enough to call home was a terrific joke. "Mister Reed will be with you in a few minutes."

"Great," Jack said as he studied a case full of mementos and trophies awarded to Montessa for their community support. Little League, Boy Scouts, Girl

Scouts, Rotary, Kiwanis, Moose, Elks, and the American Legion. Recognition for a grant they'd made to the local hospital. A decree from Roanoke's Mayor that June 1st be "hereinafter known as Montessa Chemical Corporation Day." A photo of several men in suits using shiny chrome shovels to turn over the first clumps of dirt for a new playground. Jack studied the photo to see if one of the men was Julius Reed, but his name wasn't there.

"Mister Wells," the woman said. "Mister Reed will see you now." She waved him toward a paneled wood door that stood in comforting contrast to the solid steel doors and steel jambs in the lobby.

"Thank you."

Julius Reed stood and walked over as Jack went in. He was young, handsome and black, with a thin moustache probably intended to add a few years to his age, and a fraudulent smile definitely intended to hide his suspicion of visitors. Jack noticed a diploma on the wall from Howard University that awarded Reed a Bachelor of Arts degree in public relations, and as Reed extended his hand and expanded his smile he seemed intent on proving he'd earned it.

"Welcome to Montessa, Mister Wells. Please have a seat."

Jack sat and made a show of looking around the office, then nodded as if he was very impressed. "You have a nice office. I didn't much care for the apes outside, though."

Reed glanced out his window. "Yes, they're an unfortunate necessity because of national security. If a terrorist managed to set off a bomb here, well, I'm sure you can see where I'm going with this."

"Right. Of course I can." He made an explosion with his hands. "My god, there'd be fallout of manila envelopes and printer ink all over Western Virginia."

"How I can help you, Mister Wells?"

Jack laughed. "I'm sorry. Didn't mean to make light of your security. I make jokes when I'm nervous."

"I'm sure there's no reason for you to be nervous. So...?"

"I'm doing some research for a friend. He's thinking of relocating his factory to this general neck of the woods and I'm trying to learn a little about the business climate in Western Virginia, particularly after that nasty Elk River chemical spill nearby."

Reed seemed relieved by the question, as though he already had an answer well-rehearsed. "I might be able to help with that. It's really a matter for the other side of the house, as we call the guys in Compliance, but since you're already here let's you and I talk a bit. How did you get my name, by the way?"

"I think you were mentioned in a press release my friend read, but I'm not really sure. From the looks of your lobby it doesn't look like I would have got much farther anyway, so it's probably just as well. Glad you weren't out sick today, or out taking a long lunch."

"Yes, it's just as well."

Silence. Jack suspected Reed was already pegging him as a liar, but it didn't really matter because he would be gone soon and had no intention of coming back for more fun with the SILTs. He would take whatever information he might learn and use it as data points that he hoped would point to the real reason that Jeff was dead.

"And what type of product does your friend produce?"

"Paper products. You know...well, paper products."

"Ah. By any chance is he relocating from Canton, North Carolina? I know there's a paper mill there that's been struggling with an increasing tendency to flood, due perhaps to natural erosion of the upper Pigeon River. And they're also getting pressure from developers to move. At least, I've heard a rumor that they want to relocate that mill."

Reed was testing him and Jack knew it, but since Jack had been the one to throw out paper mills he searched for everything he'd ever known or heard about them. "He wants his plans to remain confidential until he decides, but for the sake of conversation let's assume you're right."

"Canton is located in the Blue Ridge Mountains, next to Waynesville, which has a booming tourism business, especially in the fall when the leaves turn. That's really the reason I brought it up. Before the recession, a group of developers felt Canton had a shot at joining Waynesville as a vacation destination if they could force the plant to close. The developers didn't want the paper mill smell that the residents had long ago learned to accept."

Jack saw a chance to sound knowledgeable and he took it. "But the locals don't mind the smell because it's a fair economic trade-off."

"You're right, of course. That rotten egg odor is the smell of money to most of the folks who live there, because the mill provides good, safe livelihoods, and has done so for generations. They're duly proud of that, and they should be."

"Montessa shares a similar corporate dynamic, I suppose."

Reed smiled. "We try hard to be excellent neighbors, as well as a contributing part of each community in which we operate."

"My client feels the same way."

"Your client? I believe you said he was your friend."

Jack straightened his shoulders and laughed. "He's equal parts both, and he'd be very interested in your thoughts on how fully you would expect this region to accept him and his business, which, I should point out, will employ almost four hundred people."

Jack had no idea how many people might work at a paper mill. Back in the FBI he would have gone deep in the weeds and thoroughly researched an industry before having a conversation like this, but in his mind he could see Mike Roberts putting his kids to bed and getting his wife to sleep, and then cleaning his weapons and sharpening his knife and hardening his mind in anticipation of putting his hands to bloody work. Jack had seen more than enough of that work already, which dictated the urgency that made the 48-hour timer in his head tick almost deafeningly.

"Well, Mister Wells, it's always hard to predict that sort of thing while speculating about the type of industry involved, but people around here and, I think, people in most places of the world, accept the presence of industry in much the same way as they accept the presence of man. I never bought into the corporations-are-people-too silliness, but biologically we're nearly identical."

"Well that's something I've never heard before. And I can't honestly say that I follow you. Not even this much." Jack pinched his fingers together and then left a tiny gap.

Reed leaned back in his chair. "Let me help you with that. What did you have for breakfast, Mister Wells?"

"Coffee."

"Okay, then let me ask what you had the last time you ate a full meal."

"I had fish."

"Fresh fish or farm-raised?"

"Fresh grouper that I caught myself."

"Nice. I'm envious. From the shore? The bank of a river?"

"From my boat. You don't find too many grouper in rivers. Where are you going with this?"

Reed leaned back farther, settling into the comfortable pose of a professor teaching a well-rehearsed lesson. "Then please allow me a few assumptions."

"Of course."

"In order for you to catch that fish a manufacturing company, following strict environmental regulations, had to carefully produce the fiberglass and resin that went into your boat. Another company, where workers wore breathing respirators while giant fans gulped up acrid fumes, laid-up the fiberglass. An exhaust-spewing truck hauled your boat to the dealer who sold it to you. You filled your boat with fossil fuel in order to fish with rods and reels made from—"

"I get it."

"Good. But you accepted all that pollution and expenditure of raw materials without even thinking about the real cost to a town, or population, or the world for that matter. You wanted to go fishing, which is simple enough." Reed paused and smiled. "And I wish you'd invited me. But surely you see that your carbon footprint for catching that one fish was huge. I can't really speak for any corporation besides Montessa, but I do believe that most businesses, and especially Montessa, try hard to keep a good balance between needs, wants, costs, and impact, and I firmly believe that we as an industry are often more considerate of all those factors than you, Mister Wells. We've certainly studied them more, not only because we want to be good corporate citizens, but because we are required to do so by law."

"My friend's big issue is waste by-product."

"Of course it is, and there's no reason to sound ashamed of it like you just did. Waste by-product is a natural occurrence in both nature and business and there needn't be anything sinister about it."

"Tell that to people along the Elk River."

Reed ignored it. "You ate your fish, Mister Wells, and like the rest of us, in the next day or so you created a waste by-product that cost some municipality a decent amount money to treat. So you see, you and I and Montessa are all consumers as well as polluters. My job is to help communities understand that a manufacturing company is simply an entity very similar to them. Just larger, with larger responsibilities. Simply said in relative terms, Montessa would never pollute the environment to the extent you did for one single fish."

"Okay, you can act pretty high and mighty if you attribute all those costs to a single fish, but isn't that like attributing all of a paper mill's smell to a single newspaper?"

"Point taken."

"Thank you."

They both smiled, and Jack wagged a finger at him. "Reed, you're certainly good at your job."

"Thank you again. Now, was there anything else?"

"Just one thing. How do you like having Sierra Club located right here where they can constantly look over your shoulder. I don't think my friend would like that."

"Montessa welcomes the additional oversight. As you saw on the walls outside, we're closely tied to this community, all of it, including those fine people at the Sierra Club. If they bring something to our attention that we missed, we're grateful."

Jack was getting nowhere with Reed, and the longer he sat the more anxious he became to get traction somewhere else. Assuming Robyn and Preston were right, just about everyone in town potentially had some kind of a motive to kill Jeff. He wanted to talk to some of them, but mostly he wanted to talk to Claire Statler, hoping to leapfrog over Julius Reed with whatever she'd learned about Montessa in her investigation. "Sounds good. Can I come back if I have more questions?"

Reed glanced out the window and smiled. "If you're willing to put up with our unfortunately necessary security procedures, of course. Anytime. I'd enjoy it."

"Thanks."

Jack said good-bye and left, thanking the woman as he walked through the outer office and stepped into the lobby, where the SILT scanned his badge and looked at his computer. Jack followed the SILT's eyes when he looked through the front doors at a small team of SILTs out front, and then said, "Have a seat, Mister Wells," without offering any explanation.

Chapter 7

Being detained in the Montessa lobby was an intriguing experience. Jack sat patiently and let the time pass, knowing that someone, somewhere, probably right there in the building, was playing out a hand, and chances were good that Jack would learn something in the process that would keep it from being a waste of precious time. So he relaxed and waited and made a point of bugging the front desk SILT with naive questions about his weapon and his training.

After twenty minutes the SILT walked over to Jack and said, "You can go now, Mister Wells." He took Jack's badge and added, "Someone else was trying to make time to see you, but they couldn't make it work out with their schedule." Then he radioed the gate SILT that Jack was leaving.

Jack stepped out and shielded his eyes against the sunshine. When he stopped squinting he saw a police car coming to a stop right behind his rented vehicle, blocking it. A powerfully built man in a custom-tailored police uniform with lots of gold got out and leaned against it.

He was fifty, maybe fifty-five, and bald, but with the steroid-enhanced body of a dead-serious muscle-head, his slightly distended stomach counter-balanced by the disproportionate size of his massive upper body. His neck was every bit as thick as his head, bright red and veiny, giving it and his brain cage the look of an upright erection.

Jack walked purposefully toward his car and the officer, trying to get insight into the guy by thinking about the juicers he knew, and how strong they were, and how often the steroids drove one of them in particular to unpredictable, irritable, or aggressive behavior, usually all three ugly emotions at the same time. That kind of behavior could be a tool if this guy turned out to be the same way. A dangerous tool, certainly, for Jack to use against a power lifter who weighed in at 250 or 260, but something to be applied with care if needed.

He was almost to his car when a black-wheeled armored personnel carrier, identical to the Marine ones that Jack and his men used as primary transportation, roared through the gate checkpoint without stopping, the white stenciling of ROANOKE POLICE / SWAT on every possible surface gaining it immediate access. It drove right to where the big police officer with all the gold stood waiting, and squealed to a stop.

Seven police officers poured out of the personnel carrier in full battle-rattle, armed every bit as heavily as Jack and his men had geared up for their most dangerous missions of the hottest of battles in the most dangerous zones. Bullet-proof vests, elbow pads, knee pads, finger guards, Kevlar helmets, face shields, leg holsters, batons, automatic weapons, extra magazines, and tear gas grenades.

One guy had a shotgun slung over his shoulder and another had strapped a grenade launcher to his back, and all of that firepower was to ensure they were prepared to deal with one man who'd already had his car and body searched thoroughly before he'd been allowed to enter Montessa. The federal government had poured billions into local police departments since 9/11, enlisting them as warriors in the fight against terrorism. At the same time, the Pentagon had dumped as much of its surplus gear on them as possible. The predictable effect was that police departments had eagerly become militarized, and in some cases, even militant, and would probably stay that way forever, playing soldiers instead of cops-and-robbers as they bullied their way out of the Constitutional constraints of law enforcement. The Roanoke Police Department must have been near the front of the line for giveaways, so heavily armed that the misuse of that power was regrettably predictable.

The big man leaning against his car, with his ridiculous cluster of shiny gold stars on the starched white collar of his spinnaker sized shirt, didn't move as he smiled at the show his SWAT team put on, three of them taking a knee to aim at Jack while the others rushed around him in their best attempt at the time-honored Ceremony of Dominance, probably practiced in this same unjust manner by men with guns against men without guns since the first posse rode out of town in the Old West.

Jack refused to slow his pace as he walked toward the big man, and his long, fast strides had the comical effect of making the kneeling SWAT guys jump up and move, then reset, then jump up and move again, as if unsure of their ability to hit a moving target more than a few feet away.

Mr. Steroid had to be the chief of police Theodore Blanchet described, and he really did have the biggest eyeballs Jack had ever seen, like green bulls-eyes smack in the centers of altar-white targets, with the whites getting bigger and bigger as Jack approached him until he put his hand on his pistol and said, "I'm Chief Howard, Mister Wells. Welcome to my city. Are you going to be uncooperative or can we all just get along out here?"

Jack was closer to the chief than any of the black-suited SWAT guys should have allowed, close enough to reach out and snatch his weapon or twist him around as a shield, and so he took a few seconds before answering, looking around at each SWAT member in turn. One of their phones vibrated, and as Jack watched in disbelief the man stopped aiming his assault weapon at him long enough to pull out his phone to check the message.

It obviously pissed off the chief because he asked, "Anything you want to share with the rest of us, Jones?"

Jones put away his phone and once again took aim at Jack.

The chief stared at Jones a few seconds longer, then came back to Jack. "Well?"

Jack laughed. "I can't believe your man there just checked his phone." He turned to Jones and said, "Hey, do you mind Googling Attention Deficit Disorder for me while you're fiddling with that thing?" He laughed again.

Jones gripped his weapon even tighter as he pointed it at Jack, as if that somehow made him aim better.

"He needs a bit of counseling," the chief said, "and that's all. Now what about you, Wells? What are your intentions here?"

"Well, Chief, I'll be honest with you. I wasn't planning on being uncooperative with you or anyone else because I make a reasonable effort to control that part of my nature. But of course I wasn't planning on getting this kind of greeting, either, so who knows what I might do after being harassed by your merry band of idiots? Suppose you tell me what this is about and then I'll make up my mind. Does that sound fair enough?"

The chief moved around Jack, sizing him up. "That's funny," he said, the high pitch of his voice an anomaly, given his big body. "At least it strikes *me* as funny. But instead of laughing I think I'll just ask you once again what your visit to our fair city is about."

Jack pivoted around so that every member of the SWAT team could hear him. "I got a brochure in the mail from your Chamber of Commerce. Nicely done, too, with lots of pretty pictures that made Roanoke look like a great place to visit. Sorry, Jones, but you weren't in any of them. Your girlfriend might have been, though. Is she the leggy one in the short skirt with—"

"Leave him alone, Wells."

"I really liked looking at her legs, Jones. Anyway, I decided to come up to Roanoke and check this place out for myself."

He kept turning until he ended up facing the chief, who smiled as he stepped close and then nodded to Jones, who came up behind Jack and crushed a boot into the back of Jack's leg.

Jack went down to his knees and hit the ground hard, but stayed upright and still even though the pain made him want to check the places where the bomb-shattered leg had healed together to make sure the leg still held.

"Jones and the rest of my men will be more than happy to testify about how clearly they heard you threaten me just now, Mister Wells. As you might well guess, they tend to be very protective of me. Step back, Jones."

Jones didn't move. He hovered behind Jack, his rifle butt poised over Jack's head and ready to fly. The chief repeated his order to him, then nodded at another officer who stepped up and pulled Jones back into the circle.

"So you should be glad they're being gentle on account of your getting the Silver Star and all over there in Afghanistan. That wasn't your bad leg Jones hurt while searching you for a weapon, was it? The one that got blown into lots of little pieces? What's that? You say that it is? Well, that is truly a shame, Mister Wells, and I am genuinely sorry for that transgression." He smiled. Jack said nothing.

The chief took a deep breath and closed his eyes as if savoring the fresh air. "One of the more interesting things you might have read in that brochure of yours, Mister Wells, is that there is almost no crime here in Roanoke. Is there boys?"

A chorus of "No sir!" sang out.

"And whatever crime there is, well, it doesn't seem to last very long. You want to take a wild guess at why that is?"

There was no point in Jack saying anything.

The chief leaned over him. "Mister Wells," he said, in the tone of someone who'd just had their feelings hurt, "I asked you to guess why that is, but you don't answer." He stood up straight, a looming giant over Jack's kneeling body. "Now we tend to take our manners pretty seriously here in Virginia, sir, so I'm going to attend to mine and give you another minute to answer."

Jack still said nothing, just waited for whatever was coming, unable to do anything, suddenly feeling for the first time in his entire life a little of what so many peaceful protestors must have felt in the past, from marchers for civil rights to the Occupy Movement to the police brutality protesters, courageously sitting and totally defenseless, just like Jack, as law-breaking police fired at them with water hoses, pepper spray, rubber bullets, bean bags, and sound cannons.

A minute passed. "Time has just run out, boy, which means you leave me no choice but to accept your silence as proof that you intend to be uncooperative."

Jack watched the chief's eyes as he looked at the SWAT officers standing around him, as if picking the one he wanted to test or reward. He nodded at one with a baton in his hand, who took Jones' place behind Jack.

The baton went up and Jack closed his eyes as it buzzed through the air and hit his shoulder where the Veterans Administration had pinned it together. But the blow wasn't nearly as hard as he'd expected. At least nothing broke.

Jack was absolutely and totally helpless, and that kind of helplessness tended to lead people to either despair or anger. Jack was getting angry.

"What I heard about you, Wells, is that you were a trouble-maker in the Marines. Is that true?"

Nothing.

"And then some of the FBI friends you made over there in Afghanistan recommended you for a job as an Agent, where you made trouble yet again. You really don't seem to have much of the good common sense God gave most of us, now do you, Wells?"

Still nothing.

"That can only lead a righteous man like myself down one path of thinking, Wells, and here it is. You came to my peaceful little town intent on being a trouble-maker once again." He got close enough to whisper, but didn't. "But we have a way of dealing with trouble-makers in Roanoke, and as much as it pains me to say this it goes quite a bit beyond my normal praying for their souls. You got to understand that I have no choice about that if I'm truly going to protect my flock here in Roanoke."

The chief backed away. He moved to his car and leaned against it. "Now, should we show you a little more about what I'm talking about or would you just prefer to go back home and forget all about this."

"I can't go home yet."

The chief bounced off the door of his car and looked excitedly around at his men. He smiled in pretend amazement. "My God, the man speaks. Did you hear that, boys?" Then, "And why is it that you can't you go home all safe and sound? After all, that's really all I'm suggesting."

"Because if I leave now Mike Roberts will come, and you don't want Mike Roberts to come." Jack pivoted his head to take in each man. "You don't, you don't, and you don't. None of you corndogs do, whether you have the good sense to know it or not."

The chief applauded lightly. "Well, thank you, Mister Wells. Thank you so much for protecting us from…what's the guy's name? Roberts?"

"You're very welcome."

He stopped clapping. "Then I guess I'll have no choice but to arrest you."

"That comes as such a big surprise. You want to tell me the trumped-up reason your midget brain managed to invent?" Jack slapped himself lightly to see if the SWAT team would react to his sudden movement. "Shit, I didn't mean to insult midgets like that."

The SWAT team didn't react at all, just held their aim on Jack as they watched the chief, who looked embarrassed or angry or both. Then he smiled but showed no teeth.

"We recently had a nice young fella killed right here in Roanoke by a .40 caliber pistol. I bet you carried a .40 caliber pistol in the FBI, didn't you, Mister Wells?"

Jack looked around and saw a small crowd forming outside of Montessa, probably leaving for home after work. The SILTs seemed to have disappeared altogether, abandoning this mess to the locals.

"A lot of us carried the .40."

"Yeah, yeah, I imagine that's true enough. But what's also true enough is that none of them are here in Roanoke making trouble."

"Proves nothing. Maybe they didn't get the brochure yet." Jack decided to push and then gauge the chief's reaction. "Besides, didn't you already declare the man's death a suicide?"

"That's right," he said without missing a beat, "I did."

"A little wishy-washy, are we?"

"Not at all. I'm just willing to consider there might have been an error in my thinking, especially if the end result of that thinking takes a killer off my streets. I am a good and devoted shepherd who likes protecting the faithful from killers, so if I need to change my mind, I will."

"You just protect the faithful? Not the sinners?"

"We're all sinners. I protect all the good people of Roanoke."

"Do what you want, Chief-O, because to be honest I'd just as soon get arrested over this and bring a bucket full of national attention to the way you do things around here. I won't resist arrest, and since there's a nice crowd of people over there watching everything all of us do, you'll have trouble finding an excuse to kill me in front of them. You have no grounds for an arrest, and even the Buford Dumb-Nuts School of Law Enforcement you attended must have taught you that I'll get right back out."

The chief stepped back. He looked around. He searched the shielded faces of his SWAT team, all of whom probably knew more about auto repair or agriculture than police work.

"You can rise now, Mister Wells. Go ahead and get up and get out of here."

Jack stood slowly. He took in the SWAT faces once again and committed each and every one of them to memory.

"Go forth now and get out of my town before something very bad befalls you." Then, "Let's get home to dinner, boys."

The SWAT team suddenly relaxed and wandered back to the personnel carrier like actors who'd been playing very dangerous roles that suited them badly. As the chief walked to his car while his men climbed into the Army vehicle, he turned and said, "Go on back to Florida, Wells."

Jack stood there thinking about Mike and Robyn and Preston and Jeff. Thinking about a police chief who'd just given orders for him to be beaten for no lawful reason, feeling too much the way he did in the months of recovery after an Afghan safe-house exploded when he'd sat down for a meeting and tripped the wire to an American-made explosive.

And so once again Jack found himself face-to-face with the reality that some men used power corrosively. Men like the chief who, over the years, had tried to scare him or kill him or make him run. Men who were probably very much like the man who killed Jeff Roberts.

The chief was about to climb into his car when Jack shouted, "Fuck you, No-Neck!"

The chief looked back, shook his head, started his car, and drove off.

Chapter 8

At 6:10 P.M. Jack walked into The Lodge, a large two-story building with a green metal roof situated on the highest clearing of a rolling patch of old tobacco acreage. It either got its name, or lived up to it, because of its solid log walls, stone entry, and wrap-around porch. There were a dozen Kennedy rockers along the front with small round tables of woven tree branches placed between each pair of them.

Unlike most of his friends who operated on island time, Jack took pride in being punctual and was seldom late for anything, especially a pretty woman. But he'd rented a room on the outskirts of town, made two phone calls, taken a very hot bath, and closed his eyes for five minutes that turned into an hour.

"Hello," Robyn said as he approached her table.

"Hi. You look nice."

She'd changed from earlier and wore a colorful print dress, the kind women buy in the waning weeks of a hard winter in anticipation of the warmer weather ahead. Her hair was in a ponytail, adding to the casualness of her dress and making her look younger than she had in professional clothes. But her voice and poise were still professional. A manila file sat next to her plate.

"Thank you. How was your day? And why are you limping?"

He sat directly across from her, mostly to get any signal her eyes might send during their conversation, but also because he wanted to look at her. She was different from before, and that amped up his interest even more.

"My day was interesting. How about you?"

"And the limp? You were limping just now, right?"

He hadn't realized it showed, but didn't see any reason to tell her about his run-in with the chief, especially since she'd probably had plenty of them herself. "I twisted my knee at the curb out front. I'll be fine. How was court?"

She waved a hand in front of her face as if pushing away a spider web. He confirmed again there were no rings on her fingers.

"We were in and out in less than an hour."

"You don't sound like it went well."

"It went just the way we expected, because without Jeff there to support the evidence, the judge had little choice but to throw out everything we had. We'll have to start over with nearly nothing."

"I'm sorry. Was that the right thing to do, or do you think the judge was prejudiced toward Montessa and used Jeff's unavailability as an excuse?"

She looked away from Jack as she said, "No, it was probably the right decision from the bench, although it always feels like they're against us. But most of the time that's because Montessa and other target companies spend millions of dollars, whatever it costs, in order to have the best lawyers available. So they get very smart, very skilled practitioners of the law, and lawyers that good can tie a judges' hands pretty tight by objecting loudly and legally to even the slightest latitude a judge might be inclined to afford us. They kind of just wear judges down until they get what they want for their clients."

"That's not very encouraging. Will Sierra go on to something else? Or are you prepared to start over with Montessa?"

Robyn looked surprised. "Of course we'll start over with Montessa."

"Good for you."

"That's actually what makes us so dangerous to them. We know Montessa is putting people's lives at risk. And we know they're contributing to the destruction of the environment. So we're more than willing to start over, with nothing at all if necessary, and then do it again and again and again as long as it takes. Eventually we'll win at some level, and that's when we'll crack open a door that will lead us to evidence of even more violations."

"Is that why they're fighting you so hard?"

"Sure it is, Jack, because if we can get a court order giving us the right to look at their files and records and logs, they know we'll find more evidence than whatever supports our initial filing. The money they're throwing at this minor suit is a perfect example. They could admit to wrong doing and clean the tanks and get them within federal guidelines for less than one percent of what they'll pay for lawyers, but that would still force them to open their records for us. They can't let that happen."

"It doesn't sound like there's even a reason for them to stop the primary violation. The bad tanks."

She looked surprised. "Not true at all. Of course they'll stop. My guess is those storage tanks are already spotless and fully in compliance with EPA guidelines. Eventually they're going to bring an absolutely perfect inspection report to court and ask for a dismissal, which the judge will be inclined to allow. But we'll stay after them because there's so much they're hiding, and not just here. Remember, they're a global corporation."

"Preston doesn't seem very confident in your chances to win this war with them, or maybe any war, given the power these corporations have over Congress and the press."

She nodded, making her ponytail swing. "Preston's earned the right to be negative through his many years on the front line. He's still fighting the good fight, though, and I'm proud to have had the chance to fight for so many years beside a man who's built such a lifetime legend. Most would have given up long before putting in so much time, and he's only frustrated now because of all the money flowing to groups who fight against us, mostly from filthy corporations like those owned by the Koch brothers, who buy about 50,000 ads each election cycle in support of candidates they have in their pockets, including powerful ones like Senate Majority Leaders and Speakers of the House. That's big money for big power."

The waiter came over, and Jack said, "I'll order us some wine, maybe a Napa Valley Cab unless you prefer something else."

She sat up straight and looked hard at him. "You should only order that wine if you plan to drink it alone."

Jack waved the waiter away. "You don't drink wine?" He smiled, but in her eyes he saw the look of someone about to engage in a fight she would rather not.

"You should hear what I have to say first."

Jack glanced at the file on the table. "Something you read in there upset you?"

She flipped it open and said, "Yes, and it's only out of respect for Jeff that I came here to tell you in person."

It was easy to see that this was going bad, but Jeff didn't deserve to be a part of it. "Whatever this is about, don't be a coward and hide behind his name, okay? Do me and him that favor."

"Fine."

"Thank you."

"Jack, I don't have enough time in my life to spend any of it with men who lie to me."

"Nothing to argue about there."

"You lied to me about being a charter boat captain."

"I am a charter captain."

She rolled her eyes. "Don't be stupid, of course I know you're a charter captain. I went back to my office after court and looked you up. I found a link to your *Bella Sabrina* website, so I'm not saying you lied about that."

"Are you sure you don't want some wine? I could use a glass."

"What I'm saying is that you lied by not telling me you were an FBI Agent. An omission is exactly the same as a lie and a professional investigator like you should know better than most what I mean."

"I used to be an agent. I'm not anymore. It's old news."

"Having been an FBI Agent is a pretty big detail to leave out after I specifically asked if you were a detective, don't you think? You do remember my asking you that, right?"

"Of course I do. I just don't know why it matters."

"It matters because in our line of work—my kind of work, not yours—people with badges, like our local police department, are just as likely to be our enemy as our ally. We can't ever expect to count on any help from them, especially when half the time they work directly against us.

"But people who *used* to have badges are never, ever our ally. Whenever they get involved they *always* work against us, doing whatever legal or illegal work is asked of them by the companies we target. Former law officers are simply hired guns doing arms-length dirty work for companies like Montessa." She raised an eyebrow to add a look of irony to her accusation as she added, "And not surprisingly, dirty work tends to come easy to a man who's already dirty."

Jack sat back in his seat and took a breath, looked up at the beamed ceiling and around at the other people in the place, most of whom were smiling or laughing, making

Jack wish even more that this was going better. He leaned in and quietly said, "You have no right to accuse me of being dirty, and you certainly have no proof."

"You weren't dirty in the FBI?"

"Never."

She picked up the file but didn't open it, as though she'd already committed all of its contents to memory. "Is that right? I invested most of an hour into learning about you, Jack Wells. It's amazing what information's available through our search engines and subscription data bases."

Jack hated her tone, and he hated this conversation of suspicion he'd had at least one too many times before. He wanted to leave, but he wouldn't run from a proud past over which he felt no shame. Besides, he was willing to accept that Robyn was very good at digging out the truth, which could make this a chance to find out what he'd be up against with women like her in the future.

He didn't open the file, stubbornly refusing to give weight to whatever it said by doing anything that looked like he was afraid of it. "I doubt you know much about me. My guess is you know a few bits of my history and a couple of outcomes, but nothing of the many roads and paths that connect them."

"Well then let's just see about that." She flipped open the file and picked up a copy of a news article. She held it in the air but didn't read it, presenting it instead as though it were evidence she was submitting to a jury. "Here I have an article from the *Gainesville Sun* that said you changed a double-major to a single in order to graduate early from the University of Florida in December 2001, right after the terrorist attacks in September. The photo above the article is of you and a high school coach with whom you lived in Key West. He never adopted you, perhaps because your real father—" she looked up with an icy hardness in her eyes, "who has an impressive record of arrests for being drunk in public—lived so close. The article goes on to say

67

that you walked away from a chance to play professional baseball in order to fight the war on terrorism in Afghanistan."

"I'm so ashamed," he said, mocking her.

"No, Jack, you're right, this article makes you sound like once upon a time you were a good guy from a broken home. It would be a nice story if it ended there, but we both know it doesn't."

Then she smiled like she'd just dismantled a defense attorney's argument before he'd even had a chance to present it. "Because although that part of your past is something worthwhile that we should consider, it was more than a dozen years ago. We all know that people change over time."

He forced a smile and made sure it was obviously forced. "I'm going to have something to drink while I listen to you tell me the news of the past. Are you sure you won't join me?"

He motioned the waiter over as she shook her head no. "Jack Daniels, double, neat." Then, "Go on. It's obvious you want to get my reaction to all this, otherwise you just would have stayed home and written me off."

"I see this as a chance to get to know my enemies."

"You want to know what I think?"

She said nothing, which said a lot.

"Of course you do, so here it is. I think you came here tonight because you're interested enough in me to hear my side of whatever story you think you know. You sure as hell didn't come here out of respect for Jeff."

"Now who's exploiting Jeff?"

"That person would still be you, Robyn. So just let me know when you're finished making guesses about me and I'll fill you in as best I can on the details."

She sat straighter as she picked up another piece of paper." You were decorated in Afghanistan," she said flatly, with zero emotion, as if he'd done nothing more than win a sack race, "for dragging two men through heavy enemy fire."

His drink came and he took a sip. "Actually I only dragged one of them. I carried the other, since you're looking for the whole truth and nothing but the truth."

Robyn actually picked up her pen and made the note, "Dragged one, carried the other." Then, "You were transferred to intelligence and were badly wounded when a bomb brought a building down on you."

"Grievously."

"What?"

"Grievously. The medical report said I was grievously wounded, not badly. Again, just trying to stick to the truth."

She ignored it and went back to her notes. "You came back to the States and you eventually healed. You became an FBI Agent. It's all out there on the web, including the weird little fact that although you'd been a beach life guard during high school summers, you still managed to drown twice, once in a pool at a V.A. rehab center and once in the Chesapeake Bay. Pulled out and resuscitated both times." She looked up and stared at him in disbelief. "How in the world does a lifeguard manage to drown two times?"

"Maybe I just happen to like drowning." He smiled, hoping to lighten the fact that everything she said was true. But she would never know the rest of it. She would never know the important parts.

"That was fun, Robyn. Are you done?"

"Pretty much."

"And that little bit of my history is what made you insult me about being dirty? I'd be ashamed of myself if I were you. Hell, I'm sitting way over here across the table and I'm ashamed of you."

"And I could almost agree with your feeling that way because you'd be right, except for the fact that this file encapsulates absolutely everything of significance I could find out about you, using all of my many sources. You've been fairly high profile throughout your entire life, but except for what's in this file, your time in and after the FBI is almost like it never happened. That's what most makes you look dirty."

"You're not making any sense." He took another sip of Jack Daniels. "Not that you were making a lot of sense before, but now…jeez. Do you go off on witch hunts like this in court? I'll have to search YouTube."

"After you joined the FBI it's impossible to find out anything important about you. That in itself is unbelievable. I did manage to find a deeply buried criminal filing by you against two senior agents at FBI Headquarters, but it appears that nothing became of it because you withdrew those allegations."

"It was beyond my control that nothing came of my criminal charges."

"The next time you pop up is in the Collier County, Florida court records for buying your charter fishing business and a nice condo on Marco Island. No promissory notes or mortgages were recorded, even though it's very expensive property on one of the most desirable island destinations in America."

"It is a nice place. I kind of wish I was there now."

"So what happened to the patriotic volunteer who walked away from a chance to play pro ball in order to go to war? What made you become dirty enough to quash your criminal complaint in order to pay cash for a home and a business? You have to agree that it sounds like you were blackmailing those two senior agents."

He sipped again, washing his anger down with Brother Jack. "You're doing a very good job of making this sound insulting. I hope you're enjoying it."

She straightened up and looked flustered. "I absolutely hate doing this, Jack, but I don't have time to play footsy with an enemy. If it looks like you took a payoff and it sounds like you took a payoff, you probably—"

Jack was angry enough to force his focus on it just to make sure it didn't show too much. When the waiter came by to see about a refill, Jack smiled up and said, "Thanks, but no thanks." He handed him a twenty and said, "If that covers it, keep the change."

"You're leaving, Jack?"

He turned back to her. "I really don't see a reason for me to sit here and listen to your partial truths and innuendo. I did nothing to be ashamed about. Nothing."

"Ha. I imagine Hitler would've said the same thing." Then she looked hurt by her own comment. "Oh, Jack, I'm sorry. That was way over the line."

"You're suspicious of former law enforcement people, Robyn, and I get that, trust me, I get it. I would even expand that suspicion to people who are currently in law enforcement. But the one and only reason I came to Roanoke was to find out whatever I could about Jeff's death. For some reason you want to make all this about me and you, or me and The Sierra Club, so I guess there's nothing left for us to talk about."

"I'm sorry, but I just don't believe you came here to help Jeff."

"You're right. Jeff's dead. There is no helping him."

"For God's sake, Jack, you're ex-FBI. Preston shouldn't have even let you into our offices. He wouldn't have if he'd known."

Jack was already prepared to walk out, and as he watched Robyn work her way back to another attack he knew he should just get up and do it. But he would deal with the secrecy of his past for the rest of his life, so it made sense to stay a few minutes longer, using this as an opportunity to develop some good answers that wouldn't violate the sealed terms that all parties, including the Director of the FBI and the United States Attorney General, had sworn to keep secret when they'd signed the settlement.

Robyn leaned back in her seat, like a lawyer calmly laying out her closing argument. "It's quite simple, Jack. I believe you are one of *them*, just like all the other former cops who trade the bad hours and low pay of a badge for the big dollars of corporate contract work. I guess the good news is that I actually do believe you came here about Jeff's death, though."

"Well I guess that's something."

"But only to make sure his death stays covered-up so that Montessa gets away with it."

"Yeah, well, you're wrong."

"It suddenly makes perfect sense that a man like you would be hired to make sure it stays a suicide so they don't get tied to it. Come on, even you must be able to see that."

"It could make sense, I guess, but you're just plain wrong because I'm not that man."

"I don't think I am wrong, and I have no intention of letting that happen, of letting Montessa get away with killing Jeff."

"Do you hear yourself, Robyn? Earlier today you weren't even willing to say that Jeff was murdered, but now you're accusing me of covering it up and protecting his killer."

Her voice rose, not in volume but intensity. She almost sounded like she was pleading when she said, "I just want to know the truth, Jack. Please, just tell me, did you buy your home and business with payoff money? If not, then maybe you really are clean."

He took his last sip of Jack Daniels for no other reason than to once again force apart his clenched teeth and tight lips. "There were a lot of factors involved that played into what happened, and you'll never know any of them."

"Was it a payoff?"

He looked around the room, lowered his voice and leaned closer to her. "Think about everything you just said about me. I brought criminal charges against two very senior agents. Two influential men in extremely powerful positions in Washington. Men who briefed The President and Congressional Intelligence Committees and determined FBI policy. Wouldn't you expect that kind of thing to end badly for me?"

Her hard stare revealed a little curiosity, an opening, and so he said more.

"It didn't take long for me to realize I wasn't going to beat them or come anywhere close to winning. And they made it impossible for me to do my job, to be an agent. They were trying their best to disgrace me, and I'm surprised you didn't find some of that in your search because they're very good at that."

"I want to know if you were dirty, Jack? If you were a criminal?"

He ignored it. "But I wouldn't quit the Bureau, despite how miserable they made my life. To be honest I couldn't financially afford to quit. Maybe I should have done it anyway, but if I'd quit during their attack I would have been a disgraced FBI Agent, and being branded like that makes it a little hard to find work."

"Jack?"

He was rolling now, heading right to the very edge of what he could legally disclose. "I wish I'd never learned what they'd done, but once I did I had to act on it. I couldn't have lived with myself otherwise. Those men lost their jobs and an entire operation got shut down and so I'm proud of what I did, regardless of the cost. Regardless of the fact they didn't go to jail. Regardless of whatever it is you think of me right now."

"Jack?"

"Yeah, what?"

She looked like she was trying to understand, like she was hoping to understand. She leaned in, touched his hand, and quietly asked, "Was it a payoff?"

He looked her straight in the eyes and said, "Yes."

Then he stood and walked out, wishing he'd done it ten minutes earlier.

Chapter 9

Jack fumed as he drove aimlessly around Roanoke, burning fuel and bleeding off frustration. He wished Robyn hadn't been so good at digging into his past, and wished he hadn't said anything to her at all about it, because trying to explain only brought out enough of the truth to make it look like she was right.

He almost wished he'd done nothing to create the problem with Robyn in the first place. Ignore what he'd accidentally discovered and let the murderous Harvey Squad—absurdly named for the Labrador Retriever that supposedly gave homicidal orders to David Berkowitz—along with the squad's brutal wartime interrogators and the two ASACs who gave them their orders, reap the illegal benefits of Extraordinary Rendition as it played out in big and small cities in the United States, with lifelong Americans from Muslim ancestry, along with young men deemed at risk of being radicalized, snatched off the streets without any of the protections of due process, not even a criminal charge or an arrest warrant. Some of those Americans were never seen again, regardless of whether or not they actually knew anything that might keep America safe from terrorists, or had ever done anything illegal.

The Harvey Squad probably would have gone on forever if not for Jack, or someone like him, because America had slowly, slowly, slowly come to accept either one or the other of two false choices: they could live in a constant state of fear or live in a constant state of protection. Bin Laden had decisively won that battle, and anyone who argued otherwise lived a hermit's life on an isolated ranch unvisited, at least so far, by the government's surveillance drones and internet monitoring. Or they were fools. Or more likely, they were living as most of their friends did, in the comfort of doubt that it could ever happen to them, that the Federal Government would never target them, even though the odds of that happening increased daily.

Gun-toting American bravado and "Don't tread on me" flag waving aside, the stalwart citizens of the greatest nation ever conceived, a nation for which Jack would always stand willing to fight, had given up what they proudly pretended to cherish in order to feel safe. Strip searched after a K-9 made a false alert because of his handler's malicious cues? Sure thing. Forced to prove your identity when walking peacefully down a residential street? Whatever you say, officer. No-knock raid on a poorly researched address? Mistakes happen when enforcing the law. Warrantless wiretaps on millions of phones? What does it matter if you've nothing to hide?

But it did matter, because once Americans became nothing but a great big pool of suspects, anyone who might possibly know anything at all was at risk. And that meant everyone, even if the sum total of what the interrogators knew about them was that they'd Googled Edward Snowden or Mohamed Elomar.

Jack learned about Harvey when investigating the disappearance of one of his witnesses, and he'd tried hard to go along with its program. They brought him in because they assumed he was like them, and he'd actually assumed he was, too. They'd all seen war up close and seen comrades in arms killed by extremists, and therefore none of them would ever want to see that same war fought on the beachheads of Fire Island or Miami.

It was a safe bet all around, except for the fact that Jack didn't turn out to be like them. It made him sick when the men on that lethal squad laughed about their deadly mistakes, ashamed when they flaunted their immunity, and outraged when they water-boarded a Bronx realtor whose only crime was renting an apartment to a Muslim who had a brother who had a friend who had a nephew who knew a guy who'd illegally sold someone a gun.

Regardless of the cost, Jack's filing his lawsuit in closed federal court was the right thing to do. Every pay grade above him had warned him of the risks as they stood in his way, which made him even more proud that he'd gotten it done and brought Harvey to an end, at least as far as he knew.

He glanced around outside his car, trying to orient himself while he waited for the traffic light at what looked like one of Roanoke's poorer and rougher neighborhoods, built around a littered green space identified by a graffiti-covered sign as Washington Park.

But the people enjoying the park in the waning sunlight created a pleasant contrast to the apparent hardships of their lives. They sat in happy pairs or tossed balls with their kids, basking in the wonderful warm air of a fresh spring evening.

Their happiness seemed odd to Jack, weighed down by Jeff's death and Robyn's accusations, but he would always appreciate the energizing feeling of rebirth that spring brought. He missed it in the yearlong warmth of Marco Island, but he never missed the long dead winters necessary to make it feel special. Working at FBI Headquarters and the New York Field Office had given his South Florida soul enough dead winters for a lifetime.

As he looked around, a giant illuminated star caught his attention, far up on a distant mountaintop. It was so large and out of place that it made him wonder about its history, at least until the marked police car showed up in his rearview mirror, a hundred feet back.

Jack watched the traffic light. When it turned green he took off slowly, carefully obeying all laws and giving the cop no reason to stop him, even though he'd learned years earlier, and again this afternoon, that a good reason or probable cause was no longer a necessary requirement in much of America.

Several blocks ahead the streets got cleaner and better lit as the lights came on, but Jack's mood got darker and dirtier, his anger re-building, block by block, that the traffic stop he anticipated could end with him getting killed and the cop getting away with it for no other reason than that slow devolution of due process and probable cause into weak legal after-thoughts in America's post-9/11 reality, whether in tiny rural towns with good old boy sheriffs, warrantless *Stingray* and *Hailstorm* ISMI phone interceptions, or massive data-gathering operations targeting every American citizen from behind the dark veil of authority provided by a wonderfully mistitled Patriot Act.

As the cop stayed far back but still on his tail, turn for turn as though running overt surveillance on a suspect, Jack got even more pissed, and actually started to hope the cop was one of the SWAT jerks from earlier. At least that would give him some kind of an excuse for resisting him, if it came to that, because that's what he would do. He'd cooperated earlier and got beaten. Now he was on an empty city street at night where anything could happen, and he had no intention of having his name added to the list of five hundred innocent Americans murdered by cops every year. He'd already lost a career he loved over his protection of American's freedoms, and had barely survived an attempt on his life in Afghanistan for defending the very democracy America was supposedly exporting.

The cop didn't turn on his lights or siren, just continued to stay far back as Jack turned a corner and crossed the Roanoke River that noiselessly cut the city in two. He turned again, and the cop slowed, then fell back, leaving a big gap between the two cars that was quickly filled by a rusted old Chevy that dusted the cop, who turned down a side street and disappeared.

Jack hit the gas and put a little distance between him and the Chevy, just to see if it sped up. When it did, he slowed to let it catch up, glancing back to see two big men, one black with a shaved head and one white with long, blonde Hulk Hogan hair, squeezed into the front seats, and although neither of them looked familiar to Jack it was pretty easy to guess they were friends of the cop, and probably the police chief. Jack accelerated again, but whenever he turned he made sure they could see him do it. He didn't want to lose them. He wanted answers, and hoped he wasn't out for vengeance for what had happened earlier.

He parked in the first available spot in his hotel lot and popped the trunk, jumped out and dug around for the neatly stowed lug wrench. He ran to the outside stairs of the hotel, pretty sure the two men wouldn't chance going through the lobby and being seen or caught on camera. He positioned himself behind the ice machine. It wouldn't be long.

The Chevy rolled into the parking lot with its lights off and cruised slowly by the stairs and the ice machine before parking a few spots away from Jack's car. Both front doors opened and the two muscle-ups climbed out. They looked at each other as though they'd never done anything like this before, which surprised Jack because he'd already figured them for a lead or supporting role in Jeff's death.

They walked slowly, looking back and forth and all around, both acting like they'd watched this scene hundreds of times in movies. Jack heard the white guy laugh nervously and the black man tell him to shut up.

As they got close Jack saw what he most wanted to see, a weapon. A big, shiny knife that Blondie pulled from a leather sheath, which gave justification to almost anything Jack might decide to do.

As they stepped onto the walkway in front of the ice machine, Jack raised the lug wrench high in the air and said, "Hello."

Both men jumped. Then Blondie, as if by some instinct he had no idea he possessed until just that second, aimed his knife at Jack and lunged. Jack almost felt bad for the man, who looked surprised by what his body was doing. He let Blondie get close, then swung the lug wrench as fast as he could control it, hitting Blondie's forearm so hard it went from a break to a compound fracture to a useless, flopping appendage before Blondie could stop the inertia that carried him forward, which is when Jack cracked the wrench across his neck to make him go down so he could step over him and go after the black man who, seeing Jack coming for him, ran too fast for Jack to catch without giving Blondie a chance to get away.

Jack kicked away the knife as he turned back to Blondie, who was on the ground groaning as he tried to find a way to hold his dangling hand in the least painful way. Jack picked up the giant knife, admired it in the light, then knelt down beside him, still watching the black man run out of the lot and into the darkness.

"Hi," he said, friendly as could be while flashing the knife so that light bounced off it and into Blondie's eyes.

"Damn, man. Don't kill me."

"Hmm."

"I didn't mean nothing, man, there's no reason to kill me."

"Well, let's talk a bit first. I'd like to know who paid you to kill Jeff."

"What?"

"This is not going to turn out well for you if you're the one asking the questions. You do understand that, right?"

"Yeah."

"That's good. Now tell me who paid you to kill Jeff and I'll get you to the hospital. Or..." he made a quick flash with the knife, right in front of Blondie's wide-open eyes. "I think a jury of reasonable men would believe I killed you in self-defense if I cut this last minute out of your life and end the whole story with your attack."

"Who's Jeff, and damn, man, you got to promise you won't kill me. You didn't even have to hurt me this bad. We was just going to scare you."

"Jeff Roberts. I want to know who paid you to kill him?"

"I don't know no Jeff Roberts. Man, you got to take me to the emergency room." Then a look of clarity crossed his face, a quick grasp of the fact that he didn't want to go anywhere with Jack. "Dude, I want an ambulance!"

"Jeff Roberts. He was a young man who worked at the Sierra Club and got killed."

"Yeah, yeah, I heard about him dying. But news around the campfire is it was suicide and…what, you think that was me? Or us? No way, man. I'm no murderer. Damn, my arm's really starting to ache. And bleed. Shit, man, look at all that blood. Am I going to die?"

"It's just a matter of time."

"I never knew no Jeff, man."

Jack stood up and hovered over Blondie. "Who killed him if not you?"

"Beats me."

"Then explain why you came after me just now if you're not enforcers for somebody. Or for some company? Montessa Chemical, perhaps."

Blondie managed a smile. "Enforcers, huh? Oh, man, that's funny. Got a cool sound, though."

"Why did you come after me?"

"Tommy, dude."

"Tommy?"

"Tommy Jones. The cop what followed you just now. He told us that he and the other SWAT guys had fun earlier today with some dude was a badass from the war and a door-kicking son of a bitch in the FBI. We was at the gym working out with him and the chief and they both said we should have some fun, too. It's a small town, man. We find good times where we can."

"It's not that small."

"But man, I swear we never planned to hurt you. We just wanted to see if you'd cluck, you know. Get all chicken-shit at the sight of us like the guys what come to the bar and try to break bad while we're working security."

Jack stepped away and took a minute to look at the sky, all dark now but with so many stars. He had complete control over Blondie and so had time to remember plenty of people who'd lied to him over the years. And plenty who'd told the truth. Jack was good at telling the difference.

"Okay, tough guy, get up and go to the office. Have them call you an ambulance. Say you hurt your arm in a fall getting out of your car. Don't even think of saying anything that sounds like you'll sue them. You hurt your arm falling, got it?"

"Dude, no one will ever believe I did this much damage falling out of my car."

"Say you fell. Stick with that story or we'll talk again."

"A pretty hard fall is all I'm saying."

Jack walked away, went to his room, and grabbed all his gear. When he got back, Blondie was gone, but not in the office.

He drove to the long term lot at the airport and found a spot between two clean cars, which he hoped meant the owners had just flown out. He climbed into the back seat and stretched out to sleep, almost glad to know that a starting gun had been fired.

His beating at Montessa was nothing more than a line in the sand, a border he'd been warned not to cross. He'd shown his decision to ignore it when he told the chief to fuck off. Now the gloves had really come off. First blood had been spilled. Whatever cliché best applied didn't really matter, because they all meant the same thing.

Jack Wells was at war once again.

Chapter 10

A big commercial jet roared overhead toward a landing as Jack's phone rang, making it hard to hear a sweet woman's voice say, "Hi, you're Mr. Wells?" The voice almost sounded like its owner was drugged or in a trance. "I'm Claire. Jeff's girlfriend…well, Jeff's friend. Used to be. He died."

"Hello, Claire. Yes, I'm Jack. I know who you are."

"Hi," she said again, her voice meek but with a sound of purpose, like she didn't want to talk and hadn't done it in a while, but now needed to do it anyway. "You're in Roanoke? Jeff's mom said you were in Roanoke."

"I am, yes."

"Something's going to happen at the tanks tonight."

"I'm sorry, what?"

"The tanks. The tanks Jeff and I were exposing. Montessa's tanks. I got a call about them. I called you in case you're interested."

"A call from whom? And what's going on with them."

"The call was anonymous, like so many tips we get. It's dangerous to be a snitch. He said something big is going to happen there at ten tonight."

Jack looked at his watch, which showed it was nine-ten. "Okay."

"I wanted you to know. Jeff's mom said you're looking into what happened to him." She choked up and went silent. After half a minute she continued. "And what happened to him, happened to him because of those tanks. I thought you should know about tonight."

"Where are they?"

"Easy to find. Drive up 864 toward Mason Cove. There's a big sign. The tanks are big. On the right side. You really can't miss them, even at night."

"Thank you."

"Okay." Her voice slipped back into nothingness, like she was drifting off to sleep or succumbing to a sedative."

"Okay," she said again, and then hung up.

Jack checked the map on his phone as he headed out of the airport parking lot. He was actually glad to get moving toward something, anything, that might take his mind off how pissed he was about the way he'd rushed so quickly back to violence, using skills he knew too well but couldn't possibly want less. He'd come to Roanoke hoping to quietly investigate Jeff's death and then turn whatever he learned over to authorities, but it had only taken the slightest provocations of the SWAT team and Blondie, neither of which were of real merit, to make him abandon the gentle life he was sure he wanted and thought he'd found.

As he found the road and raced up it, checking his watch and wondering what might constitute "something big" at the tanks, he took comfort in the fact that he had managed to hold onto his temper with Blondie, staying calm and speaking quietly and giving the big idiot a solid option for staying alive. But Jack was honest enough with himself to admit that he'd only been pretending at the role. Blondie's attack had proven that not only was the power still in Jack's arms, the darkness would always lurk in his soul. He wasn't really surprised at how quickly he'd gone back, but his time on Marco Island had matured him to the point that he now saw it as frightening, or at the minimum, unsettling.

State Road 864 led him out of Roanoke and climbed its way up a small mountain flanked on the left by a larger mountain. It snaked left and right, and it was just after an easy curve to the right that he saw the fence and the sign and the four-story tanks, which were just as impossible to miss as Claire said they would be. A wide, high gate protected the entrance, but it was opened a foot or two. A heavy chain with a massive lock hung off it, unsecured.

He drove past the entrance and parked a few hundred yards away, then jogged to the driveway, stopping at the entrance and listening while still hanging back in the trees. He heard nothing.

9:58.

Did ten mean ten o'clock exactly? Had he already missed whatever was going to happen? Was he way too early? Should he look for a spot to hang around and wait undetected? The unlocked gate suggested he hadn't missed it, but since he didn't even know what he was expecting, the gate could mean anything.

He walked carefully into the compound, staying close to the concealment of the woods if a motion sensor light came on, or an alarm went off, moving silently toward a spot in the middle of the three big tanks, each at least the size of a water storage tank for a small city, where a luminous glow offered the best clue of where he should be looking. He crossed a bridge over a deep ditch, forcing himself to look away from the glow regularly to check the surrounding darkness, even though he couldn't see anything. Just the yellow-green glow bouncing off the enormous tanks surrounding it.

He sprinted to the first tank and pressed himself against its white metal. A row of rivets pressed uncomfortably into his back, but still he heard nothing. Not a voice in the distance or a radio or a diesel engine turning a pump.

Not even an insect. It was like everything had died, and he thought perhaps that was the point. Was it possible that Montessa had shut down the tanks and maybe the facility. They'd certainly invested enough money to make that count as something big.

As he slid around the tank, still pressed against it, he saw a pile of chemical light sticks on a small folding table, all of them glowing as though someone had prepared to hand them out to a team, which made him look around again and listen even harder. Still nothing. He moved to within fifteen feet of the table and still nothing.

He stepped carefully toward it, and five feet away he saw a manila envelope in front of the glow sticks. Another foot closer he saw his name on the front. Someone had drawn a smiley face below it.

At different times in his past his curiosity might have made him open it. But he was smarter now, and tonight he would run, get away from there as fast as he could, run for something, for anything, that might pass for safety, however slight or far away that safety might be.

He was almost to the bridge when the blast went off, so loud his hearing instantly turned to ringing as a fireball expanded out and up in all directions from the closest tank, its force pushing his whole upper body forward as the blast rolled over him with an orange fireball in very hot pursuit. He was way out over his feet and about to fall when he got to the ditch and flung himself in, rotating midair and looking up as a second fireball, and then a third, chased each other as the water swallowed him up and protected him.

His record underwater breath hold was nearly six minutes, but he'd gone into the ditch with nothing more than a short gasp that would only give him a minute or two. He stayed down for every second of it, clinging to large river rocks at the bottom, waiting and watching for more explosions. Fire was everywhere, he could tell from the bright yellow light that grew in intensity in every direction.

He rose up and gulped a breath, intending to submerge again. But he took a glance around, and what he saw wouldn't let him look away.

The three giant tanks were gone, completely obliterated from their bases. Their bent and shattered metal had spread out over three hundred yards or more, all of it on fire as the gel the tanks had stored stuck to the surface and burned. Supply pipes into the tanks shot long streams of fire like flame throwers, and an acid, acrid stench burned his nostrils and mouth. The entire facility was flattened, without even an outbuilding or pump house standing. The thick woods surrounding the facility directions were completely ablaze, and globs of fiery gel that looked something like napalm burned in dozens of patches around him, and in hundreds of small fires where it landed and set leaves and pine needles on fire, for as far as he could see.

He climbed out of the ditch, unafraid of anything now but secondary explosions because it was just too unlikely that anyone else could have survived the blast. He took another look around and then jogged toward his car, his wet clothes offering some protection from the heat of the burning woods, even as his shirt heated to the point where the steam was nearly scalding.

His car windows were all blown out, and a clump of burning gel was melting the paint of his hood while another smoldered on his roof. He grabbed a stick and scraped them off, then climbed in and turned the key. When the car started he stomped on the gas and shot up the road, looking for a place nearby to turn around in a hurry. He skidded into the parking lot of a large facility with several cars in the lot. All the windows of the cars and building appeared to be broken, and globs of burning gel had ignited fires at dozens of places where it landed in the lot and the roof and the walls, especially at the back where it was closest to the storage tanks. Two people in nursing uniforms wandered around out front, dazed or wounded or both, watching the rapidly growing forest fire burn the trees as it crackled its way to get them.

A woman at the entrance yelled to him. He couldn't hear her above his ears' ringing, but her look of determined commitment made him jump out and run over, then follow her inside, where several chunks of the storage tanks had crushed walls as they broke through the ceiling. The room directly in front of them was destroyed and already burning, while a frail, old body, contorted by time and the crushing metal, made a curious addition to the carnage.

He thought he heard a siren. Maybe several. He was pretty sure he heard the noise. Probably fire trucks, but maybe the police chief and his gang. There was no way to tell as he followed the woman through the tangle of bent metal and broken trusses to the rear of the building, where fire was devouring the now-exposed wood framing. She shouted, but he didn't hear what she said as she waved for Jack to go on, then went into a resident's room. Jack stopped to watch as she bundled an old woman in a blanket and lifted her into her arms. He moved out of the doorway as the nurse turned around, then he rushed toward the worst of the fire, figuring that within another minute or so the fire department would be too late to get that far, even if they had just arrived.

He rushed through the door of the most damaged room he could reach, his arm over his face so his sleeve could protect him a little, and ran to the bed. An old man looked up and smiled weakly with a face of grateful surprise, just as a blast of fresh air rushed through his blown out window. The air was instantly consumed by the fire it fed, creating yet another blast that hit Jack in the face and knocked him back as a shard of glass sliced deep into his arm. He scrambled back onto his feet and slid his arms under the man, but there was no muscle or resistance, and a glance at his face confirmed the man was dead.

Another loud explosion, perhaps an oxygen bottle, briefly extinguished everything in the room across the hall, but as Jack rushed toward it the fire reignited, as suddenly as it had been blown out, and every bit as dangerous as before. It covered the ceiling like a coat of yellow paint and then climbed down the walls in search of air.

He thought he heard a scream in the next room down and he ran toward it, determined to save somebody from the blast that was meant for him, and probably him alone. He went to the bed and picked up the man, carried him to the busted out window, and lowered him to the ground as gently as he could. He glanced back and saw a fireman with a booster hose at the doorway, giving him cover and a few precious seconds by holding back the fire. He looked back out the window toward the road and saw two Roanoke City police cars roll into the lot. Looked at the old man and saw he was still alive.

He jumped through the window and picked up the man, then ran toward a fire truck and put him down in front of the engineer, who turned from his panel of controls on the side of the pumper with a surprised look as he stared at the man and Jack.

When yet another Roanoke police car arrived, Jack disappeared, deep into the shroud of heavy smoke.

Chapter 11

With the busted remnants of his windows rolled down, his windshield shattered, and his car's heater blowing hard to offset the chill from his soaking wet clothes and the cold mountain air, and Claire not answering her phone, Jack headed to Atlanta to find her. She'd sent him to get killed. She'd played carelessly with his life, and maybe she'd done the same thing with Jeff's life.

He was angry just thinking about it, but not angry enough to be blind to the more likely option that Claire was being played by someone else in a game over his life. So he wanted to talk to her in person. Whoever told her about the tanks might also have killed Jeff. And they'd certainly tried to kill him. He wanted to know who, and why.

He tried to keep an open mind and give every suspect he could think of the same equal weight, but it was tempting to play favorites and hard not to, especially since the cops in Roanoke had so recently earned a top spot on his list by subverting the laws they'd sworn to uphold. But when he truly weighed those actions, the cops really weren't different from a lot of other misguided law enforcement officers around the country, including the two Assistant Special Agents in Charge that Jack got fired at

Headquarters. And it certainly didn't make the cops murderers.

Montessa had a better motive for killing Jeff, and maybe even him, since Jeff was about to expose them to a lengthy legal process that would open them up to far-reaching investigations and fines. And after all, Montessa had SILT operators working for them, and Jack was all too aware of their comfortable familiarity with killing, as well as the thick, crusty scabs that grew so naturally over their consciences. Any operator who worked for SILT would have had no trouble taking a contract to kill Jeff, or blowing up the tanks and killing innocent people.

But despite what Robyn said, it was just too difficult for Jack to make sense of Montessa doing it or having it done. Freedom Industries had been fined a mere $7,000 for polluting all the water flowing down the Elk River, so Montessa's fine for their sins would probably be even less than that. No reasonable person or corporation would run the risks of murder over that kind of fine because it made bad business sense if nothing else, especially since they had an army of high-priced attorneys that would stall indefinitely the discovery process Sierra so badly wanted.

He checked Google Maps and saw it was about eight hours to Atlanta. It would be early in the morning when Jack got there, so he tried to get a jump on things by calling the Atlanta NBC affiliate and asking to set up an early morning meeting with Claire. An operator put him through to an assistant in her office.

"I'm sorry," a youthful male voice said, "but Miss Statler isn't here right now. In fact, hardly anyone is here this late except those working on the set. Is there anything I can help you with?"

"Do you know when she'll be back?"

"I don't."

"You must have some idea. An hour? A week?" Jack tried to break through the natural caution he heard in the man's voice. "Two or three millennia?"

The young man laughed. "It won't be that long. We don't get that much vacation time."

"Especially her, being new and all."

"Right. Anyway, she had a family emergency of sorts. A death in the family, I think. I really don't know much more than that."

"Can you tell me when you saw her last? I'm a friend of hers."

"She…well, she anchored the evening news two nights ago."

"She hasn't been in since?"

"And you are...?

"My name is Wells. Jack Wells."

"I think you should probably be talking to the assistant station manager on duty, Mister Wells."

"That's fine, can you put me through?"

"He's in a sound booth on the set. I can take a message for you, though."

Jack's phone vibrated and he looked to see who it was. "I'll call him back. Thanks very much." Then, "Hello Mike, how is the family holding up?"

"Marilyn's sedated herself into zombie land," Mike said, his voice flat and professional, the voice Jack had grown comfortable with in Afghanistan, but which scared him a little now. "Her kids are still trying to figure out how to react to Jeff's death."

It troubled Jack to hear Mike putting distance between him and his adopted family. "They're your kids, too, Mike."

"It doesn't feel like I have the right to say that, 'cause a good stepdad would be in Roanoke killing a killer instead of making excuses and holding hands back here."

"A good stepdad belongs where he's needed, and they need you there. Don't underestimate how much they do. How are you holding up?"

Any tiny bit of sadness that might have been in Mike's voice was suddenly replaced by hardened determination as he slowly and carefully said, "That answer depends on you, Jack."

Jack recognized that tone and cadence from twice before. Once when Mike had slowly interrogated six enemy combatants they'd captured in house-to-house searches, and once just before slashing his knife across the throat of an enemy who'd foolishly lunged for a weapon during an interrogation, Mike saying his words now with the same powerful force he applied to the knife as it came close to severing off the man's head.

"I'm working to get rock solid facts. Still on it."

"Was it suicide? That's what I really want to know."

Mike's terrible pain leaked into his voice as a trace element, mixed with a controlled kind of rage and a bit of hope. Hope that his boy hadn't really killed himself, and if he hadn't, hope that Mike would get a chance at a few pounds of a murderer's flesh and the gallons of blood for which he thirsted.

"Mike, you've got to remember that many of our brothers have done this kind of thing to themselves. Good, strong men who never gave a clue they were capable."

"I'm talking about Jeff. Not you or anyone else. My Jeff."

"I know, but you have to accept that it is a possibility."

Jack didn't want to say any of this. He wanted to say that he knew for sure Jeff had been murdered, and that he was damned determined to find the killer and deal with him on whatever terms the murderer chose. Ideally Jack would get him arrested and safely behind bars before Mike arrived. If he removed the doubt of suicide, Mike's feet would instantly go into motion, along with his very deadly hands, and then there would be a bloodbath in Roanoke, perhaps even a war, with Mike almost certainly being the one to go to prison if he was lucky enough to live through the arrest.

"The coroner and the chief of police feel certain that he did it to himself," Jack said, sticking with what he'd been told that he could truthfully repeat. "I'm waiting for an official report. I'm heading to Atlanta now to talk to Claire."

The line was silent for a minute. Jack didn't say anything and neither did Mike, not a "Thank-you, Jack" or "Keep me posted" or "I think you're a liar." Finally, Mike just hung up, and under the circumstances that was the best Jack could have hoped for.

Jack set his phone down on his leg, ready for Mike to call back or text if he wanted, although he knew better than to believe it might happen. Which is why he jumped when the damn thing rang.

"Mike?"

"What? No, Jack, it's Grayson. I got your message from earlier about our Roanoke Resident Agent."

"Good. Hey, Gray, and thanks for calling back. How are things at Headquarters?"

"You don't really want to know, but since I'm still here working when I have theater tickets for tonight that I bought weeks ago, and they're wasting away in my jacket pocket, I'll let you consider that a clue."

"Did you find out anything for me?"

"First off, I want to know why you've got a hard-on for our guy in Roanoke. I'm sure you'll understand my bluntness, Jack, when I point out that I still have my job at the FBI and I'd really like to keep it."

Gray was right and Jack knew it. If he expected Gray to run the risk of taking shit for him at Headquarters, he deserved to know the reason.

"I don't have a problem with that. And I don't have a hard-on for him. It's more of a semi-erection. Are you ready?"

"I doubt anyone's ever been ready for you to deal one of your sleight-of-hands, Jack. And I'm willing to bet that's what you're up to."

"You're too suspicious."

"I'm in the suspicion business. Tell me I'm wrong."

"I can't. I'm not really building a game plan yet but I am working up to it by identifying all the players and motives. And since you're in the suspicion business you'll have no trouble understanding my suspicion after the crazy day I've had."

"Tell me."

"I got an undeserved beating from the Roanoke Police SWAT team. And an hour ago someone blew up some storage tanks, trying to kill me. God only knows how many people they killed in the process."

Gray didn't say anything. He just stayed quiet, professional, waiting for Jack to give up more while Jack listened for a clue that Gray might have already heard about it.

Half a minute passed, then, "I've already assigned a terrorist investigative team to Roanoke to see if the tanks were an attack. How sure are you that you were the target?"

"My name was there on an envelope that looked like an invitation."

"Okay. Shit. So, what did you do to deserve a beating and another bomb?"

Jack flinched at the ease with which Gray said it. "I asked a couple of questions about a dead kid. A friend of mine's son."

"You must have done more than that. Challenged someone, or became a threat to something someone valued? Something big enough to get you noticed on a pretty big radar screen." Gray chuckled. "But shoot, even as I say that I know from my own experience that you're seldom obvious. And what does all this have to do with our resident agent, anyway?"

"Probably nothing."

"Then why are we talking?"

"Here's what's bugging me. The police chief lectured me with facts about my past that sounded like he'd read my FBI file, maybe even some of the classified parts. He said I was a trouble-maker in the Bureau."

"No one gets to read the classified parts of your file, Jack."

"That was the deal, sure, but who knows if everyone's sticking to it?"

"If it makes you feel any better, everyone on the squad took a crack at getting a look at it. We even requested it through Langley 'cause we're sneaky little bastards like that."

"You're all assholes. And how is that supposed to make me feel better?"

"Because it's impossible to get. We have a pool going about the real reason you left, and your file would provide one of us with some nice vacation money."

"If you placed a bet, it better have been on an honorable reason."

"I did and it was. I had a hard time finding a taker."

"Good. Glad to hear it. I still don't feel better, though."

"You should because even we couldn't get it, and we're right here two floors below the Director and just down the hall from where it's kept. We're pretty clever, too. You don't have a corner on that market."

"Your mother would be so proud of you."

"My mother is proud of me."

"Terrific."

"Fletcher even dated a woman in personnel for a while, but no amount of charm got her to reveal anything."

"Fletcher isn't all that charming to start with. So maybe the chief didn't have access to my entire file. Maybe he just got some very good information from somewhere else. But he seemed to know more about me than seems reasonable in the short time I was in town." He thought about Robyn and what she'd learned. "Stuff about the FBI that couldn't be found on the internet. There's nothing online that would indicate I was a trouble-maker."

"Did you just call yourself a trouble-maker?"

"Damn, you see what I mean? Even I'm starting to believe what they say about me."

"If you care to tell me the details of your departure from this lofty perch, that might help me get some answers."

"Nice try, Gray."

"You can't blame me for taking a shot. And so you think our Resident Agent filled him in a little."

"I do. You would too. It's either that or—"

"Uh-oh, I can guess where this is going."

"Or Headquarters is involved. Have you heard anything? Has my name come up at Headquarters? More important, has word come down from the top not to talk about me at all."

"No."

"Have any of the CODE guys come around and asked questions?"

"Not to me, at least not for a while. And I don't think anyone on this squad would talk to them about you anyway."

"That's good. None of us need the trouble."

"So if we assume the chief did get his facts about you from the FBI, do we start with the assumption that it was just our local agent, at least for now? Or do you want to start at the top and work your way down. Notice I say *you* because I won't help if you decide to chew on the Director's hide."

"*We* can start with your guy here in Roanoke. And let's tread lightly. I'm not jumping to any conclusions."

"Meaning?"

"Meaning that even if he did give me up, I don't want to assume he said it to get me beaten, or with any malice, for that matter. I imagine he and the chief work together whenever crimes overlap local and federal jurisdiction, so maybe it was just a casual conversation they had once I showed up in Roanoke."

"Let's hope so. For his sake."

"What's his name?"

"Oglethorpe, and for the record, I don't think you believe a single word of what you just said."

Oglethorpe sounded familiar but Jack couldn't place it. "Was Oglethorpe SWAT or HRT? Did he work the Camshaft Group 1 with us? I sure know the name from somewhere."

He heard Gray click through screens of Oglethorpe's file. "None of the above."

"Okay. And what don't you think I believe?"

"That they had a casual conversation about you. No good agent would have talked about you casually. You're as close to an off-limits discussion as there is, and you probably always will be. Everyone knows it. We'll talk about Bigfoot and Roswell before we ever talk about you, but that's mainly because they're more interesting topics."

"I'm going to give Oglethorpe the benefit of the doubt."

"That's very generous for a guy who just got a beating and almost got his ass blown off."

"It was a quick beating and my ass survived the blast. What's Oglethorpe's story?"

"Six years in the Bureau. He was a combat vet before that, just like us except he was an E.O.D. guy."

"Explosives?" Jack wanted to lurch to a conclusion, but he wouldn't allow his mind to race in that direction on one piece of evidence, even though he would spend the rest of his life wondering about the man who blew him up in Afghanistan.

"Don't get excited. He was nowhere around when you were there. Oglethorpe deployed two years after you came back Stateside."

"Makes him a suspect for here, though."

"Maybe, but be careful calling an agent a suspect. Thousands of guys learned to blow things up in the military."

"What offices did he work?"

"Just the Miami Field Office and then straight to Roanoke. He'd put Roanoke down as his Office of Preference when he entered the Academy, and when the Roanoke R.A. retired no one else was left on the list besides him."

"Lucky for him. Unusual."

"I'll say he's lucky. The guy who had been ahead of him on the list died of a heart attack, opening the door for Oglethorpe to be around family and friends and nature while most of us fight the traffic and hassles of the city."

"All the best work is in big cities."

"Yeah. Did I mention the traffic and hassles of the city?"

"You did."

"I thought I did. Well let me know how this turns out, Jack, assuming I don't read about it first in the papers."

"One more favor."

"Isn't there always? Let me hear it."

"There's a news anchor in Atlanta named Claire Statler. Works for NBC. I need some information on her. Just basic stuff like an address, and if she's ever been arrested or suspected in anything, particularly anything radical. I have her phone number because she called me, but her address will just be a few days old because she just moved there."

"She's not in The World, Jack. She's a civilian, right? Not an agent or a criminal?"

"Yes."

"Which means I have an obligation to protect her. So do you, sort of, I guess."

"I am trying to protect her. At least I think I am. I'm not sure exactly what's happening but she's the one who got me to go out to the tanks that exploded. And the young man who was murdered here was her boyfriend. The two of them were working together on an investigation. But hey, Gray, if that isn't enough to justify your help, don't bother. I can find it easily enough."

"The young man and her, are they cops?"

"She's a reporter. Weren't you listening? He was an environmentalist."

"Murder, huh? Okay, that sounds dangerous enough to justify my help. Want to hang on?"

"No. Can you text it to me?"

"Sure, will do. Be safe, Jack."

Jack hung up and checked his watch. It was another five hours to Atlanta. He'd slept only an hour since tying *Bella Sabrina* to his Marco Island dock, grabbing some clothes, and rushing to catch the first connecting flight from Fort Myers to Roanoke.

So his plan was to roll into Atlanta, find a motel, and sleep until mid-morning. Shower, shave, and change his clothes. Eat a decent meal. Have a couple of cups of coffee and think things through. That's what he planned.

But he knew the future was turning more and more deadly, and didn't expect any of those good things to happen.

Chapter 12

The forty-eight hour timeline Jack had established with Mike died the instant Jack realized the trap, replaced by someone else's stopwatch and preferences over which Jack had no control. He learned he'd stepped into it when he approached the exit for Athens, Georgia, watching his speed, trying to keep off the radar, literally and figuratively, of the Georgia Highway Patrol.

Blue Alert! The lighted overhead sign was flashing as he passed under it on Interstate-85, meaning that a law enforcement officer had been attacked or killed in the line of duty. *White 2014 Mustang with red stripes. VA Plate ALD-671.* The sign continued on a second screen. *Suspect armed and dangerous. Do not approach.*

Jack reached into the glove box to check the license number on the rental car's papers. ALD-671, it said, and just like that, he knew he'd become a moving target in every sense of the word, because nothing brought out more fury from every Brother in Blue on the entire planet than a cop being killed or attacked. Which meant the sign was a brilliant way for someone pretty smart to get rid of Jack in a hurry.

He could only guess at whatever trumped-up lie had been told to get him onto that sign. Vehicular attack on a police officer immediately came to mind, for no other reason than the ease with which the charge could be made and then retracted. Resisting arrest was another classic. Simple assault of an off-duty officer had lots of potential, too.

But the *what* didn't really matter and so he didn't spend time on any more ideas, focusing instead on the *why* and the *who*.

The *why* was actually pretty easy. If he got stopped as a suspect in a cop-killing—which is the extreme way he suspected the lie had been told—chances of him living through the arrest were nil. As herds of Americans acclimated to the cattle chutes that slowly funneled them along the path from democracy to police state, with America shamefully joining China and Russia on the short list of countries considered "endemic surveillance societies," cops were free to employ whatever jackboot tactics they felt necessary to control the very people they'd sworn to serve.

There was growing debate about that kind of excessive police violence, and increased discussions about de-militarizing them, but a society unable to intelligently discuss keeping guns away from mentally unstable people could never have a chance of taking power and weapons away from cops. And so they would kill Jack on the spot and then, in the grand old tradition of law enforcement, sit down at their desks and come up with some kind of plausible probable cause before burying the whole incident.

But even in departments that did it right, using bicycle patrols and neighborhood policing to integrate the cops as valuable members of the communities they served, a suspected cop-killer would be delusional to expect to survive the perilous path from a traffic stop on a dark stretch of highway to a criminal trial at a courthouse. Jack wasn't delusional.

The *who* was quite a bit trickier, because although the bogus highway sign put Jack's life in extreme and immediate peril, it would take shockingly little horsepower to get his car's description on that sign, and Jack had at least four ideas about how that might have happened.

The first was that whoever rented the Mustang before Jack might have attacked a cop, which could be cleared up quickly if Jack survived the deadly first minutes of a traffic stop.

Or a law-enforcement friend of one of the Harvey defendants could have done it with a one-minute phone call. Although that would make the timing unbelievably weird, Jack would keep it on the list of possibilities simply because it was a possibility.

Blondie might even have been an undercover cop, although there was no way to construe his coming after Jack as acting in the line of duty. But he could have lied about his role in provoking the fight just to get his health insurance or workers comp to kick in. Or he could have lied to get Jack killed as retribution for breaking his arm.

Or the Roanoke police chief could have done it all by himself. Walked down whatever hall might separate him from his communications command and handed them a note with the car's description on it.

And that was what Jack hoped, because the scariest scenario of all was that someone else was involved who had far more influence in the ranks of law enforcement than a small town police chief or even a disgraced federal agent. Someone who still had the kind of power he'd confronted, and thought he'd shut down, back in the Bureau. The same corrosive kind of power that almost managed to turn Jack's reputation in Afghanistan from a patriot into one of a traitor, claiming he'd made a deal to split a pallet of hundred dollar bills with Afghan insurgents if they would help him steal it.

Jack worried about that kind of power because that would make him a national high-priority target. And since he'd done nothing since Harvey to attract that kind of attention, it meant not only did he not know who his enemy was, he had absolutely no understanding of the enemy's goals or fears or strengths, which meant he had nothing to work with.

He took the Athens exit and pulled into a 24-hour Wal-Mart parking lot. The heater had dried enough of the ditch water from his clothes for him to avoid attention, so he went to the bathroom to clean the smoke and dirt off his arms and face, and wash out his cut, before heading to the automotive section, where he grabbed black striping tape the same width as the red stripes on his door panels. There were lots of white Mustangs out there, but it was the red stripes that would get him caught, so with no way to rent another car and a soul too honest to steal one, covering the red stripes with black was his best option.

He left Wal-Mart through the grocery doors at the opposite end of the building and walked off in another direction, away from his car, checking to see if anyone approached the car or him. They didn't, and this early in the morning, anyone running surveillance would have stood out, even if they'd set up across the street with night vision gear.

The parking lot was well lit and a perfect place to apply the stripes, but Wal-Mart had security cameras rolling and even a bored guy sitting in a tiny office who knew nothing about the Blue Alert would certainly remember a guy re-striping a white Mustang when he did hear the news. So Jack drove a couple of miles down the highway and found a roadside produce stand with a mercury-vapor light out front and a wide grassy place behind it. It was a little too close to the road but at least he could hide behind it, and unlike the back sides of shopping centers, which were his next best choices, the police probably didn't patrol it.

He put on the stripes and then drove the state roads toward Atlanta, keeping off the interstate. He stopped at a closed repair garage to switch license plates with a car missing an engine.

Grayson's text said Claire Statler lived in the Buckhead area, so he drove there and found her building, then abandoned his rental car several blocks away in a hospital parking lot. First light lit the far edges of the sky as he grabbed his backpack and found a hard-to-see place in the dark recess of a neighborhood park to catch a couple hours of sleep.

He'd spent lots of great nights sleeping under the open sky on South Florida beaches, especially on uninhabited islands like Cape Romano, of which there were literally thousands. And he'd spent several cautious nights under the enormous sky at some Afghan battle sites. It seemed odd now, in the last minutes of night in a neatly manicured park of a major American city, that he was reminded more of the nights at war than of the nights in Florida.

But as he stared at the sky, hoping for sleep, his mind did what it usually did and sought out his reason for feeling that way. He wasn't surprised by the answer, because America was slowly but surely going to war with itself. The evidence was overwhelming and irrefutable and went beyond the hostilities between cops and civilians. Militias in every state were arming and training themselves, even if laughably so, to battle a federal government no longer trusted by anyone. Pro-lifers murdered fellow Americans who preferred the choice guaranteed them by law. Christian zealots jammed their beliefs down the throats of a disinterested and secular society the Christians vehemently accused of first declaring war on them. Hate and intolerance were preached from the studio pulpits of cable news networks while fringe extremists used money and media to high-jack once-respected political parties. And all the while Americans were quietly acquiescing to government's increasing intrusiveness into every possible aspect of their lives.

As Jack closed his eyes, what really surprised him was that most Americans didn't even notice.

Chapter 13

He woke up warmed by the sun, recharged by the chance to be fully alive for another day. Or as in a few times in his past, a chance to live at all. He sat up and rubbed his face, then pulled his toothbrush out of his pack, cleaned his teeth, and combed the grass out of the hair he'd grown longer than anytime since high school.

A middle-aged man walked his little lap dog in the distance, fast-paced and purposeful while the dog bounced along beside him. They weren't headed toward Jack or the park, but there was something about the athletic way the man walked that kept Jack watching. It brought back a good and familiar feeling, so Jack took out his phone and dialed.

"Hello?" The voice that answered always managed to sound gentle, even when it was loud enough to be heard from the dugout to first base above a stadium full of fans celebrating a double-play. "Is that you, Jack?"

"Yes, Coach, it's me. How are you?"

Jack never felt right just calling him Coach, but he would've felt worse calling him Dad, even though Coach had gone a long way toward earning the title. He'd made him part of his already large family when Jack's home fell apart, even paying all of his college expenses that weren't covered by scholarships or Jack's childhood savings.

"I'm doing pretty well, son. How are you?"

"I'm doing okay. Were you up?"

"Sure, you know I was." A pause. "Jill's still asleep, but you probably could have guessed that."

Jack laughed. "She still stays up late watching those cooking shows?"

"Sure, sure she does. That's never going to change, I suppose."

"I suppose not." Another pause. Then, "Hey Coach, I just wanted to call and say thanks."

Coach didn't say anything.

"Thanks…well, thank you for everything, okay? You know what I mean."

"Jack," Coach said in the tone that always made his players listen, even if they had to stop arguing with each other to hear it. "Are you scared, son? I'm watching the news and just saw you on it, so you sure have a right to be."

"Shit."

"There's no need to curse, son."

"Shoot. Sorry. Does Jill know?"

"No, not yet. She would've woken me if it had been on last night's news. She's bound to see it, though. Someone will tell her. Hard to keep secrets down here, especially about a guy as well known as you, which means the local media will climb all over this story. Do you need some money? A car? Just tell me what it is and I'll do it."

"Do you think my dad knows?"

Jack heard Coach shift the phone, scraping the whiskers that were always gone before he walked out the door. "Your dad, well, Jack, that's anybody's guess. He could be up for days in a row or lost for weeks. He might have seen it. It's impossible to guess and you know that. But if it makes you feel any better, so far all I've seen was just a quick mention."

"When did you see him last?"

"A month ago. Maybe less. At the Moose Lodge."

"Was he drunk?"

"Sure he was." Then, "I'm sorry I sounded like that was the obvious answer, son. I need to have more compassion for Carl after what he went through, what you both went through. Trust me, I'm on my knees praying for both him and you every single morning."

"I know you are. I've seen you do it and I appreciate it."

"But it's just so hard to see such a fine gentleman as your dad—"

"Stumbling drunk all the time?"

"Exactly. It's a sad, sad waste to watch him try so hard to drink himself to death. But you really should give him a call, same as you called me, don't you think? I really think you should."

"Sure thing."

"That doesn't sound like a promise, son. Listen, I know it's difficult for you but it's the right thing to do and you know that."

"Yes, sir. I'll call him."

"That's good. You're a good son, Jack, and a fine man, too. You let me know if you think of anything I can do, alright. Anything at all."

"Thanks again, Coach."

Jack stuffed his gear into his backpack and put on fresh clothes and his hat and sunglasses. He was heading out of the park as he dialed up his dad, hoping he wouldn't answer.

"You've reached the Wells family," said the voice of his long-dead mother, the hiss from the original cassette recording making it hard to understand even though Jack knew every inflection of her voice from listening to it over and over after she died. "Please leave us a message so we can call you back." Jack and his little sister were giggling in the background as the recording ended with them all saying, "Have a fun day."

Jack hung up without saying anything.

He left the park and found a coffee shop. He bought a newspaper on the way in, its front page almost entirely dedicated to the tank explosion, which was better than seeing his picture. He was surprised, in fact, that he didn't find his picture by the time the hostess seated him.

But before his coffee arrived, he did find it, a very old photo buried surprisingly deep in the sports section under a tagline about his skipping pro ball to go to war. The photo was from his Marine identification card, with his hair clipped short, which made him glad for its present length, because he now looked softer, and it would be harder to recognize him.

The placement of his photo so far back in the paper, coupled with the age of the outdated photo, didn't make sense at first. But he'd been in this kind of spot before, and with the benefit of those experiences it was easy to assume that some person – or persons – with power wanted Jack dead, but for some reason Jack didn't know, they didn't want him dead *yet*. They wanted him to stay free and on the run, but wanted him running at a panicked pace. They wanted him to worry that the first cop who saw him would shoot him, but also wanted him to feel somewhat safe knowing that the old photo made identification nearly impossible for any cop or civilian who didn't take the initiative of digging up a new one.

The heat of pure logic boiled it all down to the simple truth that someone wanted Jack to live long enough to do something. Someone wanted to benefit from his fight to survive, a fight they probably wanted him to lose.

The coffee shop felt fairly safe so he stayed there until the morning got rolling. Most people were in and out of the small shop in minutes, a to-go cup and a paper bag in their hands. But some lingered and read the paper, and they were the ones who worried Jack the most. But no one gave him a second look.

At 10:30, he walked out of the shop and headed to Claire's apartment building, a fine old colonial in a district saturated with fine old colonials, which made all that wonderful architecture look ordinary, the red brick and white columns similar to Theodore's home where Jeff lived in his rear apartment, but overdone here with an obligatory nod to Atlanta's history and heritage.

There was a buzzer in the lobby but there weren't any names on it. He checked Grayson's text for Claire's apartment number and buzzed it twice, but no one answered. He waited. He pushed the button again. Then the three-floor elevator went into gear, and Jack waited for it to come down so its passengers could get off and leave before he buzzed Claire again.

A fit man in his sixties stepped out of the elevator, square shouldered and erect, his hair cut close on the sides and flat on top. Jack was reminded of his father's joke that, for some odd reason, had inspired him to choose the Corps over the Navy. "You can always tell a Marine," his dad would laugh, "but you can't tell him much."

The man walked up to Jack and in a firm but friendly voice asked, "Young man, are you the one who's ringing the Statler residence?"

"Yes, sir, I am. I'm looking for Claire Statler. Are you her father?"

It was a chancy call because Jeff was mid-twenties, which meant Claire was probably about the same age, which meant Claire's father should probably be younger than this guy. But it felt like the right call all the same, and Jack went with it.

"Do you know my Claire?"

Jack wouldn't say that she'd called him last night. If she actually was playing him, that would definitely block the way. "No sir, I do not."

The man took a step back as if giving himself some swinging room, getting ready in case Jack meant trouble and this turned into a fight. "Then tell me why you're here. She's not accepting visitors."

Jack had come because there was a chance Claire might have some idea of who killed Jeff, or tried to kill Jack, but she might be just as much in the dark about it as anyone. So he looked the guy over and worked with what he had.

"If you'll indulge me for just a minute, sir, I'm guessing by the way you look and carry yourself that you're a veteran."

The man looked surprised, then gave a proud little smile and nodded. "Marines. Enlisted. Vietnam." He let that settle in a bit before asking Jack, "And you?"

Jack nodded along with him, two war veterans acknowledging each other's commitment. "I was a Marine too. Officer. Afghanistan. Very early in the war."

The man studied Jack hard to make sure it was true. With so many liars telling so many stories about war exploits they'd never had, Jack appreciated it. The man nodded again, and then the inbred competition between enlisted and officer got the better of him. Jack was sure the man was going to tell his story, so he waited.

"I was an embassy guard in Saigon, there at the very end of the war, and part of the largest helicopter evacuation the world has ever seen, or ever will. Two of my guys and me were among the last Marines to leave, flying out on Lady Ace 09 as the Communists rolled through the city in tanks."

He expected Jack to look curious, but Jack had studied the war and knew the brave history of the last few out. The man continued with his story when he didn't get a question.

"I was just a nineteen year old kid with written orders in my pocket from President Gerald Ford to arrest Ambassador Martin if he refused to come with us to the roof. They were back-up orders, mind you. The pilot had written the original verbal order in grease pencil on his knee tablet."

"Is it true the ambassador's wife left her baggage behind so that one additional Vietnamese could crowd aboard?"

"She saved that woman's life, for sure." Then he scratched at his chin. "I haven't said anything about any of that in quite a while. No one cares about Vietnam anymore, you know, and hell, why should they?"

Jack reached out and shook his hand. "I've got nothing to beat that, sir. I'm damned proud of you, though. Welcome home."

He smiled. "I always like that, welcome home, because we sure didn't hear it back then. Now, son, what does any of that have to do with Claire?"

"Well," Jack said, then looked around the lobby and asked, "Do you want to sit down?"

"No."

"Okay. I'm going to take a guess that you were pretty good friends with the other Marines on that embassy rooftop."

The man looked insulted. "We weren't just friends, son. We were brothers. If you really were a Marine by god you would know that." He turned slightly as though he planned to leave.

"Good," Jack said. "I do know that, and I was pretty sure you'd say that, which means you'll completely understand what it means when I say I fought in Afghanistan with Mike Roberts."

"Mike Roberts? As in Jeff's father?"

"Yes sir. He was my NCO."

The man looked Jack up and down, then stuck out his hand to shake again. "I'm Clarence Statler. My friends call me Curly. Don't bother looking for the curls 'cause they never were there."

"I'm Jack Wells. It's nice to meet you, sir."

They gripped hard, then Statler said, "Come on up with me," and turned back to the elevator.

Chapter 14

Claire Statler sat against the arm of the couch with her feet straight out and a blanket over her like she'd slept there and just woke up when Jack rang the buzzer. Her hair was a mess and she looked completely worn out, probably from crying and grieving every minute since she'd heard the news about Jeff. But even her puffy lids and bloodshot eyes couldn't take away from the fact that she was a gorgeous woman, with exactly the looks a network would want sitting behind an anchor desk.

"Hi," she said meekly after her father introduced him, in the same weak voice she had on the phone last night. "Jeff talked about you a lot. Did you go out to the Montessa tanks? Were you there for the explosions? We've been watching it on the news."

Jack ignored the questions. "It's nice to know Jeff talked about me. We go back a few years. I know all of his family pretty well, and I know his step-dad perfectly."

"Mike? He never once called Mike his step-dad. Mike was his dad."

"I'm glad he felt that way. Mike sure feels it."

She smiled sadly. "I hope you know it's all your fault I know the names of every big Southern Rock band, along with all of their greatest hits. Thank you so much for that, not really."

Jack smiled at her sad attempt at a joke. "Gimme three steps, gimme me three steps, baby," he sang, then stopped and waited.

Her sad smile got grew a tiny bit as she picked up the next line. "'Gimme me three steps, baby.'"

"Good old Skynyrd."

"That song's probably still at the top of his playlist." Then her smile disappeared as she finished the verse. "'And you'll never see me no more.'"

"Yeah. Not such a great choice of songs on my part. I'm sorry."

"No, it's alright, Jack. Can I call you Jack?"

"Of course."

"I actually think the song will become a good memory one day."

"Claire, I'm very sorry for what happened to Jeff."

She nodded but didn't speak. Her eyes stayed on him, as if they had nowhere else to go, and no energy to go there anyway.

Jack glanced over at Curly, looking for permission to push her. Curly nodded, so Jack said, "Claire, let's ignore the tanks for the moment. Do you mind if we talk a little about why you left Roanoke? I'm told you were doing some award-winning reporting on Montessa Chemicals, so it seems possible that the reason you left might have some bearing on Jeff's death."

She shrugged like none of it mattered anymore, then looked up at her father as if needing his strength or guidance. Curly sat down beside her before she said anything, and then, "I guess I did a good job there. It was…gosh, it feels so naïve now to think of what we were doing as exciting, but until Jeff died that's how we both felt. I never once considered it dangerous."

"Do you think Jeff ever did? He must have known some of the risk he was facing, just from what people said at the Sierra Club. Did he ever consider that he might die over his job there?"

"So you don't think it was suicide, either?"

Jack wasn't going to say anything to her that she might pass along to Mike. "I'm still working through it. Do you think it was?"

"No."

"Why not?"

She rolled her eyes. "Jeez, how about the simple reason that Jeff wasn't suicidal."

"You know much about suicidal people?"

"I know squat about suicidal people, but I knew Jeff better than anyone." She looked at Curly and shrugged. "Right?"

"Yes, Princess, I believe you did."

"And I'm telling you he wasn't suicidal. So take your time working through it if you want but I already know that someone killed him."

"Okay. I get that. Did Jeff ever say anything that indicated someone was threatening him? Show any worry about getting killed over what he was doing?"

She looked at her father again, and this time she seemed to find a good answer for Jack in an even better question for her father. "Dad, tell us, did you know the risks of getting killed over there in Vietnam?"

He nodded.

"But you never really expected to die, right? Isn't that what you always said?"

He nodded again. "I was scared as a little kid at the dentist the entire time I was there, but I always expected to come home safe."

Claire looked back at Jack. "I think Jeff felt the same way, and I know I did. People have died, and I suppose they will continue to die, protecting our precious environment the way Jeff did. But like my dad, I don't think any of them ever think they will be the one."

"I understand," Jack said softly, trying to be careful with her the way he always was with grieving people, especially those who made the choice to cooperate with him while suffering so. "But what I don't understand is your leaving Roanoke. I know this job is a big promotion for you, but if the environment and Montessa—"

She straightened up and forced back her shoulders. "You think I left because I wanted this *promotion*?" She said the word with absolute and intentional disgust.

"That's…that's what I was told."

"Well that's just not true. I desperately wanted to stay in Roanoke and fight Montessa with Jeff, working together against them, combining our sources as we came at that horrible company from different angles."

"I believe you. It would be hard not to believe you."

"Thank you. It's important to me that you do."

"But then why did you leave?"

She leaned back and took a deep breath. "You know what we were working on, right?"

Jack wanted to say no and let her fill him in. But she only had so much strength and he only had so much time. He wasn't going to waste any of it.

"I think I know where the story started, with the West Virginia chemical leak that polluted the Elk River and left everyone in the area without safe water to drink."

"That's right, and Montessa poses a similar risk to the residents around Roanoke. You know that, too? At least they did until the tanks exploded. Now, God, who knows what kind of damage they've done to their unlucky neighbors?"

"I knew some of that," Jack said, staying focused on what she was saying while keeping an ear to the street. A cop would discover his rental car before long and the police would start canvassing the neighborhood looking to find him or kill him.

"But I bet you don't know this. During that Elk River crisis the Charleston jail only pretended to provide potable water to its 429 inmates. In truth, they took very few of the required precautions with the water they served those poor inmates, and you can verify that by checking with the West Virginia Clean Water Hub."

She looked at Jack as if expecting him to know far more about it than he did. When she realized he didn't she went on. "The jail's staff barely even flushed the plumbing pipes after the water was finally declared safe, and fell far short of the mandated procedures issued for the municipal water supply. Inmates had all kinds of illnesses because of that, but of course they were criminals, so no one really cared."

"I didn't know any of that."

"I guess there's no reason why you would."

"But what does that have to do with Montessa? Elk River was polluted by a completely different company."

Claire straightened even more, getting herself into gear, moving away from her grief and back to being a reporter. "Three years ago there were an unusually high number of deaths at a rural Roanoke nursing home, the one destroyed by last night's blast, in fact. Everyone assumed it was just a virus being passed around from one old person to another, maybe brought in by a young and healthy staffer too strong to be affected by it, or maybe because of some food contaminant. You can imagine, I'm sure, that old people dying of sickness, just like criminals getting sick while in jail, doesn't get much news or public sympathy. Especially when the nursing home was so far out of town."

"No, I guess they wouldn't."

"But the prison's water issue got me thinking about the nursing home deaths, so I went back to take a look at those deaths, and others in the surrounding area."

"Smart investigative research."

"But it turned out that the nursing facility was too far from town to be connected to the city water supply. It was on well water."

"I'm not following."

She was most of the way back to being a professional newscaster now, building her story toward its climax. "The nursing home in Roanoke, where thirteen people of advanced age, along with a thirty-two year old nurse, died of mysterious and as-yet-unidentified respiratory problems, is located less than a third of a mile from a large Montessa storage tank facility."

"Ah. Now I'm getting it."

"Documents obtained from reliable sources provided evidence, if not proof, of a chemical leak at that storage facility, which is situated just up the aquifer that fed the nursing home. The leak occurred during the exact same time frame as the mysterious deaths but was never fully reported by Montessa Chemical Corporation. Company officials reported the incident to the EPA as 'a minor spill of a cleaning agent from a handheld container,' and the EPA didn't even bother to investigate. But in truth it was nearly five hundred gallons of highly toxic fluid spilled out on the ground and left to seep in. It leaked for two weeks before anything was done about it, and it was during those two weeks that people died in that home."

"Did you share this information with Jeff?"

She slumped, as if all her strength had gone into her reporting. "God, I wish I hadn't, but I did. And Jeff couldn't wait to put the sweet old faces of those innocent victims in front of a jury deciding the fate of Montessa's string of environmental violations."

"That was part of his court presentation?"

"He made that portion into a moving series of montages, one for each victim. Everyone who saw it cried."

"Claire, I don't want to sound insulting, but from where I sit it looks like Montessa got you this job in exchange for your dropping the news story."

She was offended and made a point of showing it. "I did not take this job for that reason. Sure, they offered it to me, but I said no without even a second's hesitation."

"But you're here now."

"Yes."

"So what changed your mind?"

"Only them intimating they would kill me if I didn't move here. Being dead or being an anchor in a major market isn't a hard choice to make."

"They didn't actually say they'd kill you, did they?"

"Of course not. As I said, they intimated it. About a month ago a guy came by my office at the Roanoke studio, poorly pretending to be a career recruiter, and talked about the benefits of this new job. Then he spoke ominously about the dangers of working big stories like mine, and making even bigger enemies, at a small town affiliate that couldn't protect me. His exact words were, 'You would be so much safer in Atlanta.'"

"That would be intimidating, for sure."

"Then he said I was wasting my skills pursuing a silly story about dead old people when I could take this new job and report on international events."

"So this guy knew you'd uncovered the reason behind the nursing home deaths. What about Jeff? I'm sure you were concerned about him."

"Of course I was. But I told the guy I hadn't mentioned those deaths to anyone else. They had no reason to suspect otherwise. And I told Jeff to keep it to himself, forever and ever and ever."

"Was this guy white? Black? Normal looking? Young?"

"He was white, somewhere in his thirties, I suppose. Probably late thirties. He really knew his way around words, too, and used them as tools the way an outstanding salesman does. He was very neat and clean. Normal except for the manicured nails and great haircut. He wasn't really metrosexual, though."

Jack smiled at her description. "By any chance is he the man who called you last night about Montessa blowing up their storage tanks?"

"No, that was a very different voice. Well polished and perfect English, but English the way a foreigner learns it, carefully pronouncing his Ts. Exact in all pronunciations of words, in fact. He still had a trace of an accent. My dorm mate in college was from Croatia. His accent reminded me of her."

Jack reacted. He couldn't stop himself. He hoped she hadn't seen it. "So you asked Jeff to keep it to himself?"

"Yes."

"But he didn't."

"No, he didn't. If he had he might still be alive. But he included all of it in the material Sierra Club prepared for trial. I'd already given him coroner's photos showing the excruciating pain on every single one of the victims' faces, as if their insides were being boiled. Jeff used those photos as the last one in each victim's montage, and they would have been absolutely devastating to Montessa in court. When Sierra turned it over during Discovery, it was like an evil wind suddenly blew across Roanoke."

Jack stood and walked to the window. "Claire, do you feel safe here?"

Her father stood up, too. "I'm going to stay with her for awhile."

Jack smiled at him, then looked out the window. Two police cars moved slowly in opposite directions down the street. There were several cops walking close to Claire's building, checking the face of every person on the sidewalk.

"I should be going. Thanks for your help."

"Jeff was murdered, right? You're sure it wasn't suicide?"

Jack looked at her and said, "Take care of yourself, Claire. You might even want to go away for awhile."

When Claire looked down, Jack caught her father's eyes and then pointed out the window. The man nodded as he stepped over for a look, while Jack opened the door and slipped out. He ran the stairs and checked the alley, then walked away, watching carefully for cops, working on the best plan he could with the few facts he knew, which were all so closely related that they didn't offer much of a range in thinking.

Claire had been threatened to the point of giving up her chance at a Pulitzer Prize by a man who was probably working for Montessa.

Jeff's investigation into Montessa and the testimony he was going to present in court gave Montessa plenty of reasons to kill him.

Whoever tried to kill Jack and then put his name on that sign wanted to get rid of him, too, or had a plan to use him, but he wasn't quite ready to attribute that entirely to Montessa, when his gut told him there was at least one other player involved.

The Roanoke Police didn't have a legitimate reason to beat him, which meant he had already done something to become enough of a threat for them to do it without one.

Itemizing those facts was an important step in allowing Jack to identify the first threads of a plan, and although it was still written in Jell-O and retained the ability to move around a lot, every conceivable iteration of the plan required Jack to have some help.

He pulled out his phone, watching for cops and moving fast as he called his radioman from Afghanistan, who answered on the second ring. "Bobby, it's Jack."

"Hi, Lieutenant. It's great to hear from you."

"I'm in Atlanta and was hoping to meet up with you while I'm here, but now I have to get back to Roanoke. Are you in town?"

"I am. What's going on in Roanoke, sir?"

"That's the reason I called. I could use your help if you want to find out. Still driving the sound van?"

"Yes, sir. And when do you want me there."

"Thanks. I was sure I could count on you. You're able to take some time off?"

"I'm sure 1 will make it happen if you need me."

"Then maybe you can even give me a lift?"

"Where and when can I pick you up? I need to make two or three calls and then I can be on the road."

Jack looked around for a landmark, anything that might be well known. "I'll wait in front of the Buckhead Theater. Do you know it?"

"Give me an hour. I'll try to be faster than that, but no more than an hour."

"Thanks, Bobby."

Chapter 15

Jack jumped into Bobby's van as soon as it pulled to the curb. As they shook hands he looked into the back at all the monitors and soundboards that made it a mobile television studio.

"The Marines really launched a career by making you a radioman."

"I chose communications when I joined the Corps, Lieutenant. I built radios as a kid, had a ten-meter single-sideband rig in my bedroom, and went into the Corp with a promise of them teaching me a lot more. Where are we headed?"

"Roanoke, Virginia. And I'm glad for your training because I could sure use some solid media help."

"I know."

"I guess that means you saw me on the news? The Blue Alert?"

"Lieutenant, I help make the news, so of course I saw it. I would have jumped to help you anyway, but with all that coming down around your ears there was no way I wouldn't be here for you. And since we're heading to Roanoke, do you know about the tank explosions?"

"I was there when it happened."

Bobby didn't even seem surprised. "Okay."

"So before you offer to help, you better understand that whoever orchestrated that alert, and maybe even blew up the tanks, has the entire law enforcement community lining up behind them. It's bound to get dicey. That's a mighty big ace they're holding."

"And you've got me," Bobby said with bold determination, but then looked embarrassed. "I'm sure you have others, too."

"I imagine you're already in trouble for taking this sound van."

"Not yet. I've told my boss I'm chasing a lead and trying to be first on the scene. They'll realize I lied pretty soon, though, and report it stolen. None of that's your worry, sir, and I'll disable the GPS tracker to buy time. Are you planning to broadcast some misinformation to throw the police off your scent?"

"Probably. I need to run a bluff or do something to confuse them, or whoever controls them. You're putting your job on the line. Maybe facing jail time. Be sure you're good with that, Bobby? I'll try to protect you but I can't promise."

"I'm good to go, sir. Knew all that when I showed up."

"Do you have all the equipment you need?"

"I do, yes, sir."

Jack looked Bobby over, remembering him in Afghanistan, afraid of dying every second he was there but never once hesitating to volunteer when a dangerous mission came up. "You don't have to help me, Bobby. You don't owe me."

"You look tired, Lieutenant. Why don't you get some sleep while I drive?"

"Thanks, I will." Jack closed his eyes, and felt like he'd just fallen asleep when his phone vibrated. He answered it without checking. "Yeah?"

"Jack, is that you? It's Robyn. Hello?"

He looked out the window of Bobby's van, shading his eyes against the bright sun while trying to recognize the landscape. He looked at his watch and was surprised it was three o'clock, which put them about halfway back to Roanoke.

He yawned and stretched as he said, "Did you call to talk some more about my past, Robyn? Maybe you found out that I once fished an entire week without a license, and ran a red light when I was sixteen."

He glanced at Bobby, who smiled and quietly asked, "A woman, Lieutenant? A girlfriend?"

"A woman, Bobby. Let's leave it at that."

"Jack, is there someone else there?"

"What do you want, Robyn?"

"I owe you an apology. I'm sorry I was such a bitch to you. Really sorry. I was way out of line."

He rubbed his eyes and looked out his window at the foothills and valleys of North Carolina as Bobby took the bypass around Charlotte. "I'm surprised. You don't strike me as a woman who leaps quickly to judgment—about me in this case—and then leaps just as quickly to an apology."

The tone of her voice changed as she said, "I am a *person* who reacts and adjusts to new facts, as should any intelligence person. The facts I had when we talked were correct, but I've adjusted my reaction to them as I've received new data."

"Jesus, you've sure got a way of making me feel like a test tube experiment. What new data?"

"I just talked to Jeff's father."

"Mike? God, he's not there is he?" Jack caught Bobby's look at the sound of Mike's name.

"He and I spoke on the phone. I called him to say how sorry all of us at Sierra are over what happened, and how good Jeff was at his job. Then Mike told me he'd asked you to come investigate Jeff's death, just the way you said. So again, I'm sorry."

A North Carolina State Trooper came alongside the van as Bobby drove off the bypass and onto I-77. Jack snapped fully awake but the trooper passed quickly and kept going.

"Forget it."

"Can we meet today? I'd like to buy you lunch and explain myself. It's important to me, even if you never speak to me again."

Jack scratched at his face and thought about Robyn, trying to work her into the facts he knew for sure, and the few things he hoped were true, building on the assumption that she was being honest right now, but open to the possibility that she was being played, or worse, acting purposefully on her suspicion that his FBI background made him a threat to her or the Sierra Club.

But the primary question at the moment was whether or not she was really sorry for attacking him. It made sense that talking to Mike could have changed her mind, but it also made sense that the person who frightened Claire, or the person who got Jack a Blue Alert, might also be exploiting her, using her to lure Jack to a meeting where he'd get arrested or killed.

Was he willing to trust her that much, and even if he did, what were the odds that she wouldn't be followed to their meeting without even realizing it? Was someone monitoring her phone as they spoke?

"Okay, let's meet, but not for lunch 'cause I have some stuff to do. Maybe dinner?"

"We have a small café in our building that's open till six, if that works. I'll meet you anytime you want."

Jack tried to think of a place to meet that was wide open, with long views from which he could watch her approach and see if she was followed. "Let's make it six. I saw a small park across from your building that might be nice. It'll be getting dark by then but it feels like too nice of a day to be inside, don't you think?"

129

Her voice lightened a bit. "I eat in that park all the time, and yes, I agree, too nice a day. There are benches near the fountain. Thank you, Jack. I'll bring some carry-out for a picnic."

"I'll see you then."

He hung up and looked over at Bobby, who shook his head and said, "Man, I am so glad I'm married. Dating, ugh. But you've always said you were never going to get serious with anybody, so you must like it."

"I don't like it, but I'm just better alone. And I always will be. It has to be that way, so let's not call it a date."

"It sure sounded to me like you just made a date."

"Just drive the van, Bobby."

"Yes, sir."

Bobby chuckled. "But you might want to take her some flowers."

"Bobby!"

"Nothing big. I mean, nothing that looks like you're trying to impress her. Maybe just a single flower. Do you know what flower's her favorite?"

"Bobby."

"Yes, sir?"

"Drive the van."

"Yes, sir."

Jack watched Bobby for half a minute. He kept smiling but didn't look inclined to make any more jokes, so Jack searched his phone for information about Robyn through *Covert Browser*. Even though he still paid a pretty heft cost to keep his phone dark, with good encryption technology, the government was always trying to find a way through every closed door or dark phone they encountered, lying about ticking-bomb scenarios to justify sweeping national signal surveillance. Jack wanted to make sure he did nothing with a traceable IP address that made him easier to catch or kill.

Covert Browser took Jack to *TOR*, which the Bureau had taught Jack to use for untraceable access to the Deep Web, where 99% of the World Wide Web's data lay hidden, just out of reach of Google or Yahoo or Bing. With his life at stake, he was grateful for the tools and training that kept him anonymous as he looked up facts about Robyn that would help him make an informed decision about meeting her or not.

What he learned was that Robyn had always been a fighter, and perhaps even a radical throughout her years at Berkeley. That, of course, depended on who applied the label. Arrested twice in lawful protests that turned terribly violent, she'd also spent long hours in volunteer offices, working the phones when she wasn't buried in a back room compiling and organizing reams of environmental data collected from scientists and naturalists.

She'd condensed a great deal of that data into a single compelling argument, footnoted with irrefutable facts, that she presented to the United Nations' Intergovernmental Panel on Climate Change, continuing the work begun in 1995 by the first team of scientists to conclude, and then bravely proclaim, that climate change was "unlikely to be entirely due to natural causes."

Barely out of law school and still studying for the bar, she'd asked to join the legal team at Sierra Club after meeting Harmon at a fundraiser, offering to work free if necessary. She quickly made a reputation for her fearless attacks on international corporate targets that showed a pattern of criminal disregard for the environment as they used it like an open sewer in their quests for profit.

She'd been warned twice by police that her life had been threatened, and Jack found one police report of her being attacked by two men as she left a restaurant. But witnesses said that she'd kicked and clawed and bit until her attackers ran away as other customers came out to help. She'd spent two weeks in the hospital, but kept up with her work during the entire time, releasing herself against doctor's orders so she could give grand jury testimony from her wheelchair.

Jack also learned that her father died in a fiery car explosion and her mother lived in a small home in Maryland, but little else besides normal background data. Nothing indicated that Robyn might be the kind of woman who would betray him, and her devotion to Sierra made betrayal seem even more unlikely. So he would assume that much, but nothing more. And even that would remain an assumption. He would still be careful.

Bobby passed the park by Robyn's office and stopped two blocks away. Jack looked in all directions before putting on his black ball cap and sunglasses and jumping out, then jogging to a parking garage across from the park and slipping into the shadows, watching Bobby pull away, waiting to see if anyone had followed the van.

His phone rang and he glanced at it. The screen displayed "No Caller I.D," which meant it could be a telemarketer, even though Jack seldom got those. More likely it was the Veterans Administration or some other governmental agency. "Hello," he said, and then went back to surveillance.

"Hey there, is this Jack Wells?" The man's cheerful voice had absolutely no accent, which actually made it sort of extraordinary. Midwestern perhaps. Great Plains. Suspiciously pleasant in a way-too-sure-of-itself kind of way.

"Who is this?"

"I called to introduce myself, Mr. Wells. Jack. Is it alright if I call you Jack? I hope so. Anyway, My name is Mark Foster. We have some business between us, Jack, and I'm calling to apologize for not being able to attend to it personally. I'm tied up elsewhere, but I sent a good man in my place." He laughed again.

"What kind of business?"

"Influence peddling."

"You or me?"

He laughed, as weirdly comfortable talking on the phone with a man he'd never met as a person could possibly be, making Jack think about Claire and the man who scared her into leaving Roanoke.

"I'm talking about me, of course, unless you also peddle influence."

"I don't."

"I thought not. Anyway, I am a salesman, and I mean that in the best sense of the word. I help people get what they want. My official title is lobbyist." He laughed again, and again there was something unnatural and sinister about it. "Although my reputation is as more of a guerilla lobbyist for the somewhat peculiar way in which I get things done. I don't mind the name. Basically it's my job to influence laws and remove obstacles so my clients can operate profitably. That is the American Way, you know. Mine is an interesting gig and I like that about it."

"Then what business could we possibly have together, Mr. Foster?"

"The security head of a client company saw you humiliate one Chief Howard in the parking lot of their facility. I want to say nicely done, Mister Wells. It's rare these days to hear of a man with your kind of mettle, and it's even more exceptional behavior from a volunteer like yourself. You are a volunteer, right?"

"Get to your point."

"Of course. I like your directness. I'm sure you can appreciate that making trouble for the chief causes my client concern that you could eventually make trouble for them. Thank you for that, by the way, because those kinds of worries create work opportunities for me. And it's that very work in which you and I will need to participate, Jack. You and I need to work together to eliminate their concern about you making trouble for them. Sound like an enjoyable experience? I hope it does." He paused, then, "Well, it's been great talking to you," and hung up without a chance for Jack to say anything more.

Jack looked down from his surveillance and stared at his phone for a few seconds. Then he waited another five minutes before leaving through the back side of the garage and walking to a place where he could observe the park. He found a safe spot from which to watch for Robyn, and waited. No one arrived early to set up surveillance, and when Robyn walked up a half-hour later in jeans and an unbuttoned flannel shirt that opened up to show a tight t-shirt, she wasn't followed. She looked around for Jack, but sat down to wait when she didn't see him.

Jack watched for ten more minutes before walking over to meet Robyn.

Chapter 16

"Hi," Robyn said meekly before Jack even sat down at her bench. "Thanks for coming. What happened to your arm?"

He glanced at the bloody gauze he'd wrapped around the cut from the nursing home. "Just a scratch. It looks worse than it really is. Are you doing okay? Have there been any new threats to anyone at Sierra?"

She looked suspiciously at his arm as she said, "No."

"That's good."

"Yes. Thank you for asking."

"You're welcome."

"I imagine you heard about Montessa's tanks."

"I did. What do you think it means?"

"I can't figure it. Doesn't make sense, at least with what little I know. I'm sure it made good sense to them or they wouldn't have done it."

"It could have been terrorists."

"Sure. Of course."

They sat awkwardly. Robyn lifted her head but kept her eyes down as she fiddled with the buttons of her shirt, while Jack kept up surveillance and tried to think of something to say.

"I wanted to trust you," Robyn said after a couple more uncomfortable minutes. "I really wanted to believe you were one of the good ones."

"Thanks. I know you mean that in a good way but it still comes off as insulting because there's really no reason for it to be so hard."

She winced. "I probably had too much emotion invested in my decision after you stonewalled my questions. The more I pressed for the truth the harder you resisted, and that pissed me off even more."

Jack took another look around and said nothing. He had nothing more to say anyway.

"It was your refusal, Jack. That's what made me mad."

"You believed what you wanted to believe and it blinded you."

"Yes, of course I wanted to believe what I'd read on the internet. It was blood in the water that naturally made someone like me predacious. I attacked almost purely on instinct."

"Like the way you attacked the San Francisco cop."

"Oh, so you've done some internet research, too. Did you happen to see the photo that went along with the story? The one where he was dragging me backward by my hair."

"Attacking is an ugly side of you. An ugly side of anyone."

"Let's not forget the fact that you admitted to taking a payoff."

He ignored her as he looked all over the park and along the road that bordered it. A Roanoke cop had followed him from a park very much like this one, and Blondie had fallen in line when the cop veered off in order to follow Jack to his motel. So even though this was a different park it still had a familiar feeling of betrayal that kept him watching.

"You can call it a payoff if you like. But it was a payoff in much the same way as any settlement from an insurance claim or a civil suit or even a divorce is a settlement. You chose to make it sound bad because you wanted to believe the worst."

"I did, that's true. But you can surely understand why, especially since most of my experiences with former law officers have been so negative." She touched his leg and grinned. "And I don't just mean being dragged by my ponytail."

He stopped looking around, feeling safer now that no one had showed, and wanting to get things back to comfortable with Robyn. "I do understand, but I told you all I could about my past. From there I just had to let you go on your instincts."

"And they weren't too good, were they?"

"How good do you think they are now?" He looked directly at her for the first time and smiled. "How am I stacking up in your head?"

She smiled too, and even though he didn't want it because of everything he had going on, he couldn't avoid feeling the same thrill he had at their offices when he'd followed her clicking heels down the hall. "I want to catch that smile," he said, raising his phone and centering her face on the screen. "Ready? Say almond milk and tofu."

She laughed, but as soon he took the picture her smile faded.

"I'm really not all that confident about the way you're stacking up, Jack. I do think it's nice that it matters to you, though."

"I didn't mean to tip my hand, but I don't really mind that I did."

"That's sweet. But if I'm going to be honest I need to say that it's hard for me to trust anyone with your kind of elite governmental background. There's no reason for you to take it personally."

Jack nodded his head in agreement because he really did understand.

"Yeah," he said, "I have a little trouble trusting people in government too, so I get it. It's your call, though. You'll either choose to trust me or you won't, and I have the exact same choice with you."

"I hadn't thought of it that way."

"But keep in mind that it's entirely possible you've seen too many movies about the FBI, because I'm not all that impressed by my background, or intimidated by it. It was a job."

She rubbed the hem of her flannel shirt between her fingers. "I've heard a lot of people say that kind of thing before, and I really don't want to sound all Big Brother-ish here, but our government really is getting hard to trust."

"No argument from me."

"And let's face it, you were one of the select few with the full force and power of the United States Government at your disposal. When you said you were FBI, things happened, right?"

She was right. Those three initials carried far too much power, but then, so did any initials that were backed up by a badge.

"And I'm sure you still have access."

"There's some truth in that. Once you're in, you're never fully out."

"Which means you can still get things done, right?"

Jack didn't answer.

"And I'm equally sure you haven't forgotten your training which, when you couple the SWAT stuff to the electronics stuff to the investigative stuff, well, you must be able to see why that makes people like you so dangerous to organizations like ours. Which is why people like you are so hard for people like me to trust."

"I do see your point."

She was silent, waiting until he looked at her before she asked, "Did you kill men in Afghanistan, Jack?"

He grimaced, and once again felt bad for not having changed Chainsaw's listing to Mike Roberts, as he'd been asked to do so many times. Mike, a career Marine, was assigned to Jack on his first day in-country. They'd choked down platefuls of violence together and vomited out just as many mouthfuls of rot. Jack no longer wanted to think about any of the men they'd killed together, and Chainsaw wanted to live down the nickname he'd earned cutting apart the enemy, worrying constantly about how he could ever explain it to his kids without telling them lies.

"I did kill men, yes."

"So you've gotten over the hurdle. You know what it's like to kill. You know for sure you can do it and you know for sure you will do it, if necessary."

"It was war, Robyn."

She softened. "I'm sorry. I do know the difference and I respect your patriotism. You should be proud of your service. I'm proud of your service. But here's the thing—"

She looked like she didn't want to continue, but Jack knew she would.

"Give me a minute, Jack. I want to say this as succinctly as possible."

Jack looked around as he waited for her to get her thoughts together, but still saw nothing threatening in the park.

"Okay, here goes. When the Sierra Club targets a billion dollar corporation, that company has a very easy choice to make. They can spend a dozen years and millions of dollars fighting us in court, getting castigated in social media, enduring discovery, facing compliance investigations, and possibly paying heavy fines for criminal environmental behavior. Exxon paid $125 million."

"That's a lot."

"It's a pittance in our opinion, compared to the damage they caused and the profits they made off that damage."

"And the choice? You said they had a choice to make."

"Yes, and thank god Exxon was honorable enough to take the path they did, at least in that instance, because the other option that every one of our targets have is to hand a few thousand dollars to a man to whom killing has lost its revulsion, with instructions for him to make the problem go away."

"Killing will always make my stomach churn."

"I'm glad it does because it should. Everyone isn't like you."

"Yours is a calloused view."

"Oh, Jack, I so wish that were true, but I've sadly learned that life, whether it's the life of a human being or a furry little animal, is just a matter of business economics, at best. My god, people kill each other in America over a traffic incident or an insult or a dog pooping on a lawn, so killing to avoid going to jail or paying an enormous fine, if you apply the road rage standard, seems reasonable."

"You based your argument on economics, but then tainted it with emotional examples."

"You're right, so let's stick with economics. Do you know how many people Ford Motor Company *knew* would die because of their exploding fuel tanks? Knew it without a doubt, had the numbers and engineering reports to make an accurate prediction with an extremely high level of confidence. That's the event that first opened my eyes. That's the reason I do what I do."

"No idea, but I'm guessing your father was one of their victims."

She flinched but just slightly. "From their own data Ford knew that at least 180 people would die horribly painful deaths, burned alive and screaming in pain as they sat pinned in their cars, for one reason and one reason alone. And that reason was that Ford, that giant, iconic American corporation, didn't want to spend eleven extra dollars per car to prevent the deaths. The actual number of deaths was even higher than they predicted."

"Disgusting."

"No, wait, because what's truly disgusting is the simple mathematics of their decision. Eleven bucks a car added up to $137 million, whereas the total value Ford put on the dead people...if you can even imagine putting a dollar value on the lives of a completely unknown group of people that would die because of you and you alone...to only be $49.5 million. So they sat down in a boardroom and made a strictly economic decision not to fix the fuel tank. They probably went out for a nice dinner afterward."

Jack reached over to touch her arm but she moved it just enough to show she didn't want his or anyone's sympathy.

"And I can cite hundreds of other examples of perverse-incentive decisions that were similarly driven by economics, from Love Canal to the Kingston Slurry Spill to Summitville to the Gulf of Mexico Dead Zone to the 1.3 billion gallons of toxic slurry gushing into Hazeltine Creek to—"

"I get it."

"I was working my way up to Louisville Gas and Electric's dumping of toxic ash into the Ohio River, and their blatantly continuing to dump those poisons into the river even after hidden cameras exposed them destroying that great resource, merely because it was so much cheaper than properly disposing of that toxic ash. Destroying our planet for their increased level of profit."

Jack wanted to add something to show he wasn't completely ignorant and out of his league. "I read recently, and I think I have this right, that the fracking in Oklahoma has moved that state almost overnight from 17th place to 1st among the Lower 48 in the number of earthquakes."

She hit her forehead. "Jesus, we're busting the earth on which we live into tiny pieces! How can we not see that as dangerous? It's like injecting thousands of gallons of corrosive fluid under the slab of a small home. Bad things *have* to happen to that slab. And by the way, the drinking water around many of those fracking sites has 17 times more methane in it than it did before the fracking. But far, far worse than any of that—and the absolute biggest threat to our survival—is the incredible amounts of money spent by outrageously rich businessmen to hide or protect what they do, primarily by discrediting the facts and science of climate change, making people think it's a hoax. As unbelievable as it sounds, those business people are actually willing to lose the entire *planet*—not just every human being and every other living organism on it, but the only home that me and you and them have in this entire universe—just to continue increasing their profits."

"Point taken."

"I hope so, Jack, but I'd be shocked if you got it so quickly."

"I'm a quick learner."

"Maybe, but I had an impossibly hard time wrapping my mind around it. It took years. But if you really did get it, then it should be easy for you to see how tiny, tiny a step it is from just doing something you know will cause deaths, like Ford, to the active orchestration of those deaths, like we saw with Montessa killing Jeff."

"You don't know that for sure. Weren't you the one who said they might only get a $7,000 fine?"

"I did, but that fine would only be for a single violation. If Jeff had lived he would have used that conviction to pull back the curtain on so many horrible things. Montessa really didn't have a good choice except murder."

"Let's eat something, okay?"

"I've bothered you."

"Yes, you have."

"Then that's a good sign. I like that it bothers you. Preston said you're a good man, and that I'd been too mean to you."

"And Harmon's opinion carries weight with you?"

She smiled. "As far as I'm concerned you couldn't get a better endorsement, because he loves me. I'm the daughter he never had. He really is like a father to me, and we both want what's best for each of us to be happy. That's nice, right?"

Jack didn't bother wasting time thinking about his own father, other than the few seconds it took to tell himself not to waste the time. "Very nice, yes."

"It was Preston who pushed me to give you another chance, and although he laughingly called this a date, I'm not ready to."

"Fair enough." He looked away and gave it a moment, hoping to indicate the end of that conversation and the start of another. "By the way, any chance the name Mark Foster mean anything to you?"

She looked up quickly while her hand moved toward her face as if instinctively catching a gasp. She caught it in time and pushed back her hair with that hand, then stared at him until it got uncomfortable. She took a breath.

"Jack, a few years back I thought Mark Foster was nothing but a myth. A legend. A bogeyman who supposedly worked for chemical and fossil fuel companies, motivating governments around the world to approve their products, even when the public demanded otherwise. An expert at bribing, cajoling, blackmailing, threatening, backslapping, getting people fired, siccing the media on them…that sort of thing."

"He pays off elected officials to pass favorable laws for his clients?"

"Yes, at least here in the States where bribes and campaign contributions work pretty well. But they're not as effective in Europe, or in many other countries where there are more ethics in government, or at least more accountability to the electorate. In those places bribing isn't always enough of an incentive."

"You said you thought he was a myth."

143

She looked uneasy. "It's kind of hard for any of us to talk about him. Law enforcement has never been able to connect him to any of the harm that's come to our people, but we feel sure he's been involved in some of it, particularly in a hit-and-run death right here in Roanoke. And we know we're constantly battling the influence he exerts over governments. He's devious, tricky, and conniving, but like a weasel with a poisonous snake, he gets the job done. The snake always dies."

"Do you suspect him in Jeff's death?"

"I don't know. It's hard to say because he's like a boxer, always probing opponents for strengths and weaknesses. It's all a very sick game to him, so if he thought Jeff's death might make us weak, maybe he would have gotten involved. But as I said, he's a difficult man to talk about. He's incredibly good at his job. GMOs would be banned in far more countries than they currently are if not for him, and wind and solar would be getting more funding, helping to slow down global warming but cutting into the profits of fossil fuel companies."

"If he's hard to talk about, then let's just skip it." Jack looked around again for something else to use as a conversation changer.

"Thank you. Why did you ask?"

"He called me earlier to introduce himself."

Now Robyn's hand shot toward her mouth and made it there with time to spare. She would never have been able to stop it. "Oh, no," she said through her fingers.

"What? Why the big reaction?"

She stared at him. He waited. Then she picked up the phone and flipped through it. "We received this film last year from our friends at Germany's Green Party. It's supposed to have been taken surreptitiously, but Foster would have never let that happen. You never see him in the video, though, so it's useless against him. The seated man wearing the blue suit is a foreign cabinet minister. It's Foster's way of warning all of us who oppose him, or them. Them being those companies who profit by killing our planet."

"He really must be good at what he does to worry you so."

"He's much too good. He's the one who convinced Texas Governor Rick Perry to ban any reference to climate change in a report on Galveston Bay, setting an example for Republican governors across the country to follow. He got Congress to investigate and disrupt the lives of our best climate scientists until they quit the environmental movement or moved to a more receptive country. There appears to be no limit to what he'll do, although I'm not sure he really even cares one way or the other about the environment. He just loves doing a job so well." She handed her phone to him. "This will show you how good he is. I can't watch it again." She got up and walked away.

The screen showed a small white boy, blonde with high cheek bones, maybe twelve years old, sitting on a chair, duct tape holding his body tightly to it. He was dirty and his worn clothes did not fit him. Homeless. A street kid. The tough look on his face probably meant he'd been there a while. Jack pushed play.

"Your son," came a calm voice off-camera, the same voice Jack had just heard an hour ago on his phone, "is about this boy's age, am I right? I've seen your son. He's a cute kid, by the way. I bet you're proud of him."

"Yes," a shaky voice said as the camera turned toward it, showing an impeccably dressed man with a flag pin on the lapel of his suit coat. Jack couldn't identify the flag for sure, but thought it might be Estonian. The man's accent seemed to confirm it.

"Phillip," Mark Foster said, "how about getting me another nail from the boy."

The camera closed in on the boy as a man's hand reached into frame and lifted the boy's right hand. Jack hadn't noticed before that it was bleeding. Then pliers went to the boy's thumbnail and pulled it out. The boy jerked violently and tears poured out of his eyes, but he didn't make a sound, not even whimper. He was even tougher than he looked.

"Now that's what we call a pity back home," Mark said, "This nice young boy suffering over your hard-headedness."

"Please stop this madness. I cannot help you. My constituents do not want your products. Our farmers do not want your products. We know you ruin lives and small farms in the United States and around the world, and we don't want that to happen here. That's why we have such strict policies against GMOs. Our people demanded it."

"Sure, sure, that's fine. You want to vote your conscience and I get that. I'm even kind of proud of you for that." He waited. Then, "Phillip, how about going ahead and taking another."

The boy, the hand, the pliers. Still no scream.

"Now, as interesting as all this is right now," Mark said, "what I'm really wondering is how well your son will hold up when we do this exact same thing to him. Go on, Phillip, take another. Get a pretty one this time."

Phillip dropped the hand with no nails remaining and picked up the boy's left hand. As the thumbnail squished off Jack thought the boy might pass out.

"Please, please stop this. This poor boy's done nothing wrong."

"Of course he hasn't. He's just a stand-in for your son. I think his name is Peter. Did I get that right? Peter? Or was it Wolfgang? I'm sorry I'm not better with names. But Phillip is. Phillip, where is Peter right now, by the way?"

The voice of the torturer said, "He leaves school in about ten minutes and heads to soccer. Then home. At least that's his plan."

"Let…" the man in the suit said, then paused, coming to terms, accepting that he had little choice…"let me see what I can do. I will try to help with what you want."

Mark sounded pleased as he said, "Why thank you so much, sir. I really do appreciate your help. How about we speak again in a week."

A chair shuffled. Footsteps. After a door closed, a knife moved in front of the camera and cut the young boy loose. A hand, different from the one that pulled out the nails, handed him a hundred Euro bill.

The boy stared at it, his eyes streaming the tears of his pain but his face still hard. It made Jack sad that boys so young could learn the look so well. He rose from the chair. "You promised me two hundred Euros."

"I did, I did. No argument there. But you promised me a good show. Remember? Yet you didn't let our guest really see how much pain you were in. You have got to get better at showing emotions."

"And for that you're going to cheat me?" The boy stepped toward the camera. "We had a deal." And then the boy stopped as if someone was suddenly aiming a gun at him, or perhaps pointing the knife that cut him loose. He began to cry, but not from pain. It was the cry of losing, of being exploited, of being worthless once again. The cry of a boy whose hunger and shame were overwhelming even the throbbing of his fingers.

"You really shouldn't have raised your voice to me, 'cause now you'll get nothing. Instead I'll use the money on a decent bottle of wine and will toast your bravery with it." The hand snatched back the bill. "Now get out."

The boy shuffled out of frame, his bleeding hands pressed into his small chest, his shoulders lurching in rhythm with his sobs.

Jack put down the phone as Robyn walked back and said, "Sickening, isn't it?"

"That poor kid."

"Yeah. In D.C. Foster just buys the votes he needs, which is lucky for those families, I guess. Still disgusting, though."

"Absolutely."

She pushed the lunches aside and sat back down. "I brought a choice of ham and cheese or tuna fish, if you're still hungry. I like both, so you choose."

The video had killed his appetite. "Not really hungry. Besides, I figured you for a vegan or vegetarian or something."

"Oh, now I get it – your almond milk and tofu line. But no, not me. In fact I love nothing more than a nice piece of fresh fish with…hang on." She slid her hand into her small purse and pulled out her phone. "Sorry. I'll turn off the ringer."

"Take the call if you want."

"Let me just check it…I should take this. You're sure you don't mind?"

"No."

Robyn smiled and gave him a flirty wink. "Hey, Theresa, did you get—"

Her smile was gone instantly. "Wait, slow down. Say that again."

She listened and nodded but didn't interrupt. Then, "Yes, of course. I'm on my way. Be there in twenty minutes."

Jack was already on his feet. "Trouble?"

"I'm sorry but I have to go."

Robyn stood and glanced around to make sure she had everything, double-checking herself like a pro who knew the value of a quick pause when you're moving fast.

"Can I help?"

"It's a co-worker with a problem."

"I'm good with problems."

"Well then I guess I've just decided to trust you, be-cause this problem happens to be right down the middle of your alley."

Chapter 17

Robyn drove away from the central business district while Jack kept watch, using the car's visor and his hat and sunglasses to conceal his face from anyone looking hard. Rush hour was over and city traffic was shifting like the tide as young suburbanites made their way to the down-town bars and sidewalk tables, joining the working profes-sionals who hung around after their work day ended.

It took about twenty minutes for them to get to a quiet neighborhood of large trees and attractive homes with small front yards but big porches. Cars and bicycles were in most of the driveways, and Jack imagined the nightly rituals of the families or couples inside, dinner and baths and home-work and maybe a game or some television before chasing cranky kids or a playful wife off to bed.

"And then," Robyn said, as she made a turn onto a street of older homes and even bigger trees, "just like I said before, Theresa was warned to be careful, and that there really wasn't anything more the FBI could do at this point except to stand by."

"Thanks for repeating it. Sometimes people remember more the second time."

"This whole business is getting kind of scary, Jack, even for me. First Jeff, and now Theresa."

"She's not a victim yet."

"Not yet, Jack, thankfully."

"She said the FBI called and warned her?"

"That's what she said. Does something about that strike you as odd?"

"Yeah, for a few reasons."

Jack went silent as he decided whether or not to trust her about the Blue Alert. If he chose wrong and she ended up doubting his innocence even a little, she could call the police and he would be done. And if she couldn't decide whether or not to doubt his innocence, she could still call the police and let them sort it out. But he didn't expect a woman in Robyn's position to do that, and even if she did, it would tell him something else about her.

"I'm a wanted man, Robyn." It sounded so funny he couldn't help but laugh.

"What? Oh, you're joking."

"I'm laughing but I'm not joking. Someone here in Roanoke, or maybe at FBI Headquarters, or maybe some-where I haven't even considered, managed to get the entire local law enforcement community looking for me."

"Why? What did you do?"

"Nothing. I showed up here and asked a few questions about Jeff. I talked to that guy at Montessa."

"That's all? Really?"

"Pretty much. I did make toothpicks out of the forearm of a local tough guy, but I have trouble believing he was a cop."

"Here in Roanoke? You got into a fight here?"

"I'd be embarrassed to call it a fight. But there's a Blue Alert out for me all the same, and that's the closest thing to a crime I've done."

"That Blue Alert sign was about you? I saw it on I-81 driving to work this morning, but would never have connected it to you. The one about a white Mustang?"

"I'm glad you didn't think of me, but now you understand why the FBI calling Theresa makes me just a little suspicious there might be a connection."

"Of course I do. There, that's her house. Do you think it's okay to park out front or should we be more careful?"

Jack looked up and down the street, always and tirelessly on the lookout for a trap or a double-cross, but he saw nothing suspicious. "It's a risk either way, but probably okay to park out front as long as I'm not recognized, which would be hard now that it's dark. Parking your car in the driveway might even be a deterrent. Whoever might be watching will see she has company."

Robyn pulled into the driveway and stopped. "Just act normal," Jack said. "Let's not set off alarms unnecessarily."

"Okay. That's Theresa at the door."

Jack made mental notes of the area as he walked to the porch, remembering cover and concealment, all the ways in and all the ways out. If he ended up in a fight there, he wanted the terrain to be more familiar to him than it was to his enemy.

"Theresa, this is Jack," Robyn said as they walked up the steps to the porch. "He was an FBI Agent. How are you?"

Jack shook her hand, which trembled just a little as he said, "We've met before, Theresa."

Robyn looked surprised and so Jack quickly added, "Yesterday in the Sierra Club lobby. She was behind the counter." He turned back to Theresa. "Remember?"

Theresa smiled, her face etched deeply by the passing of her seventy-five or eighty years, the deepest wrinkles radiating from the corners of her eyes. "Yes, yes. That was me. Yesterday, of course."

She led them inside, where just about every surface was covered with photos of a cute animal, a young person, an old man, or a younger version of the old man, including one in an Eisenhower military jacket. Lace sheers covered the windows, softening the lights from the street. But any peaceful feeling her home might otherwise have had was constantly shattered by the loud applause and clanging noises of a TV game show.

"Theresa," Jack asked, after they'd all sat in the living room, "what did the FBI Agent say to you when he called?"

"Why, just what I told Robyn, of course."

"Would you mind repeating it for me? And do you mind if I turn this off?"

"Oh, sorry. Sure, turn it off. I keep it on as company since Ralph passed. I don't really even notice it."

"Thanks." He clicked the remote. "So? The agent?"

Theresa looked at Robyn, then shrugged. "I got a call just now from the FBI—"

"I'm sorry to interrupt again, but was it a man or woman?"

"A man."

"Do you think he really was an agent? Did you get his name?"

She thought about it for a few seconds. "Well, no. He sure sounded official, but it never occurred to me to ask for proof of who he was, or even his name. He might have even said it, I'm not sure." She turned to Robyn. "When the FBI calls and says there's a threat on your life, it makes funny things happen in your head."

"I'm sure it does. Now go back to your story, Theresa, and tell it to Jack from the beginning."

"It's a short story," she said, followed by an attempt at a laugh. "I got a call from this FBI Agent who said he had information about a threat to my life because of what I do at the Sierra Club."

"What do you do there?"

Robyn leaned over to Jack and said, "She works in—"

"I'd like Theresa to tell me."

Robyn leaned back. "Of course."

"Like Robyn was probably going to say, I work in volunteer services."

"So you are just a volunteer?" It sounded insulting and Jack knew it. "I mean, you're not on the payroll? I'm asking because it might matter."

Theresa let the offense pass. "I'm proud to volunteer for a cause I believe in. No, I don't get paid. Why?"

"What is it you do there?"

"I...well, I stuff envelopes when it's my shift in the lobby. I make coffee sometimes. I take packages to the post office."

"She's the den mother of Sierra," Robyn added as she smiled and squeezed Theresa's arm. "A shoulder to cry on when you need one, and a good set of ears for listening."

"Thank you, dear."

"That's just weird," Jack said, staring at the floor. Then he looked up and said, "Not what you just said about her."

"Then what?"

"That it's weird for anyone to threaten her instead of you or Preston."

"Or Jason or Derek or any of the other people who work in legal?"

"Yeah, something like that." Jack turned back to Theresa. "Has anything like this ever happened to you before? Do you have some sort of a past before Sierra that might make someone come back at you?"

"My goodness, no, but thanks for making me sound so intriguing. I just got chills over that."

Jack smiled and Robyn laughed.

"A neighbor's dog bit my niece once and we had some not-so-nice words over that, but lord, that's been ten years now. I get along with everyone, I think."

Jack explored the room, looking for any kind of a clue while thinking through what she'd said. He felt both of them staring at him, and then Theresa asked, "Would you like some coffee or tea?"

"No, thanks."

"How about you, Robyn? To be honest, I'd like you both to stay a bit while I calm my nerves."

"Actually, a cup of coffee sounds great," Jack said, and then smiled again.

When Theresa went to the kitchen, Robyn came over. "What are you thinking?"

"I'm not sure. Maybe someone's trying to scare her enough to scare you and the others at Sierra."

"Why her. Why not me?"

"She's a better candidate because she shows fear easily, and her age will probably make every one of you want to protect her, even at the cost of backing off Montessa."

"So you don't really think someone's going to kill her?"

"I don't see how it makes sense, do you? It's possible. I mean, anything's possible. But with the facts I have I see no reason to run the risk of murdering an old woman who's only threat to a big corporation is the stamps she sticks onto envelopes."

"I don't either."

"Whereas the risks of murdering someone are always significant, regardless of how careful and well planned you are, or well-insulated by attorneys."

"So she's safe."

"I didn't say that. But if she really is a target, whether the guy who called was an agent or not, what's most likely is that she was targeted in order to send a message, probably to me. Maybe you. And if she's just delivered that message by making you react to the threat, or leave the office or, ideally, abandon your lawsuit, then she's done her job and is no longer at risk."

"And if the message was to you?"

"I'm afraid I'm slow to get messages."

"It makes sense that it's me. I mean, we're already at such a low point in our case against Montessa that one more reason might be all it takes to make us give up."

"You sounded far more determined before. You think they know how you feel?"

"Their attorneys were practically high-fiving in the corridor. I'm not proud to admit that we walked out looking pretty badly beaten."

"Then that could be what all this is about. A final scare to make you quit."

"But what if the message is something else?"

"We should move her, just in case. Will she go?"

"She seems to be frightened enough, and she's always been good at following instructions. I think she'll leave if I ask her."

Jack headed to the kitchen. "Then let's go ask her."

Theresa looked up from pouring the coffee as they walked into the kitchen. "Milk or sugar, Jack?"

"Black, thanks. Listen Theresa, Robyn and I think you're probably okay here, but we'd like to move you somewhere safer just to be sure. Will you do that for us?"

"Just to err on the side of caution. We think it's better to do too much than not enough, right?"

Theresa looked at Robyn as though reading more from her face than her words might have said, then took a sip of her coffee. With her lips still on the cup she meekly said, "Okay."

"How much time do you need to get a few things together?"

"For how long?"

"Maybe a few days."

"I don't have enough cat food. Mittens will be okay alone for a few days because Audrey loves to walk over and check on her. She'll scoop her poop, too, but I don't have enough cat food."

"Audrey can't get it for you?"

"Audrey doesn't drive anymore, the poor dear. And I can't leave Mittens without plenty of food and water."

Jack was stuck in place over the nutritional needs of a cat, but if he was right that Theresa really wasn't at risk, he had time to make a run. "Okay, pack what you need and I'll run for cat food."

"Mittens prefers the canned tuna," Theresa added hastily. "She's not too finicky about the brand. But she'll also need dry food I can leave out for her in case Audrey comes late, and she is finicky about that. They have it all at Safeway. Here's some money and my Safeway rewards card."

Jack smiled as he took the cash and the card, which he had no earthly idea how to use but assumed would be familiar to the cashier. "All right. I'll get dry and canned cat food and hurry back."

"You go with him, Robyn. You know what Mittens eats. It's the same stuff I have for her in the office."

Robyn looked at Jack, who checked his watch as he rolled his eyes. "Promise us you'll be ready to go as soon as we get back?"

Theresa scrunched up her shoulders and smiled as she said, "This is exciting, isn't it? Just like in the movies. Am I on the run? On the lam? Is that what you call it?"

Robyn touched her arm as she headed to the door. "We'll be right back."

Chapter 18

Even though it was dark Jack still wore his sunglasses and hat into Safeway, and kept his face covered as best he could as they went straight to the pet aisle and loaded up. As he and Robyn walked out of the store, sirens made Jack stop and pull Robyn aside as two police cars, lights flashing, wailed past the shopping center and squealed around the next corner in the direction of Theresa's home.

Robyn said, "Oh, my god," and tried to pull away to get to her car, but Jack held her back. He waited and watched, thinking, feeling the brute power of the trap snapping shut so very close to him, but unable to clearly define the sharp edges of its jaws.

"Come on," she said as she tugged against him, "we've got to get over there. Something must have happened that made her call the police. My God, we haven't been gone twenty minutes."

"Check your phone, Robyn."

"Let's just go!"

"Did she call you since we left?"

Robyn pulled out her phone. "No, okay? Now can we please just get over there and check on her?"

Just then an ambulance shot down the road, raced past them, and turned the corner to follow the police.

"Stop for a second and ask yourself why she didn't."

"Because she's scared, that's why, so she called the police. Probably hit 911 without even thinking about it."

"But she was also scared when she called you earlier."

"So what?"

"But that time she called you. Why not now when she knows we're already so close."

"What are you saying?"

"I'm just recognizing the possibility that someone else might have called the cops. Someone who watched you and me go into her house. Someone who knew we'd been there long enough for people to notice your car in the driveway. Someone who could probably guess we touched a few things inside and left fingerprints. Someone who watched us leave before—"

Robyn grabbed his arm. "Before that same someone went in and hurt her, or killed her? Please don't say that."

"The cops and ambulance make it hard to think otherwise."

"But why? Oh, poor Theresa. She wouldn't hurt anything. Or anyone."

Jack wished he could come up with another reason than what he believed. Any other reason. But he couldn't. "Try calling her."

Robyn nodded, grabbed her phone, and dialed. After four rings a man answered and she hung up.

"That confirms they're at her house. If she is dead, she probably died because of my coming here."

"What?" Robyn looked hard at him and said, "Now you're talking crazy." She didn't sound convincing.

"Add it up. Your police department was all over me as soon as I left Montessa. They threatened to charge me with Jeff's murder. Right after that I got a Blue Alert that has every law enforcement organization in America wanting to kill me. Twenty minutes ago I walked out of a nice old lady's home who made me coffee and now the cops are in

159

there picking up evidence of my being there and lifting my fingerprints."

"You didn't tell me the Roanoke cops threatened to arrest you."

"You were too busy attacking me to interrupt."

She looked ashamed. "We weren't exactly on the same team."

"It doesn't matter. The bigger issue is that the police were acting on someone else's behalf when they attacked me."

"They attacked you?"

"Nothing serious."

"That's why you were limping at the restaurant?"

"I assumed the police were working for Montessa, or protecting them as best they saw fit, which happens often enough, I guess. But this set-up with Theresa feels too clever for your chief of police to concoct so quickly. If Theresa's dead—and there's no reason yet to believe that she is—it has all the markings of professional tradecraft."

"Poor Theresa," Robyn said again, looking just a little less hurt but a lot more confused, like all this subterfuge was so foreign to the direct and confrontational way she liked to fight her battles. "Why would the police ever think you had something to do with Jeff's death?"

"They don't think that. At least they don't have any reason to. But they don't like that I'm here and they perceive me as a threat, even though I don't yet understand why."

"A threat to the police? Montessa? Who?"

"My guess is that the police chief's biggest worry is that I might upset some balance of power, or prove that his department had something to do with Jeff's death, or what's far more likely, prove that they helped cover it up."

"Is that what you think, that the police killed him?"

"They're on the list of possibilities, yes, although they're not on that list alone. But yeah, your chief of police was way out of line when he confronted me. I'm sure he knew it, and equally sure he knew I knew it. For all his posturing he was afraid. Of what, I still don't know, but it's the only way I can explain his overwhelming display of power."

A car pulled to the curb and it made Jack flinch, even as the young driver got out to help his wife and kid with the groceries. Jack set down the pet food and turned back to the store. "Come on."

"Where?"

"Anyplace less obvious."

As Robyn followed, she asked, "So if the police killed Jeff, wouldn't that make it possible they also killed Theresa? My God, listen to me. I've already accepted that she's dead."

"Don't jump to that conclusion, but you've got to admire the craftsmanship of whoever got me to her house, if that was the goal. The timing, the clues I left be-hind...hell, maybe they expected me to get arrested for the Blue Alert while I was there. Making a run for cat food might have been what saved me."

"If the police didn't kill Jeff, then who? I want to know what you think."

"I'm working on a few other possibilities. Maybe it was the police. I'll find out."

"How?"

"I'm chasing a lead now but I don't have long to do it. Whoever lured us there and then kidnapped or killed Theresa—"

"But for all we know the police might have been going to a completely different home."

Jack didn't have time to indulge her. "—will probably want the police to arrest me quickly now, hoping to kill me during the arrest, justifying any use of excessive force with the allegation of whatever else I'm supposed to have done."

"In order to make whatever problems you might cause here go away."

"It's time for me to get to work."

"You mean it's time for us to get to work."

Jack looked at her and for the first time saw the depth of her courage to be a fighter. She was a woman, sure, and a beautiful one at that, but a fighter who would do what she had to do and take whatever risks came with it. Like many women with whom he'd served in Afghanistan, Robyn would be a good woman to have on your side and a bad one to have against you.

"They're after me, Robyn, at least I assume they are. If this goes on for long I imagine they'll target you too, but you really don't need to make yourself part of this yet. I'm not refusing your help, just giving you an easy way out."

As Robyn took his hand she forced a smile. "If they did hurt or take or kill Theresa, then I'm already part of it, so let's go."

Chapter 19

"Give me your house key," Jack said as they walked toward her car. He was still looking around for anyone running surveillance on him, most likely from a car backed in at a far edge of the parking lot where they'd have good sightlines for their night vision gear and little interference from curious people passing by.

"Why?" Robyn reached into her purse for her key.

"I just might need it."

"What can I do to help?"

"I have to get my backpack out of your car. It has some things I need, including a knife I took off that local tough guy. Once I get it I want you to take off."

"Okay, I guess, if that's what you want. But what should I say if the cops stop me before we catch up later? We are catching up later, right?"

"Tell them I took you as a hostage but that you escaped."

"I will do no such thing!" She looked as offended as she sounded. "That will only make things worse for you."

He smiled. "They probably won't believe you, but either way, I certainly hope it makes me look worse. I need it to."

She grinned. "You're nuts, Jack. You know that, right?"

"I'm merely shuffling the playlist 'cause I'm tired of dancing to unfamiliar music."

"And if I don't get stopped by the cops?"

"Disappear. If you get the chance I want you to disappear completely until this is over." He could afford to say it, even insist on it, because he knew she would stay to protect what she loved.

"No."

"Tell Preston where you're going but don't trust anyone else. Go to the beach or to visit family. Just get out of here."

"I'm not running away. I want to help. You're here because of a Sierra matter and you'll need our help. My help."

"You'll help me most by hiding, because I can't promise to protect you if you stay. But you know I'll try and I may end up losing."

Robyn looked nervous. It was the first time he'd seen it, but it made perfect sense for anyone who did her kind of work to be nervous, so it was a good sign.

"Jack?"

"Yes."

"What's going to happen?"

He put his thoughts together as he grabbed his backpack and closed her door.

"Bad things are going to happen, Robyn. All bad things. I can pretty much guarantee that tonight's late news will broadcast the chief's reopening his investigation into Jeff's death, naming me as a suspect and broadcasting my name and photo. They'll probably claim that I had something to do with whatever happened to Theresa, too, and mention my Blue Alert, repeating whatever lie made that happen and probably branding me as a cop-killer. They might even associate me with Montessa's tanks blowing up, anything and everything in order to get me killed in a hurry. I don't intend to let that happen."

He smiled and then laughed.

"What could possibly be funny about any of that?"

"Two days ago I was fishing in the Gulf of Mexico without a care in the world. What's funny is how quickly things change."

Robyn looked like she'd gone from nervous to frightened, and it seemed a completely unfamiliar feeling as she glanced around the parking lot as if there might be an easy solution nearby. "Who's doing this, Jack? Do you know who?"

He didn't answer. He didn't want to lie, didn't want to give any clues as to how many different things he was investigating, or how he was performing so many different dances on so many different stages. It made his brain hurt to keep all his performances straight, and there was no reason to make her brain hurt, too.

"Not going to tell me? Okay then, how does my disappearing help? I don't understand."

"I want to amp things up, Robyn, either by your sudden and mysterious disappearance or by your saying I kidnapped you if the cops pick you up first. I want to look as bad as possible. I want the whole town afraid of me. I want all the gun nuts roaming the city like vigilantes, hoping to crack off a shot at me."

"You want to make yourself look worse? That doesn't make sense. You'll get yourself killed."

"I'm doing this specifically *because* it doesn't make sense. Because I can't survive by being a step behind. Because I need them reacting to my strategy, and not the other way around."

"And you want me gone."

"They'll use you against me and we both know it."

He turned and looked at her, and even with all that was going on between them, she gave him a look Jack knew he would never forget.

"I like that," she said. "I like being important enough for them to use as leverage."

"This has been one hell of a first date, wouldn't you agree? Or is this our second? Now get out of here, Robyn."

He smiled as she leaned toward him, locking up their eyes for just a second before she reached into the glove box for paper and a pen, then looked back and said, "I could go visit my sister in Virginia Beach. Here's her number. If I do go it's to do what you want, not because I'm running."

Jack watched her drive away before he walked out of the dark parking lot, using a well-worn path through the weeds of a vacant lot in order to cut through the adjoining neighborhood and into some woods, where he stopped and brought up "recent calls" on his phone and touched the screen to dial.

"Are you all set, Bobby?"

"I did everything you asked, Lieutenant. The motel is old and the room is just like you wanted. I put the key exactly where you told me."

"How many lobby cameras?"

"Two, both of them behind the counter."

"How was your afternoon?"

"I actually saved my job, I think, by getting some great video footage of those demolished tanks that exploded, along with a nursing home and several burned down houses. My boss thinks the tanks was the lead I was following, that I must have a really good source, so they're letting me stay here and work it. It was a pretty easy afternoon, all in all."

Jack breathed deep as he looked around at the sky. It was a gorgeous spring night, with the air still holding some of the warmth from the day. "That's good. Well, you already know that's about to change, Bobby, so I hope you enjoyed it."

Chapter 20

Jack's black ball cap, windbreaker, and sunglasses would be his uniform now, at least until he got everyone to consider it his uniform and be on the lookout for it. That way he would become instantly recognizable whenever he wanted to be.

But he actually felt pretty safe in it for now, and would until the photos of him dressed like that got distributed to the media, photos for which he was about to go in and pose. He wasn't completely safe, but the pool of people after him was still pretty small, and for the most part in uniforms of their own, with badges being a part of all those uniforms.

His sense of safety would change when the late news included photos of him in black when they re-broadcast his name along with the Blue Alert, and named him as a suspect in not only Jeff's death but also whatever happened to Theresa. And if the late news didn't broadcast it in enough detail to cause alarm, he would make sure the morning news did.

But for now he was safe enough to risk a cab ride to the downtown train station. He got out a block away and walked toward it, spotting the mailbox he'd noticed as he drove through town when he'd first arrived, while admiring Roanoke's architecture and the meticulous renovation of its

168

historic station. He approached the mailbox slowly, looking for the wad of chewing gum stuck along the weld at the top of the left side.

The gum was there, Bobby's signal that he'd taped the motel key under that mailbox, assuring that Jack wouldn't waste time or attract attention looking for something that wasn't there.

The key was right where it was supposed to be, taped to the bottom back left corner with a small tab of tape hanging down for easy removal. Jack barely had to slow down to get it, and walked away from the mailbox and train station without giving anyone a reason to think he'd done anything more than bend down to tie his shoe.

Bobby had written "Madison Motel Room 108" on the tape and Jack looked it up on Google Maps. Seven blocks away. He considered his choices of routes, picked the one that seemed least traveled and therefore safest, and took off walking.

The Madison Motel was old and largely un-renovated, a relic of mom and pop motels that had long ago fallen out of favor with traveling families and businessmen, and now rented mostly on a weekly or monthly basis. Low-income workers and down-on-their-luck transients seemed to occupy most of the Madison's rooms. Several of them had their doors open, and when Jack glanced into the rooms he saw worn cardboard boxes and black plastic bags. Two rooms had shopping carts full of cast-off finds. A few of the residents had expanded their tight living quarters by moving chairs out onto the walkway to enjoy the comfortable night air, and they nodded a welcome as Jack walked by, passing Room 108 without entering.

It was a first floor room, which was important. It opened directly onto the parking lot, with no halls or stairs where someone could hide. And there was a big expanse of paved parking right outside the door where the police would have to expose themselves when they arrived.

It was exactly what Jack had asked for from Bobby. When the cops came for him later, he would know the second they arrived. There was no way for them to sneak up or approach unseen. And then he might find out who he was really hunting by seeing exactly who was hunting him.

But it was still too early for him to go into the motel office, so he waited in the shadows of a Goodwill collection box until fifteen minutes after eleven, giving the local news time to broadcast their lead story, at which time he made the short walk and stepped over the motel's worn-out welcome mat. An old guy with a mess of grey hair and a nasty soul patch sat behind the counter watching television, while a tired-looking young woman sat at the far end of the lobby and stared at the road, maybe waiting for a cab.

"Hi," Jack said as he walked to the counter, checking the dusty monitors behind the desk to see where the closed-circuit cameras were aimed, their wires strung loosely across the ceiling and down the walls. He stepped precisely into their focal spot, still wearing his sunglasses and cap, which caused a double-take from the clerk.

"What can I do for you, young fellow? Too sunny in here for you?"

Jack ignored the question and laughed. "Young fellow?"

The man looked him over with a friendly sort of jealousy. "Sure. You gotta whole lotta cards left."

"Sorry? I don't understand what you mean."

The man laughed and leaned back in his chair. "I call it Dewey's Deck of Cards Theory of Life. I'm Dewey."

"Nice to meet you. Still don't understand."

"It's simple. There are 52 cards in a deck of cards, right, and 52 years that separate a young adult of 18 from an old man of 70. Which means we throw a card away every time we have a birthday. So we got to make 'em count. Don't end up like me with only a few cards left in a bust hand."

"I'll remember that. Thanks."

"You're welcome." Dewey pulled an imaginary card from an imaginary deck and flipped it away, watching as it disappeared like a dream.

Jack flashed his key. "I'm staying in Room 108, Dewey. Any chance you have any messages for me?"

Dewey scrubbed at his whiskers as he checked his old computer and then checked it again, a look of puzzlement moving across the rough landscape of his face like an eclipse. "You said Room 108? That's you?'"

"That's me," Jack said cheerfully as he waggled his plastic key tag in front of the clerk, even though the room number and whatever words had been long ago screen-printed onto it were worn off. Is there a problem?"

"Not a problem, but...well, it's just that either I'm going nuts or I checked someone else into Room 108 a little earlier today."

"You might be going nuts," Jack said, then smiled, "but this wouldn't prove it. You did rent it to someone else, my friend Robert Dotson."

"Then I guess Dotson's going to have to check for messages."

"I'm sharing the room with Bobby. He did say two people would be staying there, right? Can you check?"

The guy squinted hard at his old desktop. Jack expected him to hit the damn thing on the side, but instead he stepped over to the comfortably familiar paperwork in a file box beside it, checking Bobby's handwritten registration. "You got to understand that this all seems a little odd to me because room 108 only has one double bed, Mister..."

"Wells. Jack Wells."

His name meant something to Dewey but not enough to get a reaction. "I'm here from Florida about the Jeff Roberts murder."

"Yeah, I heard about that poor kid. Damn shame. In fact, the news was just saying that the guy who killed him…"

Jack's name suddenly meant so much to Dewey that he took an involuntary step back. He looked at Jack as his mouth fell open and showed gold. Jack waited until he was pretty sure Dewey was struggling to keep from pointing a finger and saying, "It's you," or reaching for a drink of whatever he kept behind the counter, before he said, "Then I guess I'll just go to my room if there aren't any messages."

As he turned to walk out of the lobby he laughed and said, "Although I don't expect to get much sleep."

Dewey laughed a little too, but his laugh was confused nervousness, which is exactly what Jack wanted.

Chapter 21

Jack appreciated the detail with which Bobby had done his job. He hadn't just procured a motel room with the kind of access he wanted, but one that Dewey couldn't see without walking pretty far out into the parking lot. He'd probably visited every hotel in the downtown area to find exactly the right lobby with the perfect room on the first floor facing a parking lot, but Jack would never expect anything less from Bobby.

There were two old security cameras outside of the motel office, but even if they still worked they were fixed on the parking lot and the stairs and wouldn't catch the door to his room. Bobby was much too competent and well trained not to have factored them in.

He opened the door to the room and snapped on the lights, sending a couple of roaches into hiding while a third stared belligerently from the top of the dresser. Jack picked up the night vision monocular Bobby had left on the bed, went back outside and walked slowly away, avoiding the lighted areas in the parking lot where they'd trained the camera for best nighttime visibility.

Next to the motel was a two-story Days Inn with a wrap-around balcony. Jack walked down the side it shared with the Madison Motel, scouting views of the Madison from several areas and finally deciding that the far corner of the balcony offered the best view. A camera covered the balcony and the stairs leading to it, but Jack didn't intend to be there long enough to attract much attention. Just long enough to watch the show and note all the players.

There was another problem with the far corner of the balcony. The stairs were a good thirty feet away, and that was worrisome because if the cops saw him there and charged up after him, he'd have to jump. But it was a survivable fall and he would risk it for the benefit of the view.

Jack found a spot in the shadows by a dumpster and waited. The views from there weren't good but at least he wasn't attracting any attention. It wouldn't be long before the show started in front of him, with all the performers having their backs to him as they focused on Room 108 in the other direction.

Just fifteen minutes after Jack left Dewey slack-jawed in the lobby, a SWAT van rolled into the Madison parking lot. It stopped halfway between the door to Room 108 and the Days Inn, black and menacing and polished to perfection, another of the chief's pride and joy possessions. As Jack slipped up the Days Inn stairs to the balcony corner, the chief of police arrived and parked behind the SWAT van, got out of his car, and casually stood there while his men checked weapons and talked things over as if the sheet metal of the van would protect them if a shooter actually opened up on them from Room 108 of the Madison Motel.

Jack moved along the balcony for the best view, watching the cops shame the proud precision he'd employed on the FBI SWAT team. Once used only for hostage and barricade situations, active shooter scenarios, and arresting violent felons, police SWAT teams had proliferated like dandelions across the United States and were now used mostly for embarrassing non-violent drug searches—non-violent applying only to the suspect's behavior and not the SWAT team's use of flash-bang grenades, battering rams, and military firepower. Some cities sent SWAT out on every single search warrant, even if it meant terrifying a bank's customers as the team stormed in with weapons drawn to look for an incriminating document in a bank officer's desk. At one time in the past Jack might have considered them brothers, but he now had trouble seeing these jazzed up, poorly trained but nearly bullet-proof cops as anything other than one of America's greatest threats to civil liberties, a systemic public safety epidemic.

The presence of a murder suspect in Room 108 meant that they should already be through the motel room door and finished with the entire raid by now. But to Jack's astonishment, the chief gathered his troops in a circle in the Madison Motel parking lot and led them in a prayer. During his time on SWAT, Jack and his fellow team members would have argued on the ride about who would go through the door first, even though they affectionately called the doorway a 6-foot-8 coffin because it was the place you were most likely to get killed. As soon as they opened the door of the van, or fast-roped down, they would immediately go into action as an overwhelming force. But the chief's men seemed reluctant to go until he'd finished blessing them, followed by a loud chorus of amen.

They took so much time that Jack had to wonder if there was another reason for their delay. Were they overly afraid of him, maybe pumped up with lies that he had automatic weapons or bombs? Were they waiting for a layout of the room from the building department? Expecting a second SWAT team that might be approaching from the other side of the building, and waiting for their signal to begin?

Suddenly Jack saw that he wouldn't have to stick around any longer to learn the answer, because just as the chief finally lined up his men and gave the instructions he should have given them en route, a lean man with an oddly muscular build walked out of the shadows of the Days Inn, almost directly below Jack as if he and Jack had made a joint decision on what spot was best to watch the events unfold, with only one of them willing to make the leap to the ground if necessary.

The man walked to the edge of the parking lot and folded his arms across his chest as he watched the SWAT team, his gait and demeanor so familiar that he might have been Jack's best friend or his worst enemy.

"I'll be damned," Jack muttered as he moved quietly to the stairs, down to the ground level, and around to the other side of the hotel, where he looked inside all three of the cars parked there. Only one had a radio and a briefcase on the seat, and Jack was positive the briefcase contained everything that anyone or any organization had ever known about him.

Jack memorized the license plate and the vehicle, then left a note on the windshield.

"Welcome to Roanoke, Mitch."

Chapter 22

Jack spent the night wrapped in several layers of newspaper that kept off the dew and held in some warmth. For the most part he'd slept well in the small patch of woods in a large city park alongside a fast-moving section of the Roanoke River. He always slept well when he slept outside, and slept even better around moving water. In truth, after he'd seen Mitch, sleep would have been difficult for him anywhere else but surrounded by nature.

If the police had been the only ones to show up at the motel—which Jack hadn't really expected—it would have been convincing evidence that the chief was acting alone against Jack, even if he did so on behalf of Montessa Chemical or somebody else. But from the beginning stages of his planning, Jack had expected someone else beside the chief and his men to show up. He'd just never considered that it might be Mitch Douglas, even though Claire had de-scribed his voice perfectly, and Mitch had been Jack's first thought.

But Mitch was dead. Or at least was supposed to be dead, hacked up ignobly by cartel members who lacked Mitch's professionalism, a killer with a professional killer's price tag, a price that was usually paid in cash and never less than a quarter-million.

But it could occasionally be something other than cash, if it was something Mitch needed or wanted. Jack knew of two times when Mitch had made a three-way deal, one in which he executed a hit for one client who arranged to have him paid by a third party by facilitating an escape passport, and another hit which resulted in a massive bribe that allowed Mitch to walk unquestioned over a border.

And, of course, Mitch had been guaranteed immunity from prosecution for what he'd done on the Harvey Squad, as long as he succeeded in killing Jack. That contract had been pulled as part of the settlement, but seeing Mitch below him in the Days Inn parking lot ramped up all of Jack's suspicions about who orchestrated his Blue Alert, his beating, and whatever fate had befallen Theresa that would be tied to him. As if his suspicions weren't already ramped up enough.

He rose from his bed of leaves, moving slow enough to be sure he didn't attract attention until he knew he wasn't being watched, then brushed the grass off his jacket and pants and reached into the backpack he'd used as a pillow. His hands shook from the morning chill as he cleaned his teeth and spit, brushed his hair differently from anytime before, and put away his hat and glasses. He changed back into the clothes he'd worn on the airplane, which were still pretty clean. He rolled up his black uniform and put it away too, at least for a while, because the photos from the Madison lobby cameras were bound to be on the news by now, making the uniform the primary thing people would be looking for.

He warmed his muscles as he stretched out, loosening up for the day's coming events, all the while keeping his eyes on a police officer idling his cruiser down the wide trail below, then yelping his siren at a homeless man who'd chosen a less conspicuous, or more familiar, place to spend the night. Jack appreciated the cop for waiting until morning to roust him, letting the man sleep as long as possible, bothering no one, before making him move out as the park came alive.

The cop got out of his car and talked to the man, then handed him a cup of coffee as though it was ritual, and that compassion, that cop's moment of pure human kindness, went a long way with Jack, reminding him once again that the country was full of good cops and devout priests and dedicated teachers and maybe even a rare, honest politician, all of whom had no choice but to share their professions with co-workers they held in just as much contempt as everyone else did.

Since the only photos out there of Jack would either be from his Marine ID or in his black uniform of last night, he could afford to walk casually back to the coffee shop, mimicking the pace of other people on the sidewalk so as not to stand out. He bought a paper, sat down in a booth, and listened to *Good Morning, America* as he looked around the shop for threats, waiting for a local news segment to come on one of the two televisions and say whatever the local reporters might have learned about him, perhaps detailing last night's SWAT raid at the motel that had failed to capture him.

GMA was about to go to a commercial break when George Stephanopoulos asked, "Is a rogue FBI Agent murdering people in Roanoke, Virginia?"

Jack had to fight to keep from snapping his head up to look at the screen, even though no one would have noticed because everyone else in the room did exactly that at the name of their town on national news.

"That breaking story and more when *Good Morning, America* returns."

As they went to a series of commercials Jack opened the Roanoke Times, where a photo of him in his hat and jacket and dark glasses, taken over Dewcy's shoulder by the surveillance camera at his check-in counter, was at the top center of the front page. The headline read, A TRAINED

KILLER AMONG US, and was followed by an article that recounted all the easily-discovered details of Jack's life, from his mother's accident to the University of Florida to the mountains of Afghanistan to FBI/SWAT to Marco Island and *Bella Sabrina*.

"A CAREER SURROUNDED IN CONTROVERSY" was the heading where the article continued on page four, and only there did it mention that he'd been awarded the Silver Star and had never once been prosecuted for anything, not even a parking ticket. "No criminal record of this war hero has been found to date, although our investigation is on-going."

Jack glanced around again, but no one even thought to look anywhere but at the television as they waited in reverent, fearful silence for GMA to start up again, reminding Jack of the morning the airplanes crashed into the Twin Towers. No one spoke in that coffee shop, either, while they stared with a disbelieving look of "What does this mean to me?" as the second plane removed all doubts about it being an accident and changed their world forever.

The commercials didn't seem like they would ever let GMA back on the air, but then Jack heard a newsy voice on the other television broadcasting a cable news show, and he turned enough to see a lovely blonde in a tight skirt sitting at a chair without a desk, attracting viewers with her legs while a backdrop image showed the Sierra Club logo with Theresa and Jeff's pictures superimposed.

The blonde was stating unequivocally that the Sierra Club's concern over climate change was "typical tree-hugger hyperbole from left-leaning wing nuts like Al Gore," and then, as if actually asking a question, turned to a panel of white businessmen in designer suits with a banner below that read "Climate Change Based on Flawed Science" and said, "Or are all the thousands of volumes of science that rebuke them wrong?" as if there really were thousands of volumes of refuting science, some of which could actually point a finger and rebuke anyone. Then GMA came back on, so Jack took another look at the idiot blonde's legs and turned away.

"Welcome back," said Stephanopoulos, as the photo of Jack in his black uniform of last night, the same photo that was on the paper's front page, came onto the screen, accompanied by his Marine photo. "These are photos of Jack Wells, from Marco Island, Florida. He is a former Marine Corps officer who fought in Afghanistan before joining the FBI as a Special Agent.

"Mister Wells is on many peoples' minds this morning because there appears to be a connection between him and last evening's murder of an elderly woman in Roanoke, Virginia, as well as the recent mysterious death, which was originally determined a suicide but is now presumed to be homicide, of a young man there. Beyond that, Mister Wells, who we're told took an interest in bomb making while recovering from war wounds at a V.A. hospital, also paid a visit to the Roanoke offices of Montessa Chemicals recently. We've all seen the news where three of Montessa's massive storage tanks were shredded by bombs that created enormous fireballs, destroying several nearby homes, including a nursing home, with fires those blasts ignited. So far thirty-seven people are dead, with fifty-six injured and nine missing, but we should clarify that we are not making any allegations against Mr. Wells, merely stating the facts surrounding these sad affairs. As to the woman's disappearance and the alleged suicide, both of the victims worked at the Roanoke offices of the Sierra Club, an environmental group where Mister Wells showed up unexpectedly between the times the young man and the woman died. Our local correspondent, Janice Walker, joins us live from just outside the Sierra Club's Roanoke offices. Janice?"

The screen changed to yet another attractive woman in front of the brick building where Jack met Robyn. Preston Harmon stood beside her.

"Thank you, George. I'm here with Mister Preston Harmon, the head of this Sierra Club office, who is actually responsible for all Sierra Club activities throughout most of this region. Thank you for joining me, Mister Harmon."

"I'm here to help if I can."

"Well, perhaps you can start by helping our viewers understand what the Sierra Club does that might get some-one killed?"

Harmon made an intentional show of how surprised he was by her bluntness, but answered as thoughtfully as Jack expected, saying, "There are a great many things that we, and other organizations similar to ours, do that might create enemies. We are, of course, one of the oldest environmental organizations in America, founded in 1892 by the naturalist John Muir. His commitment to protecting our planet—" he paused and looked directly into the camera, "let me repeat, we're talking about *our* planet, the only home we have—is and always will be the guiding tenet of our organization, and that commitment, unfortunately, puts us at odds, and occasionally at deadly odds, with those who have less regard for the fragility of this incredible place we call earth."

Janice Walker conjured up a smile that had no mean-ing, as if sending Harmon a direct message to skip the speech and get down to dirt. "That certainly sounds like a worthy endeavor," she said dismissively, "but can you give our audience a specific example of that work?"

Harmon adjusted his glasses the same way he did when telling Jack about all the environmentalists killed each year. "If I'm being honest, Miss Walker, I believe it's already pretty obvious to your audience what we do that puts us at risk. They all know, I'm sure, that there have al-ways been enormously profitable motives to exploit the environment, whether those motives are as obvious as a factory hosing toxic chemicals down a floor drain or into a river rather than pay for proper disposal, or as discreet as funding lobbyists who make sure laws never pass that require a reduction in factory emissions. All of them are excellent reasons, although I wouldn't blame the companies one bit for doing them."

The reporter looked surprised, which was just what Preston wanted to see before saying, "Except for the fact that the very survival of our planet depends upon someone stopping them." He smiled to highlight the sarcasm.

Janice had more caution in her voice as she followed up, clearly outclassed by Harmon's intellect and skill. "So you're saying the goals at Sierra Club are often in direct opposition to a great many companies, correct?"

"Yes."

"Can you give some examples of those companies?"

"Of course I can. Oil companies. Power and chemical companies. Even agriculture."

"Would you care to be more specific?"

Harmon showed that he knew what he was doing as he took her bait. "Yes, I would care to do exactly that. Let's name names, shall we? Let's start with Consolidated Rail, Louisiana-Pacific, Summitville Consolidated Mining, United Technologies, Rockwell International, Royal Caribbean Cruises, Chevron, Alcoa, United States Sugar, Bristol-Myers Squibb, Warner-Lambert, International Paper, Consolidated Edison, Unocal, Eastman Kodak…enough?"

He didn't wait for her to answer. "Good. Those companies are on a long list of impressive companies that paid massive *criminal* fines as a result of their environmental damage. They knew they were polluting, knew they were killing our planet, but did it anyway, fully expecting to get away with their crimes. But I suppose that's obvious to your viewers since the charges against them were criminal, not just civil. And I'm just talking about criminal charges for *environmental* violations here, totaling ignoring for the time being the numerous criminal fines so many corporations have paid for perpetrating fraud and extortion."

"And so the Sierra Club stands firmly in their way. Was your organization instrumental in bringing those criminal charges you mentioned?"

"We absolutely were. It's unpopular work that makes us quite a few enemies in the process, but don't get me wrong or misinterpret my intentions, because I recognize we need the things those companies produce in order to continue our quality of life. Our goal is merely to inspire more responsible ways of going after them. Courtrooms—especially criminal courtrooms—are a last resort."

"You told me off-camera that you know Jack Wells, Mister Harmon."

"I said that I'd met him. He came to my office to talk to me."

"About what?"

"I think the police will want to ask me the same question, so I should tell them first."

"Of course. Mister Harmon. But do you think Jack Wells killed the woman who died last night?"

"I won't speculate on that, nor will I participate in any speculation on what woman you mean, since the victim's name hasn't yet been made public."

"But you must know who she was. It's already been reported that she worked for you."

"Two women failed to come to work this morning. One, as you've just said is, tragically, dead. A homicide."

"And the other woman?"

"Missing. We've called all her relatives and every contact we have for her, but no one's heard anything since she left work yesterday."

Jack had already been listening carefully, but now he strained to hear every inflection in Harmon's voice.

"Then I can understand why you don't wish to tell me their names."

"I will mention the one."

Janice was confused, but it was clear that Preston was in control so she asked, "Why just one?"

"Because it serves no purpose to mention the name of my friend and colleague who is known to have died. But it might help the other woman if she's actually at risk in this tragedy that's currently unfolding. It might be prudent of me to let the public know because perhaps they'll see her and call the police."

"And her name, Mister Harmon?"

Preston's voice cracked as he said, "Robyn Thomas."

Chapter 23

Jack called Robyn's sister in Virginia Beach, but Robyn wasn't there. She had no idea where Robyn might be, and she was telling the truth. So Jack sat in the coffee shop wondering if Robyn had really left Roanoke as he'd asked and gone somewhere else. She was supposed to have told Preston if she did leave, but Preston was also telling the truth about not knowing where she was, so it didn't seem likely.

What did seem likely was that she couldn't bring herself to leave, since running just wasn't in her nature. Although she had considered leaving when he'd asked, he really couldn't imagine her backing away from a fight or a challenge because she was a problem solver, a fixer, a warrior, much like him, which meant that she'd decided to stay and fight, and was now in real trouble.

He forced himself to walk with confidence as he headed out the door and down the sidewalk, his head held high but not high enough to attract attention by looking cocky, which was easy because he sure didn't feel cocky. In truth he was suffering because he'd failed her. Failed to emphasize to her that whoever killed Theresa might have already been hunting her. Failed to personally put her on a train or a bus out of town, or have Bobby come get her.

Failed to keep her safe. Now she was gone, and that meant she was most likely going to be a pawn for his enemies to use against him. Enemies like Mitch Douglas who'd long ago learned that the very purpose of pawns was to be the first to die, and had become so desensitized by that fact that they probably didn't care.

Which put Jack in the kind of battle he most hated, where his success or his failure—and the self-sacrificing cost his failure would carry—hinged on the survival of a single life.

He called Sierra's office as he turned down a side street, watching carefully for a sharp-eyed cop but not expecting a normal citizen to recognize the long-haired version of him from his old Marine photo, or last night's surveillance photo in his black uniform.

"Preston Harmon, please. He might still be outside but I'll hold on until he walks back in and gets to his office."

"Can I say who's calling?"

"No."

As Jack waited on the line he found a place in the shadows to get out of sight, building plans around the various possible meanings of the news.

"This is Harmon."

"Preston, it's Jack. Tell me I'm wrong, and that you were intentionally misleading on-camera."

"Dear God, Jack, no. Please tell me you're hiding Robyn somewhere. I don't even care why, but please assure me she's safe."

Preston sounded almost in tears. The brave façade he'd shown in the interview had completely exposed Preston's fatherly love for Robyn, a love Jack had immediately assumed from the way he spoke of her that first day in his office, and the way he spoke to her when he introduced them.

"I don't have her, Preston. I thought she was going to her sister's in Virginia Beach but she hasn't heard from her."

"I called her too, which is why you were my big hope. I don't believe you killed Theresa and I'm pretty sure you had nothing to do with Jeff's death, so I was truly hopeful that Robyn was with you. I even called the local FBI office and left a message for their local agent, but so far I've heard nothing."

A name suddenly came back to Jack as Preston's words hit his ears, sharpening his senses while the turn of events pushed him to think faster and clearer, with decisions coming even faster.

"Jack, are you still there?"

Oglethorpe. The FBI resident agent who worked alone in a one-man office in a sleepy little town with very little crime that fell under Federal jurisdiction. A guy who came back to Roanoke in order to work around family and friends. A guy who probably knew everyone.

Oglethorpe. The photo in Julius Reed's office with names in the caption of the Montessa executives in suits, each of them with a chrome shovel turning over a clump of dirt in the official start of a new playground. Oglethorpe near the middle in a very expensive suit, smiling. All of them smiling.

"Jack?"

"I've got to go, Preston."

Harmon was talking as Jack hung up and redialed.

"Gray," Jack said into his phone. He'd heard him answer but he wasn't talking. "Come on, Grayson, talk to me."

Gray came back in a quiet whisper. "Hang on while I get to my office."

Twenty seconds later he said, "I can't help you again, Jack. CODE guys are giving rectal exams to every agent you ever worked with. The Bureau has to get way out in front of this story about a rogue FBI Agent being a cop-killer."

"They said I'm a cop-killer? That's what they used to justify the Blue Alert? I didn't just attack a cop, they say I actually killed one?"

"It came from a squishy source, but yeah."

"There aren't any squishy sources where cop-killing is involved. It's phony and you know it."

"And I also know I have to take a polygraph to prove I didn't help you with whatever you've been doing, and we both know I'm going to fail it, damn you. I'm looking at time on the bricks."

"Use your authority as squad supervisor to get your name last on the list. This will all be over before your turn comes up."

"What makes you think so?"

"Mitch is here."

Silence. Jack could almost see Gray clenching his jaw until it popped, the way he'd done before every raid they'd executed together, and before every testimony he ever gave in criminal court or grand jury, making himself hurt in order to use the pain as a way to prepare himself for whatever pain came next.

"Shit. Mitch. Now my fucking day is just fucking perfect. Mitch."

"Yeah, mine, too."

"I thought he was dead."

"Yeah."

"In fact I'm sure I saw an FD-302 that said he'd gotten himself killed by double-crossing a drug lord in Mexico."

"I heard the same thing. But I saw him last night. Fifty feet away from me."

"That's about two continents too close to get to a guy like Mitch."

"I left a welcome note on his car."

"You did what? Jeez, you are nuts, Jack. Want me to have that engraved on your tombstone?"

"I figured it might draw him out."

"You draw out a guy like Mitch and you end up dead. You know the odds, right?"

"I accept that possibility. He bleeds, though. He breaks. He's not a machine."

"You have proof of that, I suppose, because I'm not so sure."

"Me neither. Not so much."

"The Bureau should never have hired him. Talk about a fuck-up of Ruby Ridge proportions."

"Well, he's here in Roanoke. Maybe he'll die here in Roanoke and the Bureau can put his legacy behind them."

"One of you is going to die there. You called just to tell me this? So I can say good-bye to an old friend? Okay then, good-bye old friend."

"I called to say your Resident Agent here is dirty. Oglethorpe. Very few remaining doubts."

"What makes you think so?"

"I'm betting he had something to do with the deaths here. And probably the disappearance of a woman named Robyn Thomas."

"I've gotten continuous updates on all the bad news out of Roanoke, but you just said Mitch was on-scene so I assume those were Mitch's doing."

"Mitch is here for me. I staged my own arrest scenario at a motel to see who would show up and Mitch came to the party."

"Lucky you."

"Yeah. Feeling lucky."

"That doesn't mean he didn't kill the others."

"There's nothing of his professional signature on the kid's death. I don't know the details of how Theresa died. She was last night's victim."

"I really should hang up on you, Jack."

"That's true. Am I being targeted by Headquarters?"

"What? No. Of course not."

"Because it feels like I am, with Mitch hunting me again."

"Then maybe you are. How the fuck would I know what Headquarters is doing when it comes to you? You did make enemies of some Bureau heavyweights."

"Where does Oglethorpe live, Gray?"

Gray was silent again.

"Never mind. He'll be easy enough for me to find by myself."

"Oh, what the hell, Mitch is going to kill you and I'm going to be forced onto a beach. Might as well go out a loser."

"That's the spirit."

"Shut up. Here, write this down. Ready?"

"Yeah."

"1071 Susquehanna Drive."

"Got it. Thanks. Enjoy your polygraph."

"Go to hell, Jack." Then, to the computers recording every conversation on every FBI phone, he added. "That was the notorious Jack Wells, friends and neighbors, so maybe that will save you and me the trouble of a polygraph."

Chapter 24

A cab was still the safest way for Jack to get around, but every move he made got riskier by the minute, so he decided to wait until he saw a driver who looked foreign, maybe Indian or Pakistani, hoping they shared the same sort of cultural myopia Americans did, making all white people look the same to them. But Roanoke, lazing in the fertile foothills of the Alleghenies, wasn't a magnet of immigration like DC or New York, so it took a while for that sort of driver to cruise by. Jack waited patiently, nearly out of sight, taking all the time necessary to be safe.

1071 Susquehanna Drive was a single-family brick home with brown trim, a swing at one end of the porch, and a detached garage with a basketball hoop over the door at a below-regulation height of eight feet. Nothing about the house looked the least bit sinister, and nothing about the neighborhood looked like Oglethorpe was living more expensively than an FBI Agent's salary would allow. The big swell in the belly of the neighborhood's demographic snake was solidly middle-class, with clear visual clues pointing out the new arrivals and the pending departures in both financial directions.

There wasn't a car in the driveway, so Jack walked up the wooden steps and into the shade of the porch. The front door had a basic lock on it, the kind sold in any hardware store in America for thirty bucks, and the window screens didn't have alarm wires running through them, even though the windows were open to the breeze. Even in a safe neighborhood in a safe town, it would be careless for any FBI Agent, and particularly a dirty agent, to be so cavalier about the security of his home, which meant either Jack was wrong about Oglethorpe or that Oglethorpe did, or hid, his dirty business elsewhere.

Jack knocked on the front door, waited, knocked again, then sat down in the swing and waited, checking out the neighbor's homes but seeing no one watching him. After a few minutes of attracting no attention at all he got up and followed the concrete driveway to the back, studying the house as he made pretend notes as though writing some kind of an home repair estimate, just in case he was being watched, although it was unlikely given the large hedges that separated most of the yards from each other.

The detached garage was a different story from the house, much newer and built with concrete blocks set in place and then poured full of cement, similar to the house in which Jack had lived in Key West, built to withstand the raging powers of Force Five hurricanes, or in this case, a very determined intruder. A solid steel entry door near the middle of the sidewall was attached by heavy hinges to a solid steel jamb that was set into the concrete.

Jack looked through the high windows in the overhead door and saw a keypad, which meant the windows and doors were alarmed. But the overhead door was, most likely and as usual, the weak link in the security chain. Through the window he saw an automatic door opener and plenty of space to park a car, so Jack was willing to bet—and with Oglethorpe being an explosives guy in the military, his wager would be his life—that Oglethorpe had committed the first cardinal sin of security, sacrificing safety for convenience in order for him to come home and hit the remote in his car, then drive into the garage.

That also lowered the odds of an active motion detector inside, and indicated that the door, most likely, wasn't alarmed or booby-trapped. Of course the entire alarm system could be controlled by Oglethorpe's phone, but the typical-looking keypad made that a chance worth taking.

Jack stepped in front of the overhead door, opened the unlicensed app on his phone, and hit the scan button. A small electronic tumbler, like a tiny slot machine, went into action, transmitting two thousand code combinations every five seconds, the numbers changing so fast they were nothing but a blur. It was a simple tool, basically just a radio scanner in reverse, but it had an enormous appetite, so Jack needed the garage door to open before the power-hungry app drained his battery.

It took eighteen seconds for the tumblers to lock up. Then the door's opener engaged, a motor inside whirred to life, and the door to Roger Oglethorpe's garage went up. Jack walked in.

He felt fairly safe in the spot where Oglethorpe parked his car, and the path to the button that closed the door was probably safe from trip wires too, so he walked the ten steps and hit it. But as the door went down he got the same bad feeling he'd come to accept as normal after being blown up in a dark building once before, a sixth sense kind of thing whenever he suspected explosives, a sense on which he'd educated himself to apply some reasonable filters while bored in VA hospitals, spending long painful hours of recovery studying the most common bomb-making methods and materials, trying to insure that he never got blown up again, and trying just as hard not to be paranoid over the possibility.

The bottom of the garage door sealed against the floor and the opener stopped. Jack stood motionless, careful, wondering too late about a motion detector that might be time-activated, but putting a lot of faith in the youth-height basketball hoop and any father's understanding of his kid's natural curiosity.

He looked for anything unusual but saw nothing, at least not until his eyes fixed on the back of the garage, with rakes and tools and hedge clippers hanging off it. On the outside of the building he remembered the side door to the garage being ten feet or more from the end of the building. But inside the garage, the door opened into a corner.

Yct the back wall was covered with crap that seemed to make reasonable access impossible if a room was really hidden behind it. Jack took slow steps toward it, watching for wires or pressure plates or electric eyes. He was almost to the wall when his phone vibrated in his pocket and he jumped like hell.

"Jack!"

"Jesus, you scared the shit out of me."

"It's Chainsaw."

Everything about Mike going back to his killing personality was bad news.

"Yeah, I know it's you, Mike. What's up?"

"Time's up and I'm on my way to Roanoke. Saw your picture on the news. Don't know what's going on but I'm coming up to help."

"It's too complex for you to mangle and manhandle and then end up in prison, Mike. Please give me a little more time to sort all this out. I'm begging you."

"Jeff was my son and this is my fight. You shouldn't be taking the heat."

"You're right on both counts but I'm in it now. Besides, I can use the heat to hclp me find Jeff's killer."

"So you know it wasn't suicide."

"Pretty sure."

"And you didn't tell me."

Jack hesitated, standing in the garage, hoping Oglethorpe didn't pull into his driveway and suddenly send the door back up. Getting caught in the crosshairs of an armed federal agent opening his garage door to find an intruder standing at the back wall was near the bottom of the list of things he needed to happen.

"I only said I was pretty sure. If I was positive I would've called you."

"I'm coming up anyway."

"You'll make my job harder."

"I'll hang back. I'll be nearby when you need me. That's the best I can offer."

"Then come up and hang back."

"I want in on the kill, though. You hear me, Jack?"

Jack went back to breathing deep and forcing a smile so he'd sound sure of himself when he said, "Of course, Mike, I hear you."

Mike hung up.

Jack stared at nothing, pondering the limits of what he could do about Robyn, wondering how deep into the dark side Oglethorpe had gone, guessing at the chief's role, planning a way to survive Mitch, thinking about the additional problems of having Mike in Roanoke, and factoring him into his plans as a way of keeping him under control, rolling all those moving pieces around in his head until it hurt.

It was while thinking hard but staring at nothing that he noticed the shovel hanging on the back wall along with other hand tools. It was solidly attached to the wall with a screw through the metal shovel head and another through the wooden handle. He grabbed it and pulled and a small portion of wall swung open. A light automatically switched on in the hidden room at the back wall of Oglethorpe's garage, and Jack went in carefully.

Chapter 25

"Congratulations, Gray. You've definitely got a dirty Resident Agent in Roanoke."

Jack waited in silence for the sound of Gray's jaw popping. "You're shitting me."

"I wouldn't think of it. I've spent the last two hours going through his stuff."

"That's a big allegation, my friend."

"There's not much point in making small allegations."

"All right. Thanks a lot for something more for me to deal with." He sighed. "How sure are you?"

"That's he's breaking federal laws? I'm positive."

"That means almost nothing."

"Then how about murder."

"I'm listening."

"Possession of illegal explosives and detonators?"

"Okay, now both ears are open. What do you want me to do?"

"Nothing."

"You never call and ask me for nothing."

"First time for everything. I wanted you to know in case I get killed."

"I'm not sure you can be killed. You've survived more shit than—"

"But I don't want you to do anything yet."

"That is absolutely no *problemo*, amigo. I'll put it right at the top of my not-to-do list. What's your proof?"

"There's a false wall in back of his garage, with a hidden room behind it. He's got files in there of jobs he's done for Montessa Chemical Corporation and others. And there's also a decent cache of explosives."

"So he killed the young man, the son of your friend? He's the man you went up to find?"

"Oglethorpe didn't kill Jeff. In fact, I found nothing to indicate that any of his kills were in Roanoke."

"So the chief killed the kid?"

"No, but it looks like he killed seven others."

"Oglethorpe or the chief?"

"The chief. Oglethorpe has kept files on the chief's hits, I suppose so he can roll over on him if ever caught."

"Were they working together?"

"I doubt it, but I'm not sure. Oglethorpe did his work in South Florida."

"I told you he was stationed in Miami before Roanoke."

"So there might be others down there who were involved with him. Something for the Miami SAC to look in to after I clear from here."

"I'm going to deploy a SWAT team to Roanoke."

Jack liked the idea of showing the local cops what a professional SWAT team looked like, fast-roping out of an UH-60, making lots of noise and declaring to any bad guy who'd spent hours wearing down a hostage negotiator that the time to talk was over, that they'd come for one reason and one reason only. To end it.

"That's tempting, Gray."

"I thought you'd like the sound of it."

"But Mitch would know they're coming and he'd disappear again."

"And that's a bad thing? You don't seriously think you're up to taking him on alone, right? That certainly wouldn't be my idea of a fun time. Although I'd pay admission to see you do it."

"You know Mitch and I have history."

"Those guys on Harvey were sure he could kill you, and even I believe he would have, given more time. Hell, even now I'm willing to bet on him, because I doubt he's gotten old and slow in the short time since he was ordered to stand down."

"Yet I'm still alive."

"And yet even though Mitch was convicted in *absentia* for a couple of other murders, and risks prison just by showing his face in America, he still cares enough to come hunting you. But you still want to dance with him. I'm beginning to think you and that animal are sweet on each other."

"You're such a funny guy, but look, Mitch is here, Jeff and Theresa are dead, your resident agent is a murderer, as is the chief of police, Robyn is missing, and I've got cops hunting me down over that Blue Alert and the tank explosion. This city is crawling with state police and the governor deployed the National Guard as a precaution against further attacks, or in case they're needed to kill me. So although I wish I had time to let you have your fun frightening me about Mitch, I don't, so stop trying. Besides, a friend of mine is coming if I need back-up."

"I'll still get the SWAT team staged and ready. Even two of you probably aren't enough. Your friend's an experienced combat shooter, I hope. Not some fool overly proud of his ability to punch holes in paper targets that don't shoot back?"

"One of the deadliest guy I've ever known."

"Glad to hear it. I'm still sending SWAT."

"Don't let them get too close. A minimum thirty minute flight time."

"That's a deal, but at the first sign of trouble, my friend, look to the sky for salvation."

"Thanks. I've got to go. The chief of police and I need to have a chat."

Gray was still talking as Jack hung up and called Bobby.

"Yes, sir, Lieutenant."

"Are you set up, Bobby?"

"Getting close to finished, sir."

"Will you be up to a hundred percent? 'Cause I'm sure going to need it."

"With all due respect, Lieutenant, if you feel the need to ask that question, perhaps you called the wrong man to help."

"Sorry."

"Yes, sir, everything will be a hundred percent ready. Give me another hour or so."

"Good. Can you pick me up after you're done?"

"Just tell me where?"

"The corner of Susquehanna and Market. It's a neighborhood. There's a vacant house on the corner with a thick stand of trees in the yard. I'll wait in their shadows and watch for you."

"Two hours will give me enough time to finish here and drive over. Okay?"

"Great," Jack said, as he moved into the shadows of the trees and found a spot to wait, staying clear of any sight lines, and unobservable from pedestrians that might walk down the now-empty sidewalk.

He sat down in the grass and took advantage of the time to be peaceful, clearing his mind, seeing the whole thing work out the way he wanted. It took longer than he hoped, which always meant there were too many places for things to go wrong. But that was normal in cases when his plans got this elaborate.

When Bobby pulled up, Jack jumped in and grinned at him.

"I know that smile, Lieutenant. I'm guessing it's show time."

"Let's do it, Bobby."

Chapter 26

Jack had pretty much decided on this plan before Robyn went missing. She'd offered to help and he'd planned to use her, and with her help it would have been pretty simple and fairly safe.

Now she was gone, which could be both good and bad except that it made tangling with the chief of police and his officers a much bigger risk, because if the chief had Robyn or knew where she was he would easily spot this as a trap, and at the minimum, he wouldn't show.

But if the chief did spot it as a trap and was also a very clever man he could go all the way to the other extreme and use Jack's trap as a great opportunity to set a trap of his own in which to snare or kill Jack. And in between those diverse options were a lot of other dangerous possibilities. While Bobby drove he tried to think of all of them and then plan a counter-move for each scenario, kind of like playing chess with live pieces.

Of course the chief not coming at all would pretty much prove that he did have Robyn or knew where she was. It would be the only way to justify his lack of action. So in a way Jack's strategy was win-win. He would learn something either way, so it was clearly worth the risk.

"Are we good on time, Lieutenant? Traffic's pretty heavy but I can look for an alternate route to get back there."

"I want it to be good and dark, so we have plenty of time. Be cool and try to relax. I can feel your tension. You're giving me butterflies and I don't need them."

Bobby looked concerned. "I've been trying to get myself loose. Just not getting my breathing down, though. Been too long, maybe."

"Am I missing or overlooking something you want to mention?"

"I'm probably just out of practice. I'll be fine."

Compared to the missions Jack and Bobby and Mike and the rest of the squad had been on in Afghanistan, this didn't seem all that scary. So if it scared Bobby, it could indicate a problem with Jack's panel of warning lights that had guided all of them through war with only a couple of serious malfunctions. And if that was the case, it was also likely he'd missed something, which in turn meant it was more likely that something would go wrong. And in the lethal world of bloody battle, when things went wrong they went tragically wrong and in a whole lot of hurry.

Jack didn't say anything for the rest of the drive, testing his moves in his mind, moving the pieces across his imaginary chessboard until he reached check, and then check mate, at least for the chief.

Bobby timed it to arrive at Robyn's house at a little after dark. As they drove past, they both tried to look casual as they studied it carefully, making sure nothing had changed since Bobby left earlier.

"You'll want to go down the left side to the back door, Lieutenant. That's the way I went. The right side is more visible to neighbors."

"Left side. Thanks."

As they rounded the corner, Jack carefully typed the number for the chief he'd gotten from Oglethorpe's files into the phone Bobby had picked up at a local store, then added the text message, making sure the words sounded both desperate and honest. *Jack Wells brought me back to my house for a change of clothes. He's scaring me with crazy ideas about you being a killer. Please help. Robyn Thomas.*

Jack pressed send as Bobby stopped the van and let him out. He jogged to her back door, opened it with her key, and went inside to wait in the dark.

He didn't wait long.

The black SWAT van arrived first and stopped at the curb in front of the next door house, its flashing lights bouncing off every solid object, luring neighbors from their homes like hyenas to a kill. Jack watched from the darkened room as the chief's men poured out of the back, looking only slightly better than they had last night at the motel, perhaps having learned something useful from that futile outing of unscheduled training.

But they still showed a sad lack of professionalism that reminded Jack of the magazine photo that would always be an offense to him, where a militarized police sniper kept a close eye on an angry American crowd by aiming his weapon center-mass on them, using the weapon's scope when binoculars would have done the same job without escalating the hostility by sweeping the high-powered rifle over them.

The SWAT team took their positions around the van, beside trees, and behind cars parked on the street, using all of it as cover. Jack looked at each of them, and although they all looked the same in their black uniforms and headgear, one of them was extremely special, or at least was going to be special. Which one, Jack wondered, was going to make the kill shot.

The chief pulled directly in front of Robyn's house, parked, and stepped boldly out of his car like he was the bravest man on the planet, which probably impressed everyone watching him even though the chief had to know Jack was innocent and therefore unlikely to pose any risk to him at all.

He walked boldly to the front door wearing his well-pressed black uniform but no SWAT gear at all, not even a ballistic vest. His big shaved head seemed like a floating orb as it came toward the porch, level and steady as the juiced body that held it aloft moved with muscular stiffness.

The chief knocked hard, then knocked again even harder.

Jack waited until the chief shouted the, "I know you're in there, Wells," he expected, and then he opened the door but stayed hidden behind it.

The chief stood as still as a leopard about to pounce, black on black against the darkness. When he smiled it pulled Jack's eyes off the chief's hands and up to his giant white eyes with their luminous green dots, but Jack immediately went right back to watching the hands.

"Hello, Mister Wells," the chief said as he smiled and muscled up a little as though Jack were a gym mirror.

"You'd better come in, Chief, if you don't want your men to hear us talk about what I learned at Oglethorpe's."

"I was already planning on coming in," he said with a tone of surprise in his voice, and then he turned back to his men. Jack amped up, ready for battle if the chief jumped out of the way or spun around with a weapon drawn. But the chief just put his hands palms-down in front of him and pushed on the air, like he was telling them to be cool, before turning back around and stepping slowly inside, watching carefully as Jack stayed behind the door and aimed the pistol he'd taken from Oglethorpe's small arsenal at the chief's head.

"Now signal your men that you're safe. Turn off your radio."

"I just did signal them."

"Yeah, that's what it looked like to me, too. But for all I know it could have been a prearranged signal for them to go into action. I want you to signal you're safe."

"How do I know that I am?"'

"I didn't say you were safe, just to signal them you are. So wave to them all nice and friendly, the way you'd wave good-bye to your mother."

The chief took half a step back onto the porch and made a friendly wave. He even smiled, which proved his understanding that he and Jack were, for the moment, on the same team. Neither of them wanted the SWAT team inside to hear what was about to be said or done, and both of them knew it.

The chief moved his powerful body through the doorway, looked around the dark living room, and said, "I didn't really expect Miss Thomas to be here, and so I'm certainly not surprised I don't see her."

"Sit down."

"What makes you think you're in any position to give me orders, Mister Wells?"

"Sit down."

The chief sat.

Jack stood in front of the chief and returned his stare for half a minute before rubbing his shoulder where the chief's man hit him, just as a reminder. He kept rubbing until the chief asked, "How's the pain?"

Jack stopped. "I'll live."

"That's good."

"But I doubt you will."

The chief nodded like a man who'd been threatened for most of his life and had the well-earned confidence of a survivor. "You're planning on going all eye for an eye on me, Wells?"

"I'm considering it."

"Vengeance is mine, sayeth the Lord."

"Even the Lord made exceptions once in a while."

"The path of the wicked man—"

Jack laughed out loud. "I am so glad you brought up wicked men because you sure made the list."

The chief actually looked surprised. "How so?"

"You killed seven people on behalf of Montessa. Murders for hire. Not very Christian of you, do you think?"

The surprise turned quickly to acceptance that Jack really did know something, followed just as quickly by a weak denial. "You're lying."

"I have proof."

"I doubt it. Lots of things people believe to be proof don't turn out so convincing in court."

"Then leave. Go ahead and walk out the door. I won't stop you. But understand that I have a friend watching that front door who's ready to take it all to the press and the U.S. Attorney the second you do, just in case I die after you leave."

The chief looked at the door but didn't move.

"Good. Now we understand each other. You know, you just might live through this if you take orders from me for a while."

The chief's big head moved slightly, as if nodding to himself. "I see."

"Do you really?"

"Well why don't I take a shot at it and then we'll know for sure."

"Fire away."

"Thanks. Now for starters I'm going to guess you have no idea where Miss Thomas is. Furthermore, I'll go way out on a very thick limb and guess that you're offering to keep silent about whatever it is you think I've done in exchange for my help in finding her. Have I got that right so far?"

"Not exactly."

"Oh. Well in that case—can I have another guess? Pretty please?" The chief grinned.

"I'm feeling generous."

"Then my second guess is that you lured me here to kill me, maybe over the fun we had with you at Montessa, or maybe over some confused idea in your brain. But whatever the reason, I'm guessing—this isn't my third guess is it?"

"Go on."

"I'm guessing I still have options. Otherwise you wouldn't have given the 'you just might live through this' line. I had nothing to do with the kid dying, you know. I admit to covering up the fact that it was murder by being too quick to confirm it a suicide, but I was honestly as surprised as anyone to go into that room and find that kid dead."

"I know."

"You do? Well, that's something. You won't get away with this. My men are all around the house. You won't escape."

"Tell me, did you really kill only seven? Is that an accurate count, because it's not that impressive a number."

The chief smiled the way a too-smart criminal might as he toyed with a clumsy detective. He looked at the ceiling as if wanting to be accurate. "Let's see…one, two, three…yes, seven. That sounds right, although for all you know I could be counting seven sheep grazing in my head. But if I had killed seven people for Montessa, which of course I didn't, I'd actually be wishing I'd killed more."

"The money is that good?"

The chief leaned back in the chair, stretched out his arms and then laced his fingers behind his giant head, a man telling a good story. "The pay would be a factor, of course, and for the sake of discussion let's just say Montessa would feel that whatever I charged would be a cost effective way to eliminate problems. But if I had killed those seven people, I would have done it for more reasons than just the money."

"Personal pleasure?"

"I would have done it because I disagree with the stupidity of the environmental movement, with Sierra Club and Greenpeace and all the other tree-hugging whale lovers. Their noise-making detracts from the true answer to pollution, which is that business should be allowed to regulate itself." He leaned back and laced his fingers behind his head. "Heck, most business already self-assess their risks, like our dairy right outside of town. Old man Fremont tells me they only get inspected by the FDA once every ten years or so, and their milk is safe. But groups like Sierra keep hassling businesses, and that drives up costs."

"People die every year over contaminated food."

"Sure they do, and it's mighty easy to focus on mistakes, but the fact is we already have plenty of laws on the books that require businesses to do precisely the kind of environmental protection those groups are crying about."

"Laws on the books don't do much good if no one enforces them."

"Environmentalist don't do much good either, other than cost a lot of good people their jobs. And if the jobs go away from Roanoke, son, crime in my nice little city goes up."

"So you'll choose pollution over reduced employment."

"I'll choose to do my job, which means that I can't let the crime rate go up. I'm paid to make sure it doesn't happen. So in a very real way, if I had had anything to do with those deaths, which I didn't, I would have just been doing my job. Surely even you can see that."

"But you're only speaking hypothetically. I'd think you'd be proud to admit killing those seven?"

The chief looked around, realizing too late that there had to be microphones somewhere. He stood suddenly. "You know what, Wells? I think I'm done here."

"Sit back down," Jack said, and as he gave the command he lunged and snatched the chief's pistol out of its holster, surprising the chief with his speed. He sat slowly, looking far less in control as Jack unloaded the pistol and handed it back.

"You are a dead man, Mister Wells. You won't survive the hour."

"Where's Robyn?"

"I don't know."

"Do you know who killed Jeff Roberts?"

"Aw, yes, Jeff Roberts, your young friend. Mister Wells, I will say that I wasn't surprised by his death because he was making an enormous amount of trouble for Montessa. They hated him. And then I met that contractor who showed up a day too late to kill him. So your friend was destined to die at any rate. There was just no way he would have survived all that attention."

"You mean Mitch Douglas."

"If Mitch Douglas is the man who broke into my home and snapped my dog's neck in front of me, yes, that's exactly the man I mean. The guy who demanded absolute freedom to do whatever he wanted in Roanoke? Yes again. He's a friend of yours, I assume."

"We go back a ways."

"It's nice to know you have friends. Personally I hope I never see him again. Now are we done here, Mister Wells?"

"Not quite. Who do you work with at Montessa?"

"No one. If I actually did work for Montessa—" he stopped and turned toward a window, then waited until Jack turned with him. He smiled, comforted by the fact that his men were right outside, waiting to kill Jack.

"I know," Jack said, "I won't live through this."

"Odds are tilting severely that way, Mister Wells, so what does it matter if we speculate a bit."

"I suppose it doesn't."

"*If* what you suspect was true, a vice-president there would be the logical person to reveal who's a threat to them."

"Oglethorpe."

"He would most likely be the one to give whoever he hired their pay in cash. He would probably skim a bit too much of it, but I guess that would be the nature of this what-if game we're speculating about."

Jack dug into his backpack and pulled out his jacket, cap and sunglasses. "Here, stand up and put these on."

The chief laughed as he stood slowly to put on Jack's things. "This is your great plan of escape, using me as a decoy?"

"I want to turn myself in and get all this out in the open. You'll convince them I'm unarmed before we step out or they'll shoot you dead, thinking you're me."

"You'll notice that you and I are somewhat different builds. My men won't be fooled for long."

"How do you live with yourself?"

"Quite easily, Mister Wells, because I'm doing precisely what must be done. Even the scriptures require us to separate the wheat from the chaff."

"You mean bad people from good? With you as the judge?"

"No, I mean that quite literally. Americans demand their wheat, the products they need, but they whine about all the chaff, the by-products, the pollution, if you will." The chief exhaled hard as he strained to zip Jack's jacket. "But the chaff is there and it has to be dealt with. People who protest against it are actually the ones creating the problem. They find chaff unacceptable, but without it there's no wheat."

"Move toward the door."

"I'd rather not."

"I'm going out behind you. They'll have to shoot through you to hit me."

The chief shuffled along. "It's a silly plan and it won't work. I suppose you'll want me to aim this empty pistol at you, too."

Jack stayed to the chief's right when they got to the door. He stopped with both of them still behind the door and said, "Not exactly."

Jack quickly raised his pistol and pointed out the side lite of the door, aimed low enough to hit the ground, and fired five fast rounds, shattering the glass and hurting his ears. The chief jumped, the whites of his eyes even whiter than normal, and with the noise and confusion at its peak Jack flung open the front door but stayed behind it, leaving the chief alone in the doorway.

Dozens of shots ripped into the chief. The SWAT team never bothered to consider whether they were seeing a genuine threat that needed to be killed. If they had taken two seconds to identify their target, the chief, or an ordinary citizen in a similar situation, would have been fine. But they simply made their deadly assumptions that the chief was Jack and then acted on them, blasting away the instant a opportunity presented itself, just the way Jack expected.

What Jack didn't expect was the surprisingly large number of rounds that actually hit the chief, who looked dead before he hit the floor, the green center of his right popeye pinned on Jack, the other shredded away by the bullet that splattered through it.

Jack moved quickly to the kitchen and hid in a broom closet. He left the door cracked and waited in silence, expecting the men stationed in the back to enter first while the men out front kept cover.

Within seconds two SWAT guys crashed in, moving far too fast to secure the kitchen as they ran past him on their way to the front door and the chief, shouting into their microphones their excitement at bringing down a Blue Alert suspect.

Chapter 27

With Robyn's neighbors lured out front by the flashing lights and gunshots and shouting, it was easy for Jack to cut unseen through the neighbors' dark back yards, hopping fences and squeezing through hedges. At the side street he turned and slowed down as he walked to Bobby's CNN van, its logos covered by blank magnetic signs but its fully extended antenna towering over it, lit up by the street lights. He tapped the quick code they'd always used and Bobby let him in, pointing to his headset to indicate he was on the phone.

The truck's impressive array of audio and video gear was streaming several live images from the cameras Bobby had set up earlier in and around the house, along with a babble of dialogue. One monitor showed the front porch of Robyn's house, crowded with SWAT officers trying to get a look inside, while two other monitors showed their SWAT van and the chief's car. Another showed an area overview, and three showed all the activity happening inside, with the most interesting action being three SWAT members gathered around the chief, all of them now fully aware that they'd killed one of their own. One officer looked up and said that he hadn't actually fired at the chief, which prompted the other two to shout back that he'd been the one bragging the loudest outside about making a kill shot.

Two other SWAT members, both a little older than the rest, stood off to the side of the room, right under a camera, already building their case for self-defense. "Any reasonable man would have thought it was that Jack Wells cop-killer fellow. The chief was dressed exactly like him."

"Yeah, why would he do that? What was he thinking?"

"I've got no idea, but when he flung open the door and started shooting that pistol directly at us, of course we had no choice but to return fire. Chief or not, we clearly had no choice but to shoot to kill." They looked at each other, waiting for either one to punch a hole in their defense.

Then Bobby snatched off his headset, flipped a switch on a panel, and turned to Jack. "The car keys are right there. The rental's a silver Toyota a half a block down the street in that direction."

"Did you get all of what the chief said? It was as close as I was ever going to get him to a confession."

"That was all very cool, Lieutenant, and yes, I got it with good video and audio both."

Bobby pushed a playback button and the chief was suddenly alive again, looking smug and sounding even more so as he stood up to Jack with the confidence of a man who had a team of reinforcements outside. When he alluded to the fact that Montessa paid him to eliminate their challengers, the chief said the company's name with a proud sort of inflection that made it crystal clear.

"This is a Breaking News event if I ever saw one. I might even keep my job over this." He smiled.

"Can you feed it to Atlanta from here?"

"Ran up my antenna just before you got here. Can transmit right now if you want."

"Do it. Thanks. Good work, Bobby."

"Thank you, sir."

Bobby moved to another console, and as he did Jack called Mike.

"Mike," he said, working himself into the lie he was going to tell, not wanting to do it but willing to if it would keep Mike at a distance, "a man I think might have killed Jeff is dead."

Silence. Jack moved as Bobby reached in front of him to flip a switch. A motor outside hummed as the antenna turned. Then more silence.

"You think he killed Jeff? You're not sure?"

"I'm not done here. Just giving you a progress report, the way you asked. He did admit to covering up Jeff's death, saying it was suicide when he knew it was murder. That implicates him pretty well."

"Suppose so. Did you kill him?"

"No."

"But he's dead, right?"

"Yes."

"If not you, then who?"

"The local SWAT team."

"He's for sure dead? Not hanging onto life by a thread? I need you to be a thousand percent positive. I have to know he's dead."

"Yes, Mike, I'm sure. He was shot several times, including once through the eye. The bullet didn't come out the backside, just rattled around in his brain, I guess."

"And how sure are you he was Jeff's killer?"

"He mentioned Jeff along with seven other murders I know he committed, and as I said, he also covered it up. Pretty compelling, but like I said, I'm not done and not heading home yet."

"Oh. Okay, then." He sounded lost, like the whole purpose of his life had suddenly been taken away. Then something changed as he said, "But I'm still coming. Hell, I'm already pretty close to Roanoke."

Pushing back against Mike would just be compressing a spring, making Mike even more likely to uncoil and come out slashing with that damned knife of his. "If that's what you want," Jack said, coming to terms with reality, repositioning the pieces on his mental chessboard, looking for a way to put Mike into play without mucking up his plans, "it's probably a good idea."

Bobby held three fingers in Jack's face, excitement in his eyes and "three minutes" on his lips. Jack glanced at a monitor showing a train wreck story CNN was currently broadcasting live, and nodded that he'd be at the console soon. If Mike was coming, he had to act on that first.

"But there's something I need from you, Mike. Something I need you to do for me."

"Give it a name and you've got it." Mike sounded slightly re-energized and somewhat hopeful, glad to have something useful to do.

"Remember the guy who hunted me down over my fight with Headquarters?"

"I remember you talking about him when you stayed with us after your suicide…after your drowning."

Jack flinched because it wasn't suicide, and he knew much more than a thing or two about suicide. He'd been asked about suicidal tendencies on nearly every form he ever signed at the Veteran's Administration, and then asked again in interviews with doctors or nurses. The V.A.'s constant questioning had forced him to push for the truth about why he kept trying to drown himself, and that truth had actually surprised him. He wasn't suicidal. Even though he headed to the watery depths each time with the hopes of dying in mind, anxious, just like his dad, to end the guilt and pain he suffered for surviving when so many others hadn't, starting with his own family, he wasn't suicidal. He was merely testing his right to live. Finding out if he really deserved to be on this planet.

But all the same, he was plenty anxious for the day to arrive when no one came to save him.

"Jack?"

"The guy I fought with at Headquarters is here."

"You know I'd be proud to help you with that asshole."

"And there's a guy at Montessa Chemical who might have helped target Jeff, and definitely helped target some others."

"Montessa is the chemical company Jeff was working against, right?"

"Yes."

"I'd definitely enjoy getting up close and personal with them."

"How far away are you?"

"An hour or so."

Bobby leaned in and whispered, "They're about to go live with your story, Lieutenant."

"Thanks, Bobby."

"Bobby?" Mike asked. "Bobby Steel is there? Our radioman?"

"Yeah, Mike. It's shaping up like old home week here in Roanoke."

"Tell him I say hello. I'll call you when I get close."

"Thanks." And now to get some use out of Mike's coming. "What are you driving? I'll keep an eye out for you."

"Same old truck you borrowed last year."

"Okay, keep your head down. Check into a cheap motel in a Buy Here, Pay Here part of town and tell the clerk you're waiting for your friend Jack Wells to arrive. I'm sure you know that I plan to use you as bait."

"Sure, go ahead, that's not a problem," Mike said, as if Jeff's death had taken away everything worth living for. Then he hung up.

"It's about to go out, Lieutenant. Much of what the cameras shot in the house and some of my prep work from earlier. At least I think so. The editors rushed through it and didn't have time to let me see it first."

"Let's take a look. And Mike says hello."

"Mike?"

"Chainsaw. Sergeant Roberts."

"Oh." Bobby said, looking proud that Mike remembered him. "Cool. Way cool."

Jack pointed to one of the monitors. "This is the recording of what happened at the house after I left?"

"No, this monitor is a second live feed of what's going on in there right now, just in case the first one went down. I'm not sure how much they'll use from my background piece but I'll show all of it to you some other time if they don't air it. I'm sure someone from the Legal Department had input."

The words had barely left Bobby's lips when a "Breaking News" banner flashed up on the screen.

"This just in," the news anchor said from behind his desk, while Bobby's video of the SWAT team outside Robyn's house filled a big portion of the screen behind him.

"James B. Howard, the Chief of Police of Roanoke, Virginia, was gunned down just moments ago by his own SWAT team. Facts of the incident are not completely clear, but so far..."

The photo changed to the chief's lifeless body on the floor, the SWAT team milling around, all of them making excuses and none of them aware they were being filmed. And then that video was replaced by a photo of Montessa Chemical's Roanoke office, in the center of a collage of other Montessa operations, including farm and agriculture, petro-chemical, and defense facilities, with one photo in the collage the now-famous incinerated storage tanks.

The anchor chose his words with obvious care as he continued, "...we have unconfirmed but reliable reports indicating the late Chief Howard may have been acting illegally for quite some time on behalf of Montessa Chemical Corporation, attempting to end or dissuade grass roots environmental actions against Montessa, which has over two dozen international operations, some of which have, historically, attracted controversy.

"Over the past years CNN has covered several protests against Montessa by groups such as Greenpeace, the Sierra Club, and World Wildlife Fund over presumed violations or abuses of environmental law."

A long record of Montessa's EPA violations scrolled underneath the Montessa collage.

"However, Montessa has a great deal of support on Capitol Hill, as evidenced by the numbers of senators and congressmen who've received significant campaign contributions and voted in their favor on every environmental bill. But outside the Beltway this Fortune 500 company is viewed with suspicion. For more on this story we turn to Claire Statler, a reporter we're glad to welcome on her first day at our CNN Atlanta Bureau. Claire worked previously as a network news reporter both here in Atlanta and in Roanoke where the chief was just killed, and has been researching Montessa's environmental record for well over a year. She will present a CNN Special Report next Sunday on the evidence she uncovered that connects Montessa to several deaths at a Roanoke nursing home. It's good to have you with us, Claire."

The screen shifted to Claire, who looked confident and aggressive as she stared into the camera, her last name misspelled at the bottom of the screen by some staffer rushing to get her into the CNN fold and onto the air. Jack was glad to see her in play and wanted very much to hear what she said, but it was time to move on because Mike would be here soon.

Mitch Douglas already was.

Chapter 28

As Jack stepped out of Bobby's van his phone signaled New Mail. It was from Grayson and encrypted with normal Bureau protocol. The subject was: You need to hear this.

Gray's message said: During a break in my proctologic exam I passed your information about Oglethorpe along to the CODE ADIC, who acknowledged that the Virginia State Police are already investigating him, coordinating their case with CODE. I've been authorized to reactivate your Bureau password for a one-time, single access log-in to our server. You'll be automatically directed to an audio file of a wiretap. You won't like what you hear but you'll still owe me. Good luck, Gray.

"Bobby," Jack said as he stepped back into the van.

"Yes, Lieutenant."

"Get me a secure internet link and spool up a re-corder."

"Yes, sir, and the internet's already secure."

Jack brought up the FBI site and logged in as far as he could, locked out of all access except the one file to which he was instantly routed. The phone log was dated this morning and identified the participants as Richard and Roger Oglethorpe.

"Ready, Bobby?"

"Yes, sir."

Jack hit the play icon and leaned forward to listen.

An educated southern voice with a slight mountain twang said, "We need to talk, Richard. It's important."

"Hang on," said a voice so close to the first it was hard to differentiate. But the cadence was a bit slower and more confident, so Jack would use that to keep them straight.

Jack looked at Bobby, who confirmed he was recording.

"Hurry up 'cause I've got to get a shower and get back out in public looking normal." The first voice was shaky. Another identifier.

"Then go ahead."

"I killed the old lady last night. Really didn't have much of a choice."

"I saw the news. You bungled that. What else?"

"I'll tell you what else. What else is that I'm getting sorry I moved back to Roanoke."

"Tough, but—"

"'Cause if I hadn't, I never would have been dragged into this SILT business."

They were stepping on each other's sentences, nervous enough to be rude, making it a little harder to keep them straight.

"Tough all over again, but if not SILT, you would have signed up for something else 'cause you like the big money of killing. You did it in an Army uniform and billions of folks have done it since Cain slew Abel."

"Maybe so but maybe not, 'cause—"

Jack had the voices down now, and identified Richard's as the voice that cut Roger off with, "The only difference is the pay and you know it. A suicide bomber gets promised a bunch of virgins, a soldier gets a medal, and without SILT you'd just be getting paid government scale."

"I'm explosives, Rich. I'm no killer the way your men are. Explosives do lots of damage but I never personally killed anyone until the old lady."

"You bragged about killing those two activists working against phosphate mining up the Peace River, and those hippie-dippies protesting that development at the edge of the Everglades."

"I wasn't even around when those detonators popped."

"Boy, you really are trying your damnedest to be delusional."

"I've just never done anything like the old lady—"

"I suppose that will work in our favor 'cause you've always made it look like an accident. That's your signature, our signature, but we don't want Montessa to even consider it was us 'cause they're trying to turn down the heat. You did the old lady sloppy and that's good."

"I grabbed the other one, too. Just got back."

Jack felt Bobby look over at him, but he stayed focused on the recording by staring at the timer and twin Voice Stress Analyzers bouncing along the top and bottom of the screen.

"One of my guys met you?"

"Yeah, he's watching her."

"I'll set up a shift schedule. She knows who you are?"

"Make sure they don't go walking around the property. She knows."

"So get busy using her to get to Wells. And don't worry about her coming back at you 'cause my guys will take care of her."

"And you're sure Montessa hired Wells to kill us? It's hard for me to see him doing that."

"I'm not, no, but I am sure the SILT home office sent an independent here to make a hit, right at the same time Wells showed up at Montessa's door."

"But you're not sure we're the targets."

"Reed knew Wells was up to no good, and with the Sierra kid's death Montessa anticipates a media flare-up. So they're trying to bury everything. Public Affairs has even ordered the perimeter fence torn down and the conference rooms offered to the community for meetings and church groups, at least until things quiet down. SILT is going away, too, and it just makes sense that a smart manager would use an arms-length transaction to eliminate us, too."

"You're not sure Wells is even the contractor."

"Just keep in mind that the SILT Retirement Home is a grave, Rog. But even if I'm a hundred percent wrong, nothing good's going to come from Wells poking around. Reed was sure Wells didn't come to his office to learn about relocating a paper mill, so he's either in Roanoke to make trouble for Montessa or to kill us. Either way you need to quit stalling, use the woman to lure him out, and kill him. Do it sloppy, too, like the old woman."

"'Cause he's asking questions about that young man? I just don't see the harm. The police ruled it suicide."

"Roger," Richard said with slow intensity, "I know you're scared of him, but if you'd just killed him in the first place we'd be meeting for drinks right now. I'd even buy. But luring him to that old woman's house was stupid. And then hammering her skull—"

"It wasn't supposed to happen that way."

"—killing her in hopes the cops would think Wells did it and then kill him for you…Jesus, are you really all that afraid of this guy?"

"It's not that I'm so afraid of him, but more—"

"You best be focusing on the fact that SILT just sent a killer here."

"Jack Wells," Roger said slowly, "of all the guys they could send, I can't for the life of me figure out why they chose him, or why he'd even do it."

Richard laughed. "I'll take a shot at that. Maybe because Wells is good at killing people."

"It just doesn't make sense. Sure, he'll pull a trigger, but at Quantico he always had a big reputation for taking care of people, not killing them. He was one of those guys we called protectors, even of strangers. I once heard of him cold-cocking an agent who was being overly rough with a prisoner. Which makes me feel there's something going on here that we don't understand. That's why I'm hesitant. It's not just because I have a healthy respect for the man's skills."

"Lots of people like to protect things. Hell, that's what we do."

"We protect a giant international corporation from the insect bites of a very small and underfunded group. It's hardly the same thing."

"Who cares?"

"Wells' old man is a stumbling drunk, you know, a decorated Navy Chief who retired after his wife cart-wheeled off the Seven-Mile Bridge heading back to Key West. She took Jack's baby sister with her to a warm watery grave."

Jack instinctively looked away from the screen. His eyes met up with Bobby's, who shrugged like he was sorry to be there to hear this secret, and then turned away, still recording.

"How do you know that?"

"A bunch of us went to Key West for a lost week a while back, right after Wells left the Bureau under such a cloud of mystery, which was red meat to any investigator worth a flip. Since Wells was from Key West we poked around one afternoon and found his old man in a bar. Told him we were FBI Agents, friends of Jack's. 'You guys know Jack?' He got all excited. 'How's my boy doing?' He was already slurring and slopping his whiskey in the middle of the day. But he wanted to talk about Jack."

"That's sad."

"Are you going soft, Richard?"

"Sad is sad. I'm not an animal."

"And since Wells was a hot topic, we couldn't resist inviting the old man to join us. We kept buying him drinks and he kept talking - told us the story of his life, and Jack's life, and his wife's."

Jack stood up. He wanted to leave. He didn't want Bobby to hear any more of this, and didn't want to hear it himself. But he dug deep for the strength to do nothing but stand there in pain and listen.

"The accident that caused his wife and daughter's death seemed terribly fresh and painful to him, even though it happened when Wells was just a kid. Poor old guy was living the suffering each and every day like it was a penance. He freely admitted that he'd crawled into a bottle over it, and that he planned to hide in there 'til he got the guts to kill himself, hoping the alcohol would do it first."

"I feel bad for the old man, I really do, but right now you need to get rid of Wells. It's a shame we have to give his dad something else to suffer over, but..." Richard paused. "Wait a minute. So his dad's a drunk? Maybe we can use that instead, or maybe something else the old man said."

"What are you thinking?"

"I'm wondering if we can we go at this from another angle so you don't have to engage Wells in mortal combat." He said the words even more slowly than normal, throwing an ominous tone in for good measure.

"Or so you don't have to go kill him yourself if I fail?"

"If there's another way, that's fine. Any chance we can blackmail Wells into leaving us alone, maybe threatening to hold the old man up to ridicule, or levying his retirement, or tying up his veterans benefits? We have a guy on The Hill who can get all of that done before lunch tomorrow."

"I doubt it. The old man said he never hears from Jack anymore. He's pretty busted up that his son has nothing to do with him, although he was quick to admit that he first abandoned Jack for the bottle. Besides, I doubt the old man would even tell him. He said Child Services removed Wells from his houseboat when he was fifteen, and it was easy to understood why. We saw that floating shit-box as we headed out fishing the next day."

"Where did Child Services move Wells?"

"He became part of his baseball coach's family until he headed off to college. The old man said Jack is very proud of being part of that household. Tried to sound proud of his kid as he said it. Also said he wouldn't blame Jack if one day he decided to change his name."

"Was Wells ever married?"

"A guy on our trip said Wells was popular with the ladies in the New York office, but disappeared at the first sign of things getting serious. No, never married. I never heard that he was ever even engaged, and the Bureau's a pretty small world. Word gets around."

"A player?"

"My friend said he's not. Said Jack always seemed to hurt over the break-ups he caused."

"Broken Home Syndrome," Richard said, sounding like an academic. "I read about it in a magazine at the dentist's office. Kids from broken homes can worry they'll create nothing more than another broken home, and it keeps them alone throughout their lives. I don't see much here to use on him, do you? "

"I'm not sure. But I am sure that I'd rather not tangle with him."

"He's got no father to speak of."

"I could look into using the family he lived with."

"Too late in the game. Is there a chance there's anything shameful in Wells' past?"

"Nothing I know about, but like I said, there was quite a bit of intrigue at the Bureau when he left."

"Tell me."

"I can't 'cause I don't know. That lid is bolted down, but if he's now a contract killer, I guess that's evidence that he'd gone to the dark side."

"Then I just don't see any other leverage."

"Maybe he just went to Montessa to ask questions about the dead kid as part of an investigation. He is a trained investigator, you know, and a damned good one. Maybe he asked some questions and then moved on."

"Julius said it was clear he was lying about the paper plant. My guess is he was scouting Montessa for ways to make whatever he does look like an industrial accident so there wouldn't be an investigation that could lead back to him." Richard chuckled. "Which makes me glad we don't have vats of corrosive chemicals onsite where he could dump our bodies."

"I still can't see Wells doing anything like that."

"But are you willing to bet your life on it? Because I'm not. The facts are that, one, SILT just sent a contract killer to Roanoke. And two, a former Marine slash FBI agent with a questionable past and an impressive kill record just rolled into our quiet little town. Your Blue Alert didn't do a damned thing, and making it look like he killed that old woman won't work any better. You're going to have to do it yourself. And speaking of the Blue Alert, why did you use such old photos of Wells in the first place? It had no chance of working."

"Mark Foster told me to do it."

"Foster called you?"

"Yes."

"Wow."

"He said to give Wells a chance to prove himself. Said he wanted to toy with him a bit. Test him. See how worthy an opponent he might be."

"Why…never mind. That sick fuck could have any number of reasons."

"I couldn't guess his reasons anyway. And I sure as hell wasn't going to ask."

"I don't blame you there."

"Didn't think you would. So, what are you going to do?"

"I'm going to pack, using whatever *you* do as a diversion for *me* to get away, to get on my boat and head down to Panama where I've got a nice slip at Bocas del Toro, very close to the bar. I really don't think Montessa will care enough to chase me there. They just want me gone. You too, so if I were you I'd get packing too."

"I've got a family here. A wife with a business and a kid doing well in school. Besides, I'd like to stay in the Bureau and retire."

"You don't need any more money."

"I know, but I like the badge and my credentials. It'll sound silly to you, but if I retire I get to keep them. Hang them on a wall somewhere so I can point to them to prove I'm respectable."

"A big price to pay for a word, and a lot of years left before you can sit in a rocker and point a proud shaky finger at them, assuming you'll even survive Wells."

"Wells won't come after a fellow FBI Agent."

"Again you're being delusional. Just get this done."

"You know I've never killed like this before the old lady."

The recording stopped and the screen went blank, followed by the words "Further Access Denied."

Jack looked up when Bobby asked, "Are you okay, Lieutenant? That was some pretty hard shit to hear."

Jack managed a smile before stepping out of the trailer and walking away.

Chapter 29

The Oglethorpe recording helped fill in the map, and with Mike about to arrive, Jack decided to call FBI Headquarters and get a little help from his enemies.

"This is former Special Agent Jack Wells calling for the Director."

Even if the head of the FBI was there, he didn't expect him to take his call. But just mentioning "The Director" got people's attention.

"I'm sorry, Mister Wells, but the director isn't available."

"Any chance Assistant Director Matthews is in?"

The operator hesitated long enough for her computer to run his name and phone through its list of known crackpots and suspected threats. Jack was actually a little surprised his name wasn't on it. He was even more surprised when she said, "Please hold for Mister Matthews, Mister Wells."

Jack waited, knowing that everything he'd already said or ever might say on the call would be recorded and used against him if possible. He didn't want to violate any of the conditions of his settlement, but it was pretty hard to care since it was possible, and perhaps likely, that the FBI had sent Mitch back out to kill him. If that was the case, they'd already violated it, and he had bigger problems than a recorded phone call.

And besides, Jack would make a point of saying something during the call to make Matthews want the recording sealed as evidence or marked as previously reviewed.

"This is Matthews. What's this about, Wells?"

"We made a deal. You, me, the Director, the Attorney General, and—"

"We did, that's right, so what?"

"I lived up to my end. I left the Bureau. I moved to an island. I started a simple life working a million miles away from anything even remotely related to security or intelligence."

"I heard something about that. A charter captain, right?"

"Don't bullshit me, Matthews. You know exactly what I've been doing, which means you know I've lived up one hundred percent to my end."

"I don't currently have reasons to disagree with that."

"Then why do I feel you guys aren't living up to yours? Is our deal more trouble than it's worth?"

"I'm not following you."

"Because if you're thinking I'm trouble, then it's a small step to your thinking I might take up arms against you again. And that would logically make you try to kill me before I come after you."

"You're nuts, Wells. And don't threaten me."

"I'm promising. I'm coming for you after I kill Mitch."

Jack could almost hear Matthews straighten up in his seat and focus entirely on the conversation. "What do you mean? Are you saying Mitch Douglas is after you again?"

"For the moment. And thanks for confirming my suspicion that you knew. You're the only one who didn't think he was dead."

"Mitch. Wow." Matthews whole tone changed, because with Mitch in the game it was almost natural for everyone else to team up against him at the other end of the field. "Okay, now I see what you're driving at, but I had nothing to do with deploying Mitch. No one here did."

"It's pretty hard for me to believe you. You were his handler with Harvey and probably still have access."

"We talk from time to time, unofficially. It's not like we exchange Christmas cards."

"Doesn't matter, because I'm about to turn the tables on Mitch, whether he's your guy or not."

"That would be a mistake of colossal proportions, Wells. You should just stay away from him."

"I have no respect for your opinion."

"Listen, Wells, I suppose if I put myself in your position I could understand why you'd think that me and the other guys here on your prayer chain had something to do with this." He laughed. "Christ, if Mitch is trying to kill you again I certainly don't blame you. But just like you, all of us here have washed our hands of that whole sordid matter and buried it far too deep to even consider digging it back up. It would attract more attention than any of us want, and you know that."

There'd been a time when Jack would have believed Matthews without any hesitation, and even now, he was inclined to accept what he said as truth. But if he was telling the truth and had nothing to do with sending Mitch, Jack could still use Matthews.

"If not you, Matthews, then who?"

"Don't be stupid, Wells. Lots of smoke signals say you've been ramming a stick up the ass of one the world's largest and most powerful corporations. Are you so naïve as to think they don't know guys like Mitch?"

"You knew he was coming here."

"He called me. Said he was back in-country to do a job. I had no idea where or who. I hung up on him."

"There's more to it than that."

Matthews sighed. "There usually is with Mitch. It also turns out—and I swear I only recently found this out—that we have a bad agent in the same area of Virginia where you're clod-hopping around, and somehow he appears to have learned some of what was in your file. It seems likely that there's a connection to that agent, the data in your file, and Mitch."

"No one gets to see my file."

"I said he appears to have learned some of it. I can't guess how. It wasn't through the Director or Scott or me."

"Are you sure or are you just guessing?"

"I'm pretty sure. Anyway, this guy—"

"Oglethorpe?"

"Yes, that's him. It looks like Oglethorpe crossed paths with Mitch a couple of years ago because of something that horrible human being did once before for Montessa, which, as a good investigator like you probably know by now, is the company that lured our agent into getting dirty. Personally, I believe the only thing Oglethorpe knows about your file is whatever Mitch might have told him, that he'd been hired to kill you but lost the first round. Or he might have recognized some signatures of Mitch's work in a job he did for Montessa and put two and two together. Or hell, maybe they had drinks together and Mitch told him the whole ugly story. Like you, I'm just trying to piece it together."

"I'm about to end things with Mitch, so if you and Headquarters really aren't players on this field I'd suggest you stay way the hell out of my way."

"I wouldn't think of stopping you. And if you do somehow manage to kill him I'll be almost as happy as if he manages to kill you. Either outcome moves Harvey Squad's history farther out of reach and so I won't play favorites. But just in case you think our SWAT team will be thirty minutes away to back you up, forget it. I denied Grayson's deployment request for SWAT."

"You're a dick."

"Yes that's right I'm a dick. A dick who doesn't yet have an open case that justifies the deployment of SWAT. A dick who has no intention of getting burned for unauthorized use of those guys. A dick who's telling you all of that so you'll know you're completely on your own."

Jack swallowed hard. He hoped Matthews didn't hear it.

"I figured you should know that. This *dick* figures he owes you that much. Not sure, but I'm feeling generous."

"I'm not completely alone."

"Oh, yes, that's right. Your friend Robert Steel from CNN. A fellow brother-in-arms and all that? I saw a memo that he was there. Apparently Steele's right at the edge of committing some FCC violations, too. For you, I assume?"

"I'm not talking about Bobby. I mean Chainsaw."

"Who? And what a ridiculous nickname."

"It wouldn't sound ridiculous if you'd seen him earn that name. Staff Sergeant Michael T. Roberts will be in Roanoke within the hour, assuming his old Chevy truck doesn't break down as he makes a beeline directly from Jacksonville."

"And the two of you are up for challenging Mitch?"

"Are you planning to bet against us?"

"I'm absolutely ready to bet whiskey to water." Matthews made a mean laugh. "But either way it should make for some interesting reading. Now, was there anything else?"

"How is your wife, Matthews?"

"She's fine, Wells, she's just fine. And fuck you for asking."

"Let her know I said hi," Jack said, and hung up. He'd done what he'd needed to do because right now Matthews was classifying the recording. Then he would run a records check on Staff Sergeant Michael T. Roberts, along with a DMV vehicle ownership search. Within five minutes the

Virginia State Police would be out in force, looking for Mike but not permitted to stop him. Their orders would be to call Matthews and then do whatever he instructed.

And regardless of whether or not Matthews had anything to do with Mitch coming after Jack, he wouldn't be able to resist calling Mitch and tipping him off about Mike's whereabouts, evening up the odds a bit with the hopes of getting rid of either Mitch or Jack once and for all without getting his own hands dirty. Then if anyone got caught, it would be Mitch or Montessa, and not Matthews or the FBI, that took the fall.

And as soon as Mitch learned about Mike he would use Matthew's information to find him and follow him, fully expecting that Mike would eventually lead him to Jack, or bring Jack to wherever Mike was waiting, with Mitch somewhere out of sight but within kill range.

At least that's what Jack needed to happen.

Chapter 30

Jack drove the rental car to the motel room Mike had booked, which was exactly what Jack had asked for. Mike had left the door unlocked before slipping into the faded light of a dying sunset. He was still close, though, his empty truck parked right outside the door in the motel parking lot.

Jack went in and sat in the dark, waiting, thinking about Mitch, worrying about things going every bit as bad with Mitch as they had every reason to go. He was glad Mike was out there somewhere to back him up because he'd never seen anyone better at killing, and had never heard anyone say such a man even existed. He'd killed with guns and knives and grenades. He'd pulled Jack off an al-Qaeda soldier he was strangling just so Mike could break his neck himself, and had once walked into a non-secured cafe with nothing but a club and a pistol, killing seven men as they plotted against America, shooting until he was out of ammo and then bludgeoning their heads into mush, pounding away at the puddles until Jack and his squad arrived and shot the last two suffering bastards out of mercy.

Mike, like Jack, had learned the lesson of war, a lesson learned only at the very tip of the spear, and certainly not one that could be learned at a gun range with perfect conditions and ideal lighting, where menacing faces on paper silhouettes never shot back or bled or begged for their lives.

They'd also learned that killing needed to be left on the battlefield, or at least isolated between legitimate enemies. No one, Mike once said over drinks, should walk around America looking to kill another man, and he loathed the cowardly men and women who carried their guns into American stores and restaurants, armed to the teeth and praying for a chance to do just that. They seemed so weak and so frightened, and not only because their skill at a range had little in common with the way they'd react under fire. Rather, they were naïve because they didn't understand that killing a man wasn't the same as a winning pitch or a fistfight from which everyone healed. Taking a man's life sucked bad and haunted often, yet Jack knew people who were borderline vigilantes, proudly proclaiming after a school or theatre shooting that they would have heroically saved the day if only they'd been there, ignorant that most people in a gun fight threw their bullets in panic without accurately aiming at anything.

And even if they did manage to kill a bad guy, killing wasn't something to glory over. It left lingering doubts about the necessity, and those doubts tended to swell like wet lumber over the years. It caused guilt over the widows and families left behind, and inspired fear of retribution from the dead man's friends, forcing the shooter to look over his shoulder forever. The shallow breathing and bloody gurgling of a gunshot victim was soul-destroying and ugly. Killing a man carried costs, and Mike had paid more than his share.

Jack had paid, too, which made him glad SWAT had shot the chief for him. He'd set it up, sure, but he hadn't pulled the trigger. The difference was huge. If the SWAT team had followed the law and fired only if it became necessary, the chief would still be alive. It was as simple as that, and Jack could easily live with the fact. The chief would be in prison, and probably spend the rest of his life there, but he'd be alive. Even if his recorded testimony didn't hold up in court, it would have exposed the truth about what he'd done. The FBI would have been able to find plenty of evidence that wouldn't be tainted, and certainly enough to convict him.

But the SWAT team was made up of those very same officers who escalated routine traffic stops to violence, or swore at people who happened to know the law better than they did, or sped down the highway as they headed home. The SWAT officers acted above the law because the chief had given them free rein to do so. Maybe even encouraged them to do it. And the chief had paid for it with his life.

Jack sat in the dark hoping this next scene happened exactly according to his plan, fairly confident that the Virginia State Police would have found Mike, based on the name and vehicle description he'd given Matthews. That would have triggered the string of calls from the State Police to Matthews and then Matthews to Mitch.

The stage was set. Mike was here and he would stay close. Mike with his murderous knife in its handmade sheath, its terrible blade ready to slice and stab and puncture. Mike would sit back and watch Mitch go into the motel room. If Mitch came out without Jack, Mike would do the last thing Jack would ever ask of him, or anybody. He would kill Jack's enemy for killing him.

But if Mike had somehow slipped through, Jack was wasting precious time because Mitch had no idea where to find him, and as the minutes dragged Jack hoped that wasn't the case, and hoped it wouldn't be much longer. He was tired from lack of sleep, but he was aware of his exhaustion so he kept his mind active, assuming his plan was working and that Assistant Director Matthews had done what Jack needed. Which meant Mitch's best play would be to get to the room before Jack, kill Mike, and wait for Jack while he held the upper hand.

But Mitch was going to be the last one to the game, and as Jack waited he thought about the only other time he'd tangled with Mitch. He hadn't even known the man really existed until an informant told him.

"Some guy's in New York to kill you. He has a badge, too. Don't know his name."

"A badge?"

"Yeah, it's outside a leather case, just like yours. I imagine he has FBI credentials inside, but all I saw for sure was the badge. Hard to imagine him FBI, though, because he's foreign. Speaks English like a king but I caught an accent all the same."

"Where?"

"At Chelsea Piers. He was working out where you usually do, near the boxing ring. Dude's in good shape, too. Asked if you were around. Said he was your friend, but I can't imagine you having a friend like that."

"That doesn't mean he's out to kill me."

"You're right, it doesn't. But a dude like that isn't selling Avon. He's cold, Jack. Cold to talk to and cold to look at."

"Cold to talk to? You mean he doesn't say much?"

"Dude talks more shit than Rush Limbaugh, but nothing he says seems to matter to him. If I'd told him I'd pissed on his mother's shoes I think he might have said that's nice. He's that kind of cold. And when I shook his hand to give him a tour of the place, he was cold to touch, like life was all but drained out of him, leaving him empty. But I'd be surprised if he even feels empty."

"Again, none of that means much."

"Probably not. But I figured I'd pass it on so you'd be heads up. No harm in that."

"What's he look like?"

"Strong guy with dark hair. White but not a snowflake. More the color of that Greek guy always swimming laps. Kind of normal looking, except—"

A picture started to develop in Jack's mind of a rogue agent that a Special Agent in Charge had told him about, a Serb named Mihailo something or other who called himself Mitch Douglas, who'd gone to work in the dark, dark world of covert war and stayed in it far too long. A man who'd been so close to death for so long that he could no longer remember life. A man who apparently still had a job with the FBI.

"Except for what?"

"Well, except that for a normal guy, he stands out. Easy to spot because he looks like a man with no soul. He smiles a lot, but his dead eyes make it look creepy. Hard for a guy like me to find the words to explain, but if you see him you'll know right off what I mean."

Jack had driven straight to the sports center at Chelsea Piers after that, but no one there came close to fitting the description. He hung around all afternoon, looking for the man. At seven, as he walked to his car, a guy fitting the description approached from the other direction. If his informant hadn't warned Jack in advance, he probably wouldn't have noticed the guy, or the way he held his right hand as if palming a knife.

Jack pulled his weapon and aimed. "Drop the knife and lace your fingers behind your head!"

The man kept walking, although he looked surprised by Jack's command and angled off a little, like he was avoiding Jack the way anyone would avoid someone aiming a weapon.

"I said to drop the knife."

The man smiled and gave Jack a "Who me?" look of disbelief that made Jack doubt himself. Was that really a knife in his hand, or maybe a set of keys, or nothing at all? Was this really the Mitch of such great legend, or just a guy looking for his car in the dark?

It was during Jack's two seconds of doubt that Mitch lunged, the knife low and aimed toward Jack's guts, coming too fast for Jack to sidestep as he fired a round that hit Mitch in the stomach. Mitch stumbled, but his knife was already sinking into Jack's belly, and the man held onto it as though it were a handle, his weight dragging Jack to the ground with him.

Jack pulled the trigger to fire another shot that was muffled by their clothes and the closeness of their flesh. He didn't know if he hit the man, but they were now so close that a shot could have hit either of them, so he dropped his gun and grabbed at the knife, pulling it out of his insides, barely able to overpower Mitch, even though Mitch looked to be every bit as wounded as he was, maybe even more.

The knife came out with the sound of breaking suction, and Jack struggled to turn it. Then he raised it up so close to their faces that both of them stared at it as they fell together. Mitch hit the ground hard and Jack followed, the momentum carrying him forward and his weight propelling the knife into Mitch's mouth, the sharp blade slicing easily through his left cheek and out through the right.

Jack was suddenly pulled out of that ugly memory by a sound that was as light as air but so entirely different from anything else he'd heard outside that he sat up straight. He waited. The door knob jiggled.

There was a knock. He said nothing.

Another knock. Louder this time.

A locksmith's pick and a rake slid into the lock, and Jack heard the distinctive scraping sounds of tumbler pins being worked into position. The door handle turned. The door opened a crack and a voice immediately said, "Maintenance."

If Mike had been there he might really have thought it was the maintenance man, but there was a flat deadness to the voice that kept Jack silent in the darkness. The door opened a bit more, but not enough for Mitch to be able to shoot Jack, or for Jack to shoot Mitch with the Beretta he'd taken from Oglethorpe's hidden room.

"You might as well come in, Mihailo."

"My, my," Mitch said, sounding happy to hear Jack's voice. "Jack Wells, is it my good fortune to have you on the other side of this door?"

"Yeah. It is."

"I am well impressed, Jack," Mitch said from behind the door. "How did you know I would come here?" He still had the distinctive lisp Jack heard at their last meeting in the Attorney General's office, his difficulty in forming hard sounds with the tip of his tongue missing. "And you know I prefer Mitch to my Serbian name."

"It didn't happen by accident, Mitch. I got Matthews to lead you here."

"Are you suggesting that Matthews wants me dead?" Mitch sounded hurt.

"No idea. I tricked him into helping."

"Then I've badly underestimated you, which does not bode well for me, I'm sure. You're turning out to be quite the complex thinker."

"It's always worked out if I get people to underestimate me. And in this instance you're so far behind the power curve that I almost feel sorry for you."

"Ah, yes, but I can still ease this door closed and walk away. Are you up for chasing me?" Mitch laughed. "What a sight that would be. Two grown men playing a deadly game of tag in the parking lot."

"Of course you can make a run for it. But have you noticed that slightly sticky feel on your hand? It's a deadly pathogen I applied to the door knob. It takes a minute or two to absorb completely. Tic, tic, tic, tic."

"Hmm, I'm surprised that a man with your lofty reputation for being honorable would lie to me like that."

"Believe what you want, but I'd prefer that you neutralized it with soap and water so we can talk a bit, assuming you catch it in time. There's a sink right here and you've got about a minute left. Almost a minute."

"Why not allow me to die?"

"Because I want information."

Mitch opened the door fully, and Jack couldn't help from gasping. Whatever Mitch had done since he'd seen him last had extracted an enormous price, and not just the additional scars on his face. Not only did his eyes look dead, his whole face lacked whatever small spark of emotion it had shown the last time they'd met, when Mitch and five others sat across the conference table signing documents that Mitch, apparently, had now decided to ignore.

"If you'll allow me a moment to wash up, my friend, we'll talk. Is that okay with you?"

"You do see I'm aiming my pistol at you, right?"

"Oh, yes. And what an attractive gun it is, too."

"You know I won't regret shooting you."

Mitch hesitated, almost like he wanted to show his respect that Jack still needed to question whether or not he would regret killing.

"Yes, I know."

Jack stayed seated, keeping his pistol trained on Mitch, fully ready for him to turn and draw and try to get off a shot. If Mitch made any odd movement at all, this would end before he got any answers.

"It was you who tried to kill me at Montessa's storage tanks. I suppose if I'd shown up at midnight, the explosion would have waited for me."

"It was me, yes. And of course I would have waited. Did you get that cut on your arm there, I hope?"

"Let me guess. Hidden camera with a remote detonator?"

"Yes. I watched you from a few miles away. I really thought you would open the envelope. You must not have recognized my handwriting."

"Why?"

"Natural curiosity, of course."

"That's not what I meant. Why did you try to kill me there? Or maybe my question should be, why did you wait until now?"

"My services were requested after you stood up to the police chief in the Montessa parking lot. The vice-president for corporate security saw the entire incident from his office. It made him lose faith in that local bastion of the law, so he called Mark Foster. Since Mr. Foster was tied up elsewhere, he called me."

"Mark Foster, huh? What can you tell me about him?"

"He, my friend, is very much the animal. I know you think I'm an evil man, and I do understand your reasons, but I actually happen to have a decent set of values. Mr. Foster does not. He's slimy and friendly and absolutely insane. I mean that in a good way." Mitch smiled, but it didn't last. "I once helped him burn down his own office building. He assured me it was empty, but thirteen people were trapped in it and perished in the fire, all of them probably pretty decent people." Mitch looked down. "I'm displeased with myself for having a hand in their fate."

"Arson for profit?"

"I've never known Mark to do something so easily understood. In this case he wasn't even insured."

"Then what?"

"Mr. Foster was getting a great deal of bad press and substantial hate mail after a pivotal climate summit in Copenhagen in 2009 in which he'd pretended to be fighting for the environment. He'd gotten so much money from fossil fuel companies—by that I mean millions of dollars to make sure the conference produced nothing worthwhile—that some of that money was quickly traced back to big oil and coal. Mr. Foster was getting exposed as a fraud, attempting to discredit the science behind global warming. So what does he choose to do? He chooses to burn down his own building and recast himself as a victim, pointing his finger at major polluters and saying they did it to stop him from crusading for the environment. No one questions a victim."

"So it worked?"

"It shouldn't have, but it did. He played the victim wonderfully. He even pushed for criminal charges against some important corporations—none of which were his clients, of course. But of course law enforcement never managed to produce any evidence. For a very short while Foster was a darling of the environmental movement for his sacrifice and courage. Funny, yes? They admired a man who was really their worst adversary."

"Your explosions at Montessa also killed innocent people."

"I'm displeased with myself over that as well, but Mr. Foster said the solution stored in those tanks was mostly water that would extinguish any fires the explosion ignited. He probably just guessed badly. He doesn't lie to me often. I am sorry so many people got hurt and killed. Very sorry."

Mitch twitched and Jack did too. "Tell me, where's Robyn Thomas?"

"Who? I'm sorry, Jack, but the name Robyn Thomas means nothing to me. I'm being entirely honest with you."

It felt odd for Jack to believe him, but even a man as soulless as Mitch would still tell the truth on occasion, and this was one of them.

Jack watched Mitch wash his hands and then dry them delicately on the worn out towel. He couldn't help but wonder about Mitch, and how he became the killer he was.

"What happened to you, Mitch? I've never heard the story. Abusive father? Knuckle-busting nuns? Pedophilic Scout leader?"

Mitch chuckled as he finished drying his hands and then neatly folded the towel. "Mind if I sit? Are you truly interested? Are we going to spend some time bonding? It's okay with me, if that's what you want."

Jack made sure he looked a little doubtful about allowing Mitch to sit in the only other chair in the room, a big overstuffed antique that would be hard for Mitch to jump out of quickly. Finally, "I guess there's no harm in your sitting. Sure, let's bond. Why not?"

"Thank you. Now, my story probably goes something like yours, Jack, because we seem to be almost mirror reflections of each other. Guys like us are always—"

"Stop right there. I'm nothing like you. I'd kill myself first."

Mitch smiled and gave another small chuckle, as though enjoying this rare opportunity to sit and chat with an old friend. "I'm sorry to be the one who needs to point this out, Jack, but you are exactly like me. You're a vigilante, my friend, a gun for hire, a righter of wrongs and all that, precisely like me. The only real difference is that you absolutely believe you're on the right side of history."

"I absolutely believe that you aren't."

"But really, Jack, doesn't everyone think that way about their views? Evangelicals and atheists are both positive they're right. How about the right-to-lifers and the pro-choice crowd? Keynesian or Friedman economists? None of those folks leave any room to be wrong in their views, and neither do you. Yet we both know that everyone can't be right."

"I suppose."

"Then just suppose for another second that I'm the one on the right side of history. I'm the man doing what's best for society, and not you."

"That's a hard thing to imagine."

"But wouldn't you agree that courts are inefficient in their dealings with bad men? I mean, let's you and I sit here and face the truth together, shall we? And the truth we know is that if I got arrested tonight with a gun in my hand and your body at my feet, and the courts had my signed confession that I never retracted, it would be years before I was executed, if ever."

"Killing for hire is wrong. It's as simple as that."

"You're foolish, but I find it interesting. Now, while I admit to wearing too many of their hats in my own particular process, aren't judges, juries, and executioners also hired to kill people when it's the right thing to do?" He winced. "Wow, even I'm repulsed by saying anything is so clearly right or wrong. It's so changeable, you know. But people who cause trouble in any society are punished. They need to be. All I do is accelerate the process."

"You're not on the right side of anything, Mitch. I doubt you ever have been."

"Ah."

"Ah, what?"

"You've helped me see our problem even more clearly. You're narrow minded, Jack. God, how lucky I am to not be like you. You're cursed with such an absolute confidence in your clarity of vision that you're blind to anything that might really be true if it doesn't align with those beliefs. You're really no different than those silly Creationists who steadfastly believe Adam and Eve raised their kids around dinosaurs, in spite of all the science that disproves it." He looked around the room. "Nothing here to drink, I guess?"

"No."

"I was just thinking of the bar where I wasted an hour of my life arguing with a drunk who believed in the fable of Creationism." Mitch laughed again, actually making it hard for Jack to keep hating him. In fact, Jack was surprised by Mitch, and shocked to find him so articulate. Other than their fight at Chelsea Piers, he'd met him only the one other time, and Mitch had said very little at that meeting, which was probably why people always described Mitch as a non-thinking killing machine.

But this Mitch was different. This Mitch was trapped and probably knew he would die. And somehow, this Mitch seemed alright with it. Maybe relieved.

"If you don't know where Robyn is, Mitch, I'm not wasting any more time on you. But I would like to know why you waited until now."

"For what?"

"Why didn't you just come down to Marco Island to kill me? I'm a pretty easy target to find."

"Why would I?" Then Mitch looked off, as if spotting something on the wall that was only vaguely familiar to him. "Oh, of course, I think I see what you're getting at. You mean why didn't I come kill you for vengeance."

"Something like that."

"That really is how you think, isn't it? An eye for an eye and a tooth for a tooth and an insult for an insult, all that silly nonsense. In fact, I'd be willing to bet that vengeance is why you're here in Roanoke."

Jack had trouble wrapping his mind around the fact that he'd been looking over his shoulder for nothing, having assumed ever since they'd signed the accord that a man like Mitch, for whom killing was almost a hobby, would hunt him down for no more reason than because it was unfinished business. Or as payment for the missing tip of his tongue. Or for the bits of intestines Jack's bullet had splattered.

Jack had been safe from Mitch the whole time.

"Vengeance, my dear Jack, is quite the black-hearted affair. I know you think I'm a very bad man, but apparently I am a much better man than you. I would never stoop so low as to kill anyone for vengeance. That, my friend, belongs to the Lord, does it not?" He laughed again, enjoying himself so much that it heightened Jack's senses and doubled his guard.

"But you came to Roanoke to kill me."

"Of course I did. And I will kill you, too, if you give me just the slightest chance."

He leaned forward and Jack gasped a little. "Stay seated."

Mitch paused. He looked down at the cushy chair, then back up at Jack and smiled. "I believe I will."

"So what's the difference? Killing me here or killing me on Marco Island?"

Mitch yawned, then licked his lips like he was hungry. "I came here to kill you, and given the chance I will, but only because there's a paycheck in it. If someone had written me a check to kill you on Marco Island, I would have done that, too. But I would never kill you because you shot and stabbed me. That would…well, that would just be wrong."

"You're a real piece of work, Mitch."

"Thank you. I like to think I'm healthy of mind and body, and the thought of vengeance-killing would get in the way of that glorious feeling. Vengeance will send you to hell." Mitch smiled big, bending the scars around his mouth and distorting his ugly face more than normal.

"And it really was Montessa that paid you to kill me? Not the Bureau, at least not this time?"

Mitch rolled his eyes like a professor fielding a stupid question. "Of course it was Montessa. Who else has reason to want you dead, the Daughters of the Revolution? The National Parks Service? Bert and Ernie?"

"Then I'm going to leave, Mitch, but don't you dare move."

"You're leaving so soon? We're just getting to be friends. I like you so much more now that I've seen how clever you can be. I honestly had no expectations that you'd be here."

"Nice chatting with you, Mitch. Listen, tell me you'll walk away from all this and we can part as friends." Jack chuckled at his own words. "Okay, not really friends, I guess, but at least we can bury our roles as enemies."

Mitch looked down at the chair again. He patted his palms on the overstuffed arms. "Sorry, my friend, but as much as I'd like to comply, I can't. You know that. My reputation demands that I kill you, although I do wish things could be otherwise."

Jack walked to the door and opened it. He touched the knob and said, "That sticky stuff on the knob was shampoo from the bathroom."

"Again, clever of you. I truly am impressed. But I'll still die here, won't I, Jack?"

"You have a choice."

"I don't, not really, so can I please request a sniper shooting me outside? Or perhaps a SWAT raid as I sit here aiming at the door, maybe blasting away like in an old gangster movie?" He shook his head enthusiastically, as though either of those sounded preferable to what he expected. "At least that would provide a nice blaze of glory for my exit."

"Come on, Mitch, please, I'm offering you one last chance for peace. Take it, damn you."

"Isn't peace such a hopeful word? It's a kind word, really, and it was so very nice of you to use it." Mitch smiled warmly as he said, "But again, no thanks." He looked around the room as though deciding that this was as good place to die as any. Then he tilted his head, and very gently said, "So then, Jack Wells, I guess this is good-bye. Just keep in mind that you beat the sheriff. If you beat me, it will be Mark Foster who comes for you next. You probably won't enjoy that. He's handsome and friendly, but he's a little bit like a photo-negative of me. He's every bit as ugly as me, but every trace of it is hidden on the inside."

Chapter 31

Jack closed the door behind him and moved down the hall, waiting for Mitch to stand up to run to the door or the window, taking the weight off the trigger of the small IED he'd stolen from Oglethorpe.

He waited.

Almost five minutes passed, and he started to worry. Had Mitch escaped somehow? Gone to sleep? Found a way out of the chair without detonating the bomb? Was it even possible he was saying his prayers? Jack hadn't planned on this much time, which meant he had to start considering that the game might be going in a new direction of Mitch's choosing, and that would be a game in which Jack would have no choice but to once again play catch-up.

Just as he put his hand on the doorknob, he heard the explosion, although the overstuffed cushion under which he'd placed the bomb did a good job of muffling its sound, making it more of a whoosh than a boom.

But Mitch's scream ripped the silence to shreds and sliced time into before and after events, the *before* so much easier on Jack than the *after* in which he heard Mitch suffer horribly but die quickly.

Jack didn't want to open the door. He didn't want to see the mess. He felt exactly the same way he did when he'd shot his first man, frightened to approach as the volunteer soldier writhed on the ground at the small market of his tiny village, holding his guts in his hands, begging for life, begging for help, begging Allah for peace while he begged Jack for another bullet.

Jack put the man's head in his hands and pulled his canteen to give him water.

"Thank you," the man said in Arabic, one of the few phrases Jack had learned his short time in-country. Jack had just cut that poor, untrained, uneducated misguided son-of-a-bitch almost in half with his automatic weapon, and the man had said thank you as Jack's shaking hand sloshed water into his mouth and onto his face.

"I'm sorry," Jack said. "God, I'm so sorry."

The man moved a hand from his guts and put it on Jack's forearm, bloodying his uniform even more as the man's entrails spilled out. He managed a painful smile at Jack through his suffering and his tears.

The man struggled for air, then said, "The peace of Allah be upon you," an Arabic throw-away greeting like "How are you" said dozens of times a day in almost every personal encounter, but said with true meaning by this man who was about to meet his God.

"And the peace of Allah be upon you as well."

As Jack stared into the man's eyes he couldn't help but feel that the two of them could have been friends in any number of other circumstances. But the man's religion had demanded he fight infidels and Jack's country had demanded he kill terrorists, and no one, it seemed, had bothered to even think about building a bridge between those conflicting views. It was just like Mitch said, a narrowness of thinking had caused an enormous gulf in understanding, and lots of people were doomed to die over it.

Jack took a deep breath and pushed open the door, and what he saw almost made him vomit. He'd set the tiny bomb to go off once one hundred pounds of weight was completely off the pressure switch, and he would have shot Mitch if he'd tried to stand while Jack was still in the room. Mitch had no option but to die in that room, and he'd known it as soon as he sat down and felt the trap, probably hearing the click of the actuator. It was a smart way for Jack to do it and he took some pride in that.

But the results were shockingly ugly and impossible to feel good about.

Mitch was face down on the floor about eight feet from the chair. Both his legs had been blown off, along with much of his backside, torn open as yet another hideous example of how horribly a human being can treat his fellow man.

And Jack was the human being who'd done it.

Now that it was over, Jack found little comfort in Mitch's vow to kill him, anymore than the Afghani's wild shots in Jack's direction eased the pain of watching him die in Jack's arms. He wanted to look away from Mitch but wouldn't, because embracing the pain was the way violent people eventually learned to seek peace. At least that's what one of his commanding officers had once said.

Jack could only hope his motives were pure, even as Mitch's intellectual challenges rattled through his brain. But regardless of right and wrong, Jack was once again a violent man who lived a long, long way from peace, and peace would have to wait. Robyn still needed to be found and protected, and Montessa apparently had hired Mark Foster to send someone, or come after him personally, and finish up where Mitch failed. He hoped peace would be waiting for him when all this was over, back on his boat, rocking in the clear blue Gulf of Mexico, a few lines in the water and a beer in his hand.

Jack pulled the sandwich bags out of his pocket and reached into the bloody mess, collecting fibers from Mitch's clothes and plucking a few strands of hair from his head. He almost puked as he scooped blood out of Mitch's open cavity.

Mitch's wallet and keys had been blown out of his pockets, so Jack took the keys and left the card of Special Agent Oglethorpe in the wallet. Then he washed his hands in the sink and didn't look back as he walked out the door.

Chapter 32

"Are you okay?"

Jack barely heard Mike's words as he walked across the parking lot toward him, looking Jack up and down, searching for wounds.

"No, I'm nowhere close to okay."

"Where are you hurt?"

"I'm not hurt. I'm just a long way from being okay."

Mike looked back at the motel room. "Need me to do anything in there? Finish it? Clean up?"

"God, no. I don't want you to see it."

"You killed the man, right? And he had a hand in Jeff's death? So what's your problem?"

"He had nothing to do with Jeff. He was that killer from my past."

Mike held the truck door open for Jack to get in. "Then I'm confused."

"How about just getting us out of here."

"Where to?"

Jack knew he was staring off at nothing, and he knew Mike was waiting for an answer. He just didn't seem to have one. He really didn't care. He just wanted to keep staring out the window, his eyes blurry as his future blended itself with his past and dictated, in at least one dark and watery aspect, his future.

"Jack?"

He barely heard Mike say it. And then there was silence for more than a minute.

"Jack," Mike repeated. "Lieutenant Wells."

"What time is it?"

"Nine. Nearly nine."

"Did Bobby call while I was gone?"

"Yeah. He said Oglethorpe was home."

"Can you find 1071 Susquehanna?"

Mike dug out his phone and typed in the address. "Yeah, no problem."

"Take me there," Jack said, and then he closed his eyes and watched Mitch casually restate his deadly wisdom on the back of his eyelids. Wisdom that made too much sense while Jack looked hard for anything that separated the two men but found too little, leaving him truly dirtier than he'd ever been before. Yet knowing he would get dirtier still before this was over.

He'd found heaven in Marco Island, and this far away it seemed even more of a heaven than he'd ever realized. Found it in the clear water and fresh salt air, the Gulf's underwater escape and the sky's massive nights. But like a summer storm rolling across Florida and darkening that gorgeous sky he loved, he'd gone to Roanoke and brought hell there with him. Mitch's guts, blown all over the room, were a good image of how much bad Jack really had in him.

"We're getting close, Jack. Who lives here? This Oglethorpe character?"

Mitch's voice was still in his ears saying, "I'm sorry, Jack, but you are exactly like me." Jack heard himself say no, but it lacked conviction.

"No what, Jack?"

255

Jack shook himself as he opened his eyes. "Sorry, Mike. I was talking to myself." He forced himself away from the ugly memory. "An FBI agent lives here, Mike. A bad one."

"Did he have anything to do with Jeff's death? You promised me blood, Jack."

The thought of more blood hurt, and the idea of letting Mike finish this business seemed wonderful, especially since Mike was more than up to the challenge and anxious for the chance. But Jack was already bloody. The SWAT team killed the chief, but Mitch was different and nothing would change that. Jack had written the rules, the rules had favored him, and Jack had killed him. Obliterated him. Been absolutely inhuman to him. Even Jack's last minute offer to let Mitch live would never change that.

Jack was already in a dark place doing dark things, whereas Mike had done a pretty good job of leaving his bloody past behind. It had taken years, during which Jack had witnessed the evolution of Mike's transformation. He'd considered himself truly healed after he'd managed to quietly accept shit from an aggressive young kid at a bar, allowing the screaming asshole to get away with what would have caused him some serious fucking injuries in any earlier confrontation with Mike.

Mike had been lucky because he'd had more help than just the V.A. counselors. He'd met a nice single mother his first few months back from Afghanistan. She had some great kids and knew little if anything of Chainsaw. Together they'd built a quiet life running a simple business cleaning swimming pools in Jacksonville, raising the three kids that were now only two. The world had left Mike alone, ignored by anyone he didn't actively want in his life, and that was the way he preferred it. Jack owed him the right to continue that life.

"No," Jack said. "He had nothing to do with Jeff. He is a murderer, though, and I want to plant evidence that he killed Mitch in order to get investigators looking at what else he's done. And to throw investigators off my scent."

"It's the next block."

"Make another lap. I've got to make a call. Did you charge my phone?"

"It's right over there."

Jack nodded as he pulled up the number.

"This is Supervisory Special Agent Albert Grayson."

"Gray, it's Wells."

"Jack, I'm glad you called. Matthews cancelled SWAT. He said he told you. Is that right?"

"Yes."

"He outranks me, man. I'm sorry."

"You did your best. Is CODE all over your ass now?"

"They stopped just short of a tiny spot on my left rump when you gave up SA Oglethorpe, figuring you had to be a little better than they first thought. But yeah, other than that little spot they've been all over it. I've got a small ass, though, so it doesn't take longer than I can handle. Did you listen to the wiretap?"

"Yes. Thank you."

"It pissed me off to hear them talk about your family without knowing shit about the truth, Jack. Sorry you had to hear their stupidity, but listen, White Collar Crime ran your list of names and found lots of money from unexplained sources squirreled away in fairly hard to trace places. Without the Patriot Act and all its revisions that required overseas banking compliance, they would never have found any of it."

"I was pretty sure it wasn't just Special Agent Oglethorpe."

"Their stories aren't even close to being similar."

"Oglethorpe said on the wiretap that he took Robyn. Any ideas where he might have taken her?" Jack looked at Mike and scribbled in the air with his finger. Mike handed him a pad and a pen. "I'm ready."

"Oglethorpe and his wife own a home on Susquehanna that—"

"Robyn's not there. Where else?"

"I sent you the tape as soon as we got it. There wasn't much time to narrow the possibilities enough for a high-confidence guess. The Oglethorpe name shows up nearly a hundred times in public records, dating back to an Oglethorpe buying a farm in the late 1800's."

"Keep checking for something remote."

"Why just remote?"

"Because this area has lots of remote places. Besides, I'm betting she'd find a way to attract attention if she was in the city or around people."

"Jack, she could be gagged or…well, she could be gagged. Let's leave it at that."

"Oglethorpe took her as insurance, as leverage against me. You heard what he said. That's how Oglethorpe works. He kept stuff over the chief's head, too. Does the family still own the farm?"

"That was my first bet, but no."

"Okay, keep looking. Can you assemble a team and have them stand by with laptops when I get something?"

"You know I can, and you know I will. There's enough of our old squad still here. Every one of us will run the risk of throwing in with you on this."

"In that case have Oglethorpe arrested in exactly thirty minutes." He checked his watch for the time. "Look behind the back wall of his garage for more than enough evidence to send him away for life. Watch for explosives. Pass the word that he was EOD."

"Got it."

"Also, there's a dead guy in a motel east of town that I think Oglethorpe killed, and I don't think he's smart enough to have done it without leaving some kind of evidence."

"And how do you happen to know there's a dead guy in a motel east of town?"

"I went to a friend's room to meet him, but the dead guy was there. It's Mitch."

"Mitch. Really? And you expect me to believe that our man Oglethorpe had the stones to take him on, and then manage to kill him?"

"He was killed by a bomb. It's feasible."

"Oh."

"Just start there and see where your investigation goes."

Gray was silent, and Jack knew he was quietly pondering Jack's lie, worrying about his career, worrying about the recording device catching every word and inflection, worrying about the debt he owed Jack Wells, who he had to know killed Mitch.

"I guess I can see Oglethorpe killing Mitch. They both worked for Montessa, right?"

"Yes."

"They were rivals on some level, I suppose."

"Not just rivals, but rivals who probably knew enough about each other to send the other to prison."

"That sounds like plenty of motive to me. Okay, we'll get on it."

"Thanks, Gray. I've got to go."

"Be careful, Jack. Thirty minutes for Oglethorpe?"

"Twenty-nine now, exactly. No stopping to sightsee." As Jack hung up he turned to Mike. "Let me out here."

"Okay, but I wish I knew what you had up your sleeve."

Jack made sure Mitch's hairs, fibers, and blood were still in the plastic bags in his pocket. "I'm just making it up as I go."

"I don't believe it, not for a second."

"Just wait in your truck down the street from the house."

Jack got out and walked the rest of the way to Oglethorpe's, past trees in the fresh green of spring and plants that were plump with buds or already covered with flowers. He climbed the steps to the porch and rang the bell. It was plenty early for friends but a little late for strangers, and the look on the face of the pretty woman who answered, all smiling and pleasant, turned cautious when she realized she didn't know him.

"I'm Jack Wells."

The name meant something to her, but she couldn't place it.

"Is your husband home?"

"Why, yes he is. It is a bit late, though. Can I ask what this is about?"

He was a bad man for bringing all this to her door. She probably knew nothing of what her husband had done, and couldn't possibly anticipate that everything the two of them had built together, and everything they'd ever planned together, was about to disappear. It had to be that way, but Jack couldn't shake the feeling that he was the grim reaper or an angel of death at her door.

As if being an angel had anything to do with it.

"Just tell him Jack Wells is here to see him." Then he slowly said it again. "Jack Wells."

She recoiled. "Jack Wells? Why…why you're the one—"

As if by instinct her hand eased the door closed as she recognized the threat Jack posed. He smiled, relieved that now she knew. He tried to look unthreatening but it had no effect on her.

"He's in the garage. Wait on the porch, please, and I'll let him know you're here."

"Thank you."

Jack sat down in the swing and waited, the sun long gone and the moon sneaking over the horizon, the thought of longer days and later sunsets a good thought on Jack's mind as summer approached and the country switched to Daylight Savings Time. Jack wanted that additional light, as he always did, but now more than usual. He didn't want to accept a renewed fear of the dark and the night terrors that used to wait for him there like predators.

"What are you doing here?" came a voice from behind him.

Jack didn't move. He waited calmly as Oglethorpe came around to the front steps, stepping slowly, his gun out and carefully aimed.

"Take it easy there, Oglethorpe. There's no need for that." Now Jack stood slowly. "Unless you know something I don't."

"It's an instinct, and a good one."

"Maybe too instinctive."

"I don't think so. Not when there's a Blue Alert out for you. And I'd also be willing to bet you tricked the SWAT team into killing our chief of police, although I seem to be all alone in that opinion."

"Your chief was killed by his own men, and the Blue Alert is a lie. You were the liar, in which case you know I'm innocent. Yet you still chose to draw a weapon on me. Perhaps your instinct is driven more by guilt than intuition."

Oglethorpe glanced at the window from where his wife was watching. He lowered his weapon but didn't holster it. "You broke into my garage yesterday?"

Jack looked at the window too. "Do you really want your wife to hear all this from me? She's going to learn soon enough that you're dirty, but do you want to do that now? I was planning to let you be the one to tell her the truth."

"Keep your voice down. Let's go into my office." He holstered his weapon and walked up the steps.

"Your Bureau office is here in your home? That's unusual."

Oglethorpe opened the door and stopped, looked at his wife and then pointed Jack toward a side room with a much better lock. "Headquarters authorized it," he said as he closed and locked the door behind them.

"Lucky you."

"I had nothing to do with the Blue Alert, Wells."

"Lie to me all you want. It doesn't matter."

"I swear to you that I didn't."

"I really don't care."

"Oh." He looked shocked. "Then…well, what can I help you with? Why are you here?"

Jack put his hands in his pockets as he moved around the room. Oglethorpe was off balance, so it was time to plant evidence. "I want to find a woman and thought you might be able to help."

"A woman, huh? The FBI is now a dating service?" He made an unconvincing laugh.

"Robyn Thomas."

Oglethorpe wasn't able to hide that the name meant a great deal to him. He drew back a little, and while he struggled for words Jack dropped a couple of Mitch's hairs and some fibers from Mitch's clothes on a lightweight jacket Oglethorpe had thrown across a chair, then gently moved it so he could sit down, leaving a small smear of Mitch's blood on the zipper before wiping the excess on the inside of it.

"I heard about her disappearance on last night's news, along with that old woman getting killed."

"You know where she is," Jack said as he leaned forward in the chair and slid Bobby's transmitter under it. "Don't bother to lie about it."

"How would I know?"

"You better not have hurt her." Jack swallowed hard before saying, "You better not have killed her."

"You're talking crazy."

"I don't think so, not when I'm talking to a man making lots of money killing environmentalists who challenge Montessa."

Oglethorpe's eyes moved back and forth, watching Jack's hands, looking at the door, glancing out the window, checking Jack's eyes.

"If you're here to make some kind of half-assed citizen's arrest, you'll regret it, because I honestly don't know what you're talking about. And since I didn't do anything wrong there can't be any evidence against me."

Maybe it was just exhaustion catching up to Jack, or relief from what he'd done, but for some reason he wanted to laugh. And so he did. Oglethorpe was denying the existence of proof at the exact time Jack was planting it. Out of all the murders Oglethorpe had done for Montessa, Mitch's death, something he had nothing to do with, would be the one that opened the door to his convictions. Oglethorpe's hidden room of files and illegal explosives, and the scrutiny he would come under as a suspect in Mitch's death, would certainly reveal the other murders, and he would go to jail forever.

Jack was still laughing as he rose and walked over to Oglethorpe, his laugh and the intensity in his eyes so badly at odds that Oglethorpe looked thoroughly confused.

"Where's Robyn Thomas?"

"I said I don't know."

Jack took a step back and looked him over. Then he stepped right back into his face, his smile completely gone. "One last time, where's Robyn Thomas?"

"Nothing's changed from ten seconds ago, Wells. I said I don't know and I don't."

It was time for Jack's big gamble, a gamble so risky that it frightened Jack more than waiting for Mitch.

"I'll leave it at that for now, Oglethorpe. But if I ever find out that you lied to me, even if it's after I get her safely back, you're a dead man. I'll come back and kill you and leave the vivisected parts of your body for your family to find at breakfast. You got that?"

"You do realize you're threatening a federal agent."

"Absolutely I do. And you do realize I'm not a man who makes threats he doesn't plan to back up?"

Oglethorpe nodded, probably without even realizing he was doing it. Jack waited. Oglethorpe stared. Jack didn't move.

Finally Oglethorpe turned his head. "Yeah, I do know that about you, but listen, I had nothing to do with whatever happened to her."

"Just like the Blue Alert."

"I really had nothing to do with that."

"You're a terrible liar, Oglethorpe."

Jack walked to the door, looking around the room before opening it. "I'll find my own way out. A friend of mine with a nasty background is parked down the street with instructions to follow you if you leave here. If you call the police about my visit, I'll join them and show them what you've got hidden in your garage."

Oglethorpe was already making plans, Jack could hear it in his voice as he distractedly said, "Fine."

"Have a nice day, Special Agent Oglethorpe."

Chapter 33

Jack walked down the street and up to the open window of Mike's truck. "Are you any good at following people?"

Mike shrugged. "I've got no earthly idea. I've never done it before."

"Leave plenty of distance but not too much. Anticipate him trying to dry clean you so that you don't follow him on those dead turns. It's hard in an unfamiliar area but good luck. The map on your phone will help."

"Thanks. What am I following?"

"Any car that pulls away from the house I was just at."

"Where will you be?"

Jack wasn't exactly sure, but he was pretty confident that Oglethorpe wouldn't be stupid or brave enough to leave the house. Which meant Mike would remain safely out of the way and un-bloodied, parked on this shady residential street waiting for something that was never going to happen.

"Keep your phone handy so I can call you for help."

"Will do."

As Jack turned to walk away, Mike said, "Be careful, Jack. It can be a bad world out there."

"Don't forget it can also be a beautiful one," Jack said over his shoulder as he walked to the end of the street and turned the corner. A half block later he got into Bobby's van.

"Getting anything?"

"I hear him breathing, Lieutenant. Where'd you put the transmitter?"

"Under a chair."

"I'm getting a good signal but I'm not hearing anything."

"If it doesn't work the State Police and FBI are monitoring every phone either Oglethorpe brother owns, so we'll still get the news. This will be faster, though, I hope."

"Where's Chainsaw?"

"I asked him to stay and watch Oglethorpe's house."

Bobby shook his head. "It's your call to make, Lieutenant, but my guess is we're rushing toward trouble. Isn't that what you expect?"

"Pretty much."

"Then I'd feel better having Chainsaw along. Hell, anyone would."

"I know. I've got him standing by, though. He'll come and help if we need him."

Bobby laughed. "Sure he will if he has the chance, but you and I and Chainsaw all know better, Lieutenant. Whatever complicated scheme you've got going will all come together in minutes. You think we didn't get some insight into how your mind works?"

Jack looked at him and smiled. "I'm pretty tired, Bobby, but I hope I'm thinking straight enough to live up to your image of me. There are a lot of players, though, and even I'm having trouble managing them all."

"I'm sure you're up to it. You were tired in Kabul but pulled it off, even though every single one of us thought you were leading us to certain death."

Jack was surprised. "No one said that to me at the time. Why did you still follow?"

"Because you've got a weird way of getting things done that we'd learned to trust. Those of us who lived are alive because of it."

"It's the best way I know. Did you talk to Claire? Did she confirm with the State Police?"

"She's totally onboard, and yes she did. She has all the same facts we have and is standing by for the last few details."

"Worried about her job?"

"She says she isn't. Says she'll do whatever you ask of her. Anything to end what Montessa is doing, and to avenge her boyfriend."

"You know that her boyfriend was also Chainsaw's son, right?"

"I know. I refer to him as her boyfriend to keep people's motives straight. If I ever talk about it to Mike, I'll call Jeff his son. Makes it easier for me. I don't have your complex a brain."

Jack laughed a little. "Lucky you. It's as much a curse as. . ."

He stopped as Oglethorpe's voice came over the speakers of Bobby's sound van. "Richard," he said, which was pretty much what Jack expected, because calling his brother, his confederate, his partner in crime, is exactly what Jack would have done.

"It was a mistake to take the woman," Oglethorpe continued. "She's no leverage at all on Wells, but when he finds out I took her he'll kill me."

Jack listened, guessing at what the other Oglethorpe would say, while Bobby kept recording it all just in case Jack wanted to replay it.

"No question it needs to be done, Richard, but get the guys you have guarding her to do it, and do it now. I'm stuck here with somebody watching my house to make sure I don't leave."

Jack touched Bobby's arm. "Get ready to call Claire for me."

"Don't fuck this up, Richard. I'm not even close to kidding. This Wells asshole will cut me into little pieces if he finds any trace of her, and the only leverage I'll have then will be you. So make sure she's dead, and not just dead, but dead and gone. Have your guys make sure her body disappears far away from the cabin or I'll have no choice but to give you up to Wells."

Jack pulled himself away from Oglethorpe's conversation, picked up his phone and pushed send.

"This is Supervisory Special Agent Grayson."

"Gray, it's Jack."

"Jack, I'm ready with Stephen, Dan, and Kathryn, all here with laptops open to records and data bases."

"Thanks. State Police are standing by?"

"Standing by."

"She's at a cabin, Gray. We're looking for a cabin in or near Roanoke that Oglethorpe owns or has access to. Hurry."

He looked at Bobby and wanted to tell him to get moving. He wanted to tell the team at Headquarters to search faster. But neither would help and he knew it, so he kept his mouth shut and tried to stay calm, looking out the window at the incredible trees and the clear night sky, with two young boys having a game of catch under the street light while their mother looked on from the porch. One kid had a pretty good arm, and for just a second Jack thought about his decision to walk away from baseball.

"Kathryn's got something, Jack."

"Kathryn, go!"

"Here it is, Jack. There's a Richard Oglethorpe who owns a cabin at Smith Mountain Lake. I've got the full legal for later, but what you need right now is the address."

"Shoot."

"419 River Creek Road."

"419 River Creek Road," Jack repeated for Bobby as he punched the numbers into MapQuest.

"I've brought it up on Google Earth," Kathryn continued. "The cabin is very isolated, way up off the lake near the ridgeline. I see a fence and a heavy gate across the driveway."

"Thanks everyone. Gray, get the State Police going right now. Oglethorpe just gave orders for Robyn to be killed and her body gone. Later, Kathryn. Thanks."

"You be careful, Jack. Seven minutes and my men will be at Oglethorpe's home to arrest him."

"Bobby, call Claire and tell her to make the news public."

MapQuest located the address of the cabin and stuck a pin in it. Jack pointed his hand straight ahead and said, "And go, Bobby, go, go, go."

Bobby tore off, talking to Claire on his phone and focusing on driving while Jack said nothing to distract him. He was thinking, planning, trying to stay ahead and stay calm, analyzing the trees and weather, guessing at the vegetation at the lake, wanting to factor the density of the underbrush and the clearness of the sky into whatever he might do.

Roanoke was truly a beautiful place, like most other places he'd gone to war, whether in Battle Dress Utilities or a business suit or a SWAT uniform. Beauty really could be found everywhere. Except in what he was about to do.

Chapter 34

As Bobby raced out of town, Jack tuned Sirius XM to CNN Headline News, where an angry woman was talking about the poisoning of her dog by a drunken neighbor.

There was a special tone, followed by a very professional voice that said, "This is CNN Breaking News."

A pause, and then, "Good evening, this is Claire Statler with an update on a fast-moving story CNN has been following since a Blue Alert was issued for former FBI Agent Jack Wells."

Jack was suddenly worried because he knew the road they were traveling. He'd driven it when he'd gone to Montessa, which meant the cabin was probably close to their facility, which meant it was much too close to where SILT was stationed.

"MapQuest says to take the next right, Bobby, then go straight for two blocks and then turn. Follow that road until you hit River Creek Road, where you'll turn right."

"Robyn Thomas," Claire continued, "a lawyer and litigator for Sierra Club's Roanoke Office, was reported missing by co-workers, and police initially suspected foul play involving Jack Wells. But Miss Thomas is now believed to have been kidnapped and currently held against her will at a cabin at Smith Mountain Lake, near Roanoke, Virginia.

"A confidential but highly reliable source of this reporter," Claire said, already positioning herself to take the blame if Jack somehow managed to be completely wrong about everything, "has provided information that the cabin is owned by Richard Oglethorpe, Vice-President of Montessa Chemical Corporation, which is a frequent legal target of the Sierra Club because of its history of egregious violations of the Environmental Protection Act. The cabin is also reported to be used often by Richard's brother, Roger Oglethorpe, who is currently a Special Agent of the Federal Bureau of Investigation, assigned to Roanoke, Virginia.

"A reliable source has stated that FBI Special Agent Roger Oglethorpe is now the primary suspect in multiple murders-for-hire related to Montessa Chemicals, and will be arrested within minutes at his Roanoke home. This reporter has also confirmed that troopers from the Virginia State Police have been standing by on high-alert, ready to effect a rescue of Miss Thomas, and are at this very moment en route to the Smith Mountain Lake cabin."

"Is that what you wanted from Claire, Lieutenant?"

"You two did great, Bobby. That's sure to have ratcheted up the pressure."

"But why broadcast that the State Police are already on their way?"

"I'm hoping those SILT assholes back at Montessa are listening and will decide to stay home instead of reinforcing whoever is stationed at the cabin. Or at least hesitating a few minutes to argue about it. Now that I realize how close they are, I'm even more hopeful it works."

"I doubt they operate that way 'cause they certainly weren't trained like that. Besides, they've probably shot it out with lots of government guys around the world before."

"If nothing else it might stall them enough to work out a survivable plan. That alone might give me or the troopers enough time to get Robyn."

"I hope you're right, but I doubt you are if they're as close as you say."

"I doubt it too, but I have very few tools left to work with other than pressure. No guarantees, just doing the best I can. Here's River Creek Road so slow down. The cabin's not far."

Jack looked out the window and tried to see if there were lights up on the ridgeline, but the trees were too thick to see more than a hundred feet or so into them.

"Jesus, that cabin's going to be hard to find in those woods."

"It might be impossible," Bobby said as he slowed down to nothing. "But Kathryn said it has a driveway. Want me to drive us right up to the front door and then get out and knock?"

He looked at Jack and they both laughed. Then Jack said, "Go ahead and stop here."

Bobby eased to a stop and Jack got out. Everything was quiet. No other vehicles were on the road. There were no sirens and no helicopters. The only sounds were the buzzing of bugs, a branch scraping a nearby tree in the breeze, and a dog barking far across the lake.

"I guess we're the first ones to the party," Jack said. He dropped the magazine from Oglethorpe's Beretta and counted the rounds before slamming it back into the weapon. "You don't happen to have a gun in the van, do you?"

"I never carry, Lieutenant. Sorry."

"No problem. Now listen carefully, Bobby. I want you to park in that neighbor's driveway right over there, all the way up by their garage so as not to be noticed. Walk back to the road and wait for the State Police. When they get here, let them know I'm moving toward the cabin. Tell them what I look like and what I'm wearing."

Bobby looked him over. "You're going to need my help up there, Lieutenant. You know you are."

272

"You're unarmed, and besides, you'll be much more help to me down here." Jack swallowed hard as he looked out over the lake, appreciating the beauty of the moon reflecting off it, and thinking how much he would like to camp beside it someday. He captured that thought as a goal for his future. "If the State Police don't know I'm up there, they might shoot me by mistake."

Bobby's head was down. "Got it, Lieutenant. I'll make sure they don't mistake you for a deer." He looked up and smiled. "Or SILT."

"And make sure to tell them that Oglethorpe was EOD, and to move slowly, expecting trip wires. I'm sure expecting them."

"Yes, sir."

"And Bobby?"

"Yes, Lieutenant."

"If SILT gets here first, promise you'll stay out of sight. I'll still need you to update the State Police. You have to understand how important that is. I need you to promise me you'll stay put."

Jack turned and spotted an animal trail through the fence and into the woods. He wanted to get going but wouldn't until he had an answer from Bobby.

He turned back to the van. "Bobby?"

Bobby was up in his seat, looking like he'd just been cheated. "It's just not right, Lieutenant. We stand together or we go down as one and you know that better than anyone."

Jack hardened both his face and his voice as he said, "God damn you, Bobby, I said for you to stay here and that is an order!"

Chapter 35

"Shit," Jack said softly as he flopped into the weeds, still several hundred feet from the cabin. "You guys just couldn't stay away, could you?"

He didn't move a muscle as he listened to a big truck dieseling at the gate while someone unlocked it. Then he watched the truck roll up the long gravel drive, with SILT men jumping out of the back every twenty feet, each one taking a position to cover the others, their weapons ready and their eyes open, showing solid training, experience, and professionalism. They were true soldiers, no doubt, battle-tested and bad ass.

There was no way Jack could win this fight and he knew it. He hated to accept that, but with SILT putting more boots on the ground he had no choice but to dig in and wait for the State Police. Where were they? Had he planned things badly, or moved too fast? Had he let some feeling for Robyn or some loyalty to Mike make him a careless fool rushing ahead of good judgment?

It didn't matter if it was true or not because he sure felt that way. As the SILT team set up their fields of fire with absolute precision while a couple of others slipped toward the cabin, it was crystal clear that this was his big failure. He'd done well up to this point, but none of that mattered.

SILT would kill Robyn, take her body and any evidence that she'd ever been in the cabin, and be gone before the State Police arrived.

There was no way he could have guessed that Oglethorpe's cabin was so close to Montessa's facilities, but he was surprised they didn't care that the State Police were on their way. But as he watched them set up their lethal ambushes it was easy to understand. They simply weren't afraid. They would ambush and kill the State Police Troopers and then expatriate themselves as wealthy men, leaving Montessa, as usual, to deny its involvement in the whole affair. One, two, three, over and done.

But something about it didn't quite fit, and although Jack knew it he just couldn't put his finger on why.

He heard talking near the cabin, but no gunshots or screams or sounds of a struggle, and that's when it hit him that they wouldn't kill Robyn there. They would treat her well so she would cooperate somewhat with their moving her somewhere sterile to kill her, and they would move her as soon as they'd cleaned up every trace of her ever being there. Which meant she would go down that very road, alive. Which meant Jack still had a chance.

What tools do you have, Jack? came the calm voice in his head that he heard only at times like these. *Relax, Jack. Take a deep breath. Now, what do you have that you can use?*

"I've got Bobby," he whispered as he watched one SILT signal to another. "Assuming they didn't slit his throat as they went by him."

Bobby's definitely a well-trained combatant.

"But I don't want him killed."

Okay, the voice said without questioning the decision. *Leave Bobby out of it for now. What else?*

"Robyn might be of some help if I get to the cabin."

Maybe if you get to the cabin, but she's no help to you now.

275

"I can try to delay SILT until the State Police arrive."

How long could you hold out with fifteen rounds of ammo and Blondie's knife? How many could you pin down? How long would it take for the others to work around behind you and take you out?

"Not long."

Of course not long.

"But if I could get close enough to kill one of them with the knife, I could take his weapon and widen that window. They're all carrying MP-5s and I'm betting they're full auto. The State Police can't be far. I don't need long."

That's a bad plan, Jack.

"I know."

But if that's all you've got...

Jack pulled out Blondie's big knife and moved immediately, sliding on his belly toward the closest SILT, moving as slowly as when he'd taken out an armed Afghan sentry who turned out to be a fourteen year old kid, using the thick mountain laurel as cover, getting close to the SILT sniper in a prone position behind a blotch of brush that provided not only concealment, but also a clear shot at the road if the State Police drove up it. Jack slowed as he got closer. So close that he heard the man breathing.

Jack waited, the Beretta in his waist band, the knife in his right hand, and his left hand empty, ready to snap back the SILT's head so he could jam the knife quickly from under his chin all the way through his brain. But all his training in the technique had assumed that the enemy would be on his feet, and Jack couldn't quite work out the dynamics for scrambling the brains of an enemy on the ground.

He thought about grabbing the man's feet and jerking him back, then smashing his head with a rock, making sure to break his jaw in the process so he couldn't shout. But that was too risky. If the sniper managed to yell first or get off a shot, SILT would be all over Jack and he would die before he did any good at all.

He couldn't see much of the cabin, but he had a pretty good idea where the rest of the SILT team was, and none of them were very close to the rear guard defending the driveway. He could wait for an opportunity before he moved. With luck, the State Police would arrive and he'd get a chance to attack on whatever signal they gave.

He watched three SILTs move slowly into the trees down along the driveway, probing, looking hard, not wanting to get blown up by Oglethorpe's explosives. Jack crept ridiculously close to the sniper, the two of them watching the road together until the sniper moved and Jack froze.

The sniper eased his way up to his knees, just erect enough take a piss. His dick was in his hand as Jack lunged for him, drawing back the knife as the SILT desperately tried to swing his long rifle toward Jack, both of them getting close when the SILT slipped and fell backward and then...Boom!

The blast blew the SILT's body into Jack, protecting him even as it threw him to the ground. Jack dug into the dirt and covered his head with his hands as the bombshell of blood and dirt covered him.

God damn it, Oglethorpe really had mined the area. Jack could hardly believe it. Even as remote as the cabin was, a deer or bear could have set off a mine and got the police out there, and they would have found Robyn. Except, of course, that Oglethorpe and the police were working together.

SILTs were shouting, confused and taking wild shots while Jack wiped blood off his hands and onto his pants and then pushed aside the sniper's bull-barreled rifle so he could grab his MP-5 and his ammo. He cautiously moved ten feet away and scraped himself up against a big tree.

He wanted to get as far away from the dead SILT as possible before the others got close, make a dash through the trees to another place of concealment where it might take SILT a few minutes to find him. But he forced himself to stay tight against the back of the tree because he was safer there.

It took about fifteen seconds for the first round to hit near him, a carefully placed shot with the aid of night vision that came way too close as it tapped through the leaves and made Jack flinch. Then whichever SILT spotted him and whistled off that round told the others, and all hell broke loose as bullets splintered the bark off the tree and cut down the nearby foliage.

Jack kept tight against the tree as he stuck the barrel of the MP-5 around it and fired blindly, full auto as he sprayed the area, hoping other SILTs would duck and run, moving quickly and recklessly enough to...

Boom! Another explosion, but Jack couldn't see if a man was down or not, and he didn't have time to care. He hosed down the area with bullets to either get them moving or to keep their heads down, the suppressive fire keeping them away as he emptied magazine after magazine, not stopping as another bomb went off and a man screamed in pain.

But things got decidedly worse when he heard the order and timing of professionalism take the place of SILT's erratic and unfocused firing. Someone had assumed command and was giving orders with precision. They were coming for him now with a strategy, probably a well-rehearsed strategy involving moving, covering, and advancing, leap-frogging one another to keep their firing constant.

Jack scanned for wires as he searched for a path toward the thick walls of the cabin, but couldn't see well enough in the dark and couldn't afford to get blown up yet. He looked at the driveway and the SILT van, and thought he saw a clear path to the truck, which probably still had the keys in it and might provide him a way to the cabin. If he could get inside the cabin and kill whoever had Robyn, he could probably use the cabin's log walls to survive the attack until the State Police arrived, assuming that absolutely everything went perfectly in his favor.

He reloaded the MP-5 and put it in his left hand, his Beretta, loaded with all its rounds, in his right. He was about to make a break for the SILT van when Bobby raced up the driveway in his CNN truck, passing the van and heading straight toward the cabin, weaving through the intense rain of fire that shattered through the windshield until he lost control and crashed into a tree.

"Oh god, Bobby, no," Jack said softly, and then he suddenly jumped out into the open and started running toward the cabin, no longer worrying about trip wires or getting shot or anything other than killing the men who'd killed Bobby. Barely even thinking about Robyn, really, or Jeff, as Mitch egged him on in his head, laughing manically while shouting how motivated Jack was by vengeance.

A shooter turned away from Bobby's van to aim at him, but Jack tripped over a vine and disappeared from view into the overgrowth. He dropped the MP-5 as he went down but immediately scrambled for the gun, his hands digging into the ground as the SILT ran towards him, firing as he closed in until Jack grabbed for his Beretta and shot straight up into him, then grabbed his automatic and got on his feet and ran faster, killing another SILT who fired a burst that missed, going even faster as he shot him a second time in passing, then blasted away at another SILT who ducked behind the cabin as Jack got close, but then detonated a bomb that blew him back out into the open where Jack, still moving and still shooting and still alive, shot the man's lifeless body twice more for good measure.

Before he really even knew it, Jack was behind the cabin, protected by its walls. He looked up toward the ridge for a high-ground shooter but no SILT had had time to get there yet.

Suddenly the firing intensified as though the skirmish in the woods had escalated to war, and Jack was happy as shit to hear a helicopter roar overhead and blast its search-light into the darkness.

"Robyn," he shouted. "It's Jack! Are you in there?"

"Yes," a man's voice said. "She's in here."

"Okay listen to me. Leave. Okay? Just run away before the troopers arrive, or go out unarmed and surrender. Let her live and I promise I won't hurt you."

Nothing. Then Jack heard the door creak open.

"Run," Jack said. "Go now, but if you hurt her I'll kill you."

"Okay, I'm coming—"

A gun blast came from the inside the cabin. Jack ran to the front door, dropping the MP-5 as he drew his pistol in preparation for close quarter combat, taking the front steps in one leap, bursting through the opening, his heart pounding and his lungs burning, looking for his target, adjusting his eyes to the diminished light, having trouble seeing for a few seconds, then zeroing in on a pistol aimed in his direction. He was ready to shoot but didn't as Robyn sharpened into focus in the smoky dimness behind it.

His training demanded that he hold aim on her as he glanced at the man on the floor. "He's got to be dead," he said. "Clean head shot."

She was staring at the pistol as if amazed by what it could do.

"I sure hope he's dead. The bastard."

Jack looked in her eyes and saw the pure hate of a victim toward her kidnapper.

"You did right, Robyn. Really, you did. Are you okay?"

A voice blasted over the helicopter's speaker and demanded that SILT drop their weapons and approach the road slowly with their hands on their heads.

Robyn kept staring at the man bleeding out through the hole she'd made in his skull. "All I did was pick it up when he dropped it. I don't remember, I mean…I've never shot a man…it's just…Jack?"

Jack's mind raced as he kept his gun on her and slowly moved to get it, knowing too many stories of people shot by someone accidentally sending an auto-loaded bullet sizzling down a barrel.

"Slowly hand me the weapon, Robyn. Be gentle. No pressure anywhere on it."

She reached toward him and carefully placed it in his open hand, her stare still stuck on the dead man on the floor.

"Look away, Robyn."

She didn't look away, so he stepped between her and the body and blocked her view. She shuffled a little as she put her arms around him, and for the first time he noticed the long chain attached to shackles on her ankles.

"It's over, Robyn. It's all over."

She said nothing as she turned both their bodies in order to take another look at the man she'd killed. Jack tried to turn her back, but she wouldn't be moved.

Jack couldn't protect her from this. All he could do was warn her about the nightmares, the doubt, the regret. Regardless of how justified a shooting was, he wished he could tell her some night over wine or while staring at the stars, once you killed a man you would never be the same.

Chapter 36

State Troopers had Bobby's body out of the van and covered up on the drive when Jack walked out unarmed with his hands up. Two SILTs stood nearby in handcuffs, staring at the white sheet covering Bobby. One made a joke and the other laughed.

Jack walked over to hit him, but a trooper stopped him. "You're Jack Wells?"

"Are these assholes the only two left?"

He looked Jack over with respect before saying, "We're still collecting bodies, but you did some good shooting and we did some good shooting so I doubt we'll find more survivors."

"Good."

"I'm Trooper Williams. It's nice to meet you, sir."

"It would have been nice if we'd met earlier." He looked down at Bobby's covered body. "While Bobby was still alive."

The Trooper looked at Bobby, too. "His name's Bobby, huh? Last name?"

"Dotson. Why?"

"No big reason, really. I just like to remember the names of men like that."

"Meaning?"

"Your man there, Bobby, gave us an accurate situation report when we arrived and waited until we were squared away before saying something about creating a diversion. Then he jumped in that van of his and took off up the driveway like a madman. We couldn't stop him so we just raced along behind."

Jack bit his lip before saying, "It was stupid of him."

"Brave, though, and it made our job pretty easy." He nodded to the two SILTs under arrest. "When those guys took to firing at him it helped us identify where all of our targets were. Like I said, it was pretty easy pickings after that."

Jack turned away, searching for something else to think about. Something good. Something pretty. Something he might find hopeful. He looked through a clearing toward the lake and saw a small boat out in the middle of it. In the moonlight it looked like a man and a boy were fishing, and Jack hung onto the image like a life ring because this whole battle was now over and Jack once again had a future, and that future had his own boat in it, a boat that was back at the dock waiting to head out into the clear Gulf waters that would figure just as powerfully into the rest of his life as they always had.

"Are you all right, sir?"

"Yes, Trooper Williams. Do you know if the FBI arrested Oglethorpe?"

"They did. We sent three troopers as support but there wasn't any fight in him. He went quietly."

"How about his brother?"

"Not yet. Neither your guys or ours could find him at Montessa. He'd said he was going to his boat, so we've got men standing by at the marina. We'll get him."

Jack gave Williams a hard look. "Tell me something, Williams, and be honest because I'm far too tired for bullshit. Are you clean or are you dirty? Not just you, but the State Police."

Williams was insulted. Jack couldn't have cared less.

Williams looked at each of his men and then back at Jack. "I guess it's a fair question after what you've been through with the local police. But I think we're clean, Wells, and I know for damn sure that I am."

"How do you know about me and the chief?"

"I didn't really know for sure. We've been hearing things, that's all. Bits and pieces. Clues we were slowly piecing together."

"Williams, if you knew before now that the chief and the Oglethorpe brothers were corrupt, and you did nothing to stop it, it makes you dirty, plain and simple. There's no grey area."

"It isn't like what you think, Wells. We were already building cases to arrest them. You just beat us to it."

"But you've allowed all this," Jack swept his arm wide to take in not only the lake, but that entire region of Virginia, "to happen right under your nose. How in God's name can you live with that?"

Williams looked at Jack and then looked at the two live SILTs, the bloodied bodies of their teammates lining the road and their cache of military weapons piled up nearby.

"I don't know, sir. I really don't know. I guess I'd probably call it a disgrace if I were standing in your shoes, but we had to operate within the law so as not to be like them."

Jack was starting to realize how tired he was from getting so little sleep while gallons of adrenaline raced continuously through his body.

"Just fix it, Williams. See that it stops here."

"I will, Wells."

Jack turned and shuffled back toward the cabin. A trooper had freed Robyn from her leg irons and chain, and stood beside her on the porch.

"Wells!"

Jack turned back to Williams, suddenly so tired that his muscles were starting to shake as the go-juice flushed itself out of them.

"Yeah, Williams?"

"You're a brave man, Wells." He make another quick glance around. "And you do real good work. Thanks for your help."

"Anytime," Jack said, but he was far too tired to mean it.

Chapter 37

Jack woke up slowly in an unfamiliar bed in an unfamiliar room with unfamiliar pictures on top of the dresser and hanging on the walls. But good old familiar sunlight flooded through the windows, and a nice breeze came with it.

"Hi."

He turned slowly and was surprised to see Robyn sitting in a chair with a legal pad in her lap.

"You are quite a sleeper, Captain Jack Wells."

He rubbed the crud out of his eyes. "How long have I been I asleep? And where's Mike?"

"He's with Bobby's body at the hospital." She looked away, but then came back. "It was weird for me to meet him."

"I bet it was."

"I had no idea he was here. He's not at all the way Jeff described his father."

Jack yawned, and it felt good to have slept and to wake up refreshed. "Yeah, how so?"

"Jeff always made it clear that he loved and admired his step dad, but he always said Mike was very tough. Unyielding was the word he used more than once, although he said Mike mostly applied it to himself."

"Mike is tough. Especially on himself, just like Jeff said."

"You know him better than me, but the Mike I met seems like more of a peaceful spirit. I can imagine a bad-ass in there someplace, I guess, but to me he seemed kind of sweet."

It was good to hear her say that about Mike because it offset some of his guilt over Bobby. But what Bobby did was Bobby's choice, and so Jack would focus on having kept Mike away from the violence. He hadn't even wanted Mike to come to Roanoke, and he definitely hadn't wanted him to get bloody.

"I'll tell him you said that."

"He lost a son." She looked sad and then looked away. "He won't find much happiness in a compliment from me."

"True enough."

"He said Jeff would be cremated. Promised to let me know when they had the memorial service so that I could attend. Some others from Sierra will surely come, too. And you've been asleep almost fourteen hours."

"Damn. I wanted to be the one to tell Bobby's family what happened. I missed that chance, huh?"

Robyn looked down. "Mike called his wife. She's on her way."

Jack looked around the room and out the window again. "I don't have the slightest memory of coming here."

"The State Police dropped you off when they brought me home. You'd fallen asleep in their car and barely opened your eyes coming up the stairs."

He sat up and a slight burn in his side made him look.

"I promised to get you to a doctor, but it's really not bad. A bullet must have just barely hit you. Or shrapnel, maybe. It had wood splinters in it, so…at any rate, I put antiseptic on it and butterflied the skin together."

"Thank you. Mike's going to stay with Bobby until his wife arrives?"

"Yes. Trooper Williams called Bobby a hero and Mike wants to tell her that."

"What about Oglethorpe's brother, Richard?"

"The Georgia Patrol picked him up near Savannah. He was heading to his yacht at Jekyll Island."

Jack fell back into the bed and stared at the ceiling, emotionally drained. "My God, Robyn, is this really what you people do for a living?"

She took a breath before saying, "Are you asking if we regularly find ourselves kidnapped and at the center of gun battles in which people die? If so, that answer is no, of course not."

He turned to look at her, the soft pillow and comfortable bed feeling great, but her beautiful face in the middle of his storm seemed wildly out of place. "But you and your colleagues fight this fight every day, don't you? Fight big corporations with deep pockets and paid soldiers in a never-ending battle to protect the world we love."

"You make it sound like a big deal, but it really isn't. I mean, someone has to protect our air and water and all the beauty that's out there against Montessa and the Koch brothers and companies just like them."

"The Koch brothers are a new target for you?"

"Yes, now that Montessa already has plenty of trouble on their hands." She pointed to her legal pad. "Koch Industries dumps more pollutants into the nation's waterways than General Electric and International Paper combined, and they ranked thirteenth in the United States for toxic air pollution, generating twenty-four metric tons of greenhouse gases a year. So they really benefit from the ability to buy politicians for a fraction of what they save by having absolute control over them."

"Always the champion of the cause. Do you think you'll win?"

She looked down, then came right back up. "No, even though more and more world leaders are talking about climate change, and proposing things to do about it. I just think...I think societies all over the planet are a little like an obese person getting fatter and fatter. They know how desperately they need to lose weight, and they know they'll die if they don't. But still they eat bad and get even fatter, because it's too hard for them not too. The world is like that about climate change. But we have to fight that, to be willing to fight that. Otherwise there'll be no chance of having anything left worth protecting. People will certainly miss all of it then, but it will be too late. I can't let that happen without trying."

"It's just like Preston said. You are fighting a war."

"I guess, although what just happened isn't typical. We fight, and yes, each week a couple of us die. It's usually far more subtle, though. Or at least less obvious."

"They're dead all the same."

"I believe the price is worthwhile, and I think I speak for all of us." She hesitated before adding, "Probably the same way Bobby would feel that the price he paid was worthwhile."

Jack turned away. "I've got stuff I need to do. Are my clothes around here somewhere?"

"On that chair over there. I washed them. Most of the blood came out but not all."

"Thank you. And what are your plans?"

"I haven't been back to the office yet, so I'll go there."

"I'd like to drop by later."

"In that case..." Robyn looked down at the floor and kept her eyes there until she suddenly realized she was doing it, then raised them and said, "Well, maybe when you come to the office we can make plans for me to see your boat. Go out on *Bella Sabrina* and get close to some dolphins, like you promised."

Jack stretched to reach his clothes. He'd heard her clearly, but even if things could magically work out for them, he just didn't know how to say he was better alone, that he'd always been better alone. Or maybe it was just that people were better off without him. As much as he loved being around people, he could never fail anyone as long as he stayed alone.

The awkward silence made Robyn move toward the door. "I'm sorry, Jack. I didn't mean to be pushy."

"Don't be sorry. It's not that I don't like the idea."

"Don't worry about it. I understand. I always assumed that you named your boat after a girlfriend, but since you never mentioned her I just decided to take the chance and invite—"

"My baby sister."

"Sorry, what?"

He bit his lip, but then said it clearly. "Sabrina was my little sister."

She sat down on the bed beside him. "Was? I…gosh I'm so sorry."

"Yeah, me, too."

He went silent and Robyn did too. He didn't know what to say, didn't know how to explain how he felt about losing the people he'd held the tightest. That he'd long ago decided that he was a curse, better kept isolated. That he'd never wanted to live alone, but doing so was the only way to prevent him from failing someone else he loved.

"I read about the car accident when checking your background. I don't think it mentioned your sister."

"Not the first articles. The police didn't know she was with my mom in the car because her body wasn't in the wreckage."

"But she went over the rail with your mother?"

"Yes. You know what's funny?"

"It's hard to imagine anything about it is."

"Our car needed tires bad and my dad knew it. He had the money for them all saved up, but still she flipped off the bridge because one of the old tires blew before he could replace it."

"He must feel terrible."

"He does. He always will. You know why he didn't buy tires with the money?"

"No, of course I don't."

Jack smiled like he'd heard a stupid joke. "A guy on the base needed some fast cash and offered to sell Dad a little skiff, real cheap. He knew how badly I wanted a boat, so he bought it on the spot. Man, he was so proud of himself when he showed it to me."

"That is so sad."

Just like thousands of times before, Jack found himself back at the moment his dad walked him around to the back of their yard, his khaki Navy uniform crisp and perfect, his chest covered with ribbons and his big hand on Jack's small shoulders as he pointed to the little boat and said, "Take command of your new vessel, Captain Jack."

"He called me captain, Robyn. Then he saluted. I saluted back, and then we launched it in the canal behind the house."

"It was a good thing he did. It's not your fault what happened."

"Now Dad lives on a beat up old boat in a shitty anchorage, and every time he goes ashore he rows that goddamned skiff like it's a penance. It's an albatross, I used to tell him when he was sober. Which wasn't all that often."

Robyn managed to smile as she said, "I'm happy I got to know you, Jack."

"Don't be so sure," he said, and then he smiled too. "Lots of folks second guess the pleasure."

"And you're coming by the office before you leave? I'm guessing you'll want to say good-bye to Preston?"

"I want to catch up with Mike first, and visit with Bobby's wife, but yes."

"I'll drop you off at the hospital." She was still smiling as she asked, "Do you want me to make something to eat while you shower and get dressed?"

"Would you enjoy doing that?"

"I would, actually."

"Then that sounds great. Thanks again."

Robyn left and Jack carried his clothes to the bathroom. Pretty much everything hurt, from his scratched legs to his bloody knuckles to the sore shoulder from being struck by the SWAT team in Montessa's parking lot. But what hurt most of all was his heart, or soul, or whatever it was inside him that had the incredible power to control exactly how he felt, and was right now running in high gear to make him feel bad for having begged and begged his dad for a boat, for being a completely selfish prick about it. It was his greed that let his mom and sister go unprotected. His greed that drove his father into a bottle. His greed that hurt people.

And now he'd hurt people again, and for what? To avenge Jeff's death? Because he'd been beaten by the police? Because he'd been attacked by two idiot thugs at his motel?

He stood in the shower with the hot water pouring over him and looked for something bigger because he needed something bigger. God damn it, he was once again a man who took people's lives away from them, an act so horrible and so permanently undoable that it'd driven four of his friends to suicide, three of them leaving short notes of regret or rambling letters of shame, the other pinning his Bronze Star to his suicide note so there'd be no doubt about why he did it.

His phone was beside his clothes, and as he pushed his arm through a sleeve he picked it up and dialed.

"This is Supervisory Special Agent Grayson."

"Hey, Gray, it's Jack."

"Good lord, Jack. For once it's nice to hear from you. Are you okay?"

"Yeah, I'm okay."

"I was sorry to hear that you lost a man."

"A good man, Gray."

"I assumed he was since he was with you, so I sent a Bureau plane for his wife. She and their kids should arrive soon."

"Thanks, Gray. Listen, did Special Agent Oglethorpe cough up any names? Is there anyone else here I need to thump before I go home, or can I make plans to get out of here?"

"He hasn't yet, and I don't really think he has any. Those hidden files of his show that his big bet was to give up the chief of police for a lighter sentence if he was ever caught. So he had nothing left after..." Gray paused to acknowledge that he should never reveal even a shade of suspicion that Jack had orchestrated a killing. "After the chief was accidentally killed in that stand-off with his own SWAT team."

"Montessa is at the center of all these deaths. What Oglethorpe and the chief did were murders for hire, sure, but Montessa was their employer. You're going to ride them hard?"

"Like a thousand dollar whore, Jack. We'll find everything else they've done illegal. I've already sent special assignments out to every office and overseas legal attaché where Montessa has a facility or an employee, even if it's just some guy printing labels. We're going to dig deep."

"Don't expect it to be easy. They've got lots of layers of protection. You should expect backlash from their Washington Fan Club."

"I've already gotten a call from a California senator who wanted to make sure I wasn't unfairly targeting them. I told him to make an appointment with my secretary." Gray laughed. "But I'm sure that's just the beginning."

"I've got to go. Do you still have some agents standing by on special assignment here in Roanoke?"

"They're waiting for you to give them an after-action report and follow-up instructions."

"Yeah, but let's do it later. Give me a couple of hours. Thanks, Gray."

"My pleasure, Jack. Besides, I'll get an Atta-Boy letter for this that I hope will offset the Aw-Shit trouble you got me into at the start."

"I hope so, too. Thanks again."

"I'll be seeing you."

Jack moved slowly down the steps towards the good smells of the kitchen and the great feelings of peace they conjured up. But it was too early to feel good about anything because there was still work to do, and all Jack could hope at this point was that no one else got physically hurt. There just wasn't a reason anymore.

Chapter 38

Robyn pulled to the curb and stopped. "So I'll see you at the office later?"

Jack looked up at the hospital entrance as he opened the door of the car. He was already thinking and moving faster, his sore body picking up the pace as his mind processed scenarios for meeting Mike, and Bobby's wife, and Bobby's kids, trying to come up with something worthwhile to say.

"Let's see how this goes first. Thanks for the lift. I promise to see you before I leave Roanoke, though." He closed the door and walked up to the entrance to the lobby.

Mike was sitting alone, staring at the front doors like a sentry guarding a gate. Jack walked over and sat beside him.

"Hey."

Mike looked him over, but was silent for over a minute before asking, "You okay, Jack?"

"Yes. I'm okay."

They sat quietly together as Jack waited for Mike to give him the beating he knew was coming, a beating Mike needed to give in order for him to move on.

Mike shifted in his seat, and stayed that way until a half hour passed. Then Mike looked down the corridor in the opposite direction, like it would be impossible for him to stand the sight of Jack.

"I am so frigging pissed off at you that I can barely stand it."

"I know you are."

Now Mike turned to him, his eyes angry, but lacking the poison Jack had seen so often in Afghanistan.

"What the *fuck* were you thinking, leaving me behind like that?"

"It was a mistake, Mike."

"You're god damned right it was a mistake."

"Bobby's dead, so obviously that means you're right."

"I know I'm right. Don't tell me I'm right when we both know I'm right."

Jack nodded in agreement. "For what it's worth, Bobby wanted you there. He begged me to bring you in."

Mike's hands were clenched into fists, which was another good sign. He was absolutely consumed by his anger, but he was showing it like a normal person.

"Did I just hear that right? He begged you to let me come."

"Yes."

"But you in your infinite fucking wisdom left me baby-sitting a guy you knew wouldn't move. God damn you, Jack, I felt like such an idiot when I called Bobby for an update and found out you were about to go to war at that cabin. Shit, by the time I got there it was all over."

"I'm sorry. Like I said, I fucked up."

Mike looked him over again. "But you're okay?"

"Yes."

"Then let's do our best to get past what we can't change. How many have you killed since you've been here?"

"I don't know."

"And so now you've decided to be a liar, too?"

"I killed five, Mike. Six if you count the chief of police, but I'd just as soon not."

"Bobby was worth three times that many. At least three times. Hell, even more than that."

"I know."

Mike had probably never before been in this emotional state without someone paying a caviar price. But there was no one left to pick up the tab and Mike had to know it.

"At least one of them was the guy who killed Jeff, right? Please, God, tell me that one of those dirty rotten cocksuckers killed my son."

"Yes."

"Which one...you know what? Forget it. You're sure you got his killer?"

Jack touched his friend's arm. "I'm sure I got his killer. Positive."

Mike leaned forward and put his chin in his hands as though he was absolutely lost in this world of death in which he could play no role.

"Then I'll let Bobby go."

"Thank you."

"As long as you agree that it was a fuck up you promise never to repeat."

"I agree. And I promise. I'm going to stop trying to protect you, Mike."

"What the...you protecting me? You want to tell me what—" Mike stopped and stood suddenly as a pretty black lady with two children walked through the front doors of the hospital, elegant and wonderfully composed the way military wives would always be expected to act at terribly painful times.

Jack stood up beside Mike as the trio walked over.

"Hello Lieutenant Wells," the woman said.

"Hello, Kenya. I'm sorry to see you under these conditions."

"Me, too. Hello, Mike."

"Hello, Kenya. Hey George, how are you holding up? Gracie?"

Gracie stepped close and looked straight up into Mike's face, her big eyes tired and red from crying. "I'm sad, Uncle Mike. And I'm sorry about Jeffy too."

Mike forced a tiny smile for her benefit. "Yeah, me too, Gracie. We're all hurting an awful lot around here. You know I loved your dad."

Kenya squeezed her children's hands but never took her eyes off Jack. He braced himself for whatever horrible things she had to say, knowing he had it coming.

Kenya looked around the lobby and down the hall. "Bobby's in here someplace?"

"I know where he's at," Mike said. "I'll take you there whenever you're ready."

She nodded, still staring at Jack. He expected her to slap him or spit on him, or maybe fall into him and beat against his chest.

"Thank you so much, Lieutenant."

He was so shocked that he felt dizzy and asked "What for?" without thinking.

"After you got my Bobby safely home from Afghanistan, he always said that he owed you his life, and everything good in it, because you dragged him out of that gunfire to safety."

Jack clearly remembered doing it, but it seemed like a different lifetime and a different life.

"That was a long time ago, Kenya. Anyone there would have done the same. Mike sure would have done it. I just happened to be closest to Bobby at the time."

"He respected you so much, Lieutenant. My Bobby would have done absolutely anything for you, so thank you so much for giving him a chance to prove it because it was very important to him."

"He saved my life in return, Kenya."

"That's good," she said as she put a hand on her son's shoulder. "That's real good. Because as of right now that debt is paid in full. You agree?"

"I do agree."

She leaned toward him, her composure failing as her arms draped around him. She hugged Jack while her kids gathered close and hugged her.

Then she started to cry.

And so did Jack.

Chapter 39

A cab dropped Jack off at Sierra Club's office. Instead of running the stairs the way he normally would, Jack took the elevator to the third floor. It was a lazy decision that proved just how tired and hurt he really was.

Several bouquets of bright spring flowers covered the front counter as a welcome back to Robyn, or a tribute to Theresa, while older flowers for Jeff sat grimly on a table, reminding Jack of why he'd come in the first place, and that Theresa had died because he'd arrived in Roanoke without the first clue to understanding Montessa's fantastic return on investment for killing.

Preston and Robyn had both tried to warn him with familiar examples that he knew were true. Whether directly or indirectly, by a bullet or a fiery crash or a long-lingering sickness, Ford and Chevrolet had done exactly the same mathematics as Montessa, and so had Dow and ExxonMobil and DuPont. The list Robyn showed him was several pages long, and those were just the names Jack immediately recognized. He didn't know any of the polluters with the most lethal rankings—a representative number that factored company size into the number of deaths they'd caused.

"Hello, Mister Wells," said a receptionist Jack hadn't met before. "Welcome back to Sierra Club, and thanks for all your help."

Her gratitude was too much a contrast to Jeff's fading flowers. Jack wanted to get away from her.

"I'd like to see Robyn, please."

"Of course. Please feel free to go on back. She said you'd be coming by."

Gone was the formality of his first visit. Jack was now one of them, no longer a stranger who might mean them harm and therefore needed to be escorted. He opened the door to the offices and walked down the hall.

As he passed the open door to Preston's office he heard, "Jack, welcome back. Please come in for a minute."

"I'm looking for Robyn."

"Of course you are. Sit down and make yourself comfortable and I'll go get her for you."

Jack stepped into his office and eased into the same seat he'd sat in last time. As he waited for Robyn he looked at Preston's photos and souvenirs of a life spent in a war he now admitted to be losing.

One photo showed him cleaning crude oil off shorebirds in Alaska, while another showed him in chemical gloves, pulling a luminous blob of goo from a neon pink river. And there were several of him holding mutated animals: fish with festering boils that pushed off the scales, frogs with sick and twisted deformities, and a colony of birds with hideous birth defects that were strikingly similar to the grotesque defects of the local people who held them.

"Jack," Robyn said as she came in with Preston. "Did you see Mike? Did Bobby's family arrive?"

"I did. They did. So I'll be going home. I wanted to say good-bye."

Preston sat down and gave both of them a fatherly smile. "You're a good man, Jack. I can't thank you enough for what you've done here."

Jack thought about what he had done there, and how badly he'd thrown Roanoke into chaos. "I really don't think I deserve any thanks."

"Just the same, I'm glad you came."

Robyn sat down beside Jack and said, "We could use someone like you at Sierra Club. You'd be a great asset."

He'd already thought about it. Thought about contributing to something bigger than himself, maybe making a small difference that might not even be noticed until long after his death, or maybe not even then, as some kid reeled in a healthy fish or swam in a clean lake. It sounded like a pretty good legacy.

But he knew he wouldn't get that kind of role in protecting the environment against companies like Montessa. His role would be to cause pain, and he'd had enough of it.

"I think I'll just go back to my charter fishing business."

"Can't say that I blame you, Jack. I doubt Robyn does either."

"I don't. It sounds like a beautiful way to live."

"It is. I like it."

Preston stood up. "I'm terribly sorry, Jack, but I have a meeting to attend. I do want to thank you once again. Please drop in to see us whenever you're in Roanoke."

Jack stood up with him but stepped between Preston and the open door. "Just one thing, Preston."

Both Robyn and Preston looked surprised, not just by Jack's blocking the door, but also by the tone of his voice.

"Okay," Preston said slowly. "And what might that be?"

Jack closed the door before saying, "Right from the start there's been something about this case—if that's what it could be called—that's troubled me. All along I knew I was overlooking something, but I just wasn't able to figure out what it was."

"From where I sit it doesn't appear that you overlooked anything. You certainly saw more corruption around here than even I would have guessed existed."

"Same with me," Robyn added as she stared at him.

"But here's the thing, Preston. Montessa had the chief of police on their payroll, right?"

"Yes."

"They also had an FBI Agent on their payroll, right?"

"Yes, apparently."

"And they had the SILT mercenaries on their payroll, too."

"Okay, Jack," Preston said as he held open his hands, as if he was wasting time agreeing to the obvious. "Right again."

"And they didn't hesitate to hire Mitch."

"Once again, that appears to be accurate."

"And somehow the chief of police knew about me almost the moment I arrived. Right after I left here."

"I'm afraid I'm missing your point."

Jack picked up the photo of the deformed frogs. "I missed it too. But here it is."

Jack put down the photo and spoke slowly as he said, "Why wouldn't a company willing to spend all that money on all that firepower also hire someone on the inside? Someone to tell them when a pesky investigator showed up, or when a determined employee was getting too close."

"I don't think they'd get one of us to do it," Robyn said quickly.

Jack ignored her. "A person who worked for Sierra who could warn them when someone was building a solid case against them. Someone in an ideal position to pick their targets, to pick their victims."

Preston nodded his head in agreement. "I suppose it would make sense."

Jack glanced at Robyn, who was looking hard for his meaning, trying to anticipate where he was going. "Do you agree, Robyn?"

She shook her head slowly. "I suppose it's plausible. It does make sense that a little money spent to have a spy in here would pay big dividends. It's impossible for me to imagine someone doing it, though."

Jack turned back to Preston. "How much?"

Preston scratched at his chin and said, "I don't know how much a dividend they'd get, but it's easy to guess it would be a good investment for them."

"That's not what I mean and you know it. How much did they pay you? I want you to tell Robyn."

Robyn jumped up, staring at Jack and then slowly turning her head to see Preston.

Preston smiled. "You're really barking up the wrong tree here, Jack."

"Was it you who suggested they kill Theresa? Was that supposed to be a warning to me? Or a way to get me killed? Or was it just an enormous mistake? Honestly, did you really think that sweet old lady needed to die?"

"You're mad. I had absolutely nothing to do with her death."

Jack studied him. Then, "Okay, I believe you. You had nothing to do with Theresa."

Robyn looked back at Jack. "Why, Jack? Why did you even think Preston had something to do with it? I mean, are you even sure, and I mean really sure, that someone here is working for Montessa?"

Jack moved away from the door. He waited and watched Preston, who just stood still and stared back.

"After you were kidnapped," Jack said to her, "I called Preston to see what he knew."

Preston lurched forward. "That's right, you did call me and if you remember correctly you'll recall my saying I was totally surprised by Robyn's disappearance. I fail to see the crime in that."

"You did say that, and I know you were telling the truth when you said it."

"Wait, Jack. You're saying that Preston told you he didn't know anything about my being kidnapped, and you just agreed that he was telling the truth. I'm confused. Why does that mean something bad?"

"My dear boy," Preston said with a paternal tone, "You've been through an awful lot and with very little sleep. Please don't worry about having offended me, as it's really in everyone's best interest to consider whatever theories you have, even crazy ones."

Jack had to admire Preston's coolness. "The issue, Robyn, is not whether or not Preston told the truth when he said he didn't know where you were. The issue is that he was so surprised and caught off guard by the fact that he didn't know. I heard it clearly in his voice. Preston had absolutely no idea what had happened to you."

"I'm still confused."

"What eventually dawned on me was how weird that was. He was shocked that he didn't know."

"I was shocked that she'd gone missing. And as I just said, I fail to see the crime in that."

"That's what I thought at first and it seemed reasonable enough. But it kept gnawing at me, and I finally came to realize that it was probably the first time since you'd defected that something happened to a Sierra Club employee you didn't know about in advance."

Robyn looked like her mind was in full gear as she absorbed the allegations. "Preston?"

"And," Jack continued, "I heard a whole lot more than just surprise in your voice. I heard fear. The genuine fear of a man who'd suddenly found himself left out of a big decision. Afraid of what that meant to his own future, his own survival."

"Preston?"

"You're mad, Jack," he said again. "Well and truly mad, and this grand accusation of yours is now starting to aggravate me."

"And I'm hearing that same fear now. And that's as it should be because you have good reason to worry."

"Are these just your suspicions, Jack?"

"They're more than that, Robyn. My friend Gray had some agents from White Collar Crime dig around in Preston's finances. Do you have any idea what he gets paid?"

Now Robyn looked insulted. "We work for what we believe. It's never been about the money."

"Fifty-eight thousand dollars a year. That was his highest income year."

"I guess that sounds about right."

"There aren't any records of him ever inheriting anything, and he's never had an investment account anywhere."

"So?"

"He's never owned a home or won a lottery or declared any gambling winnings."

"Jack, where are you going with this."

"Tell her, Preston. Tell her how much money you have in that bank in Belize."

Preston flopped into his chair. Jack kept close watch on his hands.

"Not feeling too chatty, Preston?"

He glared back.

"Then I'll tell her. Two point six million dollars, Robyn, although it's been as high as five point three million dollars."

Preston continued to glare as he said, "It's a very long stretch from my having saved some money to my doing illicit work for Montessa."

"Illicit or illegal? Not that it really matters because the White Collar Crime guys and the IRS have already built a pretty sturdy bridge over that gap. I'm glad you've already spent some of that money because I doubt it will do you much good in prison."

Robyn stayed calm as she stared at Preston, but Jack could see that her mind was in full gear, as if she'd been surprised in court but was quickly recovering. Then she turned to Jack and said, "You're sure about this? I've never seen him spend a dime on anything lavish."

"I'm sure that he banked that money and I'm sure he hasn't accounted for it in any legitimate way. You know what he did with the money that's missing, why you never saw him spend it?"

"Of course I don't."

"He made anonymous donations to The Sierra Club. Harmon told me on my earlier visit that you all were losing this war, so my guess is he used the 'greater good' argument to justify himself. Losing a couple of people as collateral damage in order to better fund the war actually does seem reasonable."

"And you're sure?"

"I am, of this and more. Agents are down the hall waiting to arrest him."

Robyn shook herself out of her disbelief and then grabbed the phone on Preston's desk.

"Annette, it's Robyn. Please have the FBI Agents in the hallway come back to Preston's office. Also get security up here to make sure Preston takes nothing with him when he is escorted off the premises, and that he does not return unless and until he is cleared of all charges."

She hung up. "You're still a Sierra Club employee, Harmon, and as legal council I will strongly advise you to remain silent. Hire a lawyer. Be completely honest with that lawyer and good luck."

Preston nodded, his head down a little but his eyes still pinned on Jack.

Robyn turned and walked out. Jack sat down across from Preston and the two of them exchanged glares until the security officers led the way for two FBI agents, who handcuffed Preston and took him away.

Chapter 40

Jack sat in Preston's office until Robyn came back and threw his keys and Sierra identification onto the desk.

"I'm sorry, Robyn. I know you and Preston were close."

It was like she didn't hear him. Then she said "What? I'm sorry, Jack, what did you say?"

"That you two were close."

"I've worked for him from the start. He mentored me and over all the years we worked together became a very dear friend."

"Earlier you said you were family, and not just Sierra Club family."

"I said he's been like a father, and I will always believe he's a good man. You say he made some mistakes and I have to accept that until he's proven innocent, but he's still a good man."

"People died because of that good man and he got rich over it. I'm going to be a tough sell."

"So you say. But people are alive because of Preston, too. His impact on environmental protection is unimpeachable."

"Do you believe he killed Jeff?"

She looked away, but he wanted her answer and would wait for it.

Finally she said, "I don't know that Preston killed anyone. You said he gave Montessa some names, and again, I have no choice but to accept that for now. But nothing you said sounded like he's a killer. But maybe…gosh, maybe one thing led to the other."

The receptionist knocked quietly on the door and then opened it. "Mister Wells, your friend Mister Roberts is here to see you."

"Thank you. Can you please show him back?" He looked at Robyn. "Okay with you?"

"Of course."

Mike walked in looking like he was someplace he shouldn't be. "What's going on, Jack? Hello again, Robyn."

"Sit down, Mike. Please."

As soon as Mike sat, Jack said, "Meet the person who killed your son."

Mike's eyes shot around the room as Robyn gasped. With no one else to look at, he slowly moved his eyes to her and then locked up. Jack watched for Mike to lunge, ready to tackle him but hoping it wouldn't happen.

"What are you talking about, and how dare you accuse me of something so horrible." She got up to leave.

"State Troopers have all the exits covered. I'd like to chat first, and I think Mike has a right to hear why you did it. But if you want to leave, go ahead."

"I won't participate in this slanderous conversation without a lawyer."

"Yeah, I wouldn't either."

"What's going on, Jack?"

"I didn't want to lie to you at the hospital, Mike, but you wanted blood, and brother I get that. I just didn't really know who killed Jeff, but I wanted you to go on with your life, believing I'd killed them. Now things have changed, and although I'm not about to let you go to jail for murdering a murderer, you'll at least get to meet Jeff's killer on her way to jail. It's the best I can do."

Mike stared at Robyn, but it was a stare of confusion, not hatred.

"You did a convincing job just now, Robyn. You didn't look all that surprised by my charges against Preston but you did an excellent job of acting angry at him. Might have overacted just a bit."

"You're saying for sure my boy was murdered, Jack, and you're saying for sure she did it?"

Jack nodded. "I knew he was murdered by the way he'd gotten into the tub, which was the way anyone would have normally gotten into that tub. But in Robyn's hurry and panic she forgot that Jeff was left-handed."

"So what?"

"The entry wound would have required him to shoot himself with his right hand, which would have been too awkward and unnatural for someone so unfamiliar with guns. I'm guessing Robyn went over there under the pretext of work, or to console him over Claire leaving."

"How long have you suspected her?"

"I never really did, Mike, other than the fact that everyone starts out as a suspect. I became a little suspicious of her when she got so upset about my being an FBI Agent, because she seemed unreasonably upset, even with all the facts she threw into her argument. But then she talked to you and apologized to me, and I bought it. She fooled me, man. Sorry. Looking back now, I'm guessing she just wanted to keep an eye on what I was doing."

"But now you're sure? What made the difference?"

"I saw her lie to me at the cabin."

"About?"

"About never shooting a man. She was terrible at it. Couldn't even get the words out. Hearing her lie opened my mind to the possibility of her being the killer, and then all the pieces fit, even the incredible timing of Theresa calling her for help at the very moment I was with her, so that we would go over there together. I figured that was Preston's doing, but now I'm guessing she worked with one of the Oglethorpes on it. I'm not sure yet, but I am pretty sure he'll cough it up."

He stopped, but neither Robyn nor Mike said anything.

"I should have been suspicious when I learned she was the beneficiary on Preston's account in Belize, but I just figured it made sense for a man with no family to leave his money to her." Jack turned to Robyn. "I'm not sure you knew that, although his conviction will cause the assets to be seized. Preston has no idea what you did for him, does he?"

"You're insane."

"I'm very impressed with the aggressive hand you played and almost won. I mean, right from the start, anybody would have expected Jeff's killer, you, to enthusiastically go along with the cop's suicide story, saying Jeff was troubled and all that. But I guess you were confident you could pin the death on Montessa, adding it to their list of crimes. As I said, very bold to try to kill two birds with one stone. Sorry Mike. Bad metaphor."

Robyn sat listening, thinking. Then she smiled at Mike and said, "I don't know where this is coming from. I mean, Jack even suggested I run away from here, to go visit my sister. If he ever had the slightest suspicion of me, why would he do that?"

Mike looked at Jack as he spoke to Robyn. "He just said you fooled him. Don't push it with me."

"Truth is, I probably wouldn't have told you if I had known, Mike. Even now I don't know what you'll do, but you were totally blood-blinded those first days and I wouldn't have handed you the reason to go to jail or get killed by an arrest team. I owe that to you. You owe that to your family."

"I think," Robyn said as she stood, "I will leave now because just listening to this is an abomination. The police will agree with me."

"The first thing the police will do is arrest you. Have you ever heard of a quiet old woman named Bernadette Blanchet? The T on the end is silent, by the way."

Robyn said nothing.

"She and her husband own the home where Jeff lived. She tends to spend a lot of time at the front window. I went by there after I left the hospital and showed her the photo I took of you in the park. Her eyes got big with recognition, and with her husband's encouragement she decided to trust me enough to talk. She said you'd been there a couple of times before, although you told me you hadn't. Bernadette was at the window after the shooting, too, and is pretty sure it was you she saw go down the property line after leaving through the back door."

Robyn still said nothing.

Jack turned to Mike. "The best I can tell is that your son is dead simply because he found out about Preston. Being the kind of guy Jeff was, he had no choice but to bring it to the attention of a Sierra Club lawyer he trusted, which of course was Robyn. But Robyn and Preston were family, and that loyalty made her do whatever it took to protect him. I know you understand that, Mike. So faced with the choice of calling the police, or even sharing the secret with someone else who might kill your son, she took the job upon herself."

Mike stood with the stiffness of an old man. He started to take another look at Robyn but then angled off, slowly turned the door handle, and shuffled out the door and down the hall.

Chapter 41

It was long after midnight when Jack drove over the Judge Jolly Bridge that connected Marco Island to the Florida mainland, but from the top of the bridge, in the moonlight, he could still see some of the Ten Thousand Islands, of which his island, Marco, was the biggest. He loved the view from up there. Loved the winding creeks and flowing water and everything that lived and flourished in those backwaters that served as a nursery for Hammerheads and Snook, Tarpon and Snapper, and hundreds if not thousands of other wildlife species.

His was the only car on the bridge, so he thought about stopping at the top for a better look. But as usual, a traffic cop waited in his car at the bottom, ready to enforce the island-wide speed limit of 35 miles an hour.

Jack slowed down and waved as he passed the cop, glad the officer was there to protect his island, where people followed rules and, as far as Jack knew, life was as clean and pure as the air that blew off the Gulf.

On his flight home he'd made his plan to drive straight to the marina, so that's what he did, not yet ready to go to his condo and to bed, but not quite ready to go back to being a charter boat captain, either.

The marina was as dark and quiet as he knew it would be. The late night crowd at the Tiki Bar had gone home, even the cleaning crew. The plastic windows were rolled down and zippered up and all the lights were off.

Tomorrow, Jack's small world would come alive again. Charter parties would arrive early and excitedly meet their captains before loading the boats down with hats and coolers and sunscreen. Owners of other boats in the marina would gather on Roy's fantail and shoot the breeze over coffee. Mechanics and divers would drag gear down the docks and go in or under the boats they'd come to maintain.

Then the Key West Express would idle out, full of tourists who'd followed Interstate-75 down from Detroit or Toledo or Cincinnati or Lexington and took the very last exit before crossing the Everglades on Alligator Alley, heading south down the arrow-straight road that took them to the island town at the end of it. Jack's town, where he could live the same water-life he'd loved so much in Key West, but with less of the drunken craziness.

There was no wind at all, and Jack's boat sat still and noiselessly in the marina, just like the others. But his boat was special. It was his escape. His conduit to freedom. His life.

He stepped aboard and his weight sent a small wave radiating out as he fired up his engines, turned on his electronics and radar, and dimmed the display screens so they wouldn't blind him to the night. He threw off the lines and motored out into Factory Bay, turned to port and idled toward Big Marco Pass, a few hundred yards down the Marco River.

He passed the Snook Inn with its green underwater lights still attracting the Tarpon that Jack could see easily in the clear water, their giant scales like mirrors, their sleek bodies silhouetted against the white sand bottom.

He throttled up when he got to open water and headed straight out into the dark Gulf of Mexico, watching his radar screen for other boats even though there were no lights anywhere. The surface was so calm that his hull made a skimming sound as it moved along, a phosphorescent glow in its wake.

He ran for two hours, out until the lights of Marco were almost invisible in the distance, but still the closest lights to him. Out to where Jack was every bit alone as he needed to be. He lowered his anchor and sat in his captain's chair, waiting to make sure the anchor caught.

In the darkness he thought about Robyn, and the look they shared in her car at Safeway, and his promise to show her dolphins. Robyn, who'd done a very brave job for a very brave organization that few really seemed to appreciate enough. Robyn, who lived in a nice town in Western Virginia that Jack had turned into a bloody battleground. Robyn, a murderess.

He'd showered and scrubbed back at her house, dug hard into his skin and under his nails until he was close to bleeding. But he still felt dirty as he remembered the chief's bewildered face when Jack fired his pistol and then flung open the door. Remembered Theresa's simple innocence just before she'd been murdered. Remembered Mitch's resignation to what he had to know was his future. Remembered Bobby and his grieving family, and Mike and his grieving wife, and Jeff who was smart enough to have done anything he wanted, but chose to apply that intelligence to protecting the environment.

But what he remembered most clearly was his killing the SILTs outside Oglethorpe's cabin. He'd carefully planned everything else he'd done, and had incorporated an exacting margin of safety that had allowed him to stay human, because he'd had time to test his plan against his own set of values before doing such ugly things.

But he'd been an animal in those woods, a vicious savage who'd wanted to kill those men even more than he'd wanted to live. A terribly vindictive creature who'd shot men and then shot them again, just to be sure they were dead. Just to be sure Jack had killed them, proving that Jack Wells was still *that* Jack Wells, and would be forever, regardless of how much Captain Jack wanted that part of him gone. And like an inoperable cancer, there wasn't a damn thing he could do except live with it.

He jumped up suddenly and stripped off his shirt. Kicked off his shoes and pulled down his pants and his shorts. Stood naked in the darkness before diving off the stern and into the Gulf, swimming as hard as he could, as fast as he could, as far as he could, swimming to exhaustion and then farther, swimming until he started to sink, his arms so tired it was hard to pull them fully through the water.

He stopped and turned to look back, barely able to see *Bella Sabrina's* anchor light far away. His boat actually looked closer to the dark and distant horizon than it did to Jack.

Slowly he began to swim back, his arms too tired for anything but a slow breast stroke. Yet he began feeling refreshed as he made the two-hour swim. When he got to his boat he stopped and treaded water, looking at her high white sides reflecting the stars that provided just enough light to see.

Which was still too much light for Jack.

He dove toward the bottom, equalizing the pressure three times, then another just before his outstretched hands hit the sandy bottom and scared something awake that shot off into the absolute darkness.

A minute passed as he floated, motionless. Two. Three. Four. Then five minutes, with each second now passing slower than the one before as his oxygen-starved brain began to hallucinate and his eyes popped the white spots he would always embrace as an omen, a signal he was equally ready to leave this world or stay in it, whatever god or fate or destiny chose. He let his body settle on the bottom, his distended stomach touching sand first and his hands digging into its softness. He no longer struggled. Everything felt good. His brain expanded the white spots in his eyes to solid, and he was at peace.

And then he saw them, bright and faithful and beautiful, just above the seabed, his mom and his sister floating specter-like nearby, coming closer, smiling at him as they touched with their hands that moved to his arms, lifting him, denying him, rescuing him from himself once again as they pulled his hands free of the bottom and slowly floated toward the surface, rising through the depths together at the slow pace of his own buoyancy.

He eventually saw stars through the last few feet of water, and he admired their beauty even as it outshone their light, brighter and brighter until his mother and sister were gone. He broke free and gulped air that was once again as clean as it could ever possibly be.

Jack climbed aboard *Bella Sabrina*, far too exhausted to do anything but fall to his knees on the deck, panting until his breathing slowed, then pulling a life jacket from under a seat to use as a pillow. He stretched out naked and wet and salty in the warm darkness. And he slept.

Chapter 42

"Hey Mister Celebrity," the bartender said as Jack walked into the Tiki Bar, still too early for the night crowd but a little too late for those who'd come for Happy Hour. "I read all about you in the paper. Saw you on the news, too."

"Is that right, Jimmy? Well go ahead and tell me what you think."

"I think that a man who's been through all that most definitely needs a drink."

"I've always said you're a smart guy, despite what the rest of the crowd around here says."

"What do they know, right? You want a coke and Jack, Jack?" He laughed. "Jeez, I never get tired of saying it like that."

"Sure."

"It's on the house. Consider yourself my guest tonight so get something good to eat, too."

"Thanks. Why?"

Jimmy made Jack's drink and set it down, then opened up the New York Times. "Jack Wells," Jimmy read, "the earlier target of the unfounded Blue Alert..." He stopped and said, "This Jack Wells I'm reading about is you, right?"

"I'm afraid so."

Jimmy smiled. "Just checking before I let you eat on the house." Then, "Where was I? Oh yeah…the unfounded Blue Alert who was originally a suspect in—"

"I was there and you've already read it. How about telling me something else, like what's been going on around here?"

Jimmy put down the paper and leaned against the bar. He stuck his thumb out toward the marina. "Shelton came in late last night and banged the dock pretty hard. Michael went out fifty miles yesterday and came back with a nice bunch of keeper grouper."

"Is Joe still down in the Keys?"

"He called when he left Marathon after lunch. He should be pulling in any time now."

"Then I might wait around for him."

A noisy group of fishermen came in and sat down, fish blood still on the shorts from them wiping their hands on them.

"I'll be right back, Jack. Let me take care of that table over there."

"Take your time. No hurry."

"By the way, that guy over there's been waiting to talk to you about a charter."

"I'm not running charters now."

"Then tell him that. But last I heard, you were still a charter captain. A good one, too."

Jack smiled, having a little trouble believing it was only last week that Mike called while he was running a charter and tagging a big shark. It seemed like years had passed, and although he wasn't yet ready to go back to fishing, he wanted to make some plans to do it. So he walked over to the man, who stuffed the last of his sandwich into his mouth as Jack approached, then jumped up and smiled with his lips closed to keep in the food.

"Hi, I'm Jack Wells. If you're looking for a boat there are a couple of other good captains in the marina, but I won't be running charters for another week or so. I'll be glad to take you then."

The man looked him over, then nodded and said through his food, "Shoot, that's too bad, 'cause I'm only here for another couple days of vacation, and my friend who lives here said you're the best captain around." He swallowed, but still had a load of food in his mouth as he looked out at the marina and said, "So I guess I'll take another boat, like you suggest." He looked Jack up and down once again. "Well, heck of a pleasure meeting you. You have a great day." He wiped his mouth and walked out as Jack sat at the bar and took a sip of his drink, then looked out over the waterfront he loved so much.

A Blue Heron walked the docks, its long slender bill stabbing bait fish around the pilings, while a skimmer glided across the water farther out, its lower bill just under the surface. And near the skimmer a hundred-pound Tarpon rolled under a migrating flock of Wood Storks.

Life on Marco was perfect for Jack, but the longer he looked out over Factory Bay the easier it was to see threats he'd never thought to consider until going to Roanoke. Ships legally dumped tons of garbage, along with their massive sewage holding tanks, just a few miles offshore. Some yachts, and a few crappy derelicts, illegally dumped their sewage in the anchorage just out from his boat. Old gas docks had fuel lines and fittings corroded by salt water and time, and just a drop of their petroleum products would create a rainbow sheen on the water's surface that could suffocate life. And every golf course and most of the yards had tons of fertilizer dumped on them every year, much of which passed through the storm drains or aquifers on its way to the Gulf.

Farther off, way out of Jack's view, he knew of municipal sewage treatment plants that dumped untreated excess effluent into coastal waterways without any oversight or penalty, while agricultural pesticides from the sugar cane industry flowed over the Everglades' River of Grass on its way to the Gulf Coast or Florida Bay. Jack had long ago accepted all those things as normal, but now he saw them a little more clearly as he looked through Robyn's eyes.

He scrolled through the pictures on his phone for the one he'd taken of her at the park, the one he'd showed Bernadette. He stared at it, getting back some of the good feeling of watching her from behind as her high heels clicked down the hall of Sierra Club's office. Her calling him out for keeping his past a secret, and then her apology after Mike told her he'd asked for his help. The look on her face when Jack told what he knew about Preston, much like the way she looked after killing the SILT in the cabin, but still not as shocked as the look when she saw the bodies of the men Jack killed spread out on the side of the driveway, which was beat only by her look when Jack called her a killer.

"Dozens of us die each year for tiny little victories," Jack heard Preston say, if just in his head.

Jack felt himself nodding in agreement, but was careful to keep his words to himself. "Yes, I believe that now. I didn't before."

"We could use a man like you," Robyn added.

He studied her face in the picture. "Are you sure about that?"

"You'd have to work within the law, of course. And our rules. Don't be foolish like me. Like Preston."

Jack took another drink as he pondered what to say. Finally, "Is that really what you want? Is that really what you need from me?"

Jimmy headed over to continue his own conversation with Jack, but Jack waved him off until he'd had time to finish the one going on in his head.

"I don't know, Jack."

He could see Robyn turn away, as though trying to hide from the truth. Maybe it's not, but I don't want to say what we might really need you to do from time to time. No one should have to do it. We shouldn't even be talking about it, except that we both know it will happen again. I won't be there, of course, but the need will still be."

"I don't want to be a killer, Robyn."

"That's good. That's very good."

"But I could help people stay safe. It doesn't necessarily have to get bloody, does it?"

"Maybe not," Robyn said.

But even in Jack's own mind, with him controlling both sides of the conversation, he couldn't make her sound convincing.

He set down his phone and looked back out at his boat. He took another drink of whiskey and thought about his swim last night, and his time underwater on the pitch dark bottom, and the renewed way he felt when he woke up naked in the sunshine, all by himself, thirty miles out into the great Gulf of Mexico.

For the first time in his life Jack wanted one too many things, or maybe the right amount of things that were at odds with each other. He wasn't sure what he wanted most—a commitment to a worthwhile cause, a commitment to a real relationship that didn't keep him worried about failure, or a commitment to hold tight to someone no matter what—but he knew where he needed to start. So he picked up his phone and dialed.

"Dad," he said as soon as his father answered, "I'm running my boat to Key West tonight. Would you like to go fishing with me?"

Chapter 43

Bella Sabrina slid up and over the small waves formed by the light winds coming from behind as Jack headed his boat toward Key West. Cape Sable, so remote and unspoiled it could be an undiscovered island instead of the southwestern-most point of mainland Florida, lay a few miles off his port bow, and fifty miles of Florida Bay's beautiful emptiness lay ahead. Jack was about halfway to Key West, and more than halfway back to a relationship with his father. At least he hoped so.

He wondered what they would talk about, and how they would get along after so many years apart. He wondered how he could help his dad get sober. He wondered how his dad might help him.

But Jack suddenly stopped thinking about any of that as he finally made a match. The man who'd stuffed food into his mouth to disguise his voice was the same man who'd called Jack to introduce himself. The same man in the horrible torture video of a poor little kid loosing his fingernails.

Mark Foster was on Marco Island.

About the Author

Wes is a real-life adventurer who turns life on its head and shakes change from its pockets. A global traveler, yacht rat, intellectual, surf bum, bow-hunter, actor, romantic, former F.B.I./S.W.A.T. Agent and Security Consultant, raconteur and all-around fun guy, Wes can debate Voltaire and Rousseau while wrenching on a greasy diesel far out at sea, or drop into a point break wave as skillfully as he's crept within grasp of wild game.

Over the past fifteen years Wes (wesdemott.com) has garnered international acclaim for his novels about prisoners of war, the FBI, military assassins, and spies. In his beautiful but heartbreaking novel, *Loving Zelda*, he wrote about hope and loss and the chance to change our lives if we're fearless enough to try.

Tortuga Gold reflected a fun new chapter in Wes's own life as he was joined in his global adventures by his beautiful Belgian wife, Sabine, a human rights/refugee lawyer who spent seven of her fifteen years with the United Nations living in Africa, including full-time residency in the war zones of Rwanda, Burundi, and the Congo during their bloody genocides.

Wes's love of the ocean often plays into his short stories and novels. He's boated thousands of miles on his own boats, surfed world famous breaks, and caught or speared game fish since he was thirteen. In 2010, after sailing from the Chesapeake Bay to Florida's West Coast and selling their home, Wes and Sabine made a permanent move aboard their new boat, a trawler they named *Wasafiri* ("The Wanderers" in Swahili). After a shakedown cruise of 1200 miles, Wes and two crewmen took off for Bocas del Toro, Panama, planning to pick up Sabine in Isla Mujeres, Mexico. But the voyage was cut short when Wes shipwrecked in violent seas off the western tip of Cuba and was rescued by the Carnival Cruise ship, VALOR.

When Wes abandoned ship he left behind all their possessions except their cat and his American flag. Immediately after the Coast Guard told Sabine of the rescue, she texted a friend a message that well defines the way these two live: "Boat lost at sea. Wes and crew alive. All possessions gone, but new adventures ahead."

The couple rented a flat in a Mexican beach town, and then, in June 2011, moved to Portland, Oregon to begin exploring America's Pacific Northwest. Their shopping list of replacement items included backpacks, a good knife, Merrill hiking boots, and another adventure hat for Wes.

Serial adventurers, the pair bounced around the United States, Central and South America, Europe, the Caribbean, and Canada for a few years, and then in 2016 sold their cruising catamaran sailboat and headed from a South Florida island toward unknown adventures.

There is no way to guess where the couple will be by the time you read this, but if you happen to spot Wes or Sabine, please say hello, as they love meeting people and making new friends.

NOVELS BY WES DEMOTT

THE TYPHOON SANCTION

CIA Field Officer Cruiser is a master at manipulating people and circumstances. Be careful or he'll manipulate you in this story of vengeance, murder, and global terrorism.

Mixing spies and counterespionage with old vendettas and small town murders, The Typhoon Sanction pits the protagonist, CIA Officer Jay Stewart, against a Chinese enemy who hunts him halfway around the world to the Outer Banks of North Carolina. Stewart's mastery of misdirection provides a whodunit element to this international thriller as the reader tries to make sense of four mysterious small-town murders. The more obvious the truth appears, the further the reader gets from it, ultimately being captured by the same skills that made Stewart such a successful operative.

This novel is Wes's homage to Robert Ludlum, who graciously helped launch Wes's career by hosting his first major book signing event.

THE FUND

How deep does the conspiracy go? Who's in charge and how many more will die? Aerospace engineer Peter Jamison is determined to find out.

While trying to save his contract for a tactical weapons system, Jamison uncovers a crime of corruption, power and violence that draws him into a deadly game he cannot win but still chooses to fight, any way he can.

327

This thriller has been translated into several languages and is an international best-seller and IPPY Gold Medal Award Recipient for Best Fiction. Robert Ludlum, the wonderfully gracious man that he was, hosted the launch party for this novel.

HEAT SYNC

Heat Sync takes you through the U.S. Assassination School exposed by NEWSWEEK Magazine just prior to this novel's publication.

Experience the pain and process of sanctioned murder from Lt. Henry Thompson, who was recruited for JASPERS from the U.S. Navy SEALS. Thompson believes he's training to assassinate foreign threats to this country, and it's only after he graduates and gets his orders that he realizes his true mission is to kill the President of the United States by using the White House access his girlfriend provides, and that he's already too boxed in by his handlers to refuse. Heat Sync provides an exciting but non-traditional thriller that deeply probes the emotions and psychology of a patriotic killer.

WALKING K

America's leaders haven't faced a Prisoner-of-War crisis since the debacle over POWs left behind in Vietnam. Walking K is an exciting thriller that exposes the reasons it can't be allowed to happen again.

DeMott, a former FBI Agent, analyzed intelligence documents, Nixon's White House tapes, Congressional Records, and interviewed POWs and their commanding officers while researching this tragic story of a reluctant conspiracy lumbered upon the shoulders of each U.S. President since 1975. Crosscutting between dramatic battlefield scenes, heartbreaking torture, American businesses protecting their investments, and a continuing refusal by the White House to reveal the shameful truth, the emotional ending of this thriller sadly shows why the United States Government stopped wanting the prisoners of that war to come home, and perhaps sheds light on the government's attitude toward the POW classification in wars since Vietnam.

LOVING ZELDA

The humanity and hope of this beautiful novel makes it the work for which Wes would most like to be remembered. Loving Zelda's emotional range includes pieces of everyone's past, and provides hope that we can all find love if we're brave enough to take a chance. Loving Zelda is an extremely rare glimpse of the soft-as-cotton heart of internationally known tough guy Wes DeMott.

Loving Zelda explores the emotional pain and damage inflicted on a writer's relationship with the woman he loves as she struggles with manic-depression. Through ten years of joy and hardship he loves and cares for her with unwavering devotion, but when she marries another man he becomes a recluse on his sailboat, waiting for a chance to be together again in this or any world.

TORTUGA GOLD

Throw your sea bag aboard WASAFIRI to join Taz Keaton and the Mayday Salvage and Rescue gang in fun adventures and a chance at Blackbeard's treasure.

Tortuga Gold is a fun action story that follows Taz's fast adventures after he rejects his wealthy lifestyle and starts Mayday Salvage and Rescue in search of excitement. After Taz and his two partners race the Panamanian National Police to recover a metal case from the wreckage of a private jet in a muddy river, they meet a man with a coin from an historic but never recovered Spanish shipment that vanished in 1715. From there the adventure rolls from modern day pirates to blood-sucking leeches, exploding yachts to beautiful international competitors and a sea battle with the legendary Blackbeard himself. This is the first novel in a series involving Taz and the Mayday crew.

CNN, Fox News Network, the Huffington Post and many news outlets around the world referred to this novel after Wes' rescue off the coast of Cuba by Carnival Cruise lines. Now you can read the scene that inspired so much discussion.

THE SHRINE OF AKUMAL

A second Mayday Salvage and Rescue Adventure

Taz and the Mayday gang are back at it again, taking the reader along for a fun tangle of action and adventure as they explore scuttled yachts, tenth-century history, sweltering jungles, creationism, Mayans, astrological truths, *cenotes* and ancient aliens. The quick dialogue between the family of characters provides laugh-out-loud moments as the reader travels along through the troubles and grand adventures that Taz, Sam and Pete always seek.

www.ingramcontent.com/pod-product-compliance
Lightning Source LLC
Chambersburg PA
CBHW021303250626

47155CB00002B/354